MW00532793

The Shattered Vase

GRACIE LYNNE

Copyright 2018 by Gracie Lynne
All rights reserved. In accordance with the U.S. Copyright Act of 1976, the scanning, uploading, and electronic sharing of any part of this book without the permission of the author constitute unlawful priracy and theft of the author's intellectual property. If you would like to use material from the book (other than for review purposes), permission must be obtained by contacting the author at gracie.lynne@aol.com.
Thank you for your support of the author's rights.

Book Baby
7905 North Crescent Blvd.
Pennsauken, NJ
08110

ISBN: 978-1-54393-539-4 (print)
ISBN: 978-1-54393-540-0 (ebook)

This book is dedicated to:

God, my Father,

Jesus, my Saviour

And the Holy Spirit,

Who is my Counselor and my best friend

All characters portrayed in this novel are fictitious. Any resemblance to real persons, living or dead, is purely coincidental.

AUTHOR BIO

Gracie Lynne started writing when her children were young. The joy of relating their antics to relatives through Christmas letters was her first venture. These letters were well received and several of her family members indicated that Gracie may have talent as a writer.

Soon after her third child was born; Gracie and her husband made the difficult decision to divorce.

Gracie became involved in a Church Single's ministry and began writing, producing, directing and acting in plays for this ministry.

It was during this time that God put a calling on Gracie's life to become a Christian author. Gracie felt led to start writing a novel, to establish her writing as an occupation.

In addition to working on *The Shattered Vase*, Gracie has also launched a blog for single parents. This blog can be found at www.spotublog.com.

Gracie would like to thank everyone who has read her blog and *The Shattered Vase*. She welcomes comments and suggestions and can be reached at gracie.lynne@aol.com.

Gracie would like to acknowledge that without God's presence in her life, *The Shattered Vase* could have never been written. This is His story, much more than it is hers.

A BEAST IN THE BEDROOM

SUZIE AWOKE WITH A HORRIBLE REALIZATION THAT nothing had changed. She felt uneasy for the last couple of years. When did this start? She couldn't remember, but it was growing like a malignant cancer, consuming her thoughts and maybe, even... her heart.

She gazed at the walls of her bedroom. Jungle print was everywhere—on the border of her safari tan walls, her bedspread. Even her drapes looked like an African safari photo. It was suffocating.

The décor had been her husband's obsession for the past two years. Two years ago, her husband, Joe, had started a new hobby. He started hunting. At least, that is what he said he was doing. He left to go hunting but returned with no game. Suzie had her doubts but that changed on one fateful weekend. To Suzie's surprise, he took Friday off from work to go hunting. He had refused to leave work for a family vacation. When she married him, he hadn't shown any yearning to hunt. Now all he could talk about was his hunting trips? It seemed like Suzie and the children had become invisible.

He left before sunup, his rifle packed along with other hunting gear.

Suzie waited all weekend for a call. She didn't know who he was hunting with, or where he was hunting. What if he got hurt?

To keep her mind occupied, Suzie spent the weekend cleaning. In the pleasant and warm day, the children wore themselves out with outdoor adventures. They went to bed early, with no fight left in them.

Finally, at nine o'clock on Sunday night, she heard Joe's Ford 150 pulling into the driveway. She bristled at the sound of his new hunting boots stomping up the front stairs. She hurried to the front door, hoping to catch him before he trudged over the freshly vacuumed carpet.

Suzie greeted Joe before he could step inside. "Could you please go to the back door?"

Joe shoved her aside and stepped into the house. "Listen, I've been hunting all weekend. I really don't have the energy to walk around the house just to please you."

As he bent down to untie his Cabella boot strings, he flicked mud all over the front foyer. He strode past Suzie with defiant arrogance, leaving a trail of mud, dried grass, and brush behind him.

By the time Suzie was done cleaning up the mess, Joe was in bed. She crawled in beside him and tried to cuddle. Joe quickly turned on his side to block any kind of affection.

Suzie couldn't sleep that night. She felt uncomfortable; there was a prevailing sense of evil in the room. She tossed and turned all night. She had just started to doze off, when Joe awoke to the alarm.

He got up and made so much noise taking a shower that Suzie couldn't go back to sleep. She finally sandwiched her head between the pillows.

Before Joe left for work, he pulled the pillow away and whispered in her ear. "You need to take our wedding picture down from the wall. I shot a buck. When I get the mount back, it's going to be right where our wedding picture was."

What the hell?!! Who on earth has a buck's head in their bedroom? What has happened to my husband?

Joe was the one who had insisted that they place their wedding picture above their bed. He had tenderly said to her, "I never want to forget how beautiful you are."

Now this dead animal was going to be there?

Several months passed. Suzie hoped that Joe had forgotten about the dead deer. She was about to hang the wedding picture back up when Joe announced that the mount would be coming home.

It was a monstrosity and a bit hard for him to hang on the wall. First, he had a difficult time finding a stud, and then he couldn't figure out how to anchor the base to the wall.

He stepped into the hallway and phoned the taxidermist to ask his advice. When he came back into the bedroom, he didn't remember where the stud was, much less the stud finder. He wrenched the bed from the wall, looking for the stud finder behind the bed. After moving the bed, crawling behind it, and hitting his head on the frame, he looked up and found the device in plain view on his nightstand.

Suzie watched with a sense of amusement. She tried to engage him in conversation, asking him what she supposed were idiotic questions about hunting deer.

Joe was curt and rude in his replies.

"So, you have no problem with shooting a defenseless animal?" Suzie asked.

"Suzie, I'm doing the deer population a favor. Without hunters, the numbers would grow to such an extent they would die off from natural causes."

"Somehow I think the deer going up on our wall may have a different philosophy." Suzie bent down to pick up a sock. "I wonder what the children will think."

The children were already in bed. Suzie decided to introduce them to the aberration in the morning. After breakfast, Suzie told the children that their daddy had added an unusual piece of art to the wall in their bedroom. Michael was awestruck by the mount. Sarah was mildly amused. Baby Jonathan could have cared less.

At first, Suzie was disgusted with the mount; but in due time, her aversion to the object softened into pity.

In the mornings, Suzie talked to the buck's head, making it her confidant. It listened well, gave no condemnation for her feelings, and merely stared at her as if every word she said had meaning.

She began to act as if the mount was a friend of hers. She needed to name it. Maybe the kids could help. She corralled them in her bedroom and begged for names. There were all kinds of suggestions, from Bambi, to Rambo, to Batman. Finally, after a vote, they decided to name it "Uncle Buck."

Eventually, Suzie softened to the safari print. It was just a print, no reason to go "psycho" about it. Psycho was Joe's favorite name for her when she questioned his change in behavior.

No sooner had Suzie decided to accept the jungle décor than she received an unexpected call from Joe's secretary. The secretary asked if Suzie would mind shopping for a birthday gift for Joe's boss.

"Well, I don't think I would mind," Suzie replied. "Is this Megan we are talking about, or her boss, Steve?"

"It is Megan." The secretary said enthusiastically. "She and Joe are inseparable. The office joke is like they are two peas in a pod or bed.... Oops, well I mean not like that, you know.... they are just so compatible."

Suzie sank down on the kitchen chair and caught her breath.

"Well, anyways, I am planning a surprise birthday party for Megan. I would have gone to Joe to ask him for a contribution, but I thought he might ruin the surprise. He is always following Megan around like a lost puppy."

"Oh, really?" Suzie's stomach began to churn. "What does Megan like? Is she fond of a certain perfume? Does she prefer one specific designer?"

"I don't know her very well—at least not like Joe does. I can tell you one thing though. She absolutely loves safari print. She wears it all the time. She looks so good in it too." The secretary giggled. "I'm surprised she hasn't gotten Joe to wear safari print. They spend so much time together-behind closed doors."

Suzie wanted to throw the phone against the wall. I would like to choke this girl, the little wench. How dare she insinuate that my husband is having an affair with his boss?

"Umm, let me get back to you on this, okay? I will do some checking so that I can make sure the quality of the gift is exactly what Joe would want to give to Megan."

I wonder if the local nursery can gift wrap manure.

"Okay, that is good, but please don't let Joe know about the surprise. I am scared silly that he will let the surprise slip during one of their hunting trips."

Well, that explains his hunting fascination and his obsession with safari print. It is making sense to me now, that bastard.

"Shhh…be quiet," the secretary said. "Megan is walking towards me right now. Well, I shouldn't say "walk." She saunters. You know, like a lioness in heat. I got to go now." Click.

The secretary made sure that the phone line was dead. Then she turned, looking up at Megan. "Did I read the script the way you wanted me to, boss?"

"Yes, you did perfectly. That conversation should make it clear to Susanna that Joe and I are more than coworkers." Megan had a gleam in her eyes. "I am hoping she will give fuel to my fire by making Joe's home life so crazy that he will divorce her. Then he will be all mine."

"Give me that script." Megan tore the script up into little pieces, depositing the evidence into the trash basket.

"You will see a raise on your next paycheck."

The secretary smiled. "Thanks, boss."

"Do I really saunter like a lioness?" Megan walked away, swinging her hips with seduction riding side saddle.

"Yes, boss you do." The secretary said. The secretary waited until Megan was out of eyesight before she rolled her eyes and pretended to gag.

"Psycho" might now be an understatement for how Suzie felt. All of her "psycho" suspicions had been confirmed. Her first impulse was to burn the comforter and the drapes, and rip the safari border off the walls. How dare Joe make their bedroom into a shrine for his mistress. The nerve of him!

Suzie paced back and forth in her kitchen. No, if she did that, she would be adding fuel to the fire. She had to calm down. Think rationally. Maybe this was a phase, something Joe was doing because of a mid-life crisis.

Although the secretary insinuated that Joe and Megan were more than coworkers, that didn't mean it was true. The secretary's IQ was probably somewhere under fifty.

How do I handle this? Do I confront Joe? Do I ignore this and hope it will disappear? Or do I poke fun at it and try to demean the situation. Hmmm, that is an idea. Yes, I will make fun of the décor and mock the relationship that Joe and Megan have formed.

So, make fun of it, she did. She regaled her friends with stories from "Joe's jungle." This avenue of release helped her dissipate the anger that she had felt when conversing with Joe's secretary.

She was talking to her friend, Hope, when she said she felt like she needed to sleep with a rifle under her pillow. A hideous monster might come after her during the still of the night.

If only Suzie could have seen into the spiritual world, she would have been shocked to realize how close her suspicions were to reality.

There *was* a monster lurking in her bedroom. The Beast of Betrayal. This beast has been present since the birth of evil, taking great delight in the harvest of souls for Satan.

Horrendous in appearance, the beast sported a rotund stomach, which was covered with black, greasy hair. The legs were short, and the claws on its feet were sharp and long. The beast's eyes were blood red. Fangs a foot long extended from its mouth.

The Beast of Betrayal was relentless in its fixation to create wretched heartache in human souls. The poison of betrayal could transform a soul that had once been rich with love and forgiveness into an unforgiving and bitter wasteland of pain.

Arrogance, Deceit, Rejection and Despair wove their threads of evil into the pain of Betrayal. Arrogance set the stage for Betrayal, slipping into the mind of the perpetrator with thoughts of self-importance.

Deceit was right on the heels of Arrogance with the encyclopedia of lies such as: "We have a mandatory leadership seminar this weekend. Sorry, the spouses aren't allowed to come. They are considered a distraction."

On the other hand: "The hickey on the side of my neck? Hmmm, well.... it was a work accident. I can't tell you how exactly it happened. It just happened okay? Why are you so paranoid?"

And… "How did I get a tan while going to a leadership seminar in Wyoming in the dead of winter? Have you ever heard of a tanning salon? And yes, that is exactly where that Hawaiian lei came from."

The more deceit, the greater became the absurdity of the lies. Soon the one who was betrayed would feel the pain of Rejection seeping into their heart, and that opened the door for the last evil entity, Despair.

According to the empire of evil, Despair was a grand place for someone to be. Despair could prevent Hope, Faith, Joy, Trust, and Love from healing the pain of Betrayal. Despair could bind a person in misery.

In the spirit world of evil, the Beast of Betrayal was a giant. The Beast of Betrayal had an unusual alliance with love. Betrayal was powerless if love had not forged a path first. If a person had no capacity for love, Betrayal had no power to inflict pain.

Suzie loved Joe. She loved him with every cell of her body, and Betrayal had a bullseye on Suzie's heart.

THE SHATTERED VASE

TODAY WAS THE DAY HE WAS COMING HOME TO PACK his clothes. He had only been gone a week, but to Suzie, it seemed like a lifetime.

How many times had she reapplied her mascara? Was it five or six? Tears make a miserable mascara remover.

Joe promised to be there at 9 p.m. Suzie glanced at the living room clock as she walked back to the couch. It was 11:00 p.m. Well, she would wait thirty more minutes, and then that was it. He would have to come another day to pack his clothes. He still had a key. At least, she thought he did. If not, tough luck. He could afford to buy new clothes.

A moment later, the crunching of gravel in her driveway startled her. The screeching of Joe's brakes made her cringe.

Then the honking started—loud, obnoxious, and incessant.

What on earth was he thinking? He knew the children would be asleep.

The honking continued.

Suzie scurried to the front door, threw on her winter coat, and opened the door. She rushed onto the front porch. The layer of ice caught her heels on the first step. Her stiletto heels betrayed her as her body flew backward. She grabbed the railing on the side of the porch. The railing waffled for a moment, shaking as if it were a leaf in the wind, then held tight to the rusty bolts that secured it to the porch.

She caught the look on Joe's face as she twisted and pulled herself up. He was smirking. *Damn him.*

As Suzie walked to the truck, the smirk lingered on Joe's face. At least her near-disaster stopped the honking. *He can't be obnoxious and disrespectful at the same time. Too many thought processes required for that.*

As she started across the yard, Suzie realized that her stilettos could be a friend as well as an enemy. The heels sunk into the frozen ground and stabilized her slender frame.

Just before reaching the truck, she stopped. She used to think Joe looked like the devil when he got angry. Now, she was sure he did.

Joe rolled down his window. "Where are my clothes? I thought I told you to pack my clothes."

Suzie approached the truck. Her breath laced the truck window with fog. "They're your clothes, sir. You are an adult. Pack your own clothes."

"What a bitch you are." Joe threw open the truck door.

Suzie couldn't step back fast enough. The door hit her in the chest, knocking the wind out of her. She teetered for a moment, then lost her fight for balance to gravity. She landed with a plop on the hard-frozen ground.

Suzie swallowed hard and made a desperate effort not to cry. She had a sinking feeling this evening was not going down the path she had hoped.

Joe stared at Suzie, sprawled out like a dead bird on the ground. He recoiled, reached into his truck and grabbed some trash bags. "Get up! You're not hurt."

Joe stomped to the front porch. "The sooner I get this done, the faster I can move on with my life; make it what *I* want for a change."

Suzie took a moment to disengage from the frozen ground, then hurried to catch up to Joe. He raced up the stairs to their front door. As she reached the front porch, the door slammed in her face. She turned the door knob and pushed. The door did not budge.

"Joe, please be reasonable." Suzie struggled against the force of hate. "Joe, please. I… I… need to talk with you." Suzie choked on her words, as tears erupted.

Joe jerked opened the door, flinging Suzie into the living room.

"All I asked of you was one thing. Pack my clothes. I mean, was that so damn hard? It is not like you work or anything. Can't you help me? Just once?"

"I was hoping that maybe you would change your mind." Suzie wiped the tears from her face.

"That is not going to happen, Suzie. Wrap your mind around reality for a change. What we were…that is gone now. *There is no more us.*" Joe kicked a matchbox car across the floor. "I came for my things. I will pack them myself if I have to." Joe said, walking to their bedroom. He threw his shoes into one trash bag. His T-shirts found their home in the second, and his jeans were tossed into the third bag. He stuffed his ironed shirts and dress pants into the fourth bag.

Suzie followed him, vowing not to let defeat overcome her resolve. *This is my family and my marriage I am fighting for. No matter how much it hurts; this is worth fighting for.*

"Joe," she said softly. "Joe, please stop. I have something for you." Suzie reached toward the vase of roses with trembling fingers. "I don't know what happened to us. We had such a wonderful marriage... before Megan. I still love you." Suzie wiped a stray tear from her cheek. "The children… the children still love you, Joe. Don't you still love them? I bought these roses to symbolize the children." Suzie paused, her lower lip quivering. "The vase represents us, you and me, the parents. The roses symbolize our three children. Without our marriage, the children will not have what they need to thrive and grow," Suzie pleaded.

Joe's face softened as he took the vase and lifted it up to his nose. He inhaled deeply as if he was drinking in the fragrance of the roses.

That look in his eyes made her weak. He used to say she was breathtaking in beauty. He said she hadn't changed. She was still as beautiful as the day they had married, even after having three children. Oh, how she missed him.

Maybe she could forgive him. They could start all over! He could get another job, so he wouldn't see Megan anymore. Surely, he has some love left.

"The children have been asking every day, 'Where is Daddy?' Joe, please think about the children. Stay for them. We could... we could start all over." Suzie said, with a seductive grin.

She smiled and inched closer to the arms which she so wanted to embrace her. They could go on a second honeymoon. They could even have another wedding if that's what it took. He could buy her a new ring. Yes, she was sure she could forgive him.

Joe looked up from the vase and gazed into Suzie's eyes. The feeling of weakness was coursing through her body.

"Suzie, I am thinking of the children. I have not stopped loving them. I just don't love you." Joe released his grip from the vase. The vase plummeted to the hardwood floor, the fragile crystal vase shattering into countless tiny knives of glass.

Suzie's heart exploded with intense, shearing pain. There was a sound that escaped her lips, which startled her. It was an unusual sound; haunting and terrifying.

Her strength disappeared, and her legs felt like jelly. She found her gaze to be on the same level as the soles of Joe's shoes. Joe walked past her with his bags, his shoes crunching the splintered glass.

Joe paused in the doorway and turned back. The look of love drained from his eyes, replaced by sheer disdain.

"When the kids wake up in the morning tell them that I love them. Sweep up that broken glass, so they don't cut their feet." Joe turned to walk out of the bedroom.

He then strode arrogantly out of the home which housed his family, his hands firmly grasping the trash bags.

HOPE

THE SUNRISE KNOCKED WITH IMPATIENCE AT HOPE'S window. Concerned for her friend Suzie, Hope had wrestled with sleep, losing the match to insomnia. As she struggled to wake up, she had an unsettled feeling. Should she call Suzie? No, she would drive over to her house. It wasn't that far.

As Hope started her car, she began to panic. Something bad had happened. She was sure of it. She could feel it in her gut. She had to get to Suzie, and it had better be fast.

She pulled into Suzie's driveway and glanced at her watch: 6:30 a.m. It was too early to ring the doorbell. Phoning might wake the children. She would try the front door to see if it was unlocked.

Hope hurried out of her car and took the stairs two at a time. She reached for the doorknob expecting it to give some resistance. The door opened without a key. That wasn't good. Joe never left anything unlocked. *Too bad he didn't lock his heart against adultery.*

As Hope passed the threshold of the home, she could smell Despair, like a rotten egg. She held back the instinct to vomit.

The house looked empty. The sound of silence was threatening. No sign of life; neither the children, nor Suzie. What had happened?

Hope walked quietly through the house, checking each room. The living room, the formal dining room, the kitchen, back through the dining area again and then down the hall to Suzie's room.

At the door, Hope paused to collect herself. The stench of Despair was seeping under the door, making her feel faint.

Hope was unable to think the very worst. That a life was taken. Surely God was greater than the attack that had been waged against Suzie.

Hope slowly twisted the doorknob. She gasped. Blood was speckled like freckles over Suzie's body. When she saw the roses in Suzie's hands, she started to cry. The roses had been clenched so tightly by Suzie that the thorns had impaled her palms. Dried blood ran down her wrists like a wayward road.

Within a second, Suzie was cradled within the comfort of Hope's arms.

"What happened?"

Suzie was limp, melting like a rag doll, into the comfort of Hope. Her eyes fluttered open to catch a glimpse of Hope and then closed again, her mind scurrying back into the void of despair.

"I don't know. I don't... I don't remember." Suzie murmured, as if drunk with pain.

"That's okay, honey. Looks like it may be better to forget."

"My hands hurt. There are pricks of pain as if a porcupine has attacked me. My whole body hurts." Suzie's brow furrowed as she fought to keep her eyes open.

"I am so sorry."

"Why do my hands hurt so much?" Suzie opened her eyes to see the source of pain and then let out a mournful groan. "Oh God, now I remember." Suzie clung with desperation to Hope. "Joe left, threw his clothes in trash bags and just left."

"I am sorry he hurt you. I know you loved him."

"I did love him." Suzie hung her head. "Now I have to stop. I don't know how to stop loving that man."

"No one scales a mountain in a leap, Suzie. They reach the peak one step at a time."

"The vase of roses didn't work. He threw the vase to the floor. I thought you said that men were visual and that a symbolic picture would bring him around." A flash of anger narrowed Suzie's eyes.

"Men who are drowning in sin rarely see clearly, my dear. I was hoping he could still see some light." A tear dropped from Hope's cheek, washing away one of the freckles of blood.

"So now the broken vase is piercing my skin and causing me pain. Why am I the one who hurts? Shouldn't he be the one hurting if he is the one sinning?" Suzie spat out the words, as if they were venom.

"He will hurt in time. Sin wears the mask of happiness, but over a lifetime, it can suffocate the person who has chosen to wear it. Be patient, my dear. Let sin run its course, the hurt will come."

Suzie started crying. "I don't want him to hurt. I just want him back."

"I know. I know." Hope stroked Suzie's long silky hair and peppered her crown with kisses.

"How could God do this to me?" Suzie sobbed.

Hope flinched at the presence of Deceit. "Sin never originates with God, dear one."

"Well, then why wasn't He powerful enough to stop this from happening?"

Hope knew that Despair was gaining ground in Suzie's mind. She was starting to smell the stench again. Distraction may be the best way to handle this discussion. Suzie would be unable to understand how powerful God was in the presence of Despair.

"Um, when are the children supposed to be at school?" Hope asked.

"Shoot, I forgot about them. What time is it?"

"It is seven o'clock."

"That only leaves me thirty minutes to get them dressed and feed them breakfast. I must take a shower first. It would totally freak them out if they saw me covered with blood."

Suzie struggled to get up quickly, she was unsteady on her feet and started to sink back to the floor.

Hope shot up quick as lightning and was there to support Suzie. Suzie fell into her arms; faint from the loss of blood.

"Honey, I can get the children to school. Why don't you sit on the side of the bed for a moment and collect yourself? I will get a broom and rag and clean up the mess."

"Are you sure?" Suzie asked.

"Yes, I am sure, silly." Hope smiled and walked Suzie over to the bed. "After you feel a little more like yourself, you can take a shower and then crawl back into bed. I have missed your precious children. I intend to enjoy the time spent with them."

"Thanks, Hope. I don't know what I would do without you."

"No problem," Hope said.

Hope hurried to the kitchen and grabbed the broom, dustpan and a rag. Her mind was already in top form to make this day turn around for Suzie. As she started sweeping, she swept around the roses—avoiding them. She wiped up the blood, then turned to Suzie. "What do you want to do with the roses?"

"Throw them away, along with all the dreams for my marriage... and my life," Suzie said.

Hope turned around and began her way to the kitchen to dispose of the roses.

"No, wait a minute! Hope, don't throw them away!" Suzie said in a panic. "They symbolize my children. Wrap the stems in a moist cloth and then put it in plastic. I will keep the roses by my bed, next to my heart."

A DAY WITH HOPE

HOPE SHUFFLED QUIETLY THROUGH THE HALLWAY TO the children's bedroom and opened the door without its customary squeak. She tiptoed through the maze of toys scattered on the bedroom floor and leaned down to plant a feathery kiss on Sarah's plump cheek. "Good Morning, sweet child of God," she whispered.

Sarah's eyes popped open with excitement. She squealed with delight when she saw Hope.

Sarah sprung from the bed into Hope's open arms. The two of them giggled like young schoolgirls. Sarah looked into Hope's eyes with mock sincerity and said. "Where have you been? It seems like forever since I have seen you."

"It is not where I have been that should concern you, dear child, but it is where I am now that you should rejoice in."

"I do rejoice." Sarah said, giggling, while tightening her hug.

Michael was tangled in the covers. When he heard Hope's voice, he shot across the bed, embracing her waist in a bear hug.

In the same moment, Jonathan found comfort in Hope's right arm. His bottom, resting on her hip, as his legs encircled her waist.

"Well, darlings, I do believe you are glad to see me," Hope giggled. "I need to get two of you to school quickly. So, Sarah and Michael, I wonder, which of you can get dressed first?"

"I can! I can!" Michael said, jumping up and down with glee.

"Well, then go to it, my dear."

"Did you mean get dressed, or get dressed *correctly*?" Sarah whispered in Hope's ear.

"Both."

Sarah rushed to the closet to pick out a sweater and some leggings. She pulled her hair back into a ponytail, then slipped on her socks and shoes.

Not to be outdone, Michael dressed in record time.

While Michael and Sarah were dressing, Hope clothed Jonathan in a warm sweat suit.

"Well, I do believe the race to get dressed has resulted in a tie," Hope said. "Since everyone wins with a tie, I guess I will take *everyone* to McDonald's for breakfast on the way to school."

"Yummy." Jonathan rubbed his belly.

"Michael, are you sure you're dressed right?" Sarah gave him a critical look.

Michael looked down with doubt at his shirt, shoes and jeans. "Yeah, I think so."

"Let me check you over." Sarah turned him around to make sure he was dressed to perfection. "Well, I cannot find one thing you did wrong. I guess there is a first for everything. Good job."

"Thanks, sis." Michael beamed with pride.

"Alright, little ones, why don't you start your pilgrimage to the front door. I want to check on your mommy really quick, and then we will be on our way."

"Okay." Sarah led the progression to the door.

Hope opened Suzie's door. Although exhausted, she appeared to be at peace. So different from what she looked like an hour ago. Hope could no longer smell the scent of Despair. The miserable creature was such a coward in the presence of God's spirit.

Hope closed the door gently and started skipping through the house. Soon the children and Hope were skipping to the car. They even skipped in and out of McDonald's and left with a delicious breakfast resting in their tummies.

When Hope returned to the house with Jonathan, she knew that she had to keep his sharp mind occupied, leaving no open door for Despair to slip in. She also wanted to do some cleaning for Suzie. With creativity, she could do both. "Jonathan, I see toys on this floor, and the cabinets seem to be calling them. Can you hear the cabinets' calling?"

Jonathan looked puzzled. "I don't he' them calling."

Hope used her ventriloquist skill that she had learned at Bible camp. The cabinet said, "I am missing some matchbox cars."

Jonathan stared at the cabinets in amazement. He picked up three cars and properly placed them in the plastic box designated for such toys.

"Thank you, Jonathan," the cabinet said, "Can I please have more?"

Jonathan peered inside the cabinet. "Who is it?" Seeing no one, he grabbed four cars and placed them in the box.

"More please."

Jonathan continued to pick up more cars. With the cabinets telling him exactly what they needed, the floor was soon cleared of toys.

While Jonathan was cleaning up the toys, Hope made the bed and picked up stray articles of clothing. Within an hour, the room looked good enough for a photo op with Family Circle magazine.

"I think I am getting a teensy bit hungry. How about we make some cookies, Jonathan?"

Jonathan ran to Hope and gave her leg a hug. "I love cookies."

By the time the cookies were done and sampled, it was time to skip to the car and pick up Michael from school.

The afternoon passed quickly with an assortment of coloring, games, and a nap sandwiched in between.

When Sarah returned from school, the sounds of joy from the children lured Suzie from her deep sleep. She walked out of her bedroom with a peaceful and serene look.

The five of them played hide-and-seek until dinner time.

Hope offered to make dinner. Suzie refused, insisting that no one could make spaghetti as good as she could. Hope graciously gave in.

When the spaghetti reached the table, Hope stirred in a bit of fun. "I bet I am the only one who can eat spaghetti without getting a bit of sauce on my shirt."

"Are you kidding me?" Sarah asked. "I have never spilled sauce on my clothes before."

"Well," Michael said, "I think I may have once."

"Me too," Jonathan said.

Suzie laughed and admitted that she often missed the mark with spaghetti sauce.

Hope gave Suzie a wink. "There are some cookies on the counter. Whoever eats their spaghetti without spilling a drop of sauce gets first dibs on the cookies for dessert."

"I'm in," Sarah said.

Jonathan smiled, "Me too!"

"I don't know whether I will win, but it is worth a try," Suzie said.

Michael was already trying to corral his first bite on the fork.

By the end of the dinner, among much laughter, Hope had a face full of spaghetti sauce. Jonathan had enough in his lap to feed the starving children in Africa, and Michael's cheek was a blush with sauce.

"My abdomen hurts from laughing so much." Suzie looked down. "I must admit, I think I see some spaghetti on the floor, right next to my chair."

Sarah emerged as the winner and chose the finest of all the cookies. As Sarah looked at the cookie, Hope could feel the warmth of God's Spirit. Then she saw the Spirit of God alighting on Sarah's shoulder, like a butterfly on the blossom of a flower.

The kitchen held silence as if it was a treasure. Everyone was waiting for Sarah to take her fist bite, so they could eat the remaining cookies.

Sarah looked up from the cookie in her hand and gazed at Hope. She hesitated for a moment then handed the cookie to Hope. "Thanks for coming over. I am always happy when you are around."

Hope had tears in her eyes when she took the cookie. "Thank you, sweet child of God."

Hope looked at the cookie, wondering who needed the cookie more than she did. She looked at each of the expectant faces surrounding the kitchen table.

"Suzie, this time in your life can destroy you or transform you into a pillar of strength. It is your choice what you make of this battle." Hope offered the cookie to Suzie. "I do believe that you will make the right choice."

Suzie took the cookie, wiping tears from her eyes, and handed it to Michael. "You may not be good at hitting your mouth with spaghetti, but you are good in so many ways that count. I love you."

Michael took the cookie and handed it to Jonathan. "You are the best little brother a boy could have."

Jonathan looked at the cookie and eyed it with such desire that Suzie was scared that he would take a bite. Everyone at the table was in suspense. Jonathan looked up from the cookie and handed it to Sarah. "You good at eating spaghetti, but you betta at being my sista."

Sarah took the cookie, put it back on the plate, then took the plate full of cookies and put it on the table.

"Dig in, spaghetti eaters!" Sarah said with excitement.

The cookies were devoured in a minute, but the memory of God's presence lasted a lifetime in the hearts of those surrounding the kitchen table.

THE DEFEAT OF DESPAIR

THE CHAMBERS OF DARKNESS WERE INTENT ON destruction. The evil entities had released Deceit, Adultery, Arrogance, Betrayal, and Despair for the decimation of a family.

The breakup of the covenant agreement between Joe and Suzie was rendered a success. This put Suzie and the children at risk for fear and degradation. Now that the marriage was defeated, the forces of evil had set their sights on a new target; the life of Suzie.

On this dark night, the forces gathered to gloat about their victory and hear the current state of affairs via Despair.

"Here, here," Deceit said. "Fellow wicked ones, I believe we have cause to celebrate."

"Yes, we do," Betrayal said. "The marriage covenant between Joe and Susanna Whatley is now null and void due to our wonderful servant of lust, Megan."

Adultery fluttered her eyelashes. "Megan should be given a medal."

"Yes, she is great at seduction," Deceit paused. "I believe at last count she had seven broken marriages to her credit. I don't believe she would be impressed with a simple medal though. Her last husband gave her a mansion with a pool in the back yard. Her former husband gave her a Ferrari. The one before the Ferrari husband took her on so many trips to foreign countries that she almost forgot where home was. The only thing she hasn't had is children. She doesn't want her own children. Why waste a perfect body like hers?"

"How many abortions has she had again?" Arrogance asked.

"Eight, I think," Deceit said. "She may have slipped another one in when I wasn't looking."

Betrayal sneered, "The only obstacle to Megan having complete control over Joe's children is their mother. We eliminate her, and we have three more souls in our grasp."

"Well," Deceit said, "I think Suzie may not be an obstacle for very long if Despair had success. Despair? Where are you? You did have success, didn't you?"

Despair emerged from behind the peacock feathers of Arrogance. Her form was childlike, the belly protruding as if malnourished. Her hair was thin, long and stringy. Her eyes were brimming with fear, depression, and worry. "Well, a measure of success I may say." Despair twirled her oily hair around her fingers. "I mean I got in her mind. Yes, I got in her mind all right. I was right there when Joe packed his clothes. Yes, I—"

Deceit held up his hand, striding across the chamber to bend over Despair and glare at her with indignation. "What exactly do you mean by 'a *measure* of success?'"

"Well, you see; it was like this. Joe packed his clothes, then Susanna gave him the vase of roses. Hope was the idiot who told her to give him a vase of roses." In a mocking tone, Despair mimicked Hope's words: "The vase is symbolic of the children's need for both parents to remain together. The roses were supposed to be the children.' What a bunch of hogwash." Despair put a finger in her mouth and pretended to gag.

Despair's voice returned to its normal whiny, irritating tone. "Joe is our comrade though, so he dropped the vase and let it shatter on the floor. I heard Susanna's heart break. Oh, what a fantastic sound that was!" Despair jumped up and down with excitement.

"That is when I saw my opening, and I dove deep into her mind." Despair paused to take a breath. "I pushed Susanna's many failures, incompetence, and mistakes right to the very front of her mind. Next, I put her insecurities in the top chambers of her heart."

Despair paused to wipe the sweat off her oily forehead. "Then I started on the buffet of good. I had a feast on the good things that Susanna had done for others: the love she had shown to those unlovable, the kind acts that had been done to her. I ate them all up." Despair said, cringing at the memory of good. "I consumed all of the compliments, good words, and deeds that had been visited upon her. Then I vomited all that good right back up with the juice of Betrayal. She won't remember that any good has been done to her or by her. It will all be tainted with evil."

Deceit wasn't satisfied. "You still haven't said what you meant by a 'measure of success.'"

Despair ignored the interruption. "Once the vase had shattered, Susanna collapsed onto the floor. She was covered in blood. I mean covered." Despair gazed around the room making sure the entities had absorbed that important point. "There was broken glass all around her. I kept trying to get her to pick up a sharp piece of glass and cut some important vein. She used to be a nurse. A nurse should know how to kill herself, right?" Despair waved her thin arms up and down for emphasis. "Well, instead of using what was right by her and so convenient, she did a really weak thing ... she went to sleep."

"She went to sleep?" Betrayal screamed. "After I tainted all her good memories, she went to sleep? Are you kidding me?"

"No, but that isn't the worst of it." Despair hung her head, wrung her bony fingers and in a whisper, muttered. "Hope was the one who woke her up."

Deceit fumed, "Hope was there, and you said you had a 'measure of success?'"

"Well, I did get inside her mind." Despair said with a haughty flip of her head.

Deceit thundered as his arms whipped around and caught Despair by her hair. "One minute of Hope can destroy all our work." Deceit hurled Despair against the wall.

Despair's screams echoed through the Chambers of Darkness. The audience of evil spirits applauded the vicious attack. The assault went on for hours. Before Deceit stopped the punishment, the walls were splattered with the blackish blood of Despair.

"Next time you say you have a 'measure of success' you need to bring Susanna's death certificate with you." Deceit spat on the blackened form of Despair. Deceit paced back and forth, his black cloak billowing out behind him. "It will take some time for the memory of Hope to leave Susanna's mind. We have to develop a new strategy."

Deceit continued to pace, then stopped short and said with a menacing tone. “Who is willing to go after the children?”

“Well, I think that maybe I could possibly work it into my schedule.” Doubt said with characteristic indecision.

Insecurity said, “I have had a great amount of success with children from broken homes.”

“I need a full blown, all-out attack on their stupid, young minds,” Deceit said. “Do you understand me?”

“We will be on it tonight... I think.” Doubt was teetering on his feet, as if swaying in the wind. “Right, Insecurity?”

Insecurity was hiding behind Envy. “Well, I don’t know if we will be successful or not. Maybe Fear should take over.”

Arrogance spoke up.“Fear is currently embroiled in starting another war in the Congo of Africa. There is much bloodshed to be gained through conflict in that region. He cannot be spared for this fight, at least not now. Our greatest harvest of souls in Africa is right now.”

“Ok, well, I guess we will go then,” Doubt said. “I sure hope Faith is nowhere around.”

“Yeah, that or Love,” Insecurity whispered.

CHOCOLATE MILK

DOUBT AND INSECURITY SLIPPED IN THROUGH A crack of the foundation. They scampered through the house until their targets were found in the bedroom.

"Do you think we should try to get into the middle of their dreams and create a nightmare?" Insecurity asked.

"I don't know," Doubt said. "Sometimes, people don't remember nightmares."

"Yeah, you're right." Insecurity contemplated for a moment and then chuckled. "Hey, I just thought of a really great idea. We could knock something off their dresser and scare them half out of their wits."

"That would be fun," Doubt said. "If we do that though, the brats would go running to their mother, and we would have to deal with her."

"Yeah, she is a problem, so we shouldn't do that." Insecurity scratched his furrowed brow. "Hmmm, we could do the hover technique and just float above the bed until one of them wakes up."

"Yeah, but there are three of them and only two of us. How about we pick one of them out as our target? Then we could hover over just one." Doubt paused to consider the possibility. "But which one?"

"Well, if I remember right in our briefing on this family, Sarah is the sassy one, Michael, the smart one, and Jonathan is the one that can't pronounce his r's," Insecurity said.

"Ok," Doubt said. "I say we hover over Michael since he is the smart one."

"I don't know about that," Insecurity countered. "I believe Sarah would be the one we would have greatest access to. If she is sassy, then she may have false confidence, maybe even arrogance. You know that makes it easier for us to slide into her mind," Insecurity said.

"Good point. I sure hope we don't mess up," Doubt said. "I guess we could try Sarah. We had better do it quickly before the desolate creatures wake up."

"Okay, let's float over Sarah then." Insecurity said as the spirits swooped down from the ceiling, landing right above Sarah's chest.

The early hours of the night had passed without incident in the home, but around three a.m., Sarah awoke with a start. She had trouble breathing. She felt insecure and lost, as if the former day with Hope had been a fleeting dream.

She needed to talk. Should she wake her mother? No, her mother had enough to deal with.

The only other people she could talk to were her brothers. She looked at Michael sleeping beside her. Had she ever talked with Michael? She was constantly telling him *what* to do but that wasn't the same as talking *with* him.

Well, she had to talk to someone and it is not like God had been listening lately. If God were listening, her daddy would be in the bedroom with her mom.

Sarah patted Michael's shoulder gently. "Hey Michael, wake up. I need to talk."

Michael swatted at the air as if he were trying to ward off an irritating insect.

Sarah put her head back on her pillow trying to identify why she felt afraid. The more she thought about Michael being able to sleep, the angrier she got. She didn't need her brothers for much, but now when she needed Michael, he had the nerve to be sleeping.

Sarah positioned her mouth right over Michael's ear and used her right hand as a megaphone. "Wake up, stupid!"

Michael woke up and simultaneously started his plaintive cry for his mother. "Moooommmm!"

Sarah's hand shot out from under the covers and slapped Michael's mouth shut.

"Shhh..." She glared through the darkness at her brother. "Don't you dare wake Mom. I'm worried about her, and I need to talk. If she comes in, pretend you're asleep, and she'll go back to her room."

They both lay in bed as if they were made of stone, barely breathing and hoping that their mother had not heard Michael. After a few minutes Michael pried Sarah's hand from his mouth.

"Don't call me stupid," Michael said.

"Okay, I'm sorry. I need to talk, and you are the only person I can talk with."

"What do you want to talk about?"

"Mom."

"What about her?"

"She's different. I mean, before Dad left, she was so happy," Sarah said. "When Hope came today she was like she used to be. I want her to be the same Mom she used to be."

"None of us are the same, Sarah."

Sarah wiped a tear from her eye. "She must miss him."

"I know I miss him," Michael said. "He used to be fun. He changed though. Lately, he's just mad all the time."

"Where did he go?" Sarah asked.

"I heard Mom tell someone on the phone that he moved in with his boss." Michael turned away from Sarah, as if wanting to go back to sleep.

"What does his boss have that Mom doesn't have?" Sarah grasped Michael's shoulder, forcing him to face her.

"I don't know." Michael paused to consider the question. "Money, maybe money. Mom doesn't have any money. I mean that lady is his boss. She must have money."

"How can money be more important than Mom, or us?" Sarah asked.

Michael rubbed the sleep from his eyes. "I don't know, but I overheard her say that Dad had been fooling around with that woman for a long time; since the company picnic. At least, I think that's what she said."

"What does foolin' awound mean?" Jonathan asked, sitting up in bed.

"Well, the way I see it," Michael said. "It means ticklin."

"How could it mean that?" Sarah asked. "Why would Dad leave us to go tickle another woman?"

"What does Mom say every time we tickle each other in bed and don't go to sleep?" Michael asked.

"She says, 'Stop fooling around.'" Sarah wondered when Michael had got to be so smart. "Wow, I never thought tickling was that bad."

"Yeah, I know." Michael said with remorse. "I feel really bad for all the tickling I have done. I think we should stop."

"Yeah, Mom's probably had enough with Dad tickling his boss," Sarah said.

"Why Daddy leave?" Jonathan spoke with wide-eyed innocence.

"Well, Jonathan, I probably shouldn't tell you and Michael this, but I have to tell someone, so it may as well be you two." Sarah paused to collect her thoughts. "Back when school started, and the weather was warm enough to play outside, you both were playing in the back yard. I stayed inside because I had homework to do. Mom and Dad were in their bedroom, talking. I got nosy. I don't know why. I guess I wanted to find out why they never kissed anymore." Sarah took a deep breath. "I thought if I listened to them talk, then maybe I would have the answer. They started talking low, like they may have suspected that I was eavesdropping. Their voices started getting louder, then they started screaming at each other, using words that are bad to say."

"What wo'ds?"

"Jonathan," Sarah said. "There are some words that you shouldn't say. Mommy and Daddy were saying those words."

"Can you please go on with the story?" Michael rolled his eyes. "I need to get some sleep tonight."

"Mommy was crying. Daddy was yelling 'I don't love you anymore, Suzie! I don't have the same feelings for you that I once had.'" Sarah wiped a tear from her cheek.

"The room was silent then. All I could hear was Mommy sobbing. Then in a quiet voice she said, 'Please tell me what it is that I have done wrong in this marriage. Please tell me and I will try to fix it.'"

"There was a long pause before Daddy said, 'There's nothing you can do, Suzie. I love Megan now.'"

"Megan? Who's Megan?" Jonathan asked in wide-eyed horror.

"Megan must be Daddy's boss." Michael said with tears in his eyes.

"Once Daddy said he loved Megan, Mommy went berserk. She started calling him all sorts of names. I could hear her hitting Daddy's chest. Then I heard a loud slap. I knew that Daddy had hit Mommy. When I heard a thump on the floor, I knew he must have hit her so hard that she fell. Mommy really started crying after that. Daddy told her to 'stop crying right now!'"

Sarah shook her head. "I had to go outside because I couldn't stand to hear her crying like that. I was crying myself, so I went behind the shed to cry. I didn't want Daddy to know I was crying. He would be angry. He was mad Mommy was crying. He would have been furious if he knew I had been listening and even madder if he found out I was crying too."

"So, you not to cwy if someone stop loving you, then they slap you?" Jonathan asked.

"I guess not," Michael said.

"You think Daddy stop loving us?" Jonathan asked.

"I don't know." Sarah paused; doubt started creeping in. "He didn't say that exactly. He said, 'he stopped loving Mommy.'"

"How could you stop loving Mommy?" Michael asked. "She gives us chocolate milk every morning while we are still in bed. None of my friends' moms do that."

"Maybe she didn't give Daddy any chocolate milk in bed, or at least not enough," Sarah said.

"I don't know if he left cause of the milk thing or not," Michael wiped his tears. "I know I haven't been acting right lately. I pulled Jonathan's hair last week and Daddy got mad when I did that," Michael said.

"I not been good. I can't go pee-pee wight. I still have these." Jonathan said as he tugged on the elastic band of his pull ups. He then put his thumb in his mouth and made loud sucking noises.

"Jonathan, stop sucking your thumb!" Sarah sat up in bed. "You're going to grow thumbs instead of teeth if you keep doing that."

Jonathan whimpered. The thumb was now vacuum-packed between his upper and lower jaw.

"Stop crying Jonathan. Stop it right now," Sarah demanded.

"I can cwy if I want to. Mommy is the one who can't." Jonathan slid his words out around the contours of his thumb.

"I give up. If you want a mouth full of thumbs, then you go right ahead and have thumbs in your mouth instead of nice, pretty teeth." Sarah plopped back on the bed. "I hope we don't have to go live with Grandpa and Grandma."

"Why would we have to do that?" Michael asked

"My friend Brittany had to go and live with her grandparents when her daddy left. It happens sometimes," Sarah said.

"I don't want to live with Ganma. She is mean. She has clean house. We don't." Jonathan was still talking around his thumb.

"I don't think we have to worry about that." Michael put his hands behind his head. "I heard Mommy talking to Grandma the other day, and she said, 'no one else was going to take care of her children,' she didn't say it nice either. She yelled it. She was angry. Mommy won't leave us. She don't love anyone more than us."

"Can we still see Daddy?" Jonathan asked.

"I don't know. I hope so. I miss him and I love him," Michael said.

"Yeah, same here," Sarah said.

"Me too." Jonathan continued the sucking sounds.

"Maybe God will hear that prayer, if we pray," Sarah said. "Jonathan, if you stop sucking your thumb, you can lie down beside me, and we can cuddle."

"That not foolin' awound?" Jonathan asked.

"No, tickling is fooling around. Cuddling is ok," Sarah replied.

Jonathan jerked the thumb out of his mouth. He wiped the lingering spit on his flannel pajamas, crawled clumsily over Michael and had Sarah's arms wrapped around him, all in less than ten seconds.

THE SEESAW OF DOUBT AND INSECURITY

"WELL, I THOUGHT WE HAD THEM WHEN THEY STARTED talking about what they had done wrong." Insecurity slithered out the front door of Susanna's home.

"Yeah," Doubt said. "We may have gained a bit of ground there, but one can never have faith in humans."

"I can't believe that they're stupid enough to love their father. I mean he left their home for Megan, when he had a loyal and loving wife at home," Insecurity said.

"Yeah," Doubt chuckled. "Megan doesn't know the first thing about being loyal or loving."

"I wish we had been given the assignment to attack Joe," Insecurity said. "It would have been such an easy assignment."

"We already have Joe's soul. No reason for an attack when we have won the battle," Doubt said. "We are not allowed to celebrate our victories by being idle. There are many souls at stake. Our time is limited."

"Are you referring to the second coming of Christ?" Insecurity asked.

"Yes. Although we can't really discuss it, the prophecies have almost all been fulfilled," Doubt responded.

"Have you found out when this happens?" Insecurity was trembling now.

"No one knows," Doubt said. "Only God. If you haven't noticed, we are no longer on a speaking basis." Doubt started its customary sway back and forth. "Do you think that Deceit will consider our attempt successful?"

"I doubt it," Insecurity sniffled. "If Love hadn't slipped in I would say that we were moderately successful. I hate smelling the scent of Love. Stinks like a rose; makes me want to puke."

"I know! That is exactly why I had to get out of the house," Doubt said. "Well, I guess we had better report to Deceit."

"Yeah, but I am scared." Insecurity was shaking like a leaf. "Do you think there is any way we could get out of this? I mean you saw what Deceit did to Despair."

"I know, wasn't that the greatest?" Doubt smiled, paused a bit, and then frowned. "Oh, wait a minute, I didn't think about it like that. Deceit could do the same or worse to us."

"If we hide behind Envy and Arrogance, then maybe Deceit will forget about us. Lately, it seems that the only battle he really cares about is in Africa," Insecurity said.

"Well, one can always hope. Oh my, did I say that?" Doubt choked back his laughter. "How awful of me. Pinch me now. We can't hope."

"Yes, and joy and laughter aren't allowed either." Insecurity said, with a pitiful frown.

"Oh my goodness," Doubt said. "Wait a minute, I don't have goodness."

"You may not have Doubt either if you don't stop messing around. I wish you wouldn't be so goofy. Deceit won't be silly about punishment."

"Yeah, I know. I choose Envy to hide behind. You can have Arrogance," Doubt said. "I am always swaying from one side to the other, so I don't even know if Envy is large enough to hide me."

"Ok, but Arrogance is not as big as Envy is, so how do you expect me to hide behind him?"

"Dufus, you are Insecurity," Doubt said. "Don't you remember you can turn into a shrinking violet?"

"Oh, I forgot. Okay, then Arrogance will be fine. Let's go and get this over with."

Deceit had finished a confrontation with Fear about the war in the Congo, when the two unsavory spirits of Doubt and Insecurity slipped behind Envy and Arrogance.

"I believe," Deceit stated with pride. "We have harvested a great amount of bitterness, envy and hate on the African continent."

"Not to mention the countless souls that are now in Satan's grasp," Condemnation said.

"I love Africa!" Arrogance fanned out his peacock feathers.

Insecurity shrunk behind one of the feathers and whispered with irritation. "You can't love, stupid. That is something we cannot do."

"What is this?" Deceit said with a sly smile. "Do I hear the whisper of Insecurity?"

"Yes, it is me." Insecurity took the form of a shrinking violet.

"Where is your cohort?"

"I am here, Master." Doubt muttered, swaying behind the vomit green of Envy.

"Don't be shy. Step up and tell us about the children.

Insecurity said, "Well, they were sleeping when we..."

"Leave out the annoying, unnecessary details," Deceit said.

"I wonder," Insecurity whispered, "if he wants us to admit right off the bat that Love was there? That way, he doesn't have to wait to punish us. I don't think I could survive that. I am going to have to do my best at staving off his wrath."

"We got the children to think that they may have been the reason for Joe leaving." Doubt said puffing out his chest.

"Well done. Did you get them to blame their mother? You do realize that the enemy is Susanna, don't you?"

"They didn't exactly do that, sir. She gives them chocolate milk in bed every morning, and they think that is pretty grand." Doubt said swaying so far, he almost lost his footing.

"Let me take note of that." Envy pulled out a notebook and pen. "I can use that in some of my battles. Do any of their friends get chocolate milk in bed?"

"No," Insecurity said.

"Excellent." Envy scribbled furiously on her notepad.

"May I have the attention of all of you imbeciles?" Deceit hovered above the quivering green glob of Envy. "Number one, I am the one in command, not you, Envy. Number two, it is not my desire to make children rue the fact that they are not one of Susanna's snot-nosed little brats. It is much better to make them envious of other children--especially ones who have a Dad in the home. Get my drift?"

"Yes, Sir!" Envy swallowed the notebook in the glob of green slime.

"Did they express hate for Joe because of him leaving?" Deceit seemed to be desperate.

"Hmmm, I don't quite remember," Insecurity said.

Doubt glared at Insecurity. "I think hate may not be the exact word that I would use to describe their feelings."

"Oh, hate is not an intense enough feeling then? What would you use to describe their feelings?" Deceit asked, searching eternity for a more negative emotion than hate.

"They don't hate him, sir." Insecurity said, cowering. "They love him."

"What is wrong with this family? Why on earth do they love this horrible man who has no morals? Are they demented?" Deceit was enraged.

"Sir, hate to point out the obvious, but I believe that you would be the one to determine best whether they are demented or not. Just saying—" Arrogance fluffed out his feathers and, in the process, threw the wilted fragment of Insecurity up in the air.

Deceit caught Insecurity on the way down and threw the creature into the abyss of torture. Insecurity wailed like a wounded child.

"Doubt," Deceit said. "I believe you were a partner in this defeat, weren't you?" Deceit said whirling around to face Doubt. Doubt was swaying so erratically behind Envy that Deceit had a hard time pinpointing just which way Doubt was going to sway.

"I wouldn't say I was equally responsible. I mean, the children did think that they may have been the cause of the divorce."

"If Love was there you were ineffective," Deceit seethed.

"You always focus on the negative," Doubt said.

"Do I? Well, then why don't you find out just how negative I can be and go down to the Chamber of Torture?"

Adultery gasped in delight. "Oh, my, we haven't sent anyone down there, in like, forever; and now we are sending two!"

Doubt emerged from behind Envy, looking remorseful. "Please don't send me there. Really, is Susanna worth that amount of pain?"

"Begone!" As soon as Deceit said the words, the floor opened like a sinkhole and Doubt was swallowed in the depths of Hell, silencing the terrifying screams.

"Now that I have eliminated my two most incompetent servants," Deceit said. "I wonder who will be successful in our attack on Susanna?"

The room filled with stony silence.

"Do I have to call in Fear from Africa? If that is what it takes I will do it, but you will suffer for that decision," Deceit said.

There was a slithering sound from the far-left corner of the chamber, accompanied by a sound akin to a rattle.

Soon the snake of Rejection was center stage in the chamber. "There is no need to call in Fear, Master. I have had a home in Susanna's heart since birth."

"Since birth?" Deceit questioned.

"Yes, her mother is a perfectionist and by our good fortune, Susanna is anything but perfect."

. "Go on." Deceit said, leaning forward in rapt attention.

"Barbara, Susanna's mother, has an adequate amount of arrogance due to her successful career, her striking beauty, and her adoring husband. She was fond of Joe. Susanna doesn't know this, but Joe reminds Barbara of the son she lost when he was just an infant."

"Did she love Joe more than Susanna?"

"That would be an accurate assessment of the situation," Rejection hissed. "She worships the memory of her dead son. He didn't grow old enough to stumble upon the mountain of mistakes that Susanna has made, so he has become her idol. When Susanna married Joe, Barbara considered him a replacement for her dead son."

"Does Susanna know about her brother?" Deceit asked.

"No, he was Barbara's first born," Rejection said. "She has never told Susanna about the child."

"So, Susanna has been measured against an idol she doesn't know exists?"

"Yes, sir."

"Brilliant! Absolutely brilliant!!! This may work." Deceit's excitement caused his black cloak to quiver. "You must go quickly, make sure you get inside her mind. I want Susanna dead so that I have access to those children. This will be a glorious victory for evil."

Arrogance glared at Envy and growled. "We are not to say the word 'glorious.' This is getting out of hand."

Deceit heard the growl but chose to ignore it. He was too busy drop-kicking Rejection back to Earth.

SETTING THE STAGE FOR REJECTION

SUZIE TURNED OVER IN BED AND CUDDLED THE warmth of the morning sun. Her mind skipped childlike through the memories of the previous day with Hope. She smiled, then glanced at the alarm clock. She did a double-take. No! She overslept.

Suzie bolted out of bed and threw on dirty sweats. While pulling her pants up, she yelled, "Hey kids, get up! You have thirty minutes to get to school."

Suzie listened while tearing through her tangles with a brush. There was no sound from the children's room. She sprinted through the hallway, yelling like a lunatic, "Get up! Now!"

"Gosh, Mom," Sarah yelled back. "You don't have to yell."

"Like you would have heard a whisper." Suzie rushed to the closet and picked out clothes for Michael.

"Sarah and Michael, when you are dressed, grab a granola bar and your chocolate milk. You can eat in the car. Your lunch is in the fridge, Sarah." Suzie spit the words out as she sped to the kitchen.

After Michael had finished dressing, he went to the kitchen and grabbed a granola bar. "I thought you said we couldn't eat in the car anymore."

Suzie paused, looking at Michael. "Well, lucky you. How many moms set rules and give their children permission to break them the very next day?"

Michael shook his head.

"Don't forget your backpack, Michael." Suzie's words trailed over her shoulder as she scurried back to the bedroom. "I need to get Jonathan dressed."

Sarah was poised in front of the mirror wrangling with a barrette.

Suzie pulled Jonathan out from the covers, struggling to put his winter coat on over his thick pajamas.

"Mommy, why no clothes?" Jonathan asked.

"Sweetheart, we're in a hurry. So today you get to wear your jammies on the way to school. Won't that be fun?"

Jonathan looked confused, then broke into a smile. He skipped through the house saying, "I got jammies on today."

Sarah was still battling the obstinate barrette.

Suzie bit her lip. "Sarah, you don't have to be perfect every day. Forget the barrette. You're so pretty. You don't need it."

"Just 'cause you woke up late is no excuse for me to look like a slob." Once more, Sarah tried to place the barrette in her hair. "There, it's perfect now."

"Good darling," Suzie said. "Now sprint to the kitchen and grab your breakfast."

Suzie swept into the kitchen giving Michael a head-to-toe glance. "Honey, I think you may want to turn your shirt around and run a wet comb through your hair to get rid of that tuft. You look like a rooster."

Michael blushed and disappeared into the bathroom.

Suzie grabbed a granola bar for herself and Michael's backpack from the table. The contents of the backpack spewed onto the floor. "Michael! How many times have I told you to zip your backpack?"

"Um, like maybe a hundred," Sarah said.

Suzie's tone expressed her frustration. "Get in here and put your backpack together."

"Ok, Mom," Michael said.

"To be honest, I think it's been a thousand times," Sarah said. "Maybe you should post a sticky note on his forehead. Just saying—"

Suzie looked at Sarah, not sure whether to applaud or spank her. "This morning has been hectic enough. Making fun of your brother isn't making it any better."

Michael came out of the bathroom with hair slicked down, and shirt righted. "Sorry, Mom."

"That's okay. Just try to remember tomorrow."

"All right." Michael said, stuffing his backpack with all that had become attached to the floor.

Michael slung his backpack over his shoulder. "Are we ready to go now?"

"Yeah," Sarah said. "We would have been ready ten minutes ago if you had your head on straight."

"Sarah! Zip it." Suzie's glare was hot enough to make water boil.

Sarah and Michael jumped into the car while Suzie smashed Jonathan into his car seat, the excess of winter clothing battling back.

She had locked the car seat when she felt Jonathan patting her shoulder, his face turning pale.

"What's wrong honey?"

"Can't bweathe," Jonathan whispered.

"Poor child. These car seats should be designed better." Suzie unlocked the car seat and removed Jonathan's coat.

"Better now?"

Jonathan nodded, his thumb finding its familiar home in his mouth.

Suzie sped out of the driveway.

They were just starting on the way to school when Sarah lit the fire of dissension.

"Mom," Sarah said. "Michael is eating with his mouth open."

"Hmmm, well one must open their mouth to eat, Sarah," Suzie said.

"He is *smacking* his food." Sarah said loudly. "He sounds like a pig."

"Michael, please close your mouth." Suzie held the steering wheel with a death grip.

"MOM, he is still doing it!" Sarah screamed.

"Michael, when a person is eating, it is of primary importance that once the food has entered the vault of the mouth, the doors of the mouth shut tightly so as not to incur the wrath of screaming sisters." Suzie noted her knuckles were turning white.

"Mom, Jonathan is pinching me," Michael whined.

Suzie clenched her teeth. "Jonathan, please don't pinch."

"Michael sitting on my hand," Jonathan said. "I pinch him fo that."

“Michael, get off Jonathan’s hand!” Suzie screamed at the top of her lungs.

“Mom, now Jonathan is smacking.” Sarah’s face was turning red as her shrill voice cut the air.

Suzie slammed on the brakes, stopping in the middle of the country road.

“I have had enough.” Suzie felt cutting pain in her foot. Could it be a remnant of the shattered vase? “Ouch! Damn that hurts.”

“Daddy never used that word.” Sarah said, as if she were a Sunday school teacher.

Suzie paused for a moment and looked at Sarah. She untied her shoes, dislodged the sliver of glass and threw it out the window.

“You are right, Sarah.” Suzie pressed the gas pedal. “The words he used with me were far more vulgar.”

“What does vulgar mean?” Michael asked.

“If I ever get you to school, you can ask your teacher.”

MURPHY'S LAW

THE RED BRICK OF THE SCHOOL WAS BLOCKING THE sunrise when Michael emitted a heart-wrenching groan from the back seat.

Suzie rolled her eyes. "What's wrong now, Michael?"

Michael sobbed, "I still got my slippers on."

"Oh, great," Sarah said. "Why don't we just call the school and tell them we are sick?"

Suzie let that thought hop through her mind for a second before pushing it off the cliff of possibilities. "Sarah, that would be lying. Being late is better than being absent. I will drop you off and take Michael back to get his shoes."

"Sometimes it is an embarrassment to be a part of this family," Sarah said. "Dad was the only one who had it together. Now he is gone."

Suzie felt a pain in her chest, as tears silently caressed her cheeks. "When we get to school I suggest you get out as fast as you can, Sarah."

"Don't worry." Sarah said in an independent, grown-up tone. "Riding to school with dummies in the car is *not* my favorite activity."

"Stop! Please, Sarah stop." Suzie pulled into the school driveway, wishing the car had an ejection button.

"No wonder Dad found another woman." Sarah pulled her backpack out of the car. "You don't do anything right."

"Just go, please."

The door slammed.

Suzie crumpled over the steering wheel, dissolving into a pool of tears.

Michael knew he needed to distract his mom. "Can we go home now? I really need to get my shoes."

"Yes." Suzie lifted her head from the steering wheel and started the drive home. *If she had a delete button for life, today would be the ideal time to push it.*

"Why didn't you tell me to put my shoes on?"

Suzie wiped the snot from her nose. "Oh, my God. You're kidding me. This was my fault too?"

"Mom," Michael said. "You were the one who kept telling me to hurry."

"I was partly to blame. That's true. I overslept. When I called, nobody moved. And when I told you to hurry, you walked like a turtle." Suzie took a deep breath. "It is not my job to dress you. We decided you could be responsible for that when you turned five, remember?"

"But you told me to change my shirt and comb my hair. Why didn't you tell me to put my shoes on?"

"Someone who gets straight A's in school should remember to put his shoes on," Suzie yelled.

Michael started crying.

Suzie hated it when her kids cried. "Michael, I am not going to fight you about this. Why don't we come up with a plan to prevent it from happening again?"

Jonathan chimed in from the back seat. "I got idea. No shoes fo school!"

"No, kids can't go to school without shoes," Suzie said. "Michael, why don't we spend fifteen minutes each evening preparing for the next day? Set out your shoes, load and zip your backpack, and decide what clothes you will wear."

"I don't know, Mom. I am so busy in the evening. I have dinner, homework, then a bath; and you always read to us. I am just a kid. I need time to play too, Mom."

"Michael, I am not asking you. I am *telling* you. This is will be your new routine." Suzie spoke firmly as she pulled into her driveway.

Suzie checked on Jonathan in the car seat. He was sleeping. She closed the car door gently and raced Michael up the front stairs.

"I will search the bedroom," Suzie said. "You search the living room."

"Okay, Mom."

Suzie looked under the bed, in the closet, and behind the drapes. She even opened the cabinet doors and drawers… no shoes. Michael was already forty-five minutes late for school. Silently, she prayed for help.

"I have to go pee," Michael said. "The shoes aren't in the living room."

The bathroom door closed.

"Mom," Michael said. "Here they are, under my dirty clothes."

"Thank God!" Suzie sighed. "Now hurry, son. You're late enough already."

With shoes on Michael's feet, Suzie shot out of the driveway like a rocket.

It seemed like the next moment when Suzie was in front of the school again. "Thanks, Mom." Michael jumped out of the car.

"Sure thing, son." Suzie whipped her car around the horseshoe drive and headed home.

THE VENOM OF REJECTION

SUZIE'S STOMACH GROWLED WITH HUNGER WHEN SHE walked into her living room.

"Want a snack, honey?" Suzie turned on the TV for Jonathan.

"Yes."

Suzie opened the fridge and made a mental note to go shopping. The food was getting thin. She opened the fruit drawer. One lonely apple.

The phone rang.

"Hello?" Suzie put the apple on the cutting board and sliced it in half.

"Hello, Susanna. This is your mother, Barbara."

No kidding--really? Does she think I can't recognize her voice?

"Hello."

"Joe just called me." A long sigh. "I cannot tell you how disappointed I am in you. I don't blame Joe one bit for leaving."

Suzie stopped cutting the apple, feeling a sharp pain coursing through her chest.

"Barbara, he left me for someone else." A tear dropped on the counter.

"Well, she probably will make a much better wife than you."

Suzie groaned. "Barbara, could you please be nice? I've had a rough day. I don't need this."

"You know I loved Joe like a son," Barbara's voice choked with emotion. "Now I have lost the only living son ... That I've ever had." Silence clenched the air. "If you had just tried harder. If you had kept your house clean or if you had worked for a living. He may have stayed with you. But you did none of those things. Now, Joe is gone," Barbara said. "My son is gone, lost... dead."

"I'm sorry Barbara, I really am. I miss him, too. Nevertheless, he is not dead. I am sure you can still call him." Suzie dropped the knife on the floor.

"He was always helpful." Her tone was anything but understanding. "He never had to be asked to help. It was like he could read my mind," Barbara continued. "Your father is a good man, Susanna. I always thought Joe was like your father."

"Maybe he was like Dad. To be happy, he may have needed a wife like you. I don't know. I tried." Susanna bent down to pick up the knife. "With three children, it was hard to keep the house looking perfect."

"I wish you would have put the children in daycare. Then you could have worked and taken care of the house," Barbara said. "I told you to put them in daycare. You just wouldn't listen."

"Barbara, I love my children. I didn't want someone else to take care of them. I tried to do that, remember?" Susanna kept looking at the knife.

"That was only a week. Then you quit your job," Barbara sniffled. "Joe says the children are brats, and you don't even discipline them."

"Oh, my God. I *do* discipline them. Just because I don't whip them like you did me, doesn't mean they are undisciplined." Suzie's knees gave way to the floor, the knife still in her hand.

"You know what the Bible says about sparing the rod and spoiling the child."

"Barbara, the rod was used to *guide* sheep, *not* abuse them." The knife was now resting against the wrist of Susanna. "The only time a rod was used in violence was if the shepherd had to stop a lamb from falling off a cliff. My children are not on the edge of a cliff. I think if I used the rod of discipline in abuse they would be in danger of going off a cliff."

"I have seen your children, Susanna. They need discipline." Barbara's tone turned even harsher. "I hope that Joe's new wife sees fit to discipline my grandchildren properly."

"If she beats them with a rod, she won't be seeing them more than once. I can assure you of that." Suzie pressed the jagged edge of the knife against her wrist.

"I'm sure she will have a spotless house. Joe told me she doesn't have any children. She was too busy climbing the ladder of success," Barbara gloated. "She was so excited that he had children. He said she reminded him of me."

"They are my children, not hers." A drop of blood oozed out from beneath the knife. "Despite what you think, Barbara, a successful career is not everyone's dream. I want to be a loving mother. Probably because I never experienced love as a child."

"Well, I tried, Susanna. God, how I tried. I know Joe tried too," Barbara said. "Some people are just impossible to love. I'm surprised Joe didn't leave sooner."

Click, the phone went dead.

"God, she's as mean as the devil. I absolutely hate her. Why is she my mother? Why God?" Suzie screamed the silent prayer to a God who appeared to be deaf.

I can't deal with the pain anymore. If I cut my wrist, the pain will end. It will be over. Done. If I go to hell, so be it. Hell can't be any worse than this.

More blood dripped to the floor.

"Mommy, Mommy, what you doin?" The voice was beckoning to her. "I love you, Mommy." Tiny arms embraced her neck, and a kiss caressed her cheek. Jonathan gently took the knife out of her hands.

Suzie shook her head, trying to break free from what seemed like a trance. Then she saw the blood on the floor.

"Oh my God! Jonathan, give me the knife." Suddenly awake, she grabbed the knife from Jonathan's hand. Suzie channeled every ounce of the rage and indignation she felt into her right arm. She pulled her arm back and thrust her hand forward. The knife shot across the kitchen, carving a chunk of wood from the back door before it clattered on the floor.

Her trembling hands, which had been ready to take a life, instead, encircled Jonathan and embraced life.

THE HEAVENS REJOICE

"DID YOU SEE JONATHAN?" HOPE ASKED.

"Yeah," Faith said. "That one is ours."

"Did you notice who was in the way of the knife when it was thrown?" Hope asked.

"Hmmm," Faith said. "I believe that it was the stinking, rotten snake of Rejection. Did you see him wince when the knife cut his slippery, slimy skin?"

Hope giggled with glee. "Yeah, I saw that. I had to use every ounce of self-control to stop myself from shooting down there. I wanted to start singing the 'Hallelujah' chorus."

Faith chuckled for a moment then turned serious. "You know, she has started to break the curse."

"I know, but this is a stronghold. There will be more attacks. She still has not learned the lessons needed," Hope surmised.

"We need to work on her armor," Faith said. "With every battle if she does not have the proper protection, she will not get stronger and the battles will wear her down."

"You are referring to the armor of God?" Hope asked.

"Yes, Suzie needs to be equipped. We must teach Suzie to fight evil with the Word of God," Faith said.

"So what verse do I teach her to deal with Barbara, her mother?"

"In Psalms 45:10 it says for a woman to leave her family to focus on worshiping the Lord. Yet, I believe Suzie is strong enough to stay and fight. I think that Suzie is the one who can break the strongholds that have enslaved her mother for so long. Her mother has bitterness in her heart," Faith said. "She has never forgiven God for the son who passed away."

"Yes, but she lost her mother, too." Hope said with compassion.

"Suzie doesn't know about her grandmother, does she?" Faith said.

"No, Barbara never talks about her. Suzie has asked me several times if I knew anything about her. I think she was trying to understand Barbara. If she knew more about her, she assumed she would understand why her mother seems to hate her," Hope said.

"There have been some significant losses which Barbara has had to endure in her life, but she has hidden those losses, and they are eating away at her heart," Faith said.

"Do you think that Barbara is strong enough to reveal those losses to Suzie?" Hope asked.

Faith paused and hung her head. "No, Barbara has lived behind the veil of lies too long. It has blinded her to the truth which Suzie is so eager to discover."

"So how can Suzie know the truth of what happened to her grandmother?" Hope asked.

Faith looked up, her blue eyes ablaze with purpose. "You will tell her, but do so with wisdom. There is a way that this should be revealed. You must expose this tragedy, and amid the revelation, you must impart strength and hope to Suzie."

"Wow, what a challenge," Hope said.

"I am sure you are up to the challenge of Hope." Faith said with a grin.

"If not, I may need to ask God for a new name." Hope said with a wink and a giggle.

REJECTION'S WOUND

REJECTION HAD TO LEAVE WHEN JONATHAN UTTERED "I love you." The smell of love was suffocating him. It smelled like a rose. YUCK!

The wicked spirit started slithering to the door. Just one more look at the blood on the floor. That was all he needed to feel success. The snake raised its head, twisted its neck, and focused his beady eyes on the blood. What was that flying in the air? A knife! Crap, it was coming right at him, and before he could flinch, the knife had sliced his neck.

"Damn that woman and her disgusting little son," Rejection said.

Rejection was incensed. This was the ultimate defeat, when love between two humans could transpose the spiritual world and wreak havoc on the underworld. That a mere toddler could defeat evil, which had been so forceful in the past, was outrageous! Deceit would be livid.

Susanna had been on the cusp of defeat. She had cut her wrist, just not deep enough. Barbara was perfect, though. For some reason, Barbara felt if she loved her daughter, who was alive, she would die, just like her mother and son had. If Rejection emphasized how close he had come to the goal, maybe Deceit would spare him.

Rejection descended to the evil empire, rehearsing his speech. Deceit was in a meeting with other spirits of evil, discussing the wars in Africa.

Rejection slid into the meeting, concealing himself behind Adultery.

Adultery shivered when Rejection's cold, slimy body touched her.

Adultery flipped her head around to scowl at Rejection. "I do believe you are getting some blood on my evening gown." Adultery moved away quickly, exposing Rejection to Deceit in the process.

"Rejection?" Deceit thundered. "I am hoping you are coming to announce the end of Susanna's life." The cloak of Deceit bent down looking around Rejection as if he thought the soul of Susanna might be hidden somewhere within his slimy coils.

"Hmmm… I don't quite have that, Master. However, I almost had it." Rejection hissed, trying to hide his gaping wound from Deceit's view.

"Okay, the rest of you can clear out," Deceit said. "Let me have some time alone with Rejection."

That was not a good sign. Whenever Deceit wanted to single out an evil entity, punishment was always involved.

Rejection twisted on the chamber floor. "Barbara did magnificent in the category of Rejection. She decimated Susanna with just one phone call." That horrible wound on his neck was still bleeding. Damn it.

"Okay, tell me about the phone call," Deceit said. "And what is that running down your neck?"

"The phone call? Ah, yes, the phone call," Rejection said. "Well, the phone call was perfect. Barbara, in her narcissistic style, lamented the loss of the only living son she had. She didn't even mention the son who had died many years ago."

"Stick to the point Rejection. We don't care about the son who died right now." Deceit was becoming impatient.

Rejection's tail rattled. "She went on and on about how wonderful Joe was and then insinuated that Susanna was a horrible wife and mother. She told Susanna that she should have shuttled those children off to daycare so that she could be a Martha Stewart housewife and a career woman. Fortunately for us, she was a failure in both of those arenas." Rejection's tail rattled as he slithered around the chamber.

"If Susanna is such a failure, then where is her death certificate?" Deceit's voice rattled the chamber walls. "Rejection, what is that running down your neck?"

"Barbara even had the audacity to assume that Megan was beautiful and that her house was spotless," Rejection said hurriedly. "She said Joe deserved a better wife than Susanna. By that time, our target was sitting on the floor. When Susanna hits the floor, you know we have her, boss." Rejection quivered with fear. "Susanna was cutting an apple when Barbara called. I knocked that knife out of her hands, and it fell to the floor."

"You are getting wordy," Deceit said. "Come on, sum it up. I have other things to attend to."

"Susanna started to fight back," Rejection said. "She actually told Barbara that she hadn't felt loved as a child. When that happened, I knew Barbara would go in for the kill. I kept focusing Susanna's gaze on the knife, and she finally put it against her wrist. There was blood coming out. I thought I had her there, sir. Thought I had her."

"At least you got her to pick up the knife and start cutting her wrist; which is more than I can say about the success of Despair."

"She was fixated on the knife. Barbara said Susanna was unlovable, and she was surprised Joe didn't leave sooner. Then she hung up. Can you imagine a mother saying something like that to her daughter? Sometimes humans just strike me as evil." Rejection said with a sarcastic chuckle. "By this time, the knife was cutting through her wrist. She was thinking thoughts of death. My mouth was salivating for the end of her life."

"Was that the knife that slashed your neck?"

"Uh, yeah, I believe so, boss," Rejection said.

"So, if she is bleeding to death, then how did you end up with a wound?"

"You see, she had almost cut deep enough to hit the artery when that stinking, rotten son of hers came in. He put his arms around her neck and gave her a kiss on the cheek." Rejection turned his head and stuck his tongue out in disgust. "You know I can't tolerate unconditional love. It breaks my power. I had to leave quickly. Once my trance was broken, Suzie became an absolute crazy woman and hurled the knife at the door. I didn't get out of the way quick enough."

"So, you have been defeated by the love of a toddler. Is that what you are telling me?" Deceit said, showing anger.

"All in all, I was pretty successful. With Despair rearranging Suzie's mind, the conversation with Barbara will replay repeatedly—"

"Susanna is still alive. You have been defeated by a mere toddler?!" Deceit screamed with unrestrained rage. "Imbecile! I wish the knife had cut your head off. You will spend time in the bowels of hell."

"Master, please don't send me there. I did exactly as planned, by influencing Barbara. I have already been wounded." Rejection hissed desperately as the snake turned to show Deceit the wound.

"If you don't leave now, I will extend your stay."

"All right, but you should be more understanding." Rejection hissed and started to slide out of the Chamber of Evil, into the depths of hell.

"Understanding? Really? Do you realize that understanding is not in my nature?" Deceit reached for the pitchfork to pierce Rejection in the side.

"Okay, I am leaving." Rejection slithered quickly out of the Chamber and into the bowels of hell.

THE GENERATIONAL CURSE

SUZIE SAT FOR A MOMENT ON THE KITCHEN FLOOR, the puddle of blood turning a crimson red. Her arms locked around Jonathan, her cheeks wet from tears. She was shaking. She had to pull herself together. She looked at the clock. It was time for her to pick Michael up from kindergarten. She wrapped some gauze around her left wrist and taped it up, then slid her sweat shirt down around her wrist so that Michael would not see the wound. Jonathan reached for her hand, planting a kiss on the gauze for her "booboo." This act of love opened the flood gate of tears for Suzie. She sobbed for a moment then grabbed a tissue to blow her nose and wipe the tears from her face.

"We need to pick up your brother from school." Suzie said as she bent down to wipe up the blood on the floor. She threw the rag in the trash, as if to try and wipe this horrific scene from her memory.

"I have seen more of my own blood in the past several days, than I saw in my entire nursing career." Suzie whispered as she walked out the front door to go pick up Michael.

Soon she was back home again with both boys. She had just finished feeding them lunch when they decided that they wanted to watch a "Pooh bear" movie.

She walked to her kitchen to clean up the lunch dishes when the phone rang again. Suzie glared at the phone. She hesitated, started walking to it, and then hesitated again.

What if it was Barbara? She could always hang up or assume a foreign accent and tell her she had the wrong number.

With each ring, she got more nervous, and then on the fourth ring she decided. "Oh, what the hell. If it is Barbara, I will tell her I am busy cleaning the house." Suzie spoke out loud, trying to build up courage. "I'll tell her to call back, in a hundred years, when I am finished. That should make her happy."

"Hello?"

"Hello darlin'. How are you doing today?"

"Thank God, it is you Hope! I am not doing so well. This day has been rough."

"Oh, I am sorry. I felt the Spirit's urging to call you. I could feel that you needed a friend."

"A friend is good, but a new mother would be better."

"Oh, my goodness. Is she on the attack again?"

Suzie peeked into the living room, checking on the boys. "Well, let me go to the bedroom. I really don't want the boys to hear me recant the conversation."

"What did she say?"

Suzie laid on her bed. "It would be easier for me to tell you what she didn't say. She didn't say she loved me. She didn't ask if I needed any help. She didn't say that Joe was an idiot for leaving me for another woman. Instead, she said how disappointed she was in me for losing Joe to another woman."

"Like that was your fault?" Hope asked.

"Oh, it gets better. Then she accused me of being a worthless wife, mother, and housekeeper." Suzie paused to take a breath. "She had the nerve to say that Megan must be very pretty; and she probably had a spotless house."

"Well, what difference would that make? Joe wasn't married to her. He was married to you."

"Yeah, I know, but Barbara has always made me feel that Joe was better than me," Suzie said. "She thinks he deserved a better-quality wife than what I am or was."

"Well, that would depend upon what your definition of 'quality' was." Hope replied, knowing the sordid history of Megan. "So how did the conversation make you feel?"

"She made me feel like I was a failure. She said that my children were brats and undisciplined. That is when I kind of lost it. You know she has never been supportive of my role as a mother."

"How did you react?"

"She suggested that I should have put my children into daycare, so I could pursue my career. That is when I said that my greatest desire was to be a loving mother because I didn't receive love as a child," Suzie said. "She went on to say that I was impossible to love, and she was surprised Joe didn't leave sooner. Then she hung up."

Suzie's eyes filled to the brim with tears. "Why is she my mother, Hope? If God is a God of love, then why did He give me a mother like Barbara?"

Hope paused for a moment to consider whether Suzie was ready for her answer. "It is the common assumption among humans that parents are picked for children because of their nurturing ability. It never occurs to humans that children may be chosen to influence their parents and break the cycle of evil that has cursed their family for generations." Hope paused to let the wisdom soak into Suzie's mind. "You are your mother's daughter because you have been chosen to break generational curses."

"What?" Suzie responded in disbelief.

"The curse of Rejection has been in your bloodline for generations. You were placed in this family to break the curse."

"How the hell do I do that?" Suzie retorted, then paused to reconsider her choice of words. "Oh, I am sorry Hope, I… I... didn't mean to use that word."

"You break the curse by loving God more than you love the person who is carrying the curse."

"I don't understand what you mean." Suzie stopped for a short second then blurted out. "Something else happened, which bothers me more than what my mother said."

"Go on then. Tell me more."

"Well, after Barbara told me that she was surprised that Joe didn't leave me sooner and hung up on me, I was kind of in a trance. There was this knife that I was using to cut up fruit when she called, and I became like… obsessed with it. I wanted to kill myself, Hope. I held it against my wrist. I was thinking of ending my life, just because of Barbara."

"What stopped you?"

"Jonathan. He walked up to me and put his arms around my neck. He woke me up from the trance with a kiss on my cheek. I saw a puddle of blood on the floor, and I realized it was my blood. I was so horrified by what I had almost done that I threw the knife across my kitchen." Suzie paused for a moment to wipe the tears off her face. "I actually threw the knife so hard, it took a chunk out of my kitchen door." Suzie said with a slight chuckle.

"You threw it a lot harder than that," Hope murmured.

"What?"

"Oh, nothing." Hope replied, knowing that Suzie was unaware of the damage she and Jonathan had done to the snake of Rejection.

"So, about that loving God stuff, I was just thinking… I know my grandmother loved God. Barbara doesn't talk about her much. She died when Barbara was young. When she does talk about her, she always mentions that Grandma had a deep love for God. Now if she loved God, how could a curse come down the bloodline through her?"

"The curse didn't come from your grandmother's lineage, Suzie. It was your grandfather."

"Why couldn't she have loved God enough to break the curse?"

Hope responded with sadness. "She loved your grandfather more than she loved God."

"Wasn't she supposed to love my grandfather?" Suzie asked.

"Yes, but not more than God." Hope continued, "Pleasing your grandfather became her idol, and she started worshiping his nonexistent approval."

"So, you're saying that if you want to please your husband that you are not loving God?" Suzie asked, earnestly seeking wisdom.

"Suzie," Hope paused for a moment, contemplating how to impart important spiritual truths to a mere human. "Suzie, your grandmother loved God, but she sought the approval of your grandfather. She placed this above her love for God and His unconditional love for her. She chose rejection when she had acceptance knocking at the door of her heart."

"Ok, ok, I think I understand. God must sit on the throne, and everyone else must be second place. I know the Bible says, 'Love the Lord your God with all your heart, soul and mind.'" Suzie paused for a moment and then continued. "Can I be honest with you Hope?"

"Always, dear one." Hope said with comfort.

"It is difficult sometimes to love a God who is invisible." Suzie swallowed hard.

"Is it easier for you to love a man who can leave you for another woman?"

"Good point." Suzie paused, tears streaming down her face in a torrential downpour. "It isn't easier. It hurts like hell." Her mind kept recoiling back to the death of her grandmother as if it was a magnet. She wiped the tears from her face and continued. "I sometimes wonder how my grandmother died. I have this illusion that if she had lived Barbara would be different."

"Barbara may have been more loving if her mother had lived. Barbara absolutely adored her father though, so it may not have made a difference."

"Did my grandfather love God?"

Hope spoke with truth. "He made a show of loving God. He went to church because that was expected of him. Although he went to church, his heart was cold. He did not have the love of God in his heart. He was very hard on your grandmother. He rejected her kind and loving spirit. He was like Barbara. Perfection was his idol, and anything less than perfection was worthy of his wrath. Your grandmother was a lot like you, Suzie. She was very kind and loving. She struggled with trying to do things perfectly for your grandfather. She was exhausted with trying to meet his unreasonable demands."

"So, did she die from exhaustion?" Suzie asked.

"Exhaustion may have contributed to her death," Hope replied.

"I wonder how much exhaustion contributed to my situation this morning," Suzie said. "I may have reacted better if I hadn't been under so much stress. It was just with Joe leaving and then Barbara blaming me for it...well, I kind of cracked."

"I believe that most people would feel the same under similar circumstances," Hope said.

"So, then I'm not crazy?" Suzie asked.

"No, you are anything but crazy. In fact, you are saner than most," Hope said.

"Thanks, Hope. I have this gut feeling that you know how my grandmother died. I don't know why it is so important, but for some reason, I think it may help me understand Barbara better," Suzie said.

"It may be a good start," Hope said.

Hope sighed, “Suzie, your grandmother didn’t throw the knife when it was on her wrist. She committed suicide.”

Suzie gasped, “Oh my God!” The phone plummeted to the floor, ending the conversation with a thud.

SUZIE'S PRAYER

SUZIE FELT EXHAUSTION LAYING CLAIM TO EVERY CELL in her body. Her heart ached for the loss of her grandmother. How much had her suicide shaped the course of Barbara's life? Was this why Barbara had been so unfeeling and ruthless in her discipline?

If I am like my grandmother, is Barbara's seeming hatred for me, a displacement of her hatred for her own mother? Or is it her way of coping with pain that she could not process through as a child?

Suzie whispered a prayer. "I am so exhausted and overwhelmed with grief. First, my husband leaves me for another woman. Then I get emotionally slaughtered by Barbara. On top of that, I find out that my grandmother took her life because she did not love God more than her husband. How am I supposed to handle all of this? By breaking a generational curse. Really?!"

"I don't ask you for much, God, but right now I need to experience a miracle." Suzie muttered through the drapes of her fatigue. "I want to see a glimpse of heaven. Forgive me if this appears to be a plea based on fear or doubt. I know those two emotions bear no favor with you. I just kind of need to know there is something better than my life, as it is, right now."

As the clouds darkened in the sky, the whisper of a prayer reached the Holy One in the heavenly realm. The heavens thundered in response to the heartfelt request.

The angels were singing songs of praise when Faith entered the heavens. They became silent upon the arrival of Faith. Then they started murmuring among themselves with a joyous tone: "She wants to see where we live. She has been chosen by God to engage in war. She will become a strong fighter, a warrioress."

The archangel Michael spoke with clarity. "Take note. She approached God in the right manner also. She approached him with a humble spirit. So many Christians approach him with pride, treating Him as if He is *their* servant. They forget that He is their Creator, and the One who all will bow down to worship at the appointed time. Glory to God in the highest."

Faith's face radiated with joy. To be in the heavens when there was a reason to rejoice over a human's petition to God was a glorious experience. Faith was ushered into the presence of God. The light of His love would have blinded her, if she was human. The warmth of His love would have singed her skin. To be in God's presence was a wonder to behold.

"Suzie wants a glimpse of heaven?" The voice of God thundered.

"Yes, Master, she is wavering right now, between Doubt and me. She is just asking for a sign, Father. Please give her a sign. She has suffered so much," Faith pleaded.

"She has suffered because she has misplaced her love. There is no one who can love her as much as I." God spoke with tenderness. "I love her so much I gave my very best for her sins. I gave her Jesus' life as atonement. She chose to worship a man instead?"

"Yes, Holy One. It is a common error among humans. They tend to love their mates, but it is only because you created them to be a completion for each other." Faith spoke with respect for the Holy One.

"It was not my intention to have them exclude me from their love. Do they not understand that if they include me, their love can be supernatural in power?" God spoke; a sliver of heartache resonated in his voice.

Faith's voice began to break. "I understand you desire the love and reconciliation of all mankind through the sacrifice of your Son. I know how much you love them, Master."

"My concern regarding Suzie's request is for her, not me." The voice of God became gentle in compassion.

Faith spoke with love for her Father. "I understand you love her, Father."

"She... she is the apple of my eye. She has just been tempted to end her life by the adversary. If I show her the glory of my heavens, will she not be tempted to follow through with that act the next time she is under attack?" God spoke. "There is a time and place that revelations should happen. This is not the time for me to reveal heaven to her."

"Yes, yes, I know." Faith paused and then dared to ask the unthinkable. "Could there be something better than heaven?"

"There has been something far greater since the beginning of time. I will reveal to her the greatest love that ever existed." God thundered his reply.

"Oh, Father. You are magnificent! I believe I know what you have envisioned," Faith exclaimed.

The Spirit of God spoke firmly. "You must be there for the interpretation, Faith. This is also a revelation regarding my desire for Suzie's life, her purpose for all this pain. Pain is never allowed to be visited on my children without a purpose."

"I agree with your plan. I cannot wait to speak with Suzie and give your understanding," Faith said. "This will block Doubt and Despair from gaining hold of her."

The radiance of God grew even brighter. "If she is given understanding it may do much more than that. I am releasing the dream now to enter her consciousness. Go, be with her."

Faith shot out of the heavens on a bolt of lightning.

THE DREAM

THE AFTERNOON SKY GREW HEAVY WITH THE WEIGHT of rain as Suzie drifted into the deep valleys of slumber. Her spirit willingly tumbled into the conscious state where nightmares and dreams held court.

The land of dreams could be a path on which the Spirit of God could enter a mind. It could also be the way that the Devil could instill fear into a person's soul. Today, God was on the path to Suzie's soul.

As Suzie's mind awakened in the land of dreams, she noticed that there was a field full of women surrounding her. The black of night was the backdrop to the dream.

Suzie looked at the women and tried to gain understanding of the scene which she was in. There was an aura of expectation, excitement; maybe even just a bit of impatience. Suddenly, the lady next to her looked up at the sky and exclaimed with pure joy: "There He is! This is what you have been telling us about. There He is!"

Suzie lifted her face to gaze upon the sky and saw the image of Jesus appearing in the sky. Jesus was wearing a white, flowing robe. He had a look of peace and serenity on his face. The image was translucent and appeared as if in spirit form.

There was a cross to the left of Jesus. It wasn't wooden. It was white, and Jesus was no longer tethered to it. It looked as if it was pearly white.

As soon as Suzie's mind captured the image a thunderclap jolted her awake. As Suzie lay in bed, she struggled to recapture the memory of the dream. Had she just seen an image of the second coming? She asked for a glimpse of heaven and instead God had given her a viewing of the second coming. What was God trying to tell her? What were all those women doing in the field?

She needed to talk to someone, and that person needed to be Faith.

Suzie rolled over in bed and picked up the telephone only to have it ring in her hands.

"Hello?"

"Hello Suzie, how are you doing?" The comforting voice of Faith was like a healing balm to the wounds within Suzie's heart.

"Wow, I couldn't really say." Suzie paused for a moment. "I have had a crazy day."

"Tell me about it," Faith said.

"First off, I got the kids to school late and Sarah basically said I was worthless. Then I received a telephone call from Barbara, who confirmed Sarah's opinion of my worth, which brought me to the brink of suicide. After that, Hope told me that my grandmother *had* committed suicide, and I was supposed to be some heroic generational curse-breaking saint. Then I had a dream of what I think was Jesus' second coming." Suzie paused to catch her breath. "I feel like I have been on a roller coaster. I want to get off now."

Faith chuckled, "I don't blame you. It seems as if you have had an overwhelming day."

"I would consider that the understatement of the century, Faith." Suzie began to relax and let a giggle slip from her tense mouth. "What did the dream mean?"

"What do you make of it?" Faith asked.

"You tell me, Faith. I don't know what to make of it. I knew I was so depressed this morning when Barbara called. Then Hope said that I was put in my family to break a generational curse, and I don't have the faintest idea how to do that."

"Have you ever considered that it may not be your responsibility to break the curse but rather Christ, living through you, which would break the curse?"

Suzie's mind raced through the maze of thoughts, which were cluttering her brain. "No, I hadn't thought of it in those terms."

"Do you realize the gifts you have been given may be the gifts which are necessary to break this curse?"

"I didn't know I had been given any gifts and how can a gift break a curse?" Suzie asked.

"A gift is not always a thing you can hold. A gift may sometimes be a spiritual matter. You have been given the gift of edification, which is the opposite of criticism."

"What is edification, other than the opposite of criticism?"

"It is to spiritually enlighten or to uplift another person."

Suzie paused for a moment. "I don't think I really do that."

"You're right; you don't. Jesus does through you."

"Wow, so if Jesus can do this, then why does He need me?" Suzie asked. "I mean seriously? I am supposed to break a curse that has been going on for generations?"

"He can't do it without you. Since He returned to heaven the Holy Spirit was released on earth to work through people, so that the will of God could be done."

"Seems like if God is God, then He could do anything on his own and not pester me with His plans." Suzie stopped, wondering where all the anger was coming from. "I don't mean to be rude. I just had a rough day, and I am trying to sort it out."

"Do you really want a God who is aloof and distant? One which micromanages people's lives without their say so?" Faith retorted. "Or do you prefer a God who seeks interaction and is even dependent on interaction to accomplish the good that He wants done."

"Why does He even mess with me?"

"Love is the only word that can explain that," Faith replied. "Now tell me about your dream."

"After I heard that my grandmother had taken her life, I was at the end of my rope, Faith. I was exhausted and depressed. I prayed, no, I *begged* God to see heaven. I didn't want to die anymore; I just needed to know there was something better than this life." Suzie fluffed the pillows up on the bed and leaned back. "I wanted a sliver of light at the end of the tunnel of darkness."

"Do you feel like you got a sliver of light?"

"I don't know. I didn't get a picture of heaven, and that is what I asked for," Suzie said.

"What did you get?"

"Well, I was out in this field. It was a field of women. They were excited. They were so happy. I was looking around and taking it all in, when one of them exclaimed, 'There He is! This is what you have been telling us about!' She was pointing to the sky. I looked up and saw the image of Jesus fill the sky. It was weird though. There was a cross to the left of Him. It wasn't wooden, it looked like a gigantic pearl cross."

"So, what do you make of that dream?"

"I don't know, Faith." The tears started slowly creeping down Suzie's cheeks. "I was hoping you could tell me."

"The field signifies a harvest. Since it was full of women it signifies that you are supposed to harvest the souls of these women for the Kingdom of God."

"How on earth am I supposed to do that?" Suzie was incensed. This God of hers needed to understand that she had some limitations as a human. "I have never even had a garden. I don't know the first thing about harvesting."

Faith busted out in laughter. "I know, dear child, I know. Why do you think that Jesus was in the sky?"

"It apparently was His second coming, but I am still worried about those women I am supposed to harvest."

"Dear child, why worry about what God wants to do through you? Why not just surrender to Him and allow Him to work through you?" Faith asked.

"Why would He want to work through me?"

"I could think of a million reasons, but I will make it simple for you. He knows you, and He loves you just as you are," Faith said.

"He may be the only one right now who loves me." Suzie said wiping the tears from her eyes. "What about the pearl cross? I am having a hard time understanding the significance of that. Jesus wasn't on it. It wasn't wooden."

"Remember the prayer that you prayed to God?" Faith asked.

"Yes, I asked Him for a glimpse of heaven."

"The gates of heaven are made of pearls. The cross that you saw was made of pearls and Jesus was beside the cross. Tell me Suzie, what do you think the dream means?"

Silence lingered like a huge pendant on a minute string of sterling silver. Suzie took a deep breath and said. "I think God was symbolically telling me that the way I could get a glimpse of heaven was to believe that the sacrifice of Jesus was the key." A long pause followed suit. "I feel so ashamed. I was expecting streets of gold and spectacular beauty." Suzie's voice began to break. "God sacrificed His only Son for my sins, so I could spend eternity in His presence. I, on the other hand, was looking for a cheap thrill of glitter and gold to placate the horror of my temporary discomfort."

"God does not condemn you for being human, Suzie. If He was so intent on condemnation do you really think He would have given you Jesus?"

"No, I don't, but I know one thing: I have got to get to know this Jesus better. If He holds the key to heaven and there is a harvest of souls for me to gather before His second coming; then it is important for me to know Him and to love Him."

Faith was silent. The dream had accomplished its purpose.

OF MICE AND MEMORIES

SUZIE WOKE UP DETERMINED TO START THE DAY WITH a fresh perspective. If Jesus was going to change her heart, then she would help him by changing her bedroom décor. Looking at the jungle print made her want to scream with rage. She needed to reclaim her life and she was going to start by getting out of Joe's jungle.

The children were cooperative for a change. Michael had gotten prepared the night before, so it was a straight shot to and from school. Suzie walked into her house with a sense of purpose and then stopped cold. She didn't have any money for redecorating. What had she been thinking?

She didn't know what kind of child support she would get or when it would start, and she had not worked since Jonathan had been born.

Her shoulders deflated as she looked at the jungle inside her bedroom. What had her bedroom been before it became a jungle? She couldn't remember. A faint recollection of her former bedspread seeped slowly into her memory. Maybe if she found that she wouldn't need to spend so much money on décor.

Suzie tiptoed into the living room to see if Jonathan had become engrossed in his toys. He was oblivious to her watchful eye. Suzie then cautiously pulled the trap door to the attic, ducking as some insulation came flying at her face. As she looked up at the opening, she realized she was missing something. She needed a step ladder. Where had Joe left the ladders?

"Honey, Mommy has to go outside to the work shed to get a ladder. Will you be good and keep playing with your toys?" Suzie looked at Jonathan.

"Yes, Mommy." Jonathan did not even break his gaze from the Lego castle he was building.

Suzie threw on a coat, grabbed a flashlight and tromped on the frozen ground, making her way to the work shed. The brisk winter wind did its best to transform her ears into icicles.

The flashlight located the ladder on the west side of the shed. The shed was a mess.

What had gotten into Joe? She used to tease him saying the shed looked like a museum; it was so clean. He even kept all his tools polished. Now it looked like a tornado had blown through it.

She positioned the beam of the flashlight in front of each step. The last thing she needed was to trip and have an eye put out by the wrong end of a pitchfork. At last, she was at her destination. She grabbed the ladder, swinging it away from the wall. She had no idea a wooden ladder could be so heavy. The lightweight aluminum ladder had apparently found a new home: Megan's house.

The thought that Megan had a better ladder than she had gave Suzie a burst of anger, which transformed into brute strength. Soon she had that ladder under the opening to the attic.

She climbed up with some hesitancy. She didn't remember what was in the attic. She doubted that Joe had been up there in years. A sunbeam illuminated the small dusty room and as Suzie gazed around she could see that spiders had set up camp. It seemed as if they had had family reunions galore.

Now where would she have put her old bedroom décor? She looked around and her eyes were drawn to an end table on the edge of the sunbeam. What was laying on that table? Her heart sank as her eyes registered what her mind was struggling to avoid. A dozen dried roses were sitting on the table and the spirit of Betrayal came bustling down the path of memories.

Suzie had been eighteen years old when she had gotten the job at the local hardware store. She knew she needed to do something. Living with her parents was not on her long-term agenda for happiness.

She saw the "Help Wanted" ad in the window right after graduation and on impulse walked in and filled out an application. They called and offered her the job, without an interview, by the middle of the afternoon.

It didn't take a rocket scientist IQ to do the job, but it kept her busy and she enjoyed it. In fact, she enjoyed everything that gave her a break from her cold, indifferent mother, Barbara.

She felt as if she came alive when she was in the store. She enjoyed the people she worked with, the challenge of learning the inventory and she was a pro at customer service.

It only took her a couple of weeks to learn the store from front to back. She was an expert at stocking the shelves: except for those nuts and bolts. Ugh, they took forever. It was a wonder she was not sweating. She had been trying to sort through the small box of the little metal demons for a full hour now. She only had one more hour and then she could go home. Joy, joy, back to Barbaric Barbara.

She heard footsteps behind her. She really needed to get this done before she left. If it was a customer, she didn't mean to be rude, but they sometimes asked the most idiotic questions.

"Trying to sort through the nuts and bolts of life can be an all-consuming task, can't it?"

The deep voice startled her. She jumped, losing her death grip on the small box as it tumbled to the floor, nuts and bolts scattering, like raindrops, on the tile floor.

She whipped around, on the verge of tears, then stopped dead in her tracks. Her heart skipped a beat as she gazed into the most beautiful green eyes she had ever seen, surrounded by a handsome chiseled face.

The man's face melted into a seductive grin, as the man gently pried the one remaining bolt from her fingertips. "So, you're the new girl, right?"

Suzie could feel her face blush into a crimson red. "God, is it that obvious?"

His face crinkled into laugh lines, which gave a subtle hint of expression to his stunning eyes. "Nah, it's just that we haven't had a history of young beautiful women working here, so it was a matter of elimination."

"Thank you." Suzie replied, still star struck, as she took in the chiseled jaw line, perfect teeth and broad shoulders.

"I didn't mean to startle you." He said as he bent down to pick up the storage bin.

"Oh, no, you don't have to do that." She said as she quickly kneeled on the floor, scooping up the errant nuts and bolts.

"It's no problem. I am Joe, the owner's son. I know this store like the back of my hand."

"Hi, Joe, the owner's son. I am Suzie, the clumsy new employee." Suzie stuck out her hand and shook hands, noting the spark of electricity that surged through her body when she touched Joe.

Joe laughed, "Not only beautiful but a witty sense of humor, too. I am glad I decided to come home from college this summer."

Suzie had never been called witty or beautiful before. She didn't know how to react. She dipped her head shyly. "Ah, thanks. I guess the only thing that escapes me is putting the nuts and bolts of life back in the right place."

"Maybe that is why I had to come back home for summer." Joe winked. "So, you work till closing?"

"Yes, I was just trying to put everything back in its proper place before I left. Gerald, the assistant manager is a bit persnickety."

"Persnickety? Wow, that is a perfect way to describe the old codger," Joe said.

Suzie giggled. "I think he must come in here at three a.m. just to make sure I hung the shovels on the right hooks."

"I wouldn't put that past him." Joe said as he put all the nuts and bolts back into their bins. "There isn't anything that can slip past Gerald." Joe paused for a moment, looking at Suzie with a mischievous glint in his eye. "The only thing that has ever undone him is the store mouse."

Suzie gasped. "Seriously?"

"Yeah, a couple of years ago he swore there was a mouse that was getting into the food," Joe said.

"You must be kidding. As clean as Gerald keeps this store? I can't imagine a mouse being comfortable here," Suzie said.

"The last time he spotted it was just last week and he said it was in the janitor's closet."

"We have one of those?"

"Yes, it is next to the break room. You want me to show you?" Joe asked

"Nah, that's okay, I can pass on that. I am not really into cleaning, or mice for that matter. Thanks though. I really need to get home." Suzie turned around and felt a strong hand grabbing her elbow.

"I think you need to know where the cleaning supplies are, not because I need you to clean but you may have missed some nuts and bolts on the floor. I think it would be easier for you to have a broom, unless you want to get down on your hands and knees." Joe looked at her with an innocent and vulnerable gaze.

"Well, since you are the owner's son, I guess I can't say no. I will warn you though, if I see that mouse I will scream bloody murder."

Joe loosened his grip on her and slid his hand to the small of her back, with gentle force he guided her to the back of the store.

"So, this is the cleaning closet. I would have never noticed it if you hadn't pointed it out. Now that I know where it is, I think I will let you locate the broom. I will stay outside to make sure Gerald doesn't get upset at us being in his closet." Suzie met Joe's gaze with a twinkle of mischief and quickly turned as if to walk away from the closet.

"Oh, no you don't, little Missy." Joe caught her arm and swung her around to face him. "I have had to hear my father talk about this mouse longer than I would care to admit. If I find his location, it is just a matter of a mousetrap and some cheese and then he will be taken out to the trash."

"Ouch, poor mousie." Suzie smiled, "I will go into the closet on one condition and one condition only."

"What is that?" Joe asked.

"That you are the one who takes the dead little fella out to the trash, not me."

"Deal." Joe said as he extended his hand to shake Suzie's.

Joe opened the door slowly and pulled Suzie into the closet. "I think it may have gone in that corner." Joe said as he slyly closed the door behind Suzie, leaving only a sliver of light to illuminate the small room.

"Well, then I suggest you bend down and look in that corner. I will stand right behind you for support," Suzie said.

Joe bent down and pretended as if he was looking. Then he got up slowly, standing so close to Suzie that she could not breathe. His hand snaked around her neck and he brought her head closer, their lips were almost touching.

Suzie's heart was beating so fast, she feared it was going to pop out of her chest. She tried to divert her gaze from Joe's eyes. If she didn't look at him then maybe her knees wouldn't feel so weak. She picked a spot on an upper shelf and willed herself to fix her gaze on a roll of paper towels. But there was something wrong. The paper towel roll was rustling. She tried to focus with more concentration. Soon, two beady eyes and a pointed little nose peeked out from behind the paper towels.

"The mouse! The mouse! I found the mouse!" Suzie pushed Joe away from her with such strength that he tumbled over the mop bucket. She bolted out of the closet screaming. She almost ran right into Gerald, who had been eavesdropping on the conversation in the closet.

"Suzie! Suzie!" The clatter of brooms and brushes falling to the floor muffled the helpless cry of Joe. Soon the closet door flew open and Joe collided with Gerald head on, knocking him down. "Suzie, calm down, it's just a mouse."

Suzie was sprinting for the exit and in a flash, she was in her car, squealing her tires as she backed out and made her way home.

The next morning, Suzie was in a twist. She was embarrassed by her actions the previous night. She didn't want to see Joe, much less work at his father's store. She had no choice. She didn't have a long line of references she could call for a new job.

She took extra time to do her hair and used all of Barbara's beauty tips for her makeup. *Maybe if I fulfill his delusion of being beautiful he will forget that I pushed him into the mop bucket last night.* Suzie thought as she got into her car to go to work.

She snuck in the back door and went straight to the breakroom to clock in. She put her purse in her locker. As she was turning to walk into the store she stopped short. There was a beautiful bouquet of roses on the break table.

"Oh great, I get humiliated and someone else gets a dozen roses." She muttered and started out of the breakroom. "Wait a minute, I work with men. What kind of man gets roses at work?" Suzie did a 180 and walked to the roses. "I don't think Gerald has a boyfriend. He seems a bit odd but not in that way." She saw a little card peeking out of the crimson red and bent down to read it.

"To Suzie: Thanks so much for saving my life last night.
Hope we can be bff.

Love, your mouse."

Suzie started giggling. "How cute. I wonder who bought them?" She carefully set them back on the break table. Then she went to the front of the store and started counting the money that was in the till.

"I saw you got a dozen roses from someone." Joe said as he approached the counter.

"Yep, it was a total surprise to me." Suzie kept her eyes on the money, trying hard not to be distracted.

"So, your boyfriend doesn't normally give you flowers?" Joe asked.

"Not that one." Suzie was going to play this for all it was worth.

"So how long have you known this boyfriend?" Joe asked.

"Oh, we just met, but I guess he is pretty taken with me." Suzie finished counting the money and flashed Joe a charming smile.

"I know how he feels." Joe responded with a bit of shyness.

Suzie looked straight in Joe's eyes. She couldn't believe he just said that. No one had ever told her something like that. She had no idea how to respond. "Well, ummm, I better get to work." She started walking through the store checking the merchandise.

"So, do you date this new boyfriend on a regular basis?" Joe was trailing Suzie like a lost puppy.

"Not yet. We just met, like I said. We are getting to know each other." Suzie rearranged the garden gloves.

"So, it must be hard for you to find time to get to know someone new when you already have so many suitors right?" Joe put the garden gloves back like they were before Suzie had touched them.

"I make time for the important stuff." Suzie rearranged the garden gloves again.

"So, what does it take for a man to be considered important stuff in your book?".

"A dozen roses is a nice start." Suzie smiled warmly at Joe. She heard the bell on the front door jingle and looked up to see Barbara sashaying through the front door. "Oh God, no, not my mother, Barbara." Suzie's heart took a plummet.

Joe looked at Suzie with genuine concern. "Don't worry, I got this." He said as he walked with purpose to the front door.

Suzie watched with fascination as she saw Joe handle Barbara. He moved her through the store always keeping her an aisle or two away from where Suzie was. She heard him bragging to Barbara about how everyone was so impressed with her work ethic and punctuality. He answered every stupid question that Barbara had, giving the impression that it was the most intelligent question that could have been asked.

Barbara finally bought a pair of garden gloves and strutted out the door in her high heels and tight skirt.

Joe made sure she was gone and then let out a whistle. "Wow, she is a piece of work, isn't she?"

Suzie heaved a sigh of relief. "You have no idea."

"Did I do alright?" Joe asked.

"You were perfect," Suzie said.

"Thanks. Umm, do you think that performance would warrant a date tonight?" Joe asked with the most adorable look of innocence.

"If you wanted a date, all you had to do was ask, silly," Suzie giggled.

Suzie looked at the dried roses on the table as tears started gushing down her cheeks. *How could something that was so wonderful and romantic just evaporate? Damn that Megan.*

Now what had she come up in the attic for? Oh yes, the bedspread.

She looked to the right of the end table and saw her old bedspread in a bag.

Suzie grabbed the bag and carefully climbed down the ladder. She slammed the attic door shut with force. Wish she could slam the door to her memories like she had that attic door.

"You *can* do that." A voice inside her head said.

"No, I can't." She argued back to the unusual voice.

"If *you* can't, then who can?" The voice continued.

"Wait a minute, you got a point there. I *am* in control of my own thoughts. What I allow into my thought process is at my discretion." Suzie said as she walked into her bedroom setting the bedspread on the floor. "Let me check this new idea out with God's word."

Suzie grabbed her Bible and let it fall open to Philippian's 4:8: "And now, dear brothers and sisters, one final thing. Fix your thoughts on what is true and honorable, and right, and pure, and lovely, and admirable. Think about things that are excellent and worthy of praise."

"How do I do that when a memory changes color? At one time it was beautiful and comforting like a sunset and now when I remember the good memories with Joe it feels like a horrible thunderstorm."

"*Through forgiveness.*"

"How do I forgive a man who has betrayed me and left not only me, but our children for another woman?"

"*I died for his sins too, just as I died for yours.*"

"Okay, you win." Suzie sighed as she tore off the safari bedspread and replaced it with her old one. "Wait just one minute." Suzie stopped in mid stride. "Did I just have a talk with God?"

As she was tucking the bedspread in around the pillows she looked up at Uncle Buck and said. "Tomorrow you, my friend, are going to have to find a new home. I am now using God as my counselor and He was supposed to be my comforter in the first place. Furthermore, I just realized something. *He* talks back."

THE DEVIOUSNESS OF DECEIT

DECEIT WAS INCENSED. THE MESSAGE TO SUSANNA had been loud and clear. She is not worth loving. Her own mother didn't love her and now her husband left her. Why couldn't she get it through her thick head that she didn't need to be living anymore?

He needed another meeting. Damn those meetings. He hated them more than he hated Truth. He always felt as if he wasn't in control when the meetings were about Susanna. Nevertheless, the wench had to be put in the ground and if it took another meeting, so be it.

The alert was sounded, and all the evil entities started congregating in his chamber.

There was murmuring amongst them. Something had happened which Deceit had no knowledge of, but he sure as hell was going to find out.

"Alright will someone tell me what is going on? All of this whispering is hurting my ears."

Total silence.

Deceit towered over Despair. "Do you want to tell me what has happened, or do I need to make your blood a new coat of paint for my chamber?"

Despair was shaking. "I haven't the faintest idea master. I have just returned from Africa."

Deceit glared at Despair. Then fixed his gaze on the black greasy form of Betrayal. "I believe you have been present have you not?"

"Yes, sir. I have, but Rejection's failure is why the vision occurred."

Deceit whirled around to face the snake. "Vision?! What vision?"

"Oh, well, you know some people think that dreams are a message from God." The snake rattled his tail, turning to make sure that the wound on his neck was protected. "Susanna just had a silly dream. That is all."

"Oooh, I love getting in the middle of that." Adultery flipped her blond curly hair over her shoulder. "Dreams are my specialty."

Deceit was not to be distracted. "So, do you want to tell me what this vision was about? Or do I have to get my pitchfork and poke another hole in that neck of yours?"

Rejection put his head up as if to whisper in the ear of Deceit. "You may want to bend down for this, I don't think you want this to be common knowledge among the masses."

Deceit bent down, listening closely to Rejection's hiss. His face turned into an evil scowl. "A vision of the Second Coming of Jesus Christ? Why on earth would Susanna warrant a vision like that?"

The whole chamber exploded into chaotic dissidence. Deceit paced around in a circle as if he were a merry-go-round on speed. Doubt started throwing punches at Insecurity. Despair puked on the peacock feathers of Arrogance. Bitterness was shedding bark. Adultery started shaking so hard that her false eyelashes fell off. Betrayal lifted his leg and urinated on Envy. All semblance of reason and order had dissipated with the name of Jesus Christ being spoken.

Deceit almost crushed Insecurity in his mindless rage. "We have to do something which is shocking; something which would tear her heart into shreds. Let me think, let me think."

The murmuring was getting louder and Deceit was visibly shaken. "Quiet! I have to think." Deceit paced round and round and the circles started closing in. He slowed and lifted his head with a wicked grin spreading from ear to ear. "We will use the plan that we used on Jesus. The one which put Him on the cross. You know, accusing an innocent of a sin which they were not capable of committing."

"Oh God." Doubt whispered to Insecurity. "Is he mad? We lost that fight. Does he not remember?"

"I know. We didn't expect for Jesus to walk out of his tomb and overcome death. We thought that was our greatest victory." The shrinking violet wilted. "It ended up being the one battle which sealed our fate."

"Shut up and hear me out." Deceit said, raising his voice. "Now this is how I see it: Joe committed adultery on Susanna and left her. How about we give the impression that she has already found another man and is sleeping with him?"

Adultery clapped her hands and jumped up and down. "That would include me, right? I am so bored right now. I really need to be involved in something, or my hair is going to go limp." She bent down to dislodge the false eyelash from a fold in her evening gown.

"You will be implied but not actually present. Just as we were all implied in the case of Jesus who was crucified," Deceit said.

Condemnation spoke up. "I have some concerns about this, sir. Even though we are evil and not beyond implying guilt upon quite a multitude of innocent people; is it logical to assume that we will be successful? Wouldn't it be more logical to tempt Susanna into actual adultery?"

Deceit's smile grew wider. "Remember what we are, we are evil and we don't operate within logic. If Joe suspects Susanna of sleeping with another man, especially when the children are in the house, he will go ballistic with self-righteous indignation. He will probably fight for custody and win. The courts will view Megan and Joe as the perfect suburban couple and Susanna as the unemployed, scorned ex-wife."

"If Joe gets custody of the children then Susanna wouldn't think she had a reason to live, would she?" Despair said.

"Bingo!" Deceit said as he gave each one of the evil spirits their new assignment.

UNCLE BUCK

THE WARMTH OF THE EARLY MORNING SUN WOKE Suzie out of her slumber. She looked at her alarm clock and rolled over to go back to sleep. It was one hour before she needed to roll out of bed. She tossed and turned for a few minutes then, in defeat, got up. For some reason she felt uncomfortable with Uncle Buck gazing at her as she changed from pajamas to her clothes.

"He is just a dead animal which I used as a confidant because I didn't think God was listening to me." *Love the Lord your God with all your heart, soul and mind.* The verse echoed through her mind like a ghost.

The hardened stare of Uncle Buck kept catching her eye as she was making the bed. Suzie kept trying to avoid the gaze of Uncle Buck as she scurried around the bed, tucking in corners and fluffing up pillows.

After she was done making the bed she crawled on top of it, looking at Uncle Buck with a resolute sadness. "Listen, I know you were my friend during a hard time and it's not like I don't appreciate you listening to all my crap. But I kind of feel like I gave you a place in my life that should have been given to God. As weird as it may seem, you were an idol in my life. Instead of praying, I just talked to you." Suzie stroked the hairs on Uncle Buck's cheek. "I am sorry Joe shot you. You didn't deserve that and to be shot for your antlers is just wrong. It is like you were a trophy for him because he was trying to impress Megan." Suzie paused for a moment to think. "You weren't the only trophy Joe has; Megan is a trophy too." Suzie shrugged her shoulders. "So, after the kids get to school, I am going to put you out in the work shed so that you can feel more at home. I know I cannot give you your life back, but I need to get mine back on track and I hope you understand." Suzie patted Uncle Buck on the nose and then jumped off the bed.

Mornings were much easier since Michael had started the habit of getting ready the night before. The kids were fed and off to school without any nagging.

Suzie came back into her house feeling refreshed and ready for the challenge of dismantling an idol. Jonathan decided he wanted to watch Mommy take Uncle Buck down.

Suzie got on the bed and contemplated the challenge before her. She wasn't sure how to get the "dead head" down from the wall. She had no clue as to how heavy it would be. "It's not going to magically come off the wall with you just staring at it." Suzie said, as she tried pulling it down. She yanked and yanked and pushed and pulled but there was no moving the monstrous head. She was about ready to give up when the mount wiggled a bit.

She jumped as the phone started to ring its shrill ring.

“Honey, can you grab the phone and say “Hello?” Suzie asked Jonathan.

“Yes, Mommy.” Jonathan dropped the matchbox cars he was playing with and picked up the phone. “Hello?”

Suzie pushed up, then pulled back with determination. The mount broke loose and the weight of it was a surprise to Suzie. It was like she had dislodged a ton of bricks from the wall.

She was top heavy as she tried to hold on to it. She didn’t want it to smash her toes. She started leaning back and within a minute found herself spread eagle on the bed with Uncle Buck’s rubbery nose kissing her lips. “Who is it honey?” Suzie spit out the words through hairs that were now making way to lodge between her teeth.

“It’s Daddy!” Jonathan exclaimed. “He wants to talk to you bout vis’tation.”

“Tell him I’m busy right now.” Suzie said, trying to lift the snout of Uncle Buck off her face.

“She busy Daddy.” Jonathan said as he walked closer to the bed looking for his Mommy under Uncle Buck. “What Mommy doing? She kissing Uncle Buck, Daddy.” Jonathan had crawled up on the bed. “He has a long nose and he is haiwy, Daddy.”

Jonathan listened for a minute and then raised his voice. “I told you, she is busy. Uncle Buck is on Mommy’s face and she can’t come.” Another pause. “Ok, Daddy, I tell Mommy to call you.” Jonathan started petting Uncle Buck. “What nasty mean Daddy… Daddy… Daddy?” Jonathan’s face looked crestfallen. “Daddy hung up on me. He said you being bad, Mommy. He said you doing the nasty with Uncle Buck.” Jonathan peeked under the mount to look closely at his mother. “What nasty mean, Mommy?”

"Nasty means that someone is doing something wrong. I guess your Daddy didn't know that we named his trophy, "Uncle Buck." He must think that Uncle Buck is a man. That's all." Suzie said struggling to breathe around the whiskers and chin hairs of Uncle Buck. "Do you think that you could pull a little on the back of this so that I can stop kissing Uncle Buck?"

Jonathan straddled his mother, pulling with all his tiny strength on the back of the mount. As he was pulling, he remembered one more tidbit of information that his daddy had mentioned. "Oh, Daddy said to tell you he gonna call CPS. What is CPS?"

"What?!"

"He gonna call CPS on you!" Jonathan yelled, his face turning red with exhertion.

"The nerve of that man." Indignant rage coursed through Suzie's body. The anger gave Suzie strength to push Uncle Buck off her. "If that isn't the pot calling the kettle black."

Jonathan crawled over to pat Suzie's face. "You okay, Mommy?"

"Yes, darling I am fine." *Your daddy, on the other hand, is a total nutcase.*

Suzie turned to look at Uncle Buck on the bed. "Well now, Watson, I have a real problem on my hands. How do I get Uncle Buck out to the shed when he is clearly not a lightweight?"

Jonathan looked up at Suzie with curiosity. "My name not Watson, Mommy. My name Jonathan."

Suzie gazed at Jonathan. "I know, honey, and I am no Sherlock Holmes either." Suzie scratched her temple as if to ponder her options. "I can't imagine lifting this beast and taking him out to the shed; dragging him is going to be a chore." Suzie sat on the bed, hanging her head. "I wonder if I got a blanket and put Uncle Buck on the blanket and pulled it, if that would work? It is worth a try. Either that or Uncle Buck is going to be my new sleeping partner." She looked around her room for a suitable blanket. "I know! I will use the safari bedspread to drag him out."

Soon with a lot of huffing and puffing, Uncle Buck was put on the northern side of the work shed. Suzie almost tripped over a rope on the floor as she was walking out. She stopped and looked at it for a second, then decided to leave it alone. She didn't know what it was doing there but she had no desire to clean up the mess that Joe had left. She had enough mess inside the house.

She had just gotten back inside and was washing her hands when the phone rang again. "Oh, God. Sometimes I wish that phones were outlawed."

"Hello?" Suzie said.

"Hello, Suzie, is that you?" The sound of Joy's voice made Suzie cringe. Oh, God, no. Of all the people in the world that I want to hear from, Joy, is the last person on the list.

"Yes, Joy, it's me, Suzie." Suzie said with a lack of enthusiasm.

"How are you doing honey? I was just thinking about you. You know it has been ages since we talked." Joy said, her voice full of irritating cheerfulness.

"Yes, I know. Things aren't going too good for me right now." Suzie willed herself not to break down in tears.

"What has been going on?" The tone of Joy's voice emitted empathy and concern.

"Joe left me for another woman and now he is calling CPS on me because he thinks I had sex with someone in front of Jonathan." Suzie felt like she had just vomited up the past week in one sentence.

"Oh, my goodness. How did that happen?"

"The leaving me for another woman or the CPS allegation?" Suzie asked.

"Why on earth would he leave you? I thought you two were so compatible." Joy said with sincerity.

"We were. At least at first, we were. He was my everything, Joy. I was just remembering how we met. He was so charming, fun, and handsome. Those green eyes and blond hair used to melt me." Suzie stopped to wipe the tears from her eyes. "Then Megan, his boss, got hired at his job and things started changing. I tried to stop him from leaving but there was nothing I could do."

"How about the CPS allegation? Did you find someone new already?" Joy asked, a hopeful lilt to her voice.

"NO, I wouldn't even think of doing that. I still love Joe," Suzie said. "It all started with me trying to change my bedroom décor..."

Suzie told the story of Uncle Buck to Joy and despite her resolve not to let Joy's cheerful demeanor influence her, by the end of the story she was laughing.

"That is ridiculous that he would come to that conclusion without any evidence. He must be feeling very guilty about his relationship with Megan and he is transferring that guilt onto you," Joy said.

"You're probably right about that. Do you think I should be worried?"

Joy paused for a moment. "Yes, I think you should be very worried. For some reason CPS and the court system has changed over the past few years. They seem to be intent on taking children away from their natural mothers. It used to be that the system was in favor of the mothers but now the tide seems to have shifted."

Suzie's hand started shaking. "How do I prepare for this Joy? I have never been investigated by CPS in my entire life."

"First of all, step away from the fear. You didn't do anything wrong. It was a misinterpretation based on Joe's guilt, not yours. Second, make sure you have a relatively clean house and food in your fridge."

"I am terrified that CPS will consider me incompetent. I can't concentrate on anything, much less cleaning my house. Plus, I am almost out of food."

Joy took a deep breath. "Okay the first thing you need to do is pray, then go to the grocery store and buy some food. Pick up your house. Get a laundry basket and throw everything that is clutter in it. Then hide the basket in a closet. Make sure your dishes are done and the clothes are cleaned up, and try to spot clean your bathrooms. You don't have to go all Martha Stewart on it like Barbara does; you just have to make it look clean."

"I think I can do that." Suzie said with a sigh.

"Okay, then get to it because if Joe did call CPS they are going to be out there very soon on these false allegations. Call me when they leave. I will pray continually for you until you call."

"Thanks, Joy." Suzie said, as she started wiping her kitchen counters.

"You are welcome honey. I am sorry you have had such a hard time of it lately. I wish I had called sooner."

"You called at the perfect time, but I better get my Martha Stewart on," Suzie smiled.

"That and your Betty," Joy replied.

"Betty?" Suzie asked.

"Yes, Betty Crocker," Joy responded.

"Oh, yeah, those two women have made it so difficult for the rest of us. To think that all Megan had to do was get her Barbie doll, silicone body on to steal my husband." Suzie let a giggle slip through her lips.

"Yes, and it seems as if all men have to live up to is Ken. What a shame." Joy was laughing heartily. "Well, dear, I had better let you get to your task list now. Remember to call me."

"I will. Bye now," Suzie said.

"Goodbye, dear child of God." Joy hung up the phone.

GETTING READY FOR CPS

SUZIE GLANCED AT THE CLOCK. "OH, NO, IT IS TIME TO pick up Michael. Let me think about this for a second. I will clean up the house this evening and then do my grocery shopping in the morning after dropping Michael and Sarah off at school."

Jonathan was glued to the TV.

"Jonathan, I need you to get your coat on. It is time to pick Michael up from school." Suzie said as she grabbed her purse from the table.

Jonathan did not move.

"Jonathan? Did you hear me?"

"Mommy, be quiet. I watching Dwagons fly." Jonathan did not break his gaze from the television.

Suzie marched to the living room. "Jonathan, I have asked you twice to get ready to pick up Michael. You have chosen to ignore me, so you will lose your privileges to watch TV this afternoon."

"No, Mommy! No!" Jonathan burst into tears.

Suzie picked his coat up from the couch and quickly put it on Jonathan, grabbed his hand firmly and drug him out the front door.

The temper tantrum continued as Suzie backed out of the driveway. "If you stop crying and listen to me, I may give you a chance to win your TV privilege back."

"I neva gonna see dwagons fly again." Jonathan whimpered from the back.

"I dare say we have a flare for the histrionic in this family. First, your daddy imagines me as a harlot and now you think that PBS will cancel "Dragon Tales" if you stop watching it," Suzie whispered.

"Honey, I am sure if you are good, the dragons will be flying again tomorrow." Suzie said in a voice that could be clearly heard. "If you help Mommy clean up your toys then maybe you can even watch TV this afternoon."

"I wanna watch dwagons fly!" Jonathan screamed from the back seat. "If you do the nasty with Uncle Buck, I can watch dwagons fly!"

"Okay, stop right there. I was not doing anything nasty with Uncle Buck. Your daddy thought that Uncle Buck was a man. Now tell me, was Uncle Buck a man?"

"No," Jonathan relented.

"At this time every morning we go get Michael from school. Do you think that Michael wants to walk home in the cold, just because you want to see dragons fly?"

"No," Jonathan muttered.

"Do you want to watch television this afternoon?" Suzie asked.

"Yes." Jonathan wiped the tears from his cheeks.

"Okay, Jonathan I am giving you a way you can get out of your punishment. When we get home, if you help Mommy pick up the house you can watch TV. Okay?"

"Okay, Mommy." Jonathan was smiling now.

Michael was picked up from school and Suzie gave him the afternoon agenda. The agenda included picking up every stray article of clothing and shoes in the house. Once those items were picked up, they were to give them to Suzie, who would decide if they looked clean enough to be put into the closet or should be laundered. Once the errant pieces of clothing were collected, there was to be a sweep of the house for toys. At the conclusion of this task list, the television could be turned on again.

Suzie entered her house with every intention of becoming Martha Stewart. "Okay boys, why don't you go through the house and pick up all of the clothing."

"I'm hungry." Michael said, plopping down on the couch.

"Me too." Jonathan sat right beside Michael.

"Alright, I will get you something to eat but then we got to pick up the house okay?" She rushed to the kitchen, grabbed some peanut butter and jelly, slapped it on some bread, and cringed as she gave it to her boys. She didn't usually resort to quick fixes like this when it came to food, but her choices were limited.

She picked up the winter coats which were laying on the couch and hung them up in the closet. She glanced at Jonathan and Michael who were eating the PB and J sandwiches with a slow and methodical stubbornness.

"Boys, I need you to hurry up with those sandwiches okay? We got to clean house." Suzie looked behind the couch and found three socks and a handful of candy wrappers from last Halloween.

"Why?" Michael asked.

Suzie did not want to tell Michael about the CPS allegation. She really didn't have time to explain the whole drama of Uncle Buck. "Michael, we need to clean house today because we want to be like most people. Normal people live in clean houses."

"My friend Adam has dog poop in his living room. He is my best friend. I thought he was normal." Michael looked at Suzie with tears in his eyes.

Make mental note – Invite Adam over to our house and never allow Michael to go to his house again. "Sweetie I am sure that was just one time." Suzie wiped the coffee table off with a dust rag and put the stack of papers in a pile on the floor.

"Nope, every time I am over there, there is a pile of poop in the living room." Michael took the last bite of his sandwich.

"Well, we are not talking about Adam's house, now are we? We are talking about *our* house and *our* house needs to be cleaned up."

"I thought we were talking about who was normal. You said normal people have clean houses. My friend Adam is normal!" Michael got up with tears streaming down his face and stomped off to the bedroom slamming the door.

Suzie looked at Jonathan as if Jonathan might possibly explain what just happened with Michael. Jonathan had curled up on the couch and was snoozing.

"Okay screw CPS. Something is going on with my son and my son is a lot more important than my house." Suzie threw her dust rag down and walked with resolution to the bedroom.

She opened the door and found Michael in a fetal position on the bed. His body shaking from sobs.

"Michael, I am so sorry. I didn't mean to imply that Adam was not from a normal family. I know he is your best friend and you love him."

Michael turned over his face contorted with anger. "We are the ones who aren't normal, Mommy. Adam's mom and dad love each other. Poop doesn't matter."

Suzie felt like she had been kicked in the gut with truth and the truth hurt. "You're right Michael. Most normal families have both a mom and a dad living in the house and right now, you just have a mom living here. I wish your daddy hadn't left. I miss him, and I know you do too. I wish I could get him back, but he doesn't want to come back." Suzie's head hung down as tears flooded her lap.

"Nobody loves me." Michael said curling up tighter into a ball.

"Honey, just because your daddy left me does not mean he doesn't love you. He loves you so much." Suzie wrapped her body around Michael.

"How can he leave you if he loves me? If he leaves you then he is leaving me too. If he doesn't love you then how can he love me?" Michael asked with desperation and hurt riding on every word.

"I don't know honey. I don't know. I can't understand why your daddy left us, but I know he loves you and I know I love you."

Suzie looked at Michael and realized that her plans for the afternoon may need to be reworked. Michael seemed like a nap was in store and Jonathan was already napping. It may be that she could clean up the house better with both napping. This may be a better option than trying to get them to help. "Honey, would you like to take a nap?"

"Yeah, but I got to go to the bathroom first." Michael got up and went to the bathroom then came back and crawled on bed. He was asleep in a matter of seconds.

Suzie got up off the bed with stealth-like moves and got a throw from the closet to put over Michael. She tiptoed to the living room and laid an afghan over the small form of Jonathan. Then she got her Martha Stewart on and picked up every article of clothing and sorted through it. After the clothes were picked up she got a laundry basket and gathered all the stray toys and put them in the closet.

CONDEMNATION THROUGH CPS

DECEIT NEEDED TO MAKE SURE THAT THIS PLAN worked. He needed to micromanage every stinking detail. This was going to require what he dreaded most: A meeting.

The evil spirits sauntered into the meeting room. Betrayal was the last to enter. He did so with an air of indecision, which was very unusual for him.

"Here, here, fellow comrades in evil. I believe that the plan is progressing well, but this is only the start of the plan. We must proceed with caution in every step we take from here on out. The suspicion of Adultery has been placed in Joe's mind. CPS has been notified, now who do we have at CPS that can work for us?" Deceit focused his wicked gaze upon Envy.

Envy was distracted, looking in her book of tricks for how she could use chocolate milk to lure kids into her grasp.

"ENVY! PAY ATTENTION!" Deceit screamed.

Envy dropped her book of tricks, quivering in fear. "What did you need?"

"I need the files on CPS. I need to pick out which government idiot we are going to use to separate Suzie from her children." Deceit was simmering in fury.

"Well let me get that file. What exactly were you hoping to find?" Envy asked as she reached into her green glob and pulled out the file on CPS.

"I want someone who is blinded by prejudice." Deceit said with certainty. "Someone who believes that all single mothers are welfare recipients, abusive parents, and sluts."

Adultery threw her head back and let out a shrill bout of laughter. "Suzie is anything but a slut, sir. A prude would be a more accurate definition."

"I know that, I know that." Deceit said with a dismissive flick of his hand. "Why do you think we need the blinders of prejudice?"

"Well, sir there are quite a few to choose from that are prejudiced against single mothers. Could you possibly be more specific?" Envy said with a furrowed brow.

"I think she should be ugly," Despair interjected. "Suzie is quite a looker and that would allow Envy to be involved."

Envy gave Despair a thumbs up.

"Yes, yes, that would be a good characteristic. Do we have any CPS workers who are ugly?"

Envy heaved a sigh. "The majority of them are considered ugly. I am thinking we want a woman, not a man, right? I mean, if I am going to be involved, then I think an older, ugly woman would fit the bill." Envy flipped through her file on CPS and a look of dismay crossed her face. "Gads, that is most of the file."

Despair crept out into the middle of the chamber to get attention. "I think it should be an old ugly woman who has never had children. That way she would not only be jealous of how pretty Susanna is, but she would also resent the fact that Susanna has three snot-nosed brats and she has none."

Deceit looked down at Despair in amazement. "Sometimes you surprise me, Despair. I think you may have nailed it on the head with that suggestion."

Envy started bouncing up and down with excitement. "I think I have located the perfect servant for us. Her name is Ms. Peabody. She is scary ugly, does not have any children, has never been married, and she has one more attribute which would make her perfect for this case."

Deceit looked at Envy with suspicion. He wasn't leaving anything to chance. He needed to know *everything* about Ms. Peabody. "What is that attribute?"

"She thinks she is God and she can save the world," Envy exclaimed.

The whole chamber erupted into laughter. Deceit muttered in-between bouts of hearty laughter. "Yes, Ms. Peabody would be perfect." Then doubled over in more fits of laughter.

THE PREJUDICE OF MS. PEABODY

SUZIE WOKE UP THE NEXT DAY AND FELT AS IF SHE woke up in a stranger's home. There was no Uncle Buck to look at and no toys or clothes scattered about. "God this feels strange." She muttered as she got dressed and went to wake up the children.

Michael and Sarah were soon in the car and on their way to school. Suzie planned to go grocery shopping with Jonathan. That would be the last thing crossed off the list that Joy gave her. Although she was not sure she had overcome the fear, she intended to do everything else.

With only eighty dollars in her purse she was going to have to stick to the necessities. She said a prayer for God to help her choose wisely. It was important that CPS would be impressed with her selection. She pulled into the parking lot and glanced back at Jonathan. He was sleeping.

"Sorry, little buddy. Mommy has to wake you up so that we can go buy some food, okay?" Suzie pulled Jonathan out of the car seat and nestled him on her hip.

Suzie meandered through the grocery aisles trying to find food which was healthy and suitable for the taste buds of children. She came out of the grocery store with four full bags of produce and frozen foods, and had ten dollars left in her wallet. She felt as if she should get a gold medal for that accomplishment.

Suzie rushed home. She really wanted to get the groceries unpacked, do some detailed cleaning, and have a bit of time to relax before CPS arrived. As she pulled into her driveway she saw an old beat up car and realized her wishes were not going to happen. Her heart began to race as a feeling of dread descended upon her.

Suzie pulled Jonathan out of the car seat and grabbed all four grocery bags in her left hand. She walked to the car and waited for the driver to roll down the window.

"Can I help you?"

A wrinkled old lady snuffed out her cigarette in the ash tray and then looked at Suzie with pure contempt. "I am looking for the home of Susanna Whatley."

"Well, you are at the right place. May I ask what the nature of your business is?" Suzie asked, feeling her hands turn into icicles.

"I'm Ms. Peabody and I am here to ensure the welfare of the children in this state."

"Why don't you come in and I can explain this misunderstanding over a cup of coffee?" Suzie asked, flashing Ms. Peabody her most charming smile.

"I have already had my coffee for the day." Ms. Peabody's lips set in a firm line of haughtiness. "Let me get my briefcase out of my backseat and I will be right in." Ms. Peabody looked at Suzie as if she had a contagious disease.

"Well, okay then." Suzie made her way into her house, praying fervently with every step, struggling to keep hold of the swelling dam of tears.

Suzie and Jonathan barely got in the door before Ms. Peabody came barging in the back door.

"I am so sorry I did not show you the front door. There is no reason to use the back door." Suzie was beside herself. Going through the back door was not on her list as far as making a good impression went.

Ms. Peabody looked at Suzie as if she had lost her mind. "It matters not which door I walk through. It matters only that the children of this state are in homes which are safe. Now if I could sit down and look through your file I will determine if you are a fit mother."

"Yes, yes, of course." Suzie looked with dismay at her kitchen table. There was peanut butter and jelly smeared on the surface where Michael had sat. Toast crumbs were scattered on the top like snowflakes after a blizzard, and a splash of milk was under Jonathan's high chair.

Ms. Peabody swung her briefcase onto the table and landed it right smack dab in the middle of the peanut butter and jelly.

Suzie was mortified. The one location that she had not cleaned, was the place that Ms. Peabody was now stationed.

Ms. Peabody furrowed her brow as she opened up her briefcase. "I can't remember where I put my reading glasses. I wonder if they are in my purse which I left in my car."

Jonathan had wandered in from the living room and was staring at Ms. Peabody as if she were an alien from outer space.

"Hello, little one. How are you today?" Ms. Peabody's face transformed into a smile.

"Okay." Jonathan stated, looking up at his mother with a quizzical arch to his eyebrows.

Suzie mouthed the words, "Be good please," to Jonathan.

Ms. Peabody looked down at Jonathan, squinting, as if that would make her eyesight any better. "I have some candy in my coat pocket. If you want to reach in there you can choose a piece."

Jonathan looked at Suzie. "Mommy, can I?"

"Yes, of course you can," Suzie said.

Jonathan reached deep into the pocket of the old worn coat which Ms. Peabody was wearing and pulled out a pair of reading glasses. "That not candy, Mommy." Jonathan's face crumbled into an angry frown and Suzie knew that tears were right behind that frown.

"Oh, dear me. That is where my reading glasses are. Try again. I think if you dig a little deeper you may find some candy." Ms. Peabody said, still squinting, as she gazed at Jonathan.

Jonathan dug deeper in her pocket and came out with a Tootsie Pop.

"What do you say?" Suzie asked praying that Jonathan would choose the right words.

"Tank you," Jonathan said, his cherub cheeks bursting into a smile.

"You are welcome." Ms. Peabody put her glasses on. "My goodness you are an adorable little boy. Now I must get busy and make sure that you are safe. Okay?"

"Okay." Jonathan said with an air of indifference and made his way back to the couch to watch television.

Ms. Peabody took a stack of papers out of her briefcase and proceeded to read them. She held them at arm's length. Apparently, her reading glasses were not the right prescription. She read the first page, glancing at Suzie intermittently with disgust coloring her wrinkles. She kept reading through the five page report.

"I think if you would let me explain, you may disregard the allegations," Suzie offered.

"Ma'am. In a court of law, you are considered innocent until proven guilty. When it comes to children, I believe it should be the opposite." Ms. Peabody glared at Suzie.

"If you would just let me explain…"

Ms. Peabody put her hand up as if to stop Suzie. "I think the only person who can explain what happened is that sweet little innocent boy in the other room. Tell me, what is his name?"

"Jonathan." Suzie said, turning away so that Ms. Peabody would not see the tears creeping slowly down her cheeks.

Ms. Peabody got up slowly from her sitting position. She looked as if every bone in her body needed a good shot of WD 40. She hobbled into the living room and addressed Jonathan. "Hello, Jonathan, my name is Ms. Peabody and I need to ask you some questions okay?"

Jonathan looked at her with utter contempt. "I watching Bawney. Go away."

"It will be just a few questions, okay? Do you want another piece of candy?" Ms Peabody sat down on the couch next to Jonathan.

"No." Jonathan said, his eyes glued to the television set.

"Do you know Uncle Buck?" Ms. Peabody asked, ignoring Jonathan's request to watch television.

"I used to know him."

"What happened to Uncle Buck?" Ms. Peabody asked.

"Mommy dwug him out to the wok shed."

"Why did Mommy drag him out to the work shed?" Ms. Peabody asked.

"I guess she was done with him." Jonathan asked sucking on the Tootsie Pop.

"Wasn't it hard for Mommy to drag Uncle Buck out to the work shed? Didn't he want to stay inside with you and her?"

"He didn't have no choice. He was dead." Jonathan eyes were still glued to the television set.

Ms. Peabody's jaw dropped, and her eyes bulged out of her eye sockets. "He was dead?"

"Yep, dead." Jonathan was now chewing the Tootsie Pop with gusto.

Ms. Peabody got up from the couch as if a fire had been lit beneath her. She pranced to the kitchen and grabbed Suzie firmly by the arm. "I need to take Jonathan out to the work shed. I think we may have a crime scene here. If Uncle Buck is dead, you may be looking at a lot of long years behind bars."

Suzie was horrified. "I didn't shoot him, Joe did!"

A look of absolute horror crossed Ms. Peabody's face. She was speechless for a moment, then a wicked look of suspicion crossed her face. "Do you actually think Joe would have called for this investigation if *he* had shot Uncle Buck? I don't think so."

Ms. Peabody took her reading glasses off her face and blew hot air onto the lenses. She rubbed the lenses using a Kleenex. She put them back on her face and glared at Suzie. "Now I need you to do one thing for me. Your son is addicted to television and I need him to show me where the work shed is." Ms. Peabody stopped, furrowed her brow for a moment and then muttered just loud enough for Suzie to hear. "I may need him to actually lead me to the corpse."

"What are you talking about?" Suzie said, eyes wide with fear.

"I think you know exactly what I am talking about. Now go disengage that sweet, innocent child from the television."

"Okay, I will." Suzie said with tears streaming down her face. She brushed them aside before she leaned down to whisper in Jonathan's ear. "If you go show that old woman where the work shed is, I will let you have some cookies later."

"Weally?"

"Yes, really," Suzie replied.

"Okay." Jonathan said and jumped off the couch.

Jonathan scampered into the kitchen and winced as Ms. Peabody grabbed his hand in a death grip. He led her to the back door and down the steps across the frozen ground and out to the work shed. His little body quivering in the cold, as he stumbled over the mounds of ice on the ground.

Ms. Peabody had been so intent on gathering evidence to convict Suzie that she had plum forgotten to grab Jonathan's coat. So much for ensuring the welfare of the children in *her* state.

FINDING UNCLE BUCK

A THOUSAND FRANTIC THOUGHTS WERE FLOODING Ms. Peabody's mind. Should she call the police? No, the police regularly treated the CPS division as if they were overemotional basket cases. If there was a corpse to be found, she would find it first and then report it. Maybe then she would get some respect from those in uniform.

This crime could hit the news. Maybe she would be interviewed. She would have to get new clothes if she was interviewed on television. She hadn't bought anything new in ten years. What if it was such a huge story that it got national attention? Did Oprah still do interviews? She loved Oprah! She had always wanted to meet her. What a tragedy that it took the life of another to *finally* get her on the Oprah show.

Ms. Peabody sighed as she approached the door of the work shed. "Is this the work shed?" Ms. Peabody asked Jonathan.

"Yes." Jonathan said, his teeth chattering, as he stuck his hands into the pockets of his sweat pants.

Ms. Peabody stepped forward in fear. What if there was a gruesome murder scene behind that door? What if Uncle Buck had been shot but wasn't dead? What if he was hiding and waiting for someone to come check on him so that he could attack them in revenge? If there was one thing that she had learned in her forty years of CPS work, it was to *always* expect the worst.

She threw the door open as if it was a drug bust, then scampered to hide behind the side of the work shed. She paused for a moment then crept forward. She peeked in the work shed with caution. "Uncle Buck? Uncle Buck? Are you alive?"

The reality of silence slapped her across the face. "Well, they did say he was dead." She muttered, as she tiptoed into the dark shed. With each step the fear grew inside her. Where would someone hide a corpse? The shed had only one tiny window and it was not letting much light in.

The work shed looked like a nightmare. It was the most disorganized and dirty mess she had seen, far worse than some of the homes she had visited in the projects. She continued to take baby steps around the plethora of used tools and lawn equipment.

What was that in the far corner, under the window? It looked like a head of hair. Oh my God, it looked like he was slumped against the wall. She was appalled at the sheer brutality of parents sometimes. She inched closer to the head of hair, picking up her speed, maybe there was a chance that she could revive Uncle Buck. That would surely get her on the Oprah show. With determination she quickened her step. She was getting her speed up and almost at the window when her foot caught on something. In a split second she went from standing, to sprawling face down on the dirt floor. Screaming out in horror, she plummeted to the ground, her nose landing inches from the snout of Uncle Buck.

She lifted her head and stared straight into the glass eyes of a dead deer. Slowly, her mind disengaged from crazy and started down the path of reality. "Uncle Buck" would be a proper name for the head of a dead deer. Joe had shot him. Suzie had called it a misunderstanding and Jonathan had not shed a tear when he had said that Uncle Buck was dead. Was this the Uncle Buck which Joe claimed Suzie was having sex with? Was Joe insane?! There was no logical way to have sex with this Uncle Buck.

She spit dirt out of her mouth and with every joint screaming out in pain, pushed herself up on her knees. She looked closer at the buck head. "Uncle Buck is that you?"

"Yep, that Uncle Buck." Jonathan said as he brushed a cobweb out of Ms. Peabody's hair.

Ms. Peabody jumped with fear. She had not seen Jonathan slip into the work shed.

"Where did you come from?" she asked.

Jonathan looked at her as if she was crazy, pointing to the door.

"Why didn't you tell me Uncle Buck wasn't a person?" Ms. Peabody looked at Jonathan sternly.

Jonathan shrugged his shoulders inside the coat which Suzie had snuck out to him. "You didn't ask."

"I need to talk to your mother and get this straightened out." Ms. Peabody said as pushed herself slowly to a standing position.

Jonathan blocked Ms. Peabody with his tiny frame. “You make Mommy cwy. You don’t do that. If you do that, I take *all* the candy in yo’ pocket.” Jonathan looked at her with as much meanness as he could muster in his sweet heart.

“Oh, sweet child I have no intention of making your mother cry. I am out here to ensure that you are safe, and I think you are very safe with your mother.” Ms. Peabody tussled the hair on Jonathan’s head. “Now could you grab my hand and take me back to your house?”

Jonathan studied Ms. Peabody’s face for a moment, then sighed and grabbed her hand.

They walked hand in hand entering the back door.

“Hello, Ms. Whatley?”

Suzie came out from her bedroom, where she had cried buckets. She wiped the tears from her eyes and meekly mumbled. “Yes?”

“I think I may be ready for you to explain what exactly happened with Uncle Buck.” Ms. Peabody said with a reassuring smile.

“Well, I was just trying to change the décor in my bedroom because Joe had basically made our bedroom a shrine to his mistress. One of the things they used to do was go hunting together. Uncle Buck lost his life on one of those outings.” Suzie paused to take a breath. “When I was taking Uncle Buck down from the wall I fell back on my bed and Uncle Buck fell on top of my face. Then the phone started ringing and Jonathan answered. He told his daddy that Uncle Buck was kissing me and on top of my face.”

“It is obvious that Joe transferred his guilt from his relationship with his mistress to your supposed salacious affair with a dead animal. Am I right?” Ms. Peabody said as she scribbled furiously on the investigative report in front of her.

"Well, I don't know if that is what was behind this allegation or not. I do know that the Uncle Buck I was kissing was the dead deer that you discovered in the work shed." Suzie wiped the last tear from her cheek.

"I have been on some wild goose chases during my career but this one beats all." Ms. Peabody said as she wiped a stray hair from in front of her glasses and put the report back in her briefcase. "I have done my job. I have ensured that this precious little child of yours is safe. As far as your ex-husband is concerned, I think he should have a psychological evaluation." Ms. Peabody cleaned her glasses yet again. "Who knows, I may need one of those too." Ms. Peabody let an unusual giggle slip out.

Suzie heaved a big sigh. "I don't know what I would have done if you had taken my children from me."

"It is my job to ensure the welfare of the children of this state, Ma'am. If you are a competent parent, which it appears you are, you have no need to worry."

"Thank you." Suzie said with a smile.

"You are welcome. Now I must get on my way. I have three other investigations to pursue. I hope these are more fact-based than this one has been. Thank you for your time." Ms. Peabody picked up her briefcase and headed for the door.

Suzie watched her drive away and didn't recall that her briefcase had a layer of peanut butter and jelly on it until she had turned out of the driveway. She busted out in fits of laughter when she realized that half of the mess on her kitchen table was driving off with Ms. Peabody.

THE RETURN OF JOY

SUZIE WAS ROUNDING UP THE TOAST CRUMBS ON THE kitchen table with every intention of corralling them into the trash when the phone rang again.

"Hello?"

"Hello sweet child of God. How did the meeting with CPS turn out?" Joy's exuberance bounded through the airwaves.

Suzie breathed a sigh of relief. "Ms. Peabody showed up just as I was coming home from grocery shopping. I offered to explain to her the misunderstanding that had occurred. She refused. She insisted that Jonathan show her where "Uncle Buck" was. She actually thought that there was a crime scene because Jonathan said he was dead." Suzie paused to giggle as she heard Joy's hearty laughter. "So, she went out to the work shed. It was hilarious, now that I think about it. I was watching from the kitchen door. She threw open the door to the work shed as if she was doing a drug bust. Then she scampered to the side of the work shed." Suzie was laughing hard.

"She took Jonathan outside with her and didn't even think to put a coat on him. She didn't invite him into the shed because I guess she didn't want him to see the corpse." Suzie paused to catch her breath. "I rushed out to put a coat on Jonathan and I heard her scream. I guess she tripped over something."

"I told Jonathan to go into the shed and make sure she was alright, and I went back inside the house. Pretty soon they both came inside, and she asked me to explain. So, I told her my side of things and she said that I was a competent mother and Joe needed a psyche eval." Suzie stopped to bust out in another fit of giggles. "But you know the best thing about it?"

"No, what?"

"When she came in she put her briefcase right in the middle of some peanut butter and jelly on my kitchen table because she didn't have her glasses on. When she left she took that peanut butter and jelly with her. I didn't think to wipe it off her briefcase till she was going out of the driveway."

"So, let me get this right: Joe intended for CPS to take your kids away from you and not only did they not do that, but they cleaned up half of your breakfast mess?" Joy's laughter was an exclamation point to her statement.

Suzie was giggling so hard her tummy hurt. "Yes, yes, that is exactly what happened."

"Praise God, my prayers have been answered. I am hoping that Ms. Peabody will not only remember to wear her glasses from now on, but she will also learn that prejudice blinds many a person. Unfortunately, those who are blinded, rarely see the truth."

"Yes, sister that is so true. Would love to talk more but I got to go pick up Michael."

"Okay well, be careful and I love you sweet child of God."

"I love you too, Joy." Suzie quickly put the phone back in the cradle, threw on her coat and whisked Jonathan out to the car.

PAPERS SERVED

SUZIE DROVE TO MICHAEL'S SCHOOL WITH LAUGHTER riding shotgun. She couldn't believe how this morning had turned around. She wondered if she should say anything to Michael about the morning's events. He seemed traumatized by Joe leaving, to think that someone could take him from his mother may send him over the cliff. She wouldn't say a word, but she couldn't make any promises as far as Jonathan went.

Michael got in the front seat of the car and Suzie braced herself for what Jonathan would say. She drove home asking Michael the characteristic questions about how his day had gone. She didn't hear a peep from Jonathan. As she drove into her driveway she said a silent prayer of thanks. When she pulled up to the house on her gravel drive she realized that Jonathan had taken a nap.

When she walked into her house she looked around, feeling a strange feeling; relief. She didn't know how good it felt to have a clean house. Maybe CPS had done some good. She realized that she didn't have to be OCD like her mother, but she could be clean. Who knew? Maybe she would have time to watch Dragons fly with Jonathan if she didn't always feel like her house was a clutter landmine.

She fed the boys grilled cheese sandwiches, chips, and cookies. Then she sat on the couch to watch television with them. She had just sat down when she heard someone pounding on the front door.

"Who could that be? I don't remember inviting anyone over." Suzie said as she got up and walked to the door.

A portly man with acne scars on his cheeks stood on her porch.

Suzie didn't give him a chance. "I don't want what you are selling. Please go home and don't come back." She slammed the door in his face and sat back down on the couch.

The door shook with rage as the pounding resumed. "Oh my God! Some people can NOT take a hint." Suzie stomped to the front door and swung it open. "I told you…"

The portly man put his hand up as if to say stop. "I am not selling anything, lady. I am serving you divorce papers. I need you to sign this form to notify your husband that I have done my legal duty to set him free from you." The man glared at Suzie in contempt.

Suzie's rage did a 360. She felt shame and sorrow cascading through her body, settling in the pit of her stomach.

"Where do I need to sign?"

"Right here, Ma'am." The portly man pointed to a signature line.

Suzie scribbled her signature on the line, grabbed the manila folder and slammed the door in the face of the man again.

Michael looked at Suzie in shock. He had never seen his mother be downright rude. "Who was that Mommy?"

"Just a delivery man."

"What did he deliver?" Michael asked.

"Nothing important." Suzie made a dismissive gesture with her hand. *Only a stack of papers which will have the capacity to change your life from this moment forward.*

"Is it a Chwistmas pwesent?" Jonathan asked, his eyebrows arched in excitement.

"No, silly. We just had Christmas. Santa has to rest for a while." Suzie grinned at Jonathan and gave him a wink. She scurried to her bedroom and hid the divorce document in her nightstand, under her Bible.

She walked back into the living room trying to recapture some semblance of calm. Before she could sit down, the phone started ringing. Suzie walked to the kitchen a bit perturbed.

"Hello?"

"Hello, Susanna."

"Hello, Joe. Thanks so much for calling CPS on me. They came over this morning and the visit went well."

"Really?" There was a hint of disappointment in Joe's voice.

"Yes, they judged me and found me to be a competent and safe mother, but they didn't have the same conclusion in regards to you."

"They didn't?" Joe responded.

"Nope, they said you needed a psyche eval."

Joe paused for a moment. "Well, that is not the reason why I called. I wanted to see if you got the divorce petition."

"Yep, it just came. Is that all? Because I was sitting down to watch TV with the boys and I would like to get back to that."

"No, that isn't all. Megan and I would like to do a favor for you."

Suzie sat down on the kitchen chair and caught her breath. "Really?" She said with a doubtful tone.

"Yes, Megan has hired the best lawyer to represent me in this divorce. We talked about this last night and we decided that our lawyer should handle the divorce. There is no need for you to spend what little money you have on a lawyer."

I think I am smelling a dead rat. "Wow, how nice of Megan. First, she steals my husband and then she wants to micromanage the divorce settlement without any input from me. Did I somehow become invisible, Joe?"

"Susanna, we are just trying to help you out," Joe said.

"How nice of you Joe. If you really wanted to help me out, I have a mortgage payment due, the kids need some spring and summer clothes, a few sacks of groceries would be nice. You knew the brakes on the car were going bad way before you moved out. The house needs a new roof. The siding could use some new paint. If you took care of one, or all of those things, that would really help out, Joe. Now which one would you like to take care of?"

"I am only offering the use of Megan's lawyer, Susanna," Joe said. "If you really want all those things taken care of, I would think you would want to save money. I am offering you a way to save money."

"I don't see it that way, Joe. I think any lawyer would be loyal to the person who was paying the tab and in this case that is Megan. I am not stupid and I sure as hell did not become invisible since you left."

"You are such a bitch." Joe said with venom.

"Just because I don't fall into the trap that you and Megan have set for me does not mean I am a bitch, Joe. It just means that I am not invisible, and neither are your children. They need to be financially supported." Suzie said with more confidence than she felt.

"Why don't *you* get a job?" Joe asked.

"To be frank with you, Joe, I have not had time to get a job. I spent all day yesterday worrying about CPS doing an investigation on me and today I got served with divorce papers. I intend to look for a job soon, but I am also concerned about who will take care of the children if I work."

"Well, I hope you don't think I am going to pay for all the things that you listed. It is time you became responsible and took care of yourself. I have to take care of Megan now," Joe said.

"I understand that, Joe, but Megan is your boss. I am sure she makes a sizeable living. The children can't work, and it is important that you provide financially for their welfare."

"If you would use Megan's lawyer we could get this settled quickly and then we could both move on with our lives," Joe said.

"It appears as if you have no problem with moving on. However, I want to ensure that I am represented in a fair manner, Joe. So, the answer to your question is no, thank you."

"I am warning you that Megan's lawyer will mutilate you in court," Joe seethed.

"Like I said, Joe, I was watching TV with the boys. I think I will get back to that now." Click. The line went dead before Suzie crumbled into hysterical sobs.

Suzie crept to her bedroom with stealth. She didn't want the boys seeing her cry. She gently closed the door and sobbed uncontrollably, struggling to catch her breath. She knelt down beside her bed, crying out to God for help. She didn't know any lawyers. She sure couldn't find a qualified lawyer with the money she had in the bank. What on earth was she supposed to do?

"Call your Dad." A voice inside her head commanded her.

"He isn't a lawyer. He isn't even a banker anymore. Why on earth would I call him?" Suzie whispered back.

"Call your Dad."

"Okay. I will." Suzie caught her breath and sopped up the tears that had run down her cheeks.

GRACE AND MERCY

A MEETING OF AN URGENT MATTER WAS CALLED together in the heavens. Faith, Joy, Hope, Grace, and Mercy were present.

"Well, we won that one." Hope said giggling.

"Yes, but the evil one was right on our heels after Ms. Peabody left. Joe is being used by the evil one to put a financial burden on Suzie. He is trying to swindle her out of the support she deserves for raising the children," Faith said. "Yet we must move on with our plan. I think it is time to work on the belt of truth. I think we need to take an unusual approach in the case of Suzie."

Hope looked at Faith with eyebrows arched. "Unusual?"

"Yes, the belt of truth is commonly thought of as the Word of God. There is nothing that compares to that. Yet, I think that Suzie has been hurt by the secret idol that Barbara has worshipped for so long. If we exposed that idol to Suzie, then Suzie could confront Barbara and Barbara would be forced to work through the pain she has buried. I believe that this could start a path of healing and forgiveness for Barbara."

"Wow, that *is* unusual," Joy exclaimed. "Have you passed this by the Holy One?"

"This idea did not originate with me." Faith glanced at Joy, her eyes blazing with fire.

"Oh, I understand," Joy said. "Okay then, what is your plan? This idol has been in Barbara's heart since before Suzie was born. How are we to bring it to the surface? She just had a major meltdown because Joe threatened to mutilate her in court. I really don't think she could survive another attack from Barbara."

"Yes, I know, and I am thinking that there is only one person other than Suzie's dad who knows about the baby boy's birth," Faith said.

Grace's face transformed from a look of puzzlement to one of understanding. "I remember that man. His name is Mr. Vanderpool. I was there when Suzie's dad went to consult him about divorcing Barbara."

"Yes, you were, Grace. You helped him talk Suzie's dad into staying with Barbara when their son, Stevie, died."

"I think I may have been involved in that also, if I am remembering right," Mercy added.

"Yes, Mercy, you were. Now I need both of you to be present as the unveiling of the idol comes about. Suzie has suffered so much pain and rejection because of Barbara's unholy fascination with that child. Her common human default will be anger and despair," Faith said. "We need it to be forgiveness and understanding. Or in better terms, Grace and Mercy."

"How are we to intercede in this matter?" Grace asked.

"There is an abandoned house across the road that Suzie lives on. I want both of you to move in and set up residence. You will enter the bodies of a couple who have been foster parents. One of their sons is Jacob."

Grace looked at Mercy and Mercy gazed back at Grace, their faces alight with joy. "We would be more than pleased to move into that house."

The meeting in the heavens was adjourned.

MR VANDERPOOL

SUZIE PICKED UP THE PHONE WONDERING WHY THE whisper had commanded her to call her dad. She dialed his number, her mind swirling in Doubt. Barbara was usually the one to answer the phone at this time of day. She didn't want to talk to Barbara. In fact, she didn't care if she ever talked to Barbara again.

As the phone started dialing, she made a pact with God. If Barbara answered, she could hang up. If her dad answered, she would ask him how to find a lawyer.

"Hello?" A deep voice resounded through the airwaves.

"Hello, Daddy." Suzie sighed in resignation.

"Well, hello Suzie. How are you doing?" Steve, Suzie's dad, responded.

"Not too good, Daddy. I just got served divorce papers. Joe says he is going to mutilate me in court." Suzie started crying again.

"I am so sorry this is happening to you. Is there anything I could do to help you?"

"Do you… Do you know any lawyers? I need a lawyer. Apparently, Joe's mistress, Megan, has hired the best."

"No, I don't... wait a minute. Yes, I do," Steve said. "Let me go look through my office. I consulted with a lawyer many years ago and I had the feeling that he was a man of honor."

"I didn't think lawyers had honor." Suzie said, letting a malicious giggle slip out.

"Most don't, but this one does," Steve said. "Hold on a minute and I will see if I can find his business card. It was years ago, so I don't know if I still have it, but I will try my best."

"Thanks, Dad. Thank you so much." Suzie prayed fervently while she held the silent phone in her hand.

The minutes seemed like hours. "Wow, I had no idea my office was such a mess." Steve said, catching his breath. "I found the business card though."

"I can't believe that even one room in Barbara's house is a mess." Suzie responded with shock.

"Yeah, I know, your mother is a clean freak, but I banished her from my office. I was scared she would throw important papers away. I am so glad she didn't find this card." Steve said with relief.

"Why?" Suzie asked.

Steve ignored the question. "The name of the lawyer is Mr. Vanderpool. I don't know if he remembers me or not, but I went to him years ago, before you were born, on a very personal matter."

"Is he a family law lawyer?" Suzie asked. "I know lawyers get specialized in various legal matters."

"He was back then." Steve stopped, cleared his throat, and then continued. "Well, actually… I don't remember what kind of lawyer he is. If he can't help you maybe he can point you in the right direction. Do you want me to call and set up an appointment for you?"

"I would love it if you did that. Could you possibly set it up for the morning? That way I will only have to worry about taking Jonathan along and not Michael. I am hoping that Jonathan won't put two and two together. I know Michael would and he is having a very difficult time with Joe leaving," Suzie said.

"Yes, I will call him this afternoon. I am glad you called though. I was thinking about you. I recently cashed in some investments. Barbara wanted to do some remodeling. She didn't use all the money and I sure don't need it laying around. Could you use some help in the financial department?"

"Could I ever." Suzie said with gratitude. "I am almost out of money and I haven't had time to go look for a job."

"Well, if I send you this money maybe that will take some stress off you." Steve said with sympathy.

"Thanks, Dad. I don't know what I would do if I didn't have you." Suzie said with warmth.

"Suzie, you may never know what a difference you have made in my life. I owe you. I got to go though. Barbara will be getting suspicious and I got to hide this business card again. Bye, Suzie."

"Bye, Daddy." Suzie said with the unspoken question, "Why do *you* owe *me*?" echoing throughout the cavernous crevices of her mind. *"And why would you have to hide a business card from Barbara if she was banished from your office?"*

Suzie hung up the phone and bowed her head. "Thank you, God. I had no idea my dad had ever needed a lawyer, much less a family law lawyer. Not only is he going to set up the appointment, but I am also getting some much-needed money. Sure beats looking in the yellow pages." Suzie said as she wiped the tears from her cheeks and a smile curved her lips.

It was late in the evening when her dad called back. "Sorry it is so late. I got your appointment set for tomorrow morning at ten."

"Wow that was quick," Suzie said.

"Yes, it was. As luck would have it, Mr. Vanderpool remembered me, and we had a nice conversation. If he wasn't a lawyer, he could have been a friend of mine." Steve paused for a moment. "I never could trust lawyers."

"I don't blame you. I wouldn't want a lawyer as a friend either," Suzie said.

"I sure would like to see you and the kids sometime." Steve said with a twinge of sadness.

"I would love to see you, Dad, but the kids fear Barbara. They are terrified that they will make a mess in her sterile house. As you can guess, my house is not as perfect as the house I grew up in," Suzie said.

"I doubt many are, Suzie. Maybe we could come to your house."

"You could come, Dad, but I don't think Barbara would feel comfortable. She is only comfortable in her bubble of perfection," Suzie replied.

"Yes, I know, boy, do I know. Sometimes I wonder if she will ever change," Steve said.

"We can always hope for that, Dad," Suzie said.

"Well, I better let you go. I am sure you need sleep to take good care of my grandchildren," Steve said.

"Yes, I do need that. I love you, Dad."

"I love you too, Suzie," Steve replied.

FAMILY LAW

Suzie woke up early and rushed to get her clothes on, makeup done, and hair styled before she even woke the children up. She wanted to make a good impression on Mr. Vanderpool. If he was a man of honor she intended to show respect.

There was just one problem, she thought, as she walked into the bedroom of the children. "What am I to do with Jonathan?" She didn't know anyone on the face of the earth who could babysit for her. She knew it was unprofessional to bring a child along on a business meeting. Her mind became frantic with worry.

As she entered the bedroom, the decision to take Jonathan to the appointment became cemented in her mind. He is a family law lawyer. I'm sure I'm not the only single mom who has brought a child along with her.

The children were prepared for their ride to school. In the process, her house transitioned from a photo op for a family magazine into a cluttered mess.

She pulled into the parking lot adjacent to Mr. Vanderpool's office at 9:50 a.m.

She rushed up the stairs, carrying Jonathan in one arm, her divorce decree and purse in the other.

"Hello, I am Susanna Whatley." She said to the receptionist.

The receptionist looked up from the computer with a fleeting smile which disappeared the minute she looked at Jonathan. "Do you have an appointment?"

"Yes, I believe my dad, Steve Johnson, set it up for me yesterday."

The receptionist looked at her appointment book and breathed a sigh of disgust. "I don't see you listed."

"Could you possibly ask Mr. Vanderpool about this? I have driven a long way to come here and I would prefer it not to be in vain," Suzie pleaded.

"If you would take a seat, I will see if I can interrupt him." The secretary said with a smirk.

At that moment a door in the office opened and a very handsome elderly man walked into the waiting area. "Angie, I forgot to tell you, we are going to have to squeeze someone in." Mr. Vanderpool caught sight of Suzie in the waiting area and caught his breath. "My goodness, you are a spitting image of your beautiful mother." He said as his long legs closed the gap between him and Suzie. "Is this your son?" He asked as he reached out to touch Jonathan's hand.

"Yes, this is Jonathan." Suzie immediately warmed to this man's kind demeanor.

Mr. Vanderpool looked at Angie. "Angie, would you mind watching Jonathan a minute while I consult with his mother?"

Suzie wasn't sure that Angie would agree, it seemed as if she didn't like children. When Suzie glanced at Angie she was astounded. Her face had transformed into a gentle and nurturing façade of compassion. "Of course, Mr. Vanderpool, I was just searching the internet to see if I could find any appropriate games to play with him."

Suzie was aghast. "Yeah, I bet you were." She said, under her breath, with a heavy dose of sarcasm. She would bet anyone a $100 bill that Angie was vying for more than just a job with Mr. Vanderpool.

Mr. Vanderpool ushered Suzie into his office. It was breathtaking in elegance. The man seemed to have class oozing from every pore of his body. The wood tones of the book shelves were deep mahogany, the desk was polished and gleaming, not a speck of dust or disorder was present.

As he sat down, Suzie's eyes were drawn to a massive photo which crowned his head when he was sitting in his desk chair.

"Is that your family?" Suzie asked, pointing to the entourage of handsome men and gorgeous women.

"Yes. I have been blessed beyond measure with children and grandchildren. Which may explain the reason why I am still working at my age." Mr. Vanderpool said with a chuckle. "It is amazing what a person can do for love."

Suzie disengaged her view from the picture and looked at Mr. Vanderpool. I can see why my dad thought he was a man of honor. "Well, sir, you have a beautiful family."

"Thank you. Now I believe you came to my office to discuss a divorce decree."

Suzie shook her head slightly, realizing that the divorce decree was sitting in her lap. "Yes, I did, and you would probably like to look at it wouldn't you?" She got up and handed him the decree.

"Well, that may help, if you want me to represent you." Mr. Vanderpool winked at Suzie.

Suzie giggled. She had dreaded this day and now because of the kindness of Mr. Vanderpool she was laughing. What a surprise life could be sometimes.

Mr. Vanderpool scanned through the pages of the divorce decree with concern etching a furrow in his brow.

He looked at Suzie with empathy. "There is good news and bad news. The good news is that you are about to be free of the jerk that you were married to. The bad news is that they are filing for joint custody which will decrease the amount of child support that you will receive."

Suzie felt as if she had been stabbed in the gut. "Joint custody? Does that mean that my children have to stay at their place every other week and at mine every other week?"

"No, not necessarily. Joint custody can be as little as seeing the children every weekend. It is just a legal way for selfish people to get around paying the correct amount of child support in this state."

"Can I be honest with you, Mr. Vanderpool?" Suzie asked.

Mr. Vanderpool put down the divorce decree and looked Suzie square in the eyes. "Yes, I would prefer you be honest."

"I don't have a job, I have little money in savings and I know it is important to provide for the financial welfare of my children. I intend to look for a job as soon as I possibly can but in the meantime, I am concerned about the well-being of my children."

"I do not know this woman whom my husband has left me for. I don't know what her morals or standards are in life. I would prefer that her influence on my children be kept to a minimum until I can determine if she is a fit parent." Suzie paused to take a much needed breath. "Saying that, I want you to know that my children love their father and they miss him. Although I am not wealthy by any means I would hope that the focus of the divorce proceedings be centered on the welfare of my children, not on money."

Mr. Vanderpool looked at Suzie with a touch of wonder in his eyes. "You are the first person I have met in my long career who actually has the right perspective on divorce."

"Marriage is meant for a lifetime and is intended to provide a safe and secure environment to raise children. When a marriage dissolves it is of utmost importance to put the welfare of the children on top of the priority list. There are scads of people who think it is about revenge on their ex." Mr. Vanderpool tapped his pencil on the desk as he looked at Suzie. "You show a level of maturity that is lacking in most divorces."

"I believe it is because I truly love my children, Mr. Vanderpool. I also loved my husband when I was married to him. I don't want to hurt him or them. I believe it was you who said, 'It is amazing what a person can do for love.'" Suzie flashed a charming smile across the gleaming desk.

"Yes, I did say that." Mr. Vanderpool's eyes gave Suzie a look of warmth and understanding.

"Now that we have that settled, Mr. Vanderpool, I have one more question to ask of you." Suzie took a deep breath. "It is of a personal nature and I hope you feel comfortable in answering it." Suzie said, trying to calm her nerves.

"What would that be?"

"How did my dad come to know you?" Suzie asked with a directness that surprised even her.

Mr. Vanderpool sighed and looked down at his desk for a moment. "Suzie, in most circumstances I would not be allowed to reveal that because of attorney-client privilege. I had a long talk with your dad last night and he suspected you might want to know how he came to have my business card in his possession. He gave me his approval for what I am about to tell you."

Mr. Vanderpool looked up at Suzie. "He came to me a year before you were born. He wanted to divorce your mother. They had had a son who died of sudden infant death and your mother changed after the little boy died." Mr. Vanderpool wiped sweat from his brow.

"I think his name was Steven or Stevie. She adored that child and everyone who knew her said she was a devoted mother." Mr. Vanderpool looked out the window with a dreamy look in his eyes. "My wife and I saw her with the little boy a few months after he was born. They made the most beautiful picture. The baby was so handsome," Mr. Vanderpool said.

"When the child died she became a different person. She withdrew, and no one saw her until you were born. Your dad had intended to divorce her but then she got pregnant with you. He stayed in the marriage because he loved you and he hoped that Barbara would be like she was when Stevie was alive."

"You must have the wrong family, sir. I am the only child my parents ever had." Suzie said, getting her purse together so she could leave.

Mr. Vanderpool sighed, as his wrinkles painted concern and empathy through every line on his face. "Suzie, every family has skeletons in the closet. I have just opened the closet door for you. You can do what you want with the skeleton of your dead brother. You can ignore it, you can put it back in the closet, or you can help your mother let go of the son which has haunted her for longer than you have been alive."

Suzie caught her breath. Maybe this *was* the truth. "Wow, this is not at all what I expected."

"Secrets rarely are what we expect them to be," Mr. Vanderpool replied.

"I don't know what to do with this," Suzie said.

Mr. Vanderpool slowly rose to a standing position. "In the course of my career I have seen a lot of wicked and evil people in my office. They proceed down a path that is littered with pain and hurt for those they say they love or once loved." Mr. Vanderpool walked around his desk and held out his hand to help Suzie to a standing position. "You are different, Suzie. You are good. Whatever you decide to do with this skeleton will be the right decision."

Suzie looked up at the handsome face of Mr. Vanderpool, not even noticing that he had her hand in his grasp. "I hope you're right." She said as she blindly followed Mr. Vanderpool's lead out of his office.

She didn't realize that she was still holding his hand until Angie gave her a look that could kill. She gently disentangled her fingers from his grasp so as not to incur the wrath of a covetous receptionist and scooped Jonathan up into her arms.

THE MYSTERY OF MEMORIES

DECEIT WAS INCENSED. HE HAD THOUGHT THE BLINDers of prejudice would have been dark enough that Mrs. Peabody wouldn't have seen the truth about Susanna. He needed another attack. He paced nervously throughout the Chambers of Evil. He had to analyze what had been successful in the past. Joe leaving Susanna had been wonderful. A husband leaving his wife was always a momentous event for the entities of evil, but it had not been as successful as the verbal attack that Barbara had launched.

The pacing grew more frantic. He would have to call another meeting. Damn it! He sounded the alarm and cringed as the other entities of evil started filing into his chamber.

"Waz up boss?" Betrayal said as he came lumbering into the Chamber of Evil.

Deceit wanted to kick the beast. If he would have been more successful in the initial stages of this attack, Deceit would not have had to call another damn meeting.

"The attack on Susanna has to intensify. Any suggestions? My last brilliant idea was once again laid to waste by that stinking little brat, Jonathan."

Rejection slithered into the center of the room. "I don't mean to hog the limelight but if I recall correctly it was my work which caused the knife to draw blood from the wrist of Susanna. Am I right?"

Despair ran from the corner with rage. "It wasn't only you. You imbecile! I was there from the start. You always take all of the credit." Despair crumpled into a lump on the floor, whining and crying as if she had been stabbed.

Deceit rolled his eyes. "Yes, yes. You were there from the start. Now can you compose yourself so that we can get on with our strategy meeting?"

Rejection hissed at Despair and then raised his head to gain attention. "Susanna has many wounds from Barbara. She doesn't understand why Barbara was incapable of loving her. She doesn't even know that Barbara had another child before she was born. If you remember, we led her to the treasure chest in Barbara's closet when she was just a little girl. She saw her older brother and the thought we planted in her mind was that Barbara can love *that* baby but not her. I remember the wonderful sound of her whimpering in her bedroom after the beating."

Despair raised her head. "Oh, yes, I remember. Barbara whipped her mercilessly when she found Susanna looking through the treasure chest. Susanna couldn't understand what was so awful about looking at a little baby boy's picture."

Envy started bouncing up and down. "Yes! Yes! I remember making her envious of that little baby."

Deceit smiled and stood still for a moment. Deceit loved times like this, when the memory of successful wicked deeds came back to haunt his fellow comrades in evil.

The Beast of Betrayal got a glint in his eye. "Didn't her daddy come and find her in her bedroom? Didn't he promise to take her away from Barbara? Didn't he promise Barbara would never lay a hand on her again?"

Despair jumped up and down for joy. "Oh, yes he did, and he was only gone a few days before Barbara seduced him back into her bed. So, not only did Susanna realize Barbara didn't love her but now she had Doubt that her father ever had."

Doubt swayed erratically. "I paved the path for my friend, Insecurity, to reside in the heart and mind of Susanna."

Deceit began pacing again. "We were so successful when she was a little child. Why are we not as successful now?"

"The Holy Spirit resides in her now, Boss," Betrayal sneered.

"That didn't happen until she became a Christian which happened when she was a teenager right?"

Envy quickly fumbled through the records. "Yes, Boss, she was fourteen when she accepted Christ as her savior."

"Okay, follow my thoughts on this one. Susanna did not know Christ until she was fourteen. She discovered the treasure chest that held the memories of Barbara's idol when she was just a little girl. She did not have the helmet of salvation covering her thoughts as a little girl, so we could totally invade her thoughts at that time. If there was just a way we could have her mind return to that time when she was a little girl, we may have complete access to her thoughts."

Adultery sashayed across the room and seductively lifted the chin of Deceit in her hands, looking at him with lust. "There is a way, my doll. The way is called a flashback. I use this all the time with my conquests. Just when they think they could suffer through the marriage that they are in, I give them a flashback of the torrid affair that they once had or hoped to have."

"Susanna's mind has hidden this memory." Deceit said pushing the hand of Adultery aside. "How can we break through the helmet of salvation to get to the memory?"

"Darling." Adultery held the chin of Deceit in a death grip. "We must engage the subconscious mind of Susanna in this effort. When we do that, the memory will come rushing back like a hurricane, laying waste to all that Jesus has done in this mind. Susanna's mind will be our playground with just one memory. We will have bitterness, envy, rejection, despair, doubt, and insecurity all laying hold of every thought."

"How do we engage the subconscious?" Deceit asked, holding the gaze of Adultery.

"By luring her into the subconscious through her senses. Her sense of smell, the touch of a fabric, a taste of something which was in her mouth right before she discovered the treasure chest. A sound that she remembers. You get the idea?" Adultery said, licking her ruby red lips.

"What was Barbara doing when Susanna found the treasure chest?" Deceit asked.

Envy once again reached in her glob of green and pulled out the manual on Susanna. She flipped through the pages with frantic anticipation. "She was making apple pie."

"There is nothing more comforting than the smell of an apple pie." Adultery said as a wicked smile crossed her lips.

Suzie was relieved that the meeting with Mr. Vanderpool had gone so well regarding the divorce, but her thoughts were swirling in confusion regarding her supposed older sibling. Her parents had never hinted that they had lost a child. How could this have been hidden for so many years? Wouldn't someone have said something?

As she drove to pick up Michael from Kindergarten she decided that she had enough on her plate with the divorce and needing to find a job. Mr. Vanderpool said she could put the skeleton of her older brother back in the closet and that is just what she was going to do. She didn't need any more drama. Thanks to Megan she had enough drama for the present. Besides, he was dead anyway; no need to worry about something she had no control over.

As she was driving down the country road she was surprised to see a U-Haul truck pulling up to the house across the road.

She had always loved that house. It was a two-story and had a wrap-around porch. The white paint was peeling, and the lawn was a frozen mess. It needed a lot of work, but Suzie had always thought it looked inviting.

It would be good to have neighbors close by. She hoped they were nice. Maybe this afternoon she would bring them something to eat. She hadn't made cookies in a while. They would be easy, but she didn't have any chocolate chips. What could she make? She had bought a whole bag of green apples. Her boys loved green apples.

Maybe she could make an apple pie. It had been years since she had savored the scent of an apple pie wafting from an oven.

THE LURE OF APPLE PIE

SUZIE MADE THE BOYS CHICKEN NUGGETS AND FRENCH fries for lunch and gave them some store-bought cookies. She settled them down on the couch and turned on the television. She was hoping that they would both take a nap on the worn-out sectional that graced her living room.

She took her cutting board out and put it over her sink so that she could look out her kitchen window and watch the neighbors move in. There was a plethora of young men who were helping an elderly couple move their furniture into the beautiful home. Nobody looked stressed or frantic, they looked happy and at peace.

"How do they do that?" Suzie whispered. "I would be a total freak job if I had to move into that big of a house."

One by one, the pieces of furniture were moved from the moving van into the house. Soon Suzie could see the lights coming on in all the windows. The house and the people that were moving into the house emanated warmth and love.

"*I want what they have.*" Suzie thought as she started cutting the apples for her pie. Once she had the apples cut and sprinkled with lemon juice, she started on the crust.

She rolled the pie crust on the kitchen table and could see the collection of men laughing. She couldn't imagine what they were laughing at. She put the apples in the pie crust and sprinkled sugar and cinnamon on top, then put the top layer of pie crust on the apples and put it in the oven. She turned on the oven and set the timer. Suzie sat at her table eating from the bowl of envy as she continued to stare across the road at the house of love. She inhaled the scent of the apple pie deeply and her mind was snatched from the present. She was forced into reliving a scene from her childhood. A memory she had locked away in the caverns of her mind.

Susanna scampered to the kitchen. "What are you doing, Mommy?"

"I am making apple pie." Barbara said, intent on making the pie crust perfect. "You know your daddy loves apple pie."

"Mmmm, I do too." Susanna wandered away from the kitchen. Maybe today would be a good day. Her mommy was usually happy when she was making apple pie. Happy days were rare when it came to her mommy.

Susanna decided she would play with her Victorian dollhouse today. She skipped to her bedroom.

As she was rounding the corner to her room she noticed something unusual. Her parents' bedroom door was open. This was a strange event. She couldn't recollect that ever happening before.

A spirit of adventure laid claim to Susanna's steps. She wanted to know what had always been hidden from her. She tiptoed into the bedroom, her tiny hands in the pockets of her playful sundress.

The room was elegant and breathtaking in beauty. The bedspread was a collection of burgundy, forest green and gold. Suzie caressed the quilt and felt the silky texture slide between her fingers. Oh, it was so luxurious.

This room was a room suited for royalty. Maybe her mommy and daddy were secretly a king and a queen. If her mommy and daddy were king and queen, then *she* must be a *princess*.

If she was a princess, she needed to get ready for the ball where she would meet her prince. She rounded the bed and sat on the vanity chair, looking at her childlike face in the mirror. She took a lipstick from her mother's gold lipstick stand and applied it to her lips. She smacked her lips, like she had seen ladies on TV do. She grabbed a brush from a stand and applied blush to her cheeks. She coated her long lashes with a douse of mascara. She unleashed her pigtails, freeing her silky waves, so that they could cascade down her back.

Now that her face was transformed, she needed to do something about the sundress she was wearing. She believed that princesses wore gowns. She didn't have any gowns in her closet, but she was sure her mommy had some.

She slipped off the vanity chair and skipped playfully to the closet. She opened the door as if she had a right to. She looked up and gasped. She had never seen so many clothes. Some of them were wrapped in plastic. She didn't know why that would happen. She had never seen her parents wear plastic. She giggled, sometimes her parents were just silly. She hadn't seen anyone wear thin plastic over their clothes.

Oh well, she had to keep focused. She was preparing to meet her prince. She ventured into the closet as if it were a palace, holding her head high and her back straight. She didn't notice the chest at her feet until she stumbled over it.

The sunlight streaming in from the bedroom window alighted the gold chest. Susanna sat for a moment in wonder. She had never seen such beauty. To find a treasure chest on a day when she realized she was a princess was almost too much to absorb.

The chest had a lock on it. Tentatively, she put her hand on the lock, sneaking her fingers under the metal. She expected resistance, but it gave her none. She cautiously lifted the lid, expecting to find gold.

She peaked over the side and she began to examine the contents of the treasure chest.

There was a picture of a baby boy. Susanna picked the picture up gently and let her eyes feast on this child. He was beyond handsome. He was beautiful. His green eyes were ablaze against his golden tan and wavy golden hair.

"This must be my prince," she whispered. She kissed the photo gently and put the picture in the pocket of her sundress.

She reached into the chest and felt something soft. She grabbed a soft blue blanket and pulled it out. She rubbed the soft yarn against her cheek. It felt like heaven, so soft, so comforting.

She looked in the chest to see what other treasures it held. There was a large envelope. She opened it. She saw a lady who looked like her mommy, holding the baby boy. She was smiling. She was looking at the baby boy as if she loved him.

That couldn't be *her* mommy. Her mommy was incapable of love. Susanna smashed the picture back into the envelope. She didn't want to see any more pictures.

There was a beautiful light blue sweater with some booties to match. There were some cards and one large manila envelope at the bottom. There was something on top of the envelope. What could that be? She reached deep into the chest and grabbed it. It was a tiny bracelet. It had letters on it. Susanna took it out and held it in the sunlight. She didn't know how to read yet, but she did know the alphabet. "S-T-E-V-I-E", she whispered.

In a flash, sunlight filled the closet and she felt her arm being ripped from her side. She flew from a sitting position to one midair, her feet dangling above the closet floor.

"WHAT ARE YOU DOING?" Her mother screamed.

"I'm sorry, Mommy." Susanna pleaded as her tears dissolved the mascara on her lashes.

"You know I told you to *never* go into my room! This is MY room, not yours!" Her mommy started whipping her. Screaming at the top of her lungs. "You have no idea what you have done."

"I'm sorry. I am sorry. Please stop whipping me." Susanna begged, the whipping was beginning to feel as if knives were slicing through her skin.

"I'm sorry Mommy! I really am! Please stop hurting me!" Susanna begged and begged. But her mommy wasn't listening, so soon she fell silent and succumbed to the beating. The whipping seemed to last for hours. Blood started seeping through Susanna's sundress. That finally stopped the insane rage and Susanna was thrown into her room like a castoff.

"You are a horrible little girl!" Barbara screamed as she slammed the door and stomped off.

Susanna crawled to the corner of her bedroom, wishing she could hide or die. Dying would be preferable. If she hid, her mean mommy could find her. As she curled up in a fetal position, thoughts of despair blew into her mind like a torrential downpour.

"Who was the little baby boy? Why did her Mommy love him *so much? Why had it been wrong to look in the treasure chest? Could her Mommy actually love? If it was possible, then how come her mommy had never shown* her *love? Her Mommy must be right. She was a horrible little girl, and no one could love someone who was as horrible as she was."*

She clutched her knees to her chest and cried herself to sleep.

Susanna awoke with a start. Her parents were screaming at each other. There was a commotion coming from the kitchen. Dishes were being broken. Cabinet doors were slamming. Her mommy was screaming something about a photo.

"Oh, no," Susanna thought. "*She knows I took the picture of the baby boy."*

Susanna jumped up in terror, frantically looking for a place to hide the picture.

The thought occurred to her that she could just give it back. What if that made mommy even angrier? Would she get whipped again? She didn't think her bottom could take anymore whipping.

She needed to hide the picture. Where though?

Susanna looked at her dollhouse. Maybe under a bed in the dollhouse. She scurried across the room. Her hands were shaking as she fumbled with the picture. She tried hiding it in one of the beds, but it was too big for the miniature bed. Behind the dresser in the tiny bedroom?

No, the dresser could be moved. This was her prince. She didn't want her mommy hurting him like she had hurt her.

Could she hide it in her closet? No, her mommy was always deep cleaning her closet. She would surely find it.

The screaming from the kitchen was getting louder. She needed to find someplace to hide the picture and it had better be quick.

Susanna searched her room. The pounding of her racing heart was deafening.

Her eyes fell on her jewelry box. There was a drawer she had never used. She rushed to the jewelry box and opened the drawer. Would the picture fit? It fit perfectly. She breathed a deep sigh of relief.

The second she closed the drawer, she heard footsteps walking to her bedroom.

Susanna whipped around in terror as her bedroom door flew open. She cringed, bracing herself for another physical attack from the woman who had given birth to her. "I am sorry, Barbara." She said, her eyes shut tight.

"There is no reason to be sorry. We are leaving." Her daddy's voice filled the room.

Susanna looked up quickly, hoping her daddy was telling the truth. She searched his face. He was crying. She didn't know daddies could cry.

Her daddy scooped her up in his arms, his shoulders shaking, as his tears fell into Susanna's hair.

Susanna couldn't understand why her daddy was crying. He wasn't the one who got whipped. She felt sorry for him and hugged him tight.

"Where we going, Daddy?" She whispered in his ear.

"Somewhere far away from Barbara. You won't ever have to see her again."

"Good," Susanna replied. Her mommy didn't love her. She was a horrible little girl. Her mommy didn't need her around. She wouldn't be missed.

They left that day, but Susanna's daddy kept calling her mommy while they were gone. Susanna wondered why her daddy kept calling her mommy, if they were never going to see her again.

Her daddy cried a lot when they were gone. Susanna guessed he must have been keeping those tears locked up and once the flood gate opened… well…he just couldn't stop. He seemed to be happier when talking to her Mommy. The frequency of calls increased with each day.

Susanna did not mind him talking to her mommy but the more he talked with her, the more Susanna got ignored. The only comfort she had was to remember the beauty of the treasure chest and the picture of her prince.

The treasure chest was a big discovery for Susanna. She learned lessons from that chest.

She learned that her mommy *could* love a child, she just couldn't love Susanna.

She learned that daddies could cry.

That wasn't all that she learned about daddies though. She learned that her Daddy could also lie.

In three days they were back with Barbara.

Susanna made a vow on that day to stop calling Barbara her mother, from this point on she was merely "Barbara."

GRACE AND MR. MERCY

A NOISE BROKE THROUGH SUZIE'S CLOUDED MIND OF memories. An obnoxious noise, it sounded like a buzzer. Suzie shook her head and realized that the noise was the timer on her oven. She jumped up and pulled out a glistening, golden apple pie.

She stared at the apple pie with contempt. She wanted to throw it in the trash. She had never felt the full effect of unbridled hate until this moment in her life. She hated Barbara.

A flood of emotions filled her heart. Contempt, anger, despair, righteous indignation, and bitterness. How could Barbara have beaten her like that? She was just a little girl. She had no idea what she had happened upon. She was on fire with rage.

Wait a minute, though. Maybe this was just an imaginary scene that her mind had concocted. I mean she had been making apple pie one minute and the next minute she was transposed to a scene from her childhood? Maybe this hadn't really happened.

Suzie was startled when she heard the doorbell ring. "Who could that be? No one ever comes to visit. I really need time alone to sort things out and this is when someone decides to visit?"

She walked to the door thinking it was probably just a salesperson. She was good at being rude to salespeople. It would be a minor interruption in her day.

She glanced at her boys who were asleep on the couch. She was surprised the doorbell had not woken them up.

She opened the door to an elderly couple.

"Hello, Ma'am. We just moved in across the road and I hope you don't mind but we wanted to introduce ourselves. I am Mr. Mercy, and this is my wife Grace." The elderly man's face broke into a smile that caressed his wrinkles with kindness.

The plump elderly woman was holding a bag of cookies. "I made a ton of cookies to give to our sons. They helped us move. Those stinkers wouldn't eat them all, so I was hoping you would share them with your family." Grace patted her plump belly. "As you can see, I have had more cookies than I really need." She giggled like a little girl.

Suzie gazed for a moment at the two people who stood on her doorstep. There was a warmth and a love radiating from their smiles. It was like they held the key to the secret of happiness. She needed that key and she needed it bad.

"My name is Susanna, but most people call me Suzie. Won't you come in?" Suzie asked as she glanced at Jonathan and Michael, who were rubbing the sleep from their eyes.

"Oh, I am sorry. I should have considered that this might be nap time." Grace said, her smile turning into a frame of worry.

"No worries. I am not as stringent as some mothers are about nap times. Usually my children don't even take a nap. So, it is no big deal." Suzie said as she cleaned off a place on the sectional for Grace and Mr. Mercy to sit down. "Please sit down. You came over at the perfect time. I just finished baking an apple pie for you," Suzie said. "Let me run to the kitchen and get it for you."

"Well honey, these rolls are not going to disappear if there is apple pie." She winked at Mr. Mercy.

"You know I don't care about that one bit, sugar. Just more for me to love." Mr. Mercy said, as Jonathan crawled on his lap and fell back asleep.

Suzie came back into the living room with the apple pie and was surprised to see Jonathan had already made Mr. Mercy's lap his new couch.

Michael had sidled up as close as he could to Grace without smashing her belly. He was eyeing the cookies with a look of desire.

Suzie put the apple pie on the coffee table and was just about to dislodge Jonathan when she noticed the way Mr. Mercy was gazing at Jonathan. It was such a pure look of love she stopped dead in her tracks. Suzie looked at Grace, her eyebrows arched in an unspoken question.

Grace gave a slight nod of her head and whispered. "He's got an effect on children. They flock to him. He loves them. He misses having little ones around our house. Our grandchildren come by quite often, but he is a wreck when they leave." Grace sighed as she gazed at Mr. Mercy with compassion. "His heart is probably melting right now with your sweet little boy in his lap." She looked at Suzie, her eyes begging for understanding. "Do you mind if we don't disturb them? What is your little boy's name?"

"No, I don't mind at all." Suzie said as she turned around to sit on the couch, leaving Jonathan in Mr. Mercy's lap. "His name is Jonathan."

"My name is Michael." Michael said, still eyeing the cookies.

"Michael if it is okay with your mother, I would like you to have some of these cookies." Grace said, smiling at Michael.

"Mommy, can I?" Michael asked, pleading with his glance.

"Yes, of course you can. Let me take them to the kitchen and get you a glass of milk to go with them." Suzie got up and grabbed Michael's hand. "I think you should only have two to three so that Jonathan and Sarah can have some too. Okay?"

"Okay, Mommy." Michael sat down at the table and waited while Suzie poured him a glass of milk and gave him three cookies.

"Mmm, these are yummy. Better than yours mommy." Michael said as he devoured the cookies.

"Ouch, that hurt." Suzie winked at Michael and smiled in jest. "I may have to ask Grace for her recipe."

"Do that. These are good. You should have one." Michael said, wiping the milk off his mouth.

"Maybe later. I want to talk with Grace and Mr. Mercy right now." Suzie walked back to the living room and sat down next to Grace. "Well your cookies are a hit. I may have to get the recipe."

"I would be happy to give it. I make a large batch of the dough and then freeze it in smaller containers. Mr. Mercy and I have been foster parents for quite some time. I always liked having cookies on hand for the sweet children of God we could care for."

"Wow, that is a brilliant idea. That way you never run out of cookies, right?"

"Well I wouldn't say never. I ran out once and there was an uprising. So, I never allowed it to happen again." Grace said as she chuckled at the memory.

"So how many foster children did you take care of?"

"Quite a few," Mr. Mercy replied. "I think at last count we had over fifty that we were able to help raise."

Suzie's mouth dropped open in amazement. "Wow. I only have three to take care of and sometimes I wonder how I am going to do it."

"We relied upon God and prayed continually for His guidance, but we also had each other to depend on." Mr. Mercy gazed at Suzie with understanding and compassion.

"My husband just left me for another woman." Suzie felt the tears welling up in her eyes. "I am sorry, it just happened, and the children and I are still trying to figure out how to cope."

Michael came back in the living room and sat on the other side of Grace.

"I am so sorry." Grace reached over and grabbed Suzie's hand. "Divorce is never God's will, but He will sustain and protect you." Grace flashed a meaningful gaze at Mr. Mercy. "We felt as if God had a reason for us moving here. I hope you don't think it is presumptuous of us to offer our help. We wouldn't mind the role of foster grandparents. Your children are adorable."

"Thank you. I am sure there will be days when I could use some help. I have one more who will be coming home from school soon."

Suzie paused to wipe her eyes. A change in subject was needed if a total meltdown was to be avoided.

"What led you to become foster parents?" Suzie asked.

"Charity," Mr. Mercy said.

"Oh, of course," Suzie said.

Grace squeezed Suzie's hand. "Charity was actually our only biological child. She was a very special little girl." A cloud of sadness dimmed the sparkle in Grace's eyes.

"We only had her for fourteen years and then she was gone." Mr. Mercy said, his lip trembling. "We wandered through a desert for a few years, consumed by our grief."

"We tried again and again to have another child, but the Lord had closed my womb," Grace said.

"We were assured that Charity was in heaven," Mr. Mercy proclaimed. "But we still loved her, and we missed her."

"We spent so much time in prayer." Grace said as she massaged Suzie's hand and looked out the window with a faraway look. "The Lord comforted us in our grief."

"Then one day when we were in prayer it became apparent to us that Charity had been in our life for a reason. That reason was to open our hearts to love children who were beset with difficulties," Mr. Mercy said.

"The Lord showed us that there are many children who crave the love that we had given to Charity. These children were caught up in a system run by the state and many of them were caged in despair, moving from one home to another," Grace said.

"We felt led by the Lord to unlock that cage of despair with the key of love which had been given to us through the birth of our special daughter, Charity." Mr. Mercy said, his eyes beaming with joy.

"They weren't all easy." Grace said with honesty. "But whenever we had a difficult one, we would look at each other and say. 'We are doing this for Charity.'"

Mr. Mercy laughed. "I think we said that a million times a day with some of our sweet children of God."

Grace's eyes crinkled with fond memories. "Yes, but we always held firm to the belief that God had placed these children with us for a reason."

"What was the reason?" Suzie asked.

"We were to teach the children how to accept the unconditional love from God, their father." Mr. Mercy gazed at Suzie.

"You wouldn't believe some of the stories we heard from these children." Grace shook her head. "The beatings, the neglect and the stealing of innocence by sexual molestation."

"I had a hard time holding back when I heard the stories about sexual molestation. I wanted to find the perverts and mutilate them, as they had mutilated the innocence of our children." Mr. Mercy's face twisted in agony as his hands balled up into fists. "It was difficult to teach them forgiveness and healthy boundaries when they had been violated in that manner."

"How did you handle that?" Suzie gazed at Michael and Jonathan. She didn't want them hearing about this. Thank God, sleep had gently closed their ears to the conversation.

"We provided a safe shelter for them to grieve the sins that had been present in their parents. Then we showed them how to establish healthy boundaries with adults."

"We went to court many times to fight for these children. Some of them we adopted as our forever children," Mr. Mercy said.

"But that doesn't mean that those who weren't adopted were not forever children. We felt as if we were supposed to love all of these children as if they were going to be in God's family for eternity."

"Wow," Suzie said. She had never felt envious of foster children until she met Mr. Mercy and Grace. "I wonder sometimes why my mother didn't put me in foster care," Suzie said. "I never really felt like she loved me. For the longest time I just assumed she couldn't love children." Suzie stopped for a moment to collect herself. "Recently I learned that I had had an older brother who apparently died when he was an infant."

"Oh, that is heartbreaking." Grace said patting Suzie's hand.

"Then today I had a flashback of a time when Barbara, my mother, beat me until I was bloody." Suzie shook her head. "I don't even know if it really happened or not. This is the first and only flashback I have had."

"Many of our children had flashbacks when they were in our home. The memories would come flooding back of beatings or abuse which their mind had locked away until they were strong enough to handle them." Mr. Mercy said, his eyes emanating compassion.

"That's just it though." Suzie looked straight at Mr. Mercy. "I don't feel strong enough to handle this. My husband just left me. I found out about my older brother when I went to see an attorney about our divorce. The flashback happened when I was baking the apple pie for you."

A tortured glance bounced back and forth between Grace and Mercy.

"I have never loved Barbara but I always thought that she couldn't love me because she just couldn't love children," Suzie sighed. "In the flashback Barbara was holding a little boy in a picture. When I saw that picture I realized I was wrong," Suzie swallowed hard. "Barbara could love children; she just couldn't love me because I was a horrible little girl."

"Oh, sweet child of God. That is a lie from the devil." Grace put her arm around Suzie and tucked her into an embrace. "You are so precious to God. He loves you more than you could ever realize. You are *not* horrible. Barbara is the one who has problems." Grace stroked Suzie's hair. "Grief can take so many different pathways. For Mr. Mercy and me, it turned out to be a good thing. We followed the pathway of greater love because of our belief in God. Some follow the pathway of bitterness and become hardened."

"Have you talked with Barbara about this child who died?" Mr. Mercy looked at Suzie with such intensity she felt that she would melt if she was dishonest.

"No, this all just happened within the past week. My mind is kind of overwhelmed with misery. The divorce seemed to start an avalanche of despair." Suzie paused for a moment and her eyes got misty. "A couple of years ago I was the happiest person in the world. Now I don't even know what happy is."

"That is exactly how we felt when Charity passed." Grace looked at Mr. Mercy. "Yet we only had one event and you have had several in close proximity. I can't imagine how difficult this must be for you." A teardrop caressed the plump cheek of Grace.

"I don't know what I did wrong to deserve this punishment from God. I keep searching to see if there is a sin I have not asked for forgiveness for. I mean, God wouldn't allow me to go through this if I hadn't done something wrong, right?" Suzie asked tears streaming down her cheeks.

"Oh sweet child of God. You did nothing wrong. The marriage was not one which nourished you. That is why God allowed it to end in divorce. The rejection of Barbara stemmed from the root of bitterness which grew around her heart with the loss of her first child. You were *never* a horrible child. *She* just chose the wrong path," Grace said.

Mr. Mercy spoke with authority. "Her first child became an idol. She turned from God in anger because God had not worshipped her son as she had," Mr. Mercy paused. "Grace and I were tempted to make Charity our idol. Grief can be all consuming when it involves the death of a child."

"We are so grateful to God for each and every foster child we nurtured. Each one of them gently drew us into His love and away from an unhealthy fascination with Charity." Grace spoke with compassion.

"Why couldn't Barbara have loved me if you could love children who were foster children?" Suzie asked.

"That is something you need to ask her." Mr. Mercy said, his brilliant blue eyes gazing at her, as if he was begging her to seek truth.

Suzie shook her head. "I don't even know if she actually had another child. I mean it was an attorney who told me about my older brother and attorneys have a habit of dishonesty. The flashback came from nowhere."

"Is there any way you could find out if this child was born?"

Suzie started shaking her head, then stopped as her mind returned to the reality of her flashback. "Yes, there is. In the flashback I took a picture." Suzie paused and took a deep breath. "I put it in a bottom drawer of my jewelry box. For some reason, I demanded that that jewelry box go with me when I moved out. I haven't opened that drawer since that day I was beaten. I think the jewelry box is in my closet but I am not sure."

"A picture? What was the picture of?" Mr. Mercy asked.

"It was a picture of a beautiful baby boy. My older brother, Stevie."

Sarah came busting through the door and both boys woke up.

Grace handed a tissue to Suzie. "Well, this must be the beautiful child of God you had mentioned to us. My goodness she is a pretty girl."

Sarah blushed, "Hi, my name is Sarah."

"Hi, Sarah. My name is Grace and this is my husband, Mr. Mercy." Grace spoke with a gentleness that soothed the hearts of everyone in the room. "We really should go. I am sure you have things to do." Grace looked at Suzie with an understanding smile.

"Yes, I do have things to do but I am so very glad you both came over. It is so nice to have neighbors. It can be very lonely out in the country." Suzie got up from the couch and picked up the apple pie from the coffee table. "Please take the pie."

"Are you sure?" Grace asked.

"I am positive. This pie is what triggered my flashback," Suzie responded.

"We would be glad to take it from you." Mr. Mercy gently put Jonathan on the floor and in one swift fluid motion took the apple pie out of Suzie's hands.

"Please call us if you ever need a babysitter or any help. We are frankly bored to tears without little ones at our feet." Grace said as she bent down to hug Michael.

"Oh, don't worry. I will." Suzie said as she smiled.

As Suzie closed the door, she felt a change within her heart. She had been so mad when she had pulled the apple pie out of the oven. Now she felt a strange sense of peace. What Barbara had done to her had not been right but she wanted to walk the greater pathway of love like Grace and Mr. Mercy had. She didn't know what the first step would be on that pathway. She had a suspicion it would start with forgiveness.

THE PICTURE OF STEVIE

SUZIE TUCKED THE FLASHBACK INTO THE RECESSES OF her memories for the evening. Barbara may have been a tyrant, but Suzie was determined to maintain her nurturing ability.

The children were amazing once Grace and Mr. Mercy had visited. They listened, didn't fight, and went to bed without any complaint. Suzie was shocked. They had never been this good.

Suzie considered herself blessed to have been visited by such lovely neighbors but she really needed to talk with Faith to understand what had transpired in the last few days. She needed more than understanding, she needed wisdom as to how to proceed.

She settled into bed and picked up the phone, praying as she dialed Faith's number.

"Hello?"

"Hello, Faith. This is Suzie."

"How are you doing sweet child of God?" Faith asked.

"I wish I knew. I need to talk to you about something."

"Go ahead. Start talking."

"Okay. Well, today I was making an apple pie to take over to the neighbors who just moved in. As the apple pie was baking I remembered something from my childhood." Suzie brushed a stray hair out of her eyes.

"Yes, go on… what did you remember?" Faith asked.

"I remembered my mother beating me till I was bloody."

"Oh, my goodness, that is a horrible memory," Faith cringed.

"Yes, it was, but it happened when I was just four-years-old so it doesn't hurt anymore. What hurts is the reason why I was beaten," Suzie said.

"Why would anyone beat a four-year-old child till they were bloody?" Faith asked.

"I had stumbled upon a chest in my mother's closet, and she found me looking in the chest," Suzie said.

"That doesn't seem to be a good enough reason, dear. I am sorry but I don't have any stomach for child abuse."

"I don't either but I think my mother had hidden something in that chest that she didn't want me to find." Suzie said, smoothing out the bed covers.

"What could that have been?"

"A picture of my older brother, Stevie. The lawyer that I went to yesterday was the same one that my father had gone to when he thought about divorcing my mom. He said she had changed because Stevie had died as an infant."

"You had an older brother?" Faith paused. "Wow, that is heartbreaking that he died as an infant."

"Yes, it is. I am glad that Sudden infant death did not claim any of my children. I don't know how I would have responded if that had happened. There was more than just a picture of Stevie though. There was a picture of him and my mother. When I looked at that picture I realized something."

"What was that?"

Suzie swallowed hard. "She truly loved him. So all of my thinking about my mother has been wrong. It's not that she couldn't love children. It's just that she didn't love me."

Faith paused for a moment as silence settled into the phone line. "Maybe she did love you but in a different way."

"No, she didn't love me. I realize that now. She told me I was a horrible little girl after beating me."

Faith gasped. "You didn't believe her did you?"

"I was four, Faith. Of course I believed her."

"Oh, my goodness. There is no reason to believe that old witch. NO reason at all."

"I kind of think that she was crazy. So, I don't really believe her now. I think the reason I hadn't remembered this until now is because as a child I couldn't process it. It didn't make any sense." Suzie said, with a pondering lilt to her voice.

"So true," Faith replied.

"It is interesting what happened after the flashback," Suzie continued.

"What happened?" Faith asked, hoping that Grace and Mercy had been on cue.

"My neighbors came over. Their names were Grace and Mr. Mercy. Before they arrived I had so much hate towards my mom, it was like a raging fire coursing through my veins. After they left I didn't feel that anymore," Suzie paused. "My feelings changed. My concern was for my mother. I don't know what happened to her when Stevie died. I know I wasn't a horrible little girl. I was just curious. I have three living children whom I adore. She has only one whom she can't seem to love. I look at the beauty of my life filled with love and I see the coldness of her life, filled with bitterness and I realize… I am the blessed one."

"So you see now from my vantage point, sweet child of God. You are immensely blessed and favored by God because you can love. It is a choice my dear and you have chosen well." Faith said with sincerity.

"So how do I proceed forward with my mother?"

"What are your thoughts on that?" Faith asked.

"I think I need to first make sure that the flashback was not a figment of my imagination. I can do that by looking in the drawer of a jewelry box I had as a child," Suzie said.

"I don't understand," Faith said.

"Oh, I didn't tell you. I stole a picture of Stevie from the treasure chest and hid it from Barbara in the drawer of a jewelry box."

"You still have that jewelry box?" Faith asked with amazement.

"Yes, it is weird but I demanded I take that jewelry box with me when I married Joe. I didn't remember about the picture."

"Do you know where it is?"

"Yes, it is in my closet."

"Do you want to check now while I am on the line?"

Suzie paused, wondering if she was strong enough to search for the answer which had been beyond her reach all of her life. She took a deep breath. "Yes, I want to know. Can you hold on?"

"Certainly, sweet child of God."

Suzie got up from her bed, tears streaming down her face. Her mind was a whirl. With one thought she hoped the drawer was empty but if it was, did that mean her mind had created the flashback? If Stevie's picture was there, she would have to bring his skeleton out of the closet and deal with it, and her mother.

Her steps were wobbly, her hands shaking, as she dug through the piles in the back of her closet. There it was: the jewelry box. She walked slowly back to the bed, holding the jewelry box with her heart racing. She sat down on her bed, nestling the box in between her slender legs. She picked up the phone. "Faith are you there?"

"Yes, dear child, I am here." The soothing sound of Faith calmed the shaking heart of Suzie.

Suzie slowly pulled the knob on the drawer towards her and the beautiful smile of Stevie caught her breath. Tears poured out of her eyes as her heart broke. "He is here, Faith. My brother was a reality. What do I do now?"

"You help Barbara forgive God for the death of her firstborn."

"How am I supposed to do that, Faith? I don't even like my mother. I don't want to talk with her anymore."

"You pray first and start by asking God to help you forgive her for all of the bitterness and rejection you have had to face because of her. Then when you are at peace, you approach her with your discovery. The memory of Stevie has become an idol in her heart. If you have idols which you worship it is difficult, if not impossible, to accept the love of God."

"Wow, so she beats me till I am bloody when I was a little girl and I am supposed to forgive her and help her experience the love of God? I'll be honest with you Faith. I don't know that I can do that."

"Sweet child of God, you have already started."

"How on earth have I started to forgive my mother?"

"This is the first time since I have known you that you have called Barbara your mother, instead of Barbara."

"No, I didn't. I couldn't have." Suzie dissolved into sobs, frantically searching through her memory for the words she had just spoken. A long pause held the phone line in suspense. "You're right, Faith. I didn't realize it. I did call her my mother."

"You have started on the right path my dear. Now you need to get some sleep. You will need your strength in this battle."

"Good night, Faith."

"Good night, sweet child of God."

THE BOWELS OF HELL

DECEIT HAD BEEN GLOATING. HE KNEW THAT THE plans for Suzie would come to fruition. To have used a flashback to tap her mind before Christ had entered was a brilliant plan. He would have to remember to use flashbacks more often. Especially in the case of those stinking Christians.

He couldn't wait to hear how Suzie had come to her end. He needed to call another meeting. This was the first meeting regarding Suzie that he was actually looking forward to.

The alarm sounded and pretty soon the entities of evil filled the chamber. Despair was first, her greasy head gazing at the floor. Doubt and Insecurity came in throwing punches at each other. Envy bounced in, without her normal exuberance for evil. Rejection was wrapped around the trunk of Bitterness, trying to blend in. Betrayal was the last to enter and he avoided the glance of Deceit.

Deceit started to feel a little less sure of himself. The evil spirits did not indicate by their demeanor that they had been successful. Surely they didn't get trounced again by a stupid single mom. Surely not.

"Well, I believe at our last meeting we happened to come to a collective decision that Suzie would be transported on the back of Despair to a place where she was being beaten by Barbara." Deceit stood over Despair.

"Wait a minute boss. I don't remember that I was supposed to carry her on my back. Does anyone else remember that being said?" Despair glanced furtively around the chamber.

"Well, I really don't remember. I kind of thought it was Insecurity which was supposed to carry the nasty woman on her back." Doubt said as he kicked Insecurity across the room and hit Deceit right in the smacker with the entity.

Deceit was incensed. "I meant it figuratively, not literally."

Despair sidled up to Envy. "What does "figuratively not literally" mean?"

Envy quickly reached into her glob to pull out the dictionary.

"STOP! JUST STOP!!!" Deceit screamed with rage. "All I want to know is how the flashback caused Suzie to end her life. Now who is going to be the lucky one to tell me?"

Silence filled the room. Dead silence. Despair shuffled over to the corner, plopped down and started chewing on her split ends. Doubt was shaking instead of swaying, which was a new low. Insecurity had hopped over to Rejection and was trying desperately to slide under the slimy snake. Bitterness stood stoically in the corner opposite Despair, his gnarled branches quivering in fear. Envy had the dictionary in front of her face, pretending to be absorbed in definitions.

"I see I have no volunteers. So I will ask each one of you to relay what part you should have successfully accomplished and then decide who gets the prize," Deceit said.

"We don't get prizes, you ain't fooling anyone. All we get is punishment." Despair said as she spit some dead hair out of her mouth.

"Despair, you will be the first. Tell me about the flashback."

Despair crossed her legs and started tearing her worn and dirty dress into shreds. "Suzie decided she was going to make an apple pie for her new neighbors. They moved in right across the road from her. They are an elderly couple. They don't have any kids around anymore. They moved into a nice house." Despair paused to pick a buger out of her nose and ate it. "But boy is it run down. That house needs paint, a new roof, some landscaping…"

"ENOUGH! I do NOT need to know about the neighbors you imbecile! I need to know about how Suzie did during the flashback," Deceit yelled.

"I lured her down the road of pain, causing her mind to skip back through history to the day when she was just a four-year-old. On that special day she deluded herself into thinking she was a princess." Despair got up and did a pirouette. Then the numbskull started twirling as if she was a ballerina.

Deceit caught her in the midst of one twirl and bent down to glare in her eyes. "Thinking you are a princess is not exactly what I call a road of pain."

"Well of course it isn't, but when Barbara comes in and finds you messing with her treasure chest, then you get snatched up by your arm and get beaten till your bloody… Well, sir… it can be a horrifying fall from an imaginary throne." Despair looked up at Deceit and smiled when she saw the gleam in his eye. "Now *that* can be a road of pain." Despair paused and bowed to applause, even though no one was clapping.

Deceit looked at Despair with awe. "Sometimes I swear you are more than an imbecile."

"Thank you, I think." Despair went back into her corner and started chewing on her toenails.

"Alright. So the flashback was in full swing. Let's back up a little bit. I want to savor every morsel of this devastation. What happened when Suzie discovered the treasure chest?"

"She thought she would find gold but she found a picture of a beautiful baby boy instead." Envy started jiggling with excitement.

"Good, good. Did she realize that this was her dead brother?"

Despair began twirling again. "No, she thought he was her prince."

Deceit furrowed his brow. "I am thinking that so far we do not have much to go on for Bitterness and Envy to reside in her soul. Someone had better come forward to prove me wrong."

Rejection swung down from one of Bitterness's branches. "That wasn't the only picture Suzie saw. In fact, it was not the most important picture she saw."

Deceit was seething now. " Damn it, I do not know why you are telling me this story as if it were a suspense novel." Deceit started to pace, which was never a good sign. "I just want to know how we finally caused this disgusting wretch to take her life. We have to work on the children as soon as she is out of the picture. So tell me and make it fast."

Insecurity hopped to the middle of the chamber eager to get in on what appeared to be a good thing. "I lured her into opening an envelope which had a picture of Barbara holding Stevie, her dead brother. I put the thought in her mind that her mother loved Stevie but she didn't love her."

Envy started bouncing up and down with glee. "Yes, yes! I was there too. I made her envious of dead little Stevie."

"Good, good. Now I can go down and start working on the minds of the children. With Suzie out of the way I will have full access to their thoughts." Deceit said starting to turn and walk out of the chamber.

The tree of Bitterness stopped him by extending a branch to block the exit. "That would be a wasted trip, sir. Suzie is still alive. What these idiots didn't tell you is something very important about the neighbors. They had something very unusual in their hearts."

Deceit whipped around, his eyes filled with fury. "What the hell could be in the hearts of her neighbors?"

"Grace and Mercy, sir. We didn't even get a sliver of Suzie's heart or mind, much less her life," Bitterness exclaimed.

The screams of Deceit echoed through the bowels of hell; striking terror in those who were slaves to evil.

OPENING THE CLOSET DOOR

SUZIE WOKE UP THE NEXT MORNING FEELING refreshed. She was amazed at how effective tears were as a sleeping agent. She glanced at the alarm clock and realized she had woken up early.

She had a lot of thinking to do but that wasn't what Faith had told her to do. Faith had told her to pray.

Suzie wondered if she could think and pray at the same time. She felt like she needed to lay all of her burdens down. She remembered a verse in the Bible where Jesus said something like, "we should cast all of our cares upon Him."

What did He know about a mother not being able to love? Suzie thought that Mary was probably a good mother.

A nagging recollection crept forth in her mind. She remembered a passage in the Bible where Jesus had been called crazy by his mother and brothers.

Maybe He did know how it was to have a dysfunctional family.

Suzie knelt beside her bed and poured out her heart to God. She confessed and recounted all of the memories that she had kept hidden in the dark recesses of her heart. The ones which had been bound by the roots of Bitterness. With each memory confessed, the pain started to dissipate. Tears flowed freely down her cheeks as she told God how difficult it had been for her to accept His love when she had never felt love from her mother. She knew that she had built up walls around her heart because of her mother's icy demeanor. She begged God to tear down those walls so that she could accept the love which He so freely gave.

The phone started ringing. Suzie glanced at the clock, it was almost time to wake up the kids.

"Hello?"

"Hello, sweet Child of God. Faith asked me to call you. How are you doing?"

Suzie sighed. "Hi, Hope. I was just praying. Did Faith tell you I had a flashback?"

"Yes, Suzie, she did; and I am so sorry you went through that as a child," Hope said.

"Yeah, me too. My childhood has always seemed like a puzzle to me. I had a hard time understanding why some things had changed. I am starting to put the puzzle pieces back together now."

"What do you mean?" Hope asked.

"Well in prayer this morning, I realized that now I know why my dad quit a successful banking career. He gave up a wonderful job because he didn't want to leave me alone with my mother. After that beating, she became the breadwinner," Suzie said.

"Wow, that is quite a revelation. Have you asked your dad about this?" Hope asked.

"No, not yet. It's just a guess. I've been thinking about my mother a lot. I think I'm beginning to understand why my mother couldn't love me. I think she loved her mother very much. When her mother committed suicide, some of her heart must have died. Then when her first born child died, she may have decided that anything she loved would die. If she wanted me to live she couldn't show me love," Suzie stated.

"Wow. That is pretty deep," Hope said.

"Yes it is." Suzie paused to collect her thoughts. "But I was also the person who thought she just couldn't love children. I was wrong on that count so I may have come to the wrong conclusion."

"How are you going to resolve this?" Hope asked.

"I am going to take the advice of Faith and pray until I have peace. Then I will invite my mother over for coffee and try to gently pry her heart open with Stevie's picture. I have to dismantle the idol of Stevie according to Faith."

Hope cleared her throat and said, "How do you intend to dismantle the idol?"

"Initially, I wanted to attack her in anger. I think she was a horrible and cold-hearted mother for having beaten me like she did. I think I had a right to that kind of rage. She beat me till I bled and all I was doing was being a kid."

"You have every right to feel that way." Hope said in a soothing tone.

"After Grace and her husband, Mr. Mercy, came over, my feelings changed. I began to think about what my mother has gone through in her life. I may not have felt love from my mother but at least I *had* a mother. She didn't have one. Then to lose a child… I can't even imagine how awful that would be."

"Sweet child of God, you have come so far to be able to grasp the deeper wisdom of God. To care about someone else's pain more than your own is a sign that Grace has taken up residence in your heart. Once you step out of your own pain to understand the pain of someone else, you achieve a deeper intimacy not only with them but also with God." Hope paused for a bit to let this truth sink in. "If you understand this, you will be able to understand that Jesus becoming human was the most gracious gift that God has ever given."

"I never thought of it that way, Hope," Suzie said. "I guess Jesus coming down to earth and becoming human was a way for God to understand us better, wasn't it?"

"Yes, and that is why He intercedes for you to the Father. He brings your petitions before the Father reflecting on the reality that He faced when He was on earth." Hope spoke gently with no condemnation.

Suzie continued, "I will be honest with you. I am terrified that I won't be able to dismantle that idol. I don't really know how to talk with my mother. All she has ever done is tell me what I am doing wrong. It is not like we have ever been friends."

"I know, I know. She has built up walls around her heart," Hope said. "She has isolated her love in a chamber, loving only the memory of her dead son."

"I am scared that this won't work. When she finds out that I know about Stevie she may retreat even more."

"That is always a possibility. Can I suggest a way to approach this?"

Suzie breathed a sigh of relief. "Yes, Hope, please do. I am worried sick about this."

"Continue to pray about this discussion. Pick out a verse from the Bible about forgiveness and memorize it. Any time you want to back down, quote that scripture. You must realize that the only thing which is effective against evil is the Word of God." Hope paused so that Suzie could grasp this concept. "When you have peace, approach your mother with love, not condemnation; and leave the outcome to God. If your mother refuses to tear down her idol then that is *her* choice. If that happens, you can dust your feet off and walk away. If she realizes she needs to let go of her dead son, Stevie, and start loving her daughter, who is still living, then that is when the real work begins."

Suzie busted out in giggles. "More work, that is exactly what I *don't* need Hope."

Hope joined Suzie in her laughter. "Yes, I know but this will be exciting work because the Holy Spirit will be in the midst. I can guarantee that once you start working with Him you won't want any other boss."

"I think you may be right about that Hope." Suzie glanced at the clock. "I had better sign off now. My kids need to get ready for school. Goodbye Hope."

"Goodbye sweet child of God." Hope said as she hung up the phone.

SUZIE'S IDOL?

SUZIE RUSHED TO GET THE CHILDREN READY FOR school. They had been so much better since Grace and Mr. Mercy had come over that Suzie actually enjoyed the hustle and bustle. She teased Sarah about being such a beauty queen and complimented Michael on how well he had done at getting ready the night before. She delighted in the sweet innocence of Jonathan.

As she was loading them in the car, she caught her breath. The picture of Stevie reminded her of someone. She couldn't identify who though. She would have to look at it again. She also needed to search the Bible for a scripture.

Then there was that task that she had been avoiding; the search for a job. The money from her dad had not arrived yet. If she didn't spend any money on extras, the money she had would last her one to two months. She had no idea how much child support she would get but she didn't expect that Joe would give her much. Apparently taking care of Megan had become his first priority.

She knew she should be worried but what would that do to help her? It would only make her cross with the children.

She started driving the children to school. Their banter back and forth bringing a smile to her lips.

When she got home she checked the clock to see what kind of shows were on TV. It was a good hour before those stinking dragons started flying again. Maybe if she got Jonathan engaged in some coloring he wouldn't make such a fuss at leaving to go pick up Michael from school.

"Hey honey. Why don't you sit at the dining room table and color in this coloring book?" Suzie asked. "Mommy needs to do a few things in her bedroom okay?"

"Okay, Mommy," Jonathan said as he climbed up on a chair and grabbed a color to start coloring.

Suzie went to her bedroom and sat Indian style on the bed. She opened the Bible and searched for verses on forgiveness. She needed something that was simple and to the point. After searching through the scriptures, she settled on Ephesians 4:32, "And be kind to one another, tenderhearted, forgiving one another, even as God in Christ forgave you."

She needed to write that verse down. She went to the kitchen to get a recipe card and wrote it down so she could take it with her until it was memorized.

Where had Jonathan gone? He wasn't sitting by the table anymore. She peeked in the living room and he wasn't there. Where was he? Maybe he had gone to her bedroom when she was in the kitchen. She walked to the bedroom and saw him pulling out the drawer to her jewelry box that she had left on her nightstand.

"Oh, no. Honey, please don't do that." Suzie scurried across the room just as Jonathan was taking out the picture of Stevie.

"Who's this?" Jonathan asked, holding the fragile picture in his hand.

Suzie picked him up gently and sat on her bed. Should she tell him who Stevie was? She didn't really want her children knowing about Stevie before she had talked with her mother.

"This is someone from Mommy's past."

Jonathan looked at her with a grin on his face. "No, it isn't, Mommy. That Daddy as a baby."

Suzie caught her breath as the knife of reality stabbed her chest. She looked at the picture closer, studying each nuance in the photo. She *knew* he reminded her of someone. She hadn't realized how much he looked like Joe until this very moment.

"No, honey. That isn't Daddy but it looks a lot like him doesn't it? Can Mommy have that picture back please?"

Jonathan looked one more time at the picture and then gave it back to Suzie. "That baby looks like Daddy."

"Yes, you are right, he does look like Daddy. Thank you so much for giving it back to me. This picture is very important to me. I am so glad you were a good boy and gave it back to me."

"You have been so good this morning that I am going to let you watch the dragons fly for a little bit before we go pick up Michael. Would you like to do that?"

"Yes, Mommy, I would." Jonathan jumped down from her lap and started for the living room.

Suzie turned on the television and made sure Jonathan was settled.

She crept back to her bedroom, her mind whirling with thoughts. If Stevie looked like Joe, had she married Joe hoping to capture her prince? She knew she had loved Joe. She felt it when they had been together. Yet she hadn't dated anyone other than Joe, so how did she know that he was the one she should marry?

She remembered how her mother had gone on and on about Joe from the first time she met him. It had been the only time that Suzie had seen her mother with a sparkle in her eye. Did her mother love Joe more than her because Joe was a replacement for Stevie?

Suzie picked up a few things in her bedroom and as she bent over to pick up a stray sock a thought exploded into her reality. Maybe the reason why she had married Joe was because she was trying to gain the love of Barbara. Had the elusive love of cold-hearted Barbara become the idol which she had worshipped to such an extent that she had married a replica of her dead brother?

Furthermore, was her desire to heal Barbara just another attempt to gain her love or was it something that was actually centered on the purity of Grace and Mercy?

Suzie walked over to the phone and dialed Faith.

"Hello?" Faith said.

"Hello, Faith. This is Suzie, do you have time to talk?"

"Yes, of course I have time to talk. What is going on?" Faith asked.

"I just realized something today. That picture of Stevie is similar, if not a perfect replica, of the baby pictures of Joe. That got me thinking," Suzie said.

"Go on," Faith said.

"When I found Stevie's picture as a little girl I called him 'my prince.' He was such a beautiful baby. I know I loved Joe when I was married to him but I am wondering if in some way, big or small, I was trying to replace Stevie," Suzie said.

"That's a possibility," Faith said.

"I wonder if I was either trying to find my prince or trying to heal my mother by marrying Joe."

Faith cleared her throat. "Wow, you *have* been thinking."

"Then I got to wondering about *my* idols. I intend to tear down the idol of my dead brother for my mother but could it be that my idol has been the approval of my mother? I mean, I think about how hard I am on myself about the house. If it isn't perfect, I feel as if I am a failure but I don't like cleaning house. I would much rather play with my kids. I don't know Faith. Is my desire to confront my mother about Stevie just a selfish move on my part to finally gain her love? Or do I really want her to tear down that idol so that she can accept the love of God?" Suzie asked.

"You are not selfish, Suzie. To want a mother to love you unconditionally is not selfish. That is the way that God loves you. It is natural." Faith paused a bit before she went on. "You may have been attracted to Joe because he reminded you of Stevie. He became a favorite of Barbara but that doesn't mean it was wrong to love him. He was your husband and God would want you to love him. An idol is anything that draws you away from God. To crave the love of your husband and your mother is not a bad thing if it draws you closer to God." Faith said with conviction.

"To be honest, I don't think Joe did draw me closer to God. He fulfilled my flesh. At first we had such a romantic and playful relationship. Then the kids came and the romance and playfulness seemed to disappear." Suzie stroked the picture of Stevie gently. "It always seemed as if there was something missing, though. I couldn't put my finger on it but in a way it was like a chocolate bunny. It looked good on the outside but the inside was hollow. I know now what I was missing. I was missing God. Reading God's word and praying with my husband would have filled that hollow bunny with delicious chocolate," Suzie said.

Faith giggled, "You have such a way with words. The analogy of a chocolate bunny is priceless." Faith held on to silence for a moment, considering her words. "I would encourage you to go forward with your mother. It is important for many reasons. She needs to let go of the bitterness that has taken root within her heart. Remember I told you that you were destined to break generational curses?"

"Yes, I remember that," Suzie said.

"The root of bitterness blocks the Holy Spirit from having full access to a heart. That is a very strong generational curse that is easily passed from one generation to another. I thought you may become bitter when Joe left you, but I am amazed at how you have overcome the attacks of the evil one. Instead of being consumed with grief you are more concerned about the grief that your mother has suffered," Faith said.

Suzie smiled, "Do you think I am just in denial? I mean that *is* the first stage of grieving."

"No, you are definitely not in denial. You are searching for truth and that is the polar opposite of denial. Sweet child of God, you have come so far in this journey."

"Thanks, Faith. So even if Stevie was somewhat of an idol for both me and my mother, it is not selfish or wrong to want my mother to love me like God does, is that right?" Suzie asked.

"Yes, that is right. Every child wants their parents to love them and that is a God-given need," Faith said.

Suzie glanced at the clock. The time to pick up Michael from school was fast approaching.

"I have to pick Michael up from school. Thanks so much for your wise counsel, Faith."

"Anytime dear," Faith replied.

"Good bye." Suzie said as she grabbed her keys and made her way to the living room.

"Goodbye sweet child of God." Faith said before hanging up.

BREWING A CUP OF COFFEE

SUZIE WOKE UP THE NEXT MORNING ON A SEESAW. ONE moment she wanted to call her mother and ask her over for coffee and the next moment she wanted to avoid the whole stinking mess of Stevie.

Why was it her responsibility to break generational curses and dismantle idols? I mean really, didn't God know that her husband had just left? Wouldn't it be a bit more realistic for her to search for a job so that her kids could keep eating?

She couldn't shake the sense of urgency though. She carried the verse from Ephesians 4:32 around with her as she picked up the house. "And be kind to one another, tenderhearted, forgiving one another, even as God, in Christ, forgave you."

She needed to confront her mother in order to conquer her own fear. What did she fear? She feared that if her mother couldn't love her and her husband couldn't love her, then maybe she *was* unlovable. To get to the root of her mother's bitterness was essential to her own self-worth.

She would make the call. Maybe her dad would answer. Barbara was usually at work during the week. Her dad could ask Barbara about having coffee with her and if she said "No" then she could dust her feet off and walk away.

She sat at the kitchen table and said a prayer. Then picked up the phone and dialed.

"Hello?"

"Hello, Barbara," Suzie said.

"Well, hello Susanna! How are you? You never call unless you want something. What do you want now?" Barbara said, with an icy tone to her voice.

Suzie wanted to slam the phone down but took a deep breath instead. "I was wondering if you would like to come over for coffee sometime this week."

"Hmmm. Let me think about that for a minute." Barbara paused and then continued on as if thinking out loud. "I just ordered the new spring line to put in my store but it won't be coming in till next week. I have been training a new sales person and she is coming along very well." She stopped and let out a big sigh. "Yes, I think I could come over this week. What day were you referring to?"

"How about tomorrow?" Suzie asked.

"This must be an urgent matter. You have never invited me over to your home." Barbara took a deep breath. "This comes as a bit of a surprise to me. Could I… Could I bring something to go with the coffee?" Barbara asked.

"You can bring whatever you want. I will provide the coffee. How about you come over at nine in the morning?" Suzie said, looking at her house and wondering just how she was going to get it clean enough for a white glove test.

"Okay, I will be there at nine. Thank you for the invitation, Susanna. I have wanted to see your home ever since you and Joe bought it. By the way, have you heard from Joe?" Barbara asked.

"No." Susanna cut the conversation short. If she had to hear Barbara go on and on about how much she missed Joe, she may not have the courage to confront her about Stevie. "I will see you tomorrow morning. Goodbye, Barbara."

"Goodbye, Susanna." Barbara said as she hung up the phone.

Suzie was seized by panic the minute she hung up the phone. Her eyes darted from one cluttered mess to another. Why on earth had she said tomorrow? She had so much to do and only half of a day to do it in. She hadn't even thought about what she was supposed to do with Jonathan. She didn't know how this confrontation would turn out but she did know that she didn't want any of her children to be present.

She quickly flitted from one mess to another, not able to concentrate enough to get anything put away. Why hadn't she kept her house clean after CPS had come to visit? Her mother was sure to condemn her for the piles of schoolwork left on the coffee table, the dishes in the sink, and the clothes on her children's bedroom floor. What was she to do with Jonathan during the coffee confrontation?

She was cleaning off the kitchen table when she looked up and saw the lights of Grace and Mr. Mercy's house shining across the country road. They were like a beacon, slicing through the cloudy mist.

She took a deep breath. They had said they would love to watch her children. Mr. Mercy had said she needed to talk to her mother. Maybe they would be available to watch Jonathan tomorrow. She would run by their house on the way to go pick up Michael from school and ask them.

Just thinking of those two wonderful people helped calm the panic that was seizing the mind of Suzie. She slowed down to concentrate on one room at a time. She glanced at the clock while she was wiping the kitchen counters. It was time to leave and she had only gotten the kitchen cleaned. With both of the boys being home in the afternoon she was not sure how she would get the rest of the house done.

She whisked Jonathan out to the car and drove over to the home of Grace and Mr. Mercy.

She rang the doorbell and waited on the porch. It took just a bit for the door to open. When it opened Suzie was surprised. It was a nice looking young man standing in the doorway.

"I'm sorry I didn't mean to bother you. It's just that Grace and Mr. Mercy came over to my house the other day and they said that they wouldn't mind babysitting for me." Suzie caught her breath and went on. "I don't mean to impose but I kind of need someone to watch my youngest son, Jonathan, tomorrow morning."

The man's eyes crinkled in a compassionate grin. "Well they went to the store this morning. I am Jacob, their son." Jacob held his hand out for a shake.

"Ooops. I am such a ninny. I always forget to introduce myself. I am Suzie, the neighbor across the road." Suzie shook Jacob's hand

and flashed him a winning smile. "Do you have any idea when they will be back?"

"Soon. They should be back soon. Would you like to come in for some coffee?" Jacob asked.

"No, I am on my way to go pick up my other son from school. Would it be okay if I stopped by after I picked him up?" Suzie asked.

"Sure that wouldn't be a problem at all. They adore children and if they can watch yours maybe they will stop trying to get me married off," Jacob chuckled. "They are always pestering me about marriage… but I think what they really want is some more grandchildren."

"They do seem to have a way with children," Suzie said. "My children took to them instantly."

"I know they had a way with me. I was blessed to be adopted by them at a young age." Jacob's face melted into a smile of gratitude.

"Oh, so you are one of the foster children that they adopted?" Suzie asked.

"Yes," Jacob replied.

"Well, I am jealous. I think that they were the most perfect parents ever."

"I can't argue with that but their love is available for everyone. I am sure they would be more than willing to look after your son tomorrow morning," Jacob said.

Suzie looked at her car with a bit of anxiety. "I better go. I will be late to pick up my son if I don't leave right now. I will stop by on the way home okay?" Suzie asked.

"That sounds like a plan. Be careful," Jacob said.

"Thanks. I'll see you later." Suzie said as she skipped down the steps and trotted to her car.

As Suzie drove to the school, she reflected on Jacob. He seemed like such a nice man. There was nothing spectacular about him in the looks department but his demeanor was comforting to her. Maybe he could be a friend. She could always use more friends.

Suzie picked up Michael from school and drove over to the Mercy house. Michael and Jonathan were so excited to be there that Suzie could not make them stay in the car. They ran up the stairs, jumping up and down as she rang the doorbell.

Mr. Mercy opened the door and as soon as he saw the boys, his face exploded into a grin. Jonathan raised his arms up, as if it was a reflex and soon he was nestled in Mr. Mercy's embrace.

"Hello, Suzie. I am so glad you came over. Jacob told Grace that you had stopped by and she went to making some cookies."

"Cookies?!" Michael exclaimed as he slid around Mr. Mercy's legs and walked right into the house.

"Michael, come back here right now." Suzie didn't want to presume an invitation.

Mr. Mercy chuckled as he turned to watch Michael sprint for the kitchen. "I think he may not have heard you." Mr. Mercy said with a grin. "The kitchen is in the back of the house, little guy."

"I am so sorry. I haven't gotten to the point of teaching them proper manners yet. It will be on the top of my list for this week." Suzie said, blushing with embarrassment.

"Don't worry about it. We were expecting you and I am sure Grace is thrilled that her cookies are such a hit." Mr. Mercy opened the door to let Suzie in. "Jacob had mentioned that you needed us to babysit for you tomorrow?"

"Yes, if you don't mind. I need to talk to my mother," Suzie said.

"Grace and I have been praying for you in that regard." Mr. Mercy said with compassion. "We would be happy to babysit for you tomorrow morning. In fact, we were just saying that we didn't know what we were going to do tomorrow. Our unpacking is all done and everything is put in place. If you want, we could watch them for a couple of hours this afternoon also."

"Are you kidding? I would love that. I have to pick up my house. My mother has the Martha Stewart gene and somehow I got skipped when they were handing out OCD genes," Suzie chuckled. "I could pick them up right before Sarah gets home. This would help me out so much."

"That wouldn't be a problem at all. Do they need some lunch? I think Grace has some homemade pizza cooking in the oven right now. She usually makes pizza while the cookies cool," Mr. Mercy said.

"I didn't even think about lunch. I am sorry. Would it be an inconvenience for you to feed them lunch?" Suzie asked.

"Not a bit. We have plenty to share." Mr. Mercy said with a smile.

"That would be great then. Thank you so much," Suzie said. "You both are life savers."

"I am glad you appreciate us but we truly enjoy your children as we do all children."

"Thanks again." Suzie said as she literally flew off the porch.

Suzie drove across the country road to her home and bounded up her stairs with renewed vigor. She did three loads of wash and picked up all of the toys in the living room. Then she dusted the furniture and vacuumed the carpet in the dining room and living room. She deep cleaned the toilet and scrubbed the bathtub and sink.

There was no reason for Barbara to go into the bedrooms so she didn't worry about those three rooms. Sarah's room was always perfect because Sarah hardly used her room. She finished the whole house in three hours and went to get Michael and Jonathan.

Grace answered the door and welcomed her into her home. Suzie stepped inside and breathed in deep. There was a beautiful fragrance wafting through the air, it smelled like roses. The house was clean but not sterile and the beauty of the furnishings seemed to beckon a guest to explore further.

"I hope the boys were good," Suzie said.

"They were wonderful. They are playing outside with Jacob and Mr. Mercy." Grace said with a smile. "Jacob would be such a wonderful father but he is so particular when it comes to women." An out of place furrow of worry crossed her brow. "I know that God has a very special lady for Jacob. In due time, he will find her." Grace said, giving Suzie a wink, as she led her to the kitchen in the back of her house.

The back porch door flew open and the house was filled with laughter. The men and boys stomped the snow and mud off of their shoes in the porch and came inside the kitchen. Suzie's heart warmed to see her boys so happy. She didn't realize how much they missed the companionship of an adult male until this moment.

Her gaze settled on Jacob. He was so happy with her boys. She hadn't remembered Joe ever being that happy. In fact, she hadn't remembered Joe playing with Michael or Jonathan within the past two years. What a shame that their own father could not enjoy the sons that God had given him.

"Hello, Suzie." Jacob said with a smile. "These boys you have are pretty good at throwing and catching a ball."

"Are they?" Suzie realized that she hadn't ever played ball with them herself. She was too busy trying to be a Martha Stewart clone. "Well, when it gets warmer I may have to go out and play catch with them."

"Mommy, do we have to go home?" Michael asked.

Suzie looked down at him in amazement. "Of course you have to go home, silly. Grace and Mr. Mercy have been so nice to take care of you but we don't want to overstay our welcome."

"Awww, shucks." Michael hung his head. "I was having so much fun over here."

"I want to thank you for taking such good care of my children." Suzie's gaze scanned from Jacob to Grace to Mr. Mercy. "You have been such a gift from God. I really don't know what I would have done without you."

Grace's face softened into a warm smile. "We seek to show God's love and mercy to anyone whom He places in front of us. Not everyone accepts the love we have to share, nor do they accept the love of God. You have an open and willing heart. It is a delight for us to share the love of God with you and your family."

Suzie could not identify how this family did it, but every time she was around them she felt accepted and loved. Those were two emotions which had been nonexistent in her childhood.

"Thank you, and it is a delight for us to spend time with you." Suzie gazed at her sons. "Michael and Jonathan, I need you to get your coats and shoes on. Sarah will be coming home to an empty house if we don't make our way across the road." Suzie said with as much authority as she could muster.

Jacob was getting Jonathan's coat and shoes on him and Michael had the hands of Mr. Mercy assisting him with his outer garments. Soon the boys were ready to go and there was not an ounce of disobedience in their demeanor.

The evening whisked by as if it was a brisk wind on an autumn day. Suzie tried to keep busy with detailing her house, making dinner for the children and their nighttime rituals. Her mind was tormented with worry, though. She didn't know what would happen tomorrow when she met with Barbara. She feared the worst and hoped for the best.

As she settled in for the night she sought comfort in the Bible. She opened the Bible to Ephesians 4:29 "Do not let any unwholesome talk come out of your mouths, but only what is helpful for building others up according to their needs, that it may benefit those who listen."

Then she started praying. "God, I don't know why you think I am so strong that I can break generational curses, dismantle idols and win this battle that you have set before me. I am hoping it is not my strength that has to win this battle but yours. Please keep me on the right path to forgiveness of my mother. Guard my heart and my lips. Stop my words when I want to use them to hurt her, like she has hurt me. Please give me courage to expose the things which are hidden. I am worried that finding the truth may cause me more pain than living with a lie. I know you are a God of truth and I believe it is your will for me walk in truth. Give me courage, Dear Lord, because frankly, I am terrified of my mother. I love you, God. Amen."

FEAR

DECEIT WAS INFURIATED! HE HAD TO CALL FEAR IN from Africa for that sniveling wench, Suzie. Now that Grace and Mercy were involved, the battle had just been elevated to a whole new level. The forces of God were intent upon making Suzie's life a testimony. Deceit was just as determined to snuff out her very existence.

She hadn't gone to church much, if any, she had only recently started to pray in earnest, she had rarely read the Bible and yet God favored her? It didn't make sense but now that Fear was on hand maybe he could relax a little. Fear was a great master of evil. Humans were so easy to overcome when Fear was present.

Another meeting was in order. There was no time to waste. The meeting with Barbara was in the morning and the strategy had to be clear.

Deceit sounded the alarm and the idiots from the underworld started lumbering into the Chamber of Evil. Everyone had assembled before the dark cloud of Fear made its grand entrance.

"I thought you were supposed to stay in Africa." Despair said, shaking like a leaf.

"I have spread misery throughout that continent like frosting on a chocolate cake. The fruits of war leave only death for its victims to eat. Do not worry, my effects on that continent will be felt for generations to come. It seems as if I am needed here now because certain evil entities have failed to destroy one simple single mother." The cloud of Fear enveloped Despair and she crumpled into a shivering mass of tears.

Despair looked up through her greasy hair and said, "I did what I could master. I swear I did what I could."

"That wasn't good enough."

Deceit could see that this was going nowhere fast. So much for his relaxing. Apparently Fear had been around war so much he had forgotten that not everything was a conflict… or was it?

"Attention! I don't believe we have any need to rehash the past. We need to focus on the opportunity which is presented to us. Suzie has invited Barbara over for coffee," Deceit stated.

"Well, if she is trying to get on the good side of Barbara, I think she should scrap the coffee idea and try chocolate milk. If I remember right she is an ace in the chocolate milk department." Envy winked at the cloud of Fear.

Deceit rolled his eyes. *Oh, no, not again.* They were already slipping from his grasp and the meeting had only started. "Envy, the primary reason for us to have Suzie meet with Barbara is to dig the fissures of pain and hurt deeper into Suzie's heart. How would getting on the good side of Barbara accomplish that?"

"Ummm, not sure , but I am just saying she is an ace at chocolate milk." Envy started bouncing up and down with excitement.

Deceit waited until she bounced close to him and then drop kicked her across the chamber to get her to shut up.

The cloud of Fear turned into a dark ominous presence. The room was silenced. "Bitterness, how deep have your roots burrowed into Barbara's heart?"

The huge tree bent a branch and seemed as if it was scratching an imaginary forehead in contemplative thought. "Master, very deep. I started burrowing deep into her heart when her mother committed suicide."

The cloud of Fear directed its wicked wind at Despair. "How often have you been present in the thoughts of Suzie and when did you start?"

"I have been present since she had understanding. I have told her that she wasn't worth loving. She would never be perfect enough to gain the love of her mother." Despair cowered in the presence of Fear.

Fear turned its attention to Deceit. "How easy has it been to infiltrate the heart and mind of Suzie?"

"Sir, she has been the most difficult of subjects. Every time we think we have an edge and have set up residence in her thoughts or her feelings, she opens up her Bible and seeks the presence of God," Deceit said.

"That is problematic. Could we possibly cause her to lose her Bible?" Fear asked.

Envy looked through the records to see if Suzie had a history of losing things. "Yes! That would be good. Suzie is always losing her keys." Envy jiggled with excitement then stopped jiggling and became quiet.

"What is wrong, Envy? Why the change in demeanor?" Fear asked.

"At last count, Suzie had ten different Bibles in her home. It may be difficult for her to lose all ten while she is sleeping. I mean the meeting is in the morning and I don't think…"

"Yes, yes. You are right. Would someone explain to me exactly what the purpose of this meeting is?" Fear asked.

The room became still and silent. "I need to know the purpose if I am to intervene. I am most effective against Faith which is the foundation for courage. As we all know there are other aspects of God's character which can be attacked more effectively by others in this room." Fear was swirling around the room in anger. "So *what* is the purpose?" "

Deceit hung his head. "She is searching for truth and understanding. She is hoping that a confrontation with Barbara will open the door to healing for both of them."

The fury of Fear sucked the life out of the cavern. The dark cloud threw Deceit against the stone wall, crushing his throat with a choke hold. "You mean to tell me you interrupted my work in Africa for this nonsense? A mere sniveling single mother has brought you to this point? Whatever possessed you? YOU ARE DECEIT! YOU ARE THE ARCH ENEMY OF TRUTH!"

Fear brought Deceit to the point of passing out and then released the choke hold. Deceit gasped for air, bending over to hide his shame. He paused a moment to collect his thoughts and then rose up to face Fear head on. A distraction was necessary."The reason why we called you in from Africa is because Suzie is favored by God.

She has received visitations from Hope, Faith, Joy, and now Grace and Mercy. Every time we launch an attack there is a counter attack. It would be different if she was more open to our influence but our attacks have slid off of her heart like butter on Teflon. We just cannot stick. She has the heart and soul of the apostle Paul."

Despair started wailing in the corner. "Please, please... *don't* say that name. Once Jesus entered that man I lost complete control. Singing praise songs when being imprisoned leaves me no open door." Despair started fidgeting as she rocked back and forth with anxiety. "I hate that man!"

The tree of Bitterness was losing leaves. It was common knowledge that the names of those who had gained victory over the evil empire were not to be spoken. Deceit had just committed a grave error. Someone had to take charge and it was clear that Deceit was not the one elected. "I know we have been at a loss with Suzie. However, I have had my roots entwined in Barbara's mind since her mother, Sarah, committed suicide. That death opened wide the path for me to enter in."

Insecurity sidled up to Doubt and whispered. "I do believe we are becoming redundant. I swear I have heard enough about what Bitterness has done in the mind of Barbara. If I have to hear one more word, I am going to barf."

The brisk wind of Fear started swirling. "Good, very good. So there is an opportunity for a generational sin to be passed along right? I do believe that bitterness crosses the generational gap quite frequently. So this should be a piece of cake, right?" The cloud of Fear lightened, if ever so slight, in its darkened tone.

"Yes, yes. This should be a piece of cake. I do love cake." Adultery sashayed across the room as if she was in a beauty pageant. "Why has it been so very hard for us?" She glared at Deceit with a mixture of contempt and lust.

"To be honest, she is beginning to love God more than she loves her mother," Deceit said.

A current of dissension wove invisibly throughout the evil cavern. Doubt gasped in horror and started swaying erratically. "You cannot tell the truth! That is not your place to tell the truth. How dare you even speak the word."

Despair started screaming as if she was being knifed. Betrayal opened his mouth baring his teeth. Rejection rose its slimy head up and hissed at Envy who was bouncing up and down, bumping into everyone in her path. Adultery lost her wig, revealing the horror of a skull which was riddled with maggots of lust. Insecurity had wilted into a violet which could easily be crushed with one step. Bitterness was shedding it's bark like a Persian cat in a hot desert. The whole lot of evil entities had come undone with the unusual event of Deceit speaking the word, "honest." Deceit crumpled in shame and tried to hide behind the small form of Despair.

Fear was in a rage. He had come back from Africa for this? It was apparent that Susanna Whatley had defeated every attack soundly through her wavering faith in God. Damn it! How God could take the most unlikely person and then transform them into a pillar of strength in His army, was beyond the logic of Fear. God had done this repeatedly throughout time. The majority of the prophets were not wealthy. The Bible was full of people who had been murderers, adulterers, and downright miserable creatures of evil until they decided to follow God. Fear had to regroup the entities of evil and collect their distracted minds into one focus; the decimation of one single mother, Susanna Whatley. He stood close to the peacock of Arrogance, almost trouncing his beautiful feathers.

"It is apparent to me that I have come back from Africa under false pretense. If this is truth we are fighting then it is you, Deceit, who needs to fight this fight. I will be present for a short time this morning in the heart and mind of Suzie but then I am going back to my current home, Africa." The cloud of Fear thundered and shook the cavern of evil.

BREWING COURAGE

SUZIE AWOKE WITH DREAD CLOUDING HER THOUGHTS. She really didn't want her mother to come over. Why had she asked her? She knew her mother would look down on her for the home in which she lived. It was run down. It wasn't exactly clean either. At least not by Barbara's standards.

Suzie glanced at the clock. She needed to get Michael and Sarah off to school and then drop Jonathan off at Grace and Mercy's house. She didn't have time for fear. If she focused on the task at hand, then maybe fear would leave.

She hadn't been able to sleep and had woken up much earlier than normal. Maybe she could pick up the house before the children got up. She rushed to the kitchen and started brewing coffee. As she looked out the kitchen window, she could see the lights shining forth from the house of Grace and Mercy. It warmed her heart to think of those two people. If things began to go down the wrong path with Barbara, Suzie promised herself she could glance across the road.

She started bustling around the house, putting it in order and before she knew it, the time to wake the children had arrived.

She didn't mention the morning plans she had to the children. She didn't want to tell them about Stevie unless her mother gave her permission.

After she dropped Michael and Sarah off at school, Suzie decided to broach the idea of going to Grace and Mr. Mercy's house to Jonathan.

"Hey, Jonathan. Mommy has a lot to do this morning. How would you like to spend the morning playing with Mr. Mercy and Jacob?"

Jonathan's face exploded with joy. "Yes! Mommy, I love that! Jacob teaching me catch."

"Well, then that is settled. I will take you right over there." Suzie heaved a sigh of relief.

As she drove down the long driveway to the house of Grace and Mr. Mercy she noticed that the house didn't look run down anymore. The paint was still peeling off of the siding but it was a house which looked inviting. Grace had put up some lovely lace curtains and the lamps shining through the windows gave such an appealing tint to the home.

As soon as Suzie got Jonathan out of the car seat, he sprinted up the stairs of the front wrap around porch; jumping up and down with impatience, as Suzie got out of the car to ring the doorbell.

It took just a moment for Jacob to open the door. "Well, hello there!" Jacob said, as he bent down to pick up Jonathan.

"Hello, Jacob. How are you doing?" Suzie said with a hint of shyness.

"I am doing just fine and how are you?" Jacob said meeting Suzie's gaze with a smile.

"Okay, I guess." Suzie considered that a blatant lie. She was anything other than okay. She was apprehensive and scared about the meeting with her mother. Every cell in her body wanted to back out.

Jacob let Jonathan down gently. "Hey, little guy. Why don't you see if you can find Mr. Mercy? I have been looking for him all morning and haven't been able to find him yet." Jacob winked at Suzie as he walked out onto the front porch and closed the door behind him. Then he tenderly took hold of Suzie's hand and led her to the porch swing.

"Grace told me a bit about your mother. I hope you don't mind." Jacob said, as they both relented to the lure of the porch swing.

"No, I don't mind at all. I know the motivation for anything that Grace does is love. How can I be offended by love?" Suzie asked.

"You know what you're doing demands a lot of courage," Jacob said.

"I know and I am not sure I have that," Suzie responded.

"You don't have what?" Jacob asked.

"Courage. I don't think I have courage," Suzie said.

"The basis of courage is Faith. From what Grace told me she said you had a deep faith in God."

"I don't know if I would consider it a deep faith. I do believe in God. I just wonder if He believes in me," Suzie said.

Jacob chuckled. "I think with all that you have gone through and how well you have handled everything, I could almost guarantee God believes in you." Jacob paused and took a deep breath. "So you are meeting with your mother to confront her about the son she had who died?"

"Yes. I think she adored that little boy. I always wondered why she couldn't love me. Was I unlovable? If your own mother can't love you than who can?" Suzie leaned her head back and gazed up at the ceiling of the porch.

"I know how you feel. I didn't feel any love from my natural parents either. It wasn't until I met Grace and Mercy that I felt true love. They loved me unconditionally and because of their love I was able to start the process of forgiveness." Jacob said holding Suzie's hand. "So what do you hope to attain through this meeting?"

"I want my mother to love me for who I am, not who she wants me to be. It is hard for me to accept myself when I feel that my own mother doesn't accept me," Suzie said.

"Do you realize that love is a choice based upon your own sense of self worth?" Jacob asked. "The one person who loved more than anyone else was Jesus. Even when He had been beaten, mocked and hung on a cross, His concern was not for himself but for those who had nailed Him to the cross."

Suzie gazed at Jacob with amazement in her eyes. "I never thought about it in that way."

"Your self-worth is much greater than that of your mother because you are willing to love," Jacob said. "She has suffered a great loss and because of this she is scared to love, because when you love you take a chance."

Suzie raised her eyebrows. "You take a chance?"

"Yes, you take a chance that your heart could be broken if you lose that love."

Suzie nodded slowly. "I am not scared anymore. I place this meeting into God's hands. He is the reason why I asked my mother over for coffee. It is my responsibility to show her love and forgiveness even if she does not accept it or want it. I am a grown woman, not a small child anymore and I have forged a path of love even when I was not shown any love." Suzie stopped and took a deep breath.

The porch door swung open and Jonathan pulled Mr. Mercy out on the front porch. "I found him! He was behind the couch." Jonathan said giggling.

A look passed between Jacob and Mr. Mercy. Without a word being spoken, Mr. Mercy lured Jonathan back inside to give Jacob some privacy.

Suzie looked at her watch. "I better rush over and make a new pot of coffee. Barbara will be arriving in fifteen minutes and she is never late." She bounded up from the porch swing, hesitated a moment and then threw herself into Jacob's waiting arms for a bear hug.

"Thank you so much, Jacob. I may not have had courage when I dropped Jonathan off. After talking with you, I think I may have gained a bit of courage." Suzie said, hugging his tall frame with a firmness that held no fear.

"Remember you are amazing and that God has favored you to fight in this battle." Jacob whispered in Suzie's ear.

"Thanks again. I better go now." Suzie slipped out of the embrace and bounded down to her car.

Jacob stood on the porch, watching her go, trying desperately to catch his racing heart.

"HOT" COFFEE

SUSANNA BOUNDED UP THE STAIRS TO HER HOUSE AND went in with a new perspective. Her house may not be perfect like her mother's had been but her house was full of love. She knew it was run down and not that clean but she would much rather have this house, than the cold house of perfection that she was raised in.

She picked up a stray matchbox car on her way to the kitchen and started brewing a fresh pot of coffee, praying for a heart of forgiveness with each step.

The doorbell rang and Susanna opened the door. Her mother was on the front porch with a perfect pecan coffee cake in her hands.

"Hello, Susanna." Barbara said, a bit of smugness lingering in her gaze.

"Hello, Barbara. Won't you please come in." Susanna said opening the door wide and stepping aside. "That coffee cake looks sinfully delicious."

Barbara looked a bit surprised at the compliment. "It kind of does, doesn't it? You know I am not much of a cook but I found this recipe that you put in the oven the night before. The bread rises over night and then you cook it in the morning. It is so simple; you could even do it."

Ouch that hurt. Susanna let that insult slide. This meeting wasn't about coffee cake or who was the best cook. "Well, you never know, maybe I could. If you want, you can share the recipe with me after we eat every last crumb of it."

Barbara continued to walk through the house with a look of contempt. "I wish you and Joe would have taken my advice when you bought this house and just bulldozed it."

"Well, Barbara, that would have taken more money than we had in the bank. We didn't want to live in debt and now that Joe has left, I am glad that we lived within our means."

"That reminds me, your father gave me this envelope. He insisted I give it to you first thing." Barbara took an envelope out of her designer purse and gave it to Susanna. Susanna took the envelope and walked quickly to her bedroom. She put the envelope in her lock box.

As she turned to go out the door she noticed the jewelry box on the night stand. She hesitated for a moment, then slowly opened the drawer. She gazed down at the beautiful smile of her older brother and picked the picture up, tucking it in the pocket of her sweater.

She rushed back into her kitchen.

Barbara was standing at the table looking as if she was lost.

"Why don't you sit down at the table?" Susanna asked.

"Where is Jonathan?"

"I dropped him off at the neighbors." Susanna said as she poured coffee into the cups on the table and got two small plates for the coffee cake.

"You have neighbors?" Barbara asked.

"Yes, they just moved in. They are the sweetest couple and the children have really taken to them." Susanna replied, as she cut some coffee cake and put it on a plate for Barbara. "How is your boutique doing?"

"It is fabulous. I have a new spring line coming in that is selling like hot cakes. The new sales girl I just hired is out of this world. I was telling your father the other day that I think she could sell ice to an Eskimo. She is such a pretty young thing too. She really has the traits of a manager more than a sales clerk. I think I may start grooming her for a promotion." Barbara said cutting her coffee cake into minuscule pieces.

"Haven't you had the same manager taking care of the store for a while now?" Susanna asked, taking her first bite of the coffee cake. "Mmmm, this is really yummy."

"Thank you. Yes, I have had Sally for way too long. She was good at first but she is boring my customers. She goes on and on about the divorce that she is going through. It is really affecting the atmosphere in my boutique. I hate to fire her when she is going through such a hard time, but it is affecting my profit line and that is unacceptable." Barbara took her first tiny bite of coffee cake.

"Have you discussed this with her? I mean her tendency to talk about her divorce with the customers?" Susanna asked before digging into the coffee cake again.

"No, I won't do that until I have mentored the new sales girl so that she can take over when Sally leaves. I don't think Sally is open to criticism," Barbara said. "She has had enough of that from her ex."

"Isn't it customary to give a verbal warning, then a written warning before terminating someone?" Susanna asked, feeling compassion for Sally's situation.

"It may be customary in a corporation but I own this boutique and I make the rules regarding what happens there. In addition to boring my customers with her pathetic tale of woe she has also attached herself to your father. Any time he walks through the door she is on him like glue. You would think she would have better sense than that." Barbara speared a pecan with the tong of her fork.

Yes, of course." Susanna could tell that this conversation was not leading to Stevie. She needed to redirect.

"Barbara, I need to be honest with you. I asked you over to my house for a specific reason and it wasn't to discuss how you manage your boutique," Suzie said.

"Thank God, because Susanna you wouldn't have the faintest idea how difficult that boutique has been for me. It is not all fun and games." Barbara said, spearing another caramelized pecan.

"I am sure it isn't. I asked you over to my home because I took something from you years ago and I need to give it back." Susanna took the picture out of her pocket and slid it across the table to Barbara.

Barbara's brow furrowed with tension. "Who on earth is this?" Barbara took the picture and tried to remain calm.

"I believe that beautiful baby is Stevie…your firstborn son. He was adorable, wasn't he?"

Barbara looked at Susanna with a mixture of horror and hate. "No, you couldn't… this isn't Stevie." Barbara dabbed her mouth with a napkin. "This baby looks like Joe. You must be mistaken. You are my only living child."

"The opportune word in that sentence is 'living.' Mom, I know about Stevie. There is no reason for you to lie." Suzie looked down at her plate in defeat. Then slowly lifted her head and gazed out the window at the home of Grace and Mr. Mercy. With tender resolve she continued. "Mr. Vanderpool told me about him. Why don't you talk to me about him? He was a beautiful little boy wasn't he?"

Barbara's silence was stoic. Susanna feared that Stevie would have to remain in the closet. She reached her hand across the table and stroked Barbara's hand to comfort her.

"Yes, yes, he was." Barbara said, holding the picture near her heart as tears started streaming down her face. "He died… so unexpectedly. The night before he died he was full of life." Barbara cupped the picture in both of her hands, gazing at the picture with grief clouding her gaze. "We were inseparable. I loved him more than life itself. I tried to commit suicide several times after his death. Then I got pregnant with you and resigned myself to living."

"Do you want to talk about him? I really want to know more about my older brother. I think his death changed you and I am trying hard to understand."

"Your father demanded that I stop talking about him as soon as he found out I was pregnant with you. He bought me a chest that I could put in my closet. He told me that I had to get rid of his toys and the pictures of him. He told me I was obsessed. Whatever didn't fit in that chest had to go." Barbara broke down in sobs. "How do you let go of love without breaking your heart? I know your dad was trying to help me, but when he took all of the toys and the pictures...."

Suzie moved around the table to embrace her mother. "I had no idea, Mom. It doesn't seem like Dad would do something like that."

"He has changed so much since you were born. You softened his heart. You were always a daddy's girl. Stevie was my little boy and you were daddy's little girl. You softened your daddy's heart and Stevie softened mine. When Stevie died my heart turned hard."

"I am so sorry he died, Mom. I am so sorry. You can talk to me about him, though. I won't tell Dad."

Barbara looked up, with mascara streaming down the river of tears. "Are you sure you want to know? Do you promise you won't tell your father?"

"Yes, I promise. Come, let's sit on the couch. It will be more comfortable for us." Suzie gently pulled Barbara out of the chair and led her to the living room.

Barbara sat down on the couch and hung her head with the weight of memories. "Well, I didn't think I could get pregnant. Your dad and I had tried for several years with no luck. Then we went on a vacation to Hawaii. When I returned I felt different. I was so exhausted all of the time. You know me, I have always been energetic and driven."

"If I know anything about you, it is that," Suzie said.

"I couldn't understand what was happening. I was sick in the mornings. Even though I vomited every single morning, I was gaining weight. I went to the doctor thinking I had some fatal disease." Barbara grabbed a tissue from the coffee table and proceeded to smudge the mascara all over her cheeks. A smile of remembrance crossed her face. "He told me I was pregnant."

"When Stevie was born I was crazy about him. He was so adorable. He had those beautiful green eyes, wavy blonde hair and perfect skin tone. I used to call him 'my angel' because he was perfect. The picture that you took was two days before he turned six months old. He died when he was six months old… to the day." Barbara shivered with the memory. "I still remember going in to wake him up and feeling his stiff, cold body."

Barbara dabbed her eyes with a tissue. "His death changed me. I used to be a lot like you. I didn't care whether or not my house was clean." Barbara glanced around the living room with understanding. "After Stevie died, a lady at my church said that he had probably died due to germs. She said my house was a mess." Barbara's shoulders shook with sorrow and tears rushed down her cheeks. "I felt so guilty. I almost lost my mind. Then I got pregnant with you." Barbara squeezed Suzie's hand. "When you were born I made two promises to myself: I would keep a perfect house and I would never walk into a "house of condemnation" again." Barbara lifted her chin in haughty defiance. "That is what I called that church. The old ladies in that church were there only to criticize and condemn others. They weren't there to worship God."

"Why didn't you ever talk about him?" Suzie asked.

"Your father told me that I could never talk about him. I was obsessed with Stevie. When you were born he told me to stop. Remember that day you found the chest?" Barbara looked at Susanna with fear in her eyes.

"Yes, recently I had a flashback of that day. It was horrible. I would never beat a child like that."

"I know, I know. I am so sorry I did that. I hope you can begin to understand my reaction that day. That chest was all I had left of Stevie. If you would have ruined that, then I wouldn't have had anything to remember him by," Barbara sighed. "There were days I would just sit and cry. I missed him so much. I tried to love you like I loved him. I don't think I did a very good job of loving you." Barbara squeezed the hand of Suzie and gave her a wistful glance. "I was scared that if I loved you, you might die too."

"I had no idea when I was a little girl what significance that chest held for you. I thought it was a treasure chest," Suzie said.

"I didn't let anyone touch it, not even your father. That is why my bedroom door was always locked as soon as you knew how to walk. I was distracted the day you found the chest. It was Stevie's sixth birthday. My mind was twisted with memories of him. I am so sorry I beat you like that. It was horrible. If I could change anything in my life, it would be my reaction that day. I lost so much… on that day." Barbara gazed out the window, with regret clouding her vision.

"Daddy told me that we were going to leave you. I am sorry to say this, but I was happy that we were leaving you. You told me I was a horrible little girl." Suzie said gently.

"Did I say that?" Barbara looked at Suzie with a tortured gaze.

"Yes, that is what you said in the flashback," Suzie said with a bit of confusion. "I didn't remember anything though… until the flashback, so I'm not really sure."

"I probably did say something to that effect." Barbara shook her head. "You weren't a horrible little girl. You were just curious."

Barbara reached out and took Suzie's hand in hers. "Will you please forgive me for beating you that day?"

"Yes, of course I will Mother." Suzie opened her arms and tenderly embraced her sobbing mother with arms of Grace and Mercy.

GRIEF CAN LAST A LIFETIME

SUZIE COULDN'T HAVE SAID HOW LONG IT WAS THAT her mother cried in her embrace. The thought occurred to her that this was the first time in her mother's life that she had been allowed to grieve Stevie. She didn't think she had a right to tell her mother to stop crying tears that had been caged inside of her for more than thirty years.

She was a bit upset with her father for the way he had handled Stevie's death. She didn't know if her mother had been aware that he was considering divorce. She had always thought her father was the warm-hearted individual in their family. After talking with Barbara, she was beginning to sway the other way.

She needed to know more. She looked at the clock and realized that time had evaporated quickly. In another hour, she would need to go pick up Michael.

"Mom, can I ask you something?"

Barbara nodded her head. "Yes, ask anything you want."

"Did Daddy take me away for a few days after you beat me?"

"Yes, he did. I begged him to come back. I threatened suicide again. I know it wasn't the right way to handle the matter, but back then it seemed as if it was my only option. First, I lost Stevie. If I lost my husband and my daughter, I would have nothing left."

"When we were away you talked quite a bit on the phone right?"

"Yes, we talked every day."

"What things did you discuss?" Suzie asked.

"At first he was furious with me and threatened to file charges against me for abuse. Then he calmed down a bit and told me he was going to commit me to a psychiatric ward. I don't blame him. I think I was crazy." Barbara stopped to blow her nose in a tissue. "Once we both calmed down, we came up with a solution. Your father offered to give up his position in the bank after he bought the boutique. I was to become the bread winner, and he was to take care of you. It was a sacrifice for him but he never once complained. He adored you, and he enjoyed every minute with you. I wish I could say that I enjoyed every minute in the boutique."

"Did you miss staying home with me?" Suzie asked.

Barbara looked at Suzie with pain etched in her wrinkles. "God, yes. I missed you. I may not have been a good mother but you were not a horrible child; you were a delight."

"Really? You thought I was a delight?" Suzie could not believe this.

"Yes, I know I fussed at you about not being clean enough, but I didn't want you to get sick or die like your older brother. You always had such a natural beauty, and you were so dainty. I would just sit and watch you sometimes."

"I think I remember you doing that. It made me nervous. I thought you were watching me because you thought I was going to make a mess," Suzie said.

Barbara let a slight chuckle escape. "I think I was a bit OCD. I am sorry for all the times I over-reacted."

"That is okay. I know now why you acted the way you did, and I am amazed about one thing." Suzie said with a twinkle in her eye.

"What is that?" Barbara asked.

"You said you used to be like me. I don't know how you did it." Suzie smiled.

"Did what?" Barbara asked.

"I don't know how you became OCD. I couldn't fathom how to be that." Suzie said hoping to lighten up the atmosphere.

Barbara's eyes clouded with remorse. "It was a battle every day. I changed who I was because of those nasty old women in the church." Barbara sighed deeply. "The sad thing is that in changing who I was created to be, I think I lost the most important part of me. I lost some of my ability to love and maybe even my will to live." Barbara paused for a moment. "I became cold-hearted through the death of Stevie. It is hard to love someone else when you don't love who you are. I failed miserably in loving you."

"Oh, Mom. Don't say that. You did as best as you could. I will be honest though; I didn't feel like you loved me, and you never said you did. However, you did keep a clean house, and if you thought that was important for my safety you get an A+ in that department." Suzie said with hope that Barbara could smile.

"I can't get those years back, Suzie. I would like to see if I can work on developing a loving relationship with you now." Barbara hesitated and reached for Suzie's hand with shaking fingers. "If you are open to that, if not, I completely understand."

"Of course I am open to that. I would love to spend more time with you and talk with you, and maybe you could teach me how to become OCD." Suzie looked at Barbara with tenderness.

Barbara looked at Suzie with love. "Can we put the OCD task on the back burner? I have been trying to teach you how to be OCD all of your life." Barbara sighed with exasperation. "To be honest, it has been a futile venture." Barbara started laughing and then Suzie started laughing. Pretty soon mother and daughter were laughing so hard they could barely catch their breath.

Suzie glanced at the clock, dismayed that the time with her mother had passed so quickly. It was time to pick up Michael from school.

"Mom, I have to go pick up Michael from school. I have enjoyed this morning. Could we please talk again soon?"

"Yes, I would love that." Barbara paused for a moment, glancing at the picture of Stevie. "If there is any way you would trust me to spend time with your children, I would like to try to become a grandmother to them. I know you would have to be close by … in case I lost control."

Suzie looked at Barbara as if she had lost her mind. "Of course you can spend time with them. I am not worried that you would lose control either."

"Would you mind if I kept this picture of Stevie? I only have one other picture of him." Barbara asked, holding the picture with trembling fingers.

"I meant it when I said I was giving it back to you. It is yours, Mom. It wasn't mine to begin with."

"Thank you, and thank you for one more thing." Barbara said getting up from the couch and grabbing her purse to leave.

Suzie couldn't fathom what else Barbara could be grateful for, the coffee had not been that good. "What's that?" Suzie asked as she got up from the couch.

"Thank you for calling me 'Mother.' You have no idea how I detested being called 'Barbara.'"

"Oh, yes I do. I hate being called 'Susanna.' Most of my friends call me 'Suzie.' You and Joe are the only ones who have called me 'Susanna.' So from now on, you are 'Mom,' and I am 'Suzie.' Is that a deal?" Suzie put her hand on her hip in a show of mock indignation.

"Okay, Suzie. Now I had better get going so you can pick up Michael from school. Why don't you keep the rest of the coffee cake? You can give the plate back next time we meet."

Suzie glanced toward the clock. "Yes and I need to hurry, or I will be late."

The two women parted ways having entered the meeting as Barbara and Susanna and leaving as mother and daughter.

THE PRAYERS OF MR. MERCY

SUZIE JUMPED IN HER CAR AND SPED OFF TO GO PICK up Michael. As she drove she reflected on the morning. She could not fathom, in her wildest dreams, that Barbara would ever ask for forgiveness. She had never seen her mother cry before this morning. There was so much more she wanted to know about her mother. She suspected this was just the first step on a long journey of emotional and spiritual healing for her mother. She hoped that she could be a part of this journey with her mother. Who knew? Maybe they would even start loving each other.

Suzie picked up Michael from school and drove straight to Grace and Mr. Mercy's house. Michael literally flew up the porch steps just as Jacob was coming out the front door with a trash bag. A head on collision between the two was averted at the last minute with Jacob making a quick step to the side.

Suzie skipped up the steps with a smile, as wide as the sky, crossing her lips.

"How did it go?" Jacob asked, putting the trash bag down on the porch beside him.

"Wonderful! I couldn't have wished for anything more. She asked forgiveness for how she treated me, Jacob. She has never once said she was sorry in the past."

"Did you forgive her?" Jacob asked with concern.

"Yes, of course I did. She shared so much with me. Things which had been hidden… for so long. I think I am beginning to understand her." Suzie walked over to the porch swing and sat down, motioning for Jacob to sit beside her. "You know it is kind of funny, the more I seek to understand her, the more my pain dissipates. I went into the meeting this morning with every intention of confronting my mother and somehow the axis turned. When I said goodbye to her, all I could think about was the pain she had gone through. To lose a child must be a horrible thing to go through."

"Wow, I am so impressed with how you handled this challenge. The amazing thing about forgiveness is that it is a gift. It is not like any other gift; it is a gift which always gives back. As you learn to forgive, you loosen the roots of bitterness from your own heart and you can love more freely," Jacob said.

"You know I think you are right about that. I feel as if a weight has been lifted from my shoulders. My mother has had such a negative impact on my life and I never had the courage to confront her. I had assumed that if I did confront her that she would just become more vicious in her attacks." Suzie paused to look at a cricket crossing the porch floor. "She has been so horrible to me all of my life but I don't believe she meant to hurt me. In her twisted reality she was protecting me with her criticism, rejection, and her sterile environment. I really believe that God was involved in this confrontation. It had a supernatural quality to it. I prayed a lot about this and I did one other thing I have never done before." Suzie looked up and gazed straight into Jacob's eyes. "I claimed a verse from the Bible and prayed that verse over this situation before I walked into it."

"What verse was that?" Jacob asked, a gentle smile caressing his kind face.

"Ephesians 4:32, "Be kind to one another, tenderhearted, forgiving one another, even as God, in Christ, forgave you." Suzie was beaming.

Jacob started laughing. "You are amazing. You fulfilled the Word of God this morning. You have broken down strongholds that the devil has erected to separate your mother from love."

"So this wasn't really about me, was it?" Suzie asked.

"In a way, it was. God loves you deeply Suzie and when you hurt, He feels the pain because you have Christ in your heart. You are good though. Your mother, on the other hand, appears to have stopped believing in God after Stevie died."

"If you had two sheep and one was nestled in the hay, safely in your barn, with enough food to last several days. While the other one was on the edge of the cliff, with wind and hail slashing its hide into shreds, and you were the shepherd, which one would you be more concerned about?"

"The one on the cliff of course," Suzie exclaimed. "But I don't feel like I am nestled safely in a barn with enough food to last several days. I barely have enough food for the week."

Jacob busted out in laughter. "If you could only see yourself through God's eyes, you would see it differently. You have just been given the opportunity to learn the power of God's Word. In the Bible, Mark 4:4 says; "Man shall not live on bread alone, but on every word that comes from the mouth of God.'"

Suzie furrowed her brow. "I don't understand."

Jacob paused for a moment. "Let me see if I can explain it to you in a way you will understand. You believe in heaven, right?"

Suzie nodded her head. "Yes, I believe in heaven."

"You believe that Jesus is the Son of God. You believe that He died on a cross to cover our sins with His blood. Believing this is necessary to reach God, right?"

"Yes, I do believe that," Suzie responded.

"So you believe there is a mortal life and an immortal life right?"

"Yes, I believe I will live on this earth until my earthly purpose has been achieved, then I will die and go to heaven," Suzie said.

"So how long do you expect to live on earth?" Jacob asked.

"I would like to live till I am eighty or ninety years old," Suzie said.

"What things are you going to do to ensure you live that long?" Jacob asked.

"I will eat healthy. I used to exercise but I don't have time anymore. I don't drink, smoke or do drugs," Suzie said.

"The first thing you said that you were going to do was to eat healthy food, is that right?"

"Yes," Suzie replied.

"That is for your mortal life. How long do you expect to live in eternity?" Jacob asked, grinning at Suzie.

"Well, that is a bit of a silly question. I will live forever," Suzie responded.

"When you consume God's word, as you did for this meeting, you are feeding the part in your mortal body that is immortal. You have connected with God in a deeper way because you have chosen to let His light and His word guide your path. When you did this you not only fed your own soul but lured your mother back from the cliff of bitterness and unforgiveness."

Suzie paused to contemplate. "Wow, how come every time I am with you I feel challenged and affirmed at the same time? You have given me a lot to think about Jacob. I appreciate your wisdom."

"Thank you for allowing me to share my wisdom and my faith with you. So many have shut the doors of their heart to words of faith." Jacob gently took the hand of Suzie. "Why don't we go inside? I think Grace is making lunch for us."

"She didn't need to do that. Taking care of my boys is enough. I need to ask her how much she charges for babysitting. I don't want to take advantage of her generosity and kindness."

Jacob looked at Suzie and chuckled. "She won't take a penny. Taking care of children is her calling in life. It is her passion. She has been lost without little feet pattering through the hallways. I am so grateful that you have shared your children with my parents. They have the sparkle back in their eyes now."

"Well, then maybe I can do something else for her." Suzie paused to contemplate what she could do and realized that Grace didn't need any help.

Jacob smiled. "I have been trying to repay the love I have received from Grace and Mr. Mercy all of my life and it has been a futile venture. Every time I think I have slipped in a kindness that they did not notice, they outdo me. I have finally learned that they are the greatest example of the unconditional love of God and I have just learned to accept their love; no payback needed."

Suzie sighed, "Well, I am still going to try."

As Jacob and Suzie crossed the threshold Jonathan started jumping up and down. "Yay! Mommy is home. I can go get Mr. Mercy now." He bounded up the stairs with pure joy and knocked on a door.

Suzie looked at Jacob with curiosity. She saw Mr. Mercy coming down the steps, Jonathan pulling on him with impatience. "Honey, don't pull too hard. You may make Mr. Mercy trip and fall."

"He been pwaying for you all this time and I wanted to play ball." Jonathan said with angst.

Suzie looked at Mr. Mercy and noted that he had been crying. She crossed the living room in silence and stood in front of Mr. Mercy. "Thank you. Thank you so much." Then she crumbled into the waiting embrace of Mr. Mercy, dissolving into tears; letting all of the bitterness, anger and hurt flow out of her that had been caged in her heart since the moment she was born.

Mr. Mercy held her gently and whispered in her ear. "You are deeply loved, sweet child of God."

THE HEAVEN'S REJOICE

THERE WAS AN ELECTRICITY IN THE ATMOSPHERE; A current of joy sparkled as Grace and Mr. Mercy entered the heavenly realm.

Hope was so excited she was bouncing up and down. "She did it! She did it! She forgave her mother."

Grace entered the meeting with a heart full of gratitude. "If not for God's mercy, we may have lost them both." Mercy crept in looking war-torn. "The prayers of Mr. Mercy were relentless on behalf of Suzie. There was no way that the devil had a chance. Suzie did everything right. She prayed, she stood on God's word, she didn't take offense when Barbara insulted her. Most important of all, she forgave. I thought it was too quick and may be superficial but when Mr. Mercy was embracing her, he felt all of the roots of bitterness being torn off of her heart. She has gained the belt of truth and has used the sword of the Spirit, God's Word, effectively. She has shattered strongholds and is blocking the effect of generational curses so her children will not stumble."

"She is a mighty woman of God. Yet her heart is still exposed to attacks of the evil one. She has not learned the lessons of the breast-plate." Faith said with sincerity.

"But she hasn't really sinned. I mean she hasn't murdered anyone or committed adultery. In fact, she hasn't even lied." Hope spoke her piece, hoping to spare Suzie.

Faith looked at Hope with a gaze that silenced her. "I know her thoughts. She has murdered Megan a thousand times over in her thoughts. 'All have sinned and fall short of the glory of God.' She is no different than anyone else. She is just highly favored by God."

"How can we, who are entwined with the righteous and holy God tempt her?" Mr. Mercy asked, his wrinkles creased with worry.

"We are unable to tempt her. I can guarantee that the spirits who are subject to the evil one already have a plan to target her heart and lead her into temptation," Faith said.

"Oh, this makes me want to cry. If they are successful then Suzie will suffer more heartache. Hasn't she had enough heartache?" Hope pleaded.

"If we are watchful and she is relying on the Word of God for guidance, the temptation will not render heartache. Instead, she will gain the breastplate of righteousness." Faith said, her eyes ablaze with determination.

REGROUPING

DECEIT WAS EAGER TO FIND OUT HOW THE MEETING had gone between Barbara and Susanna. He was in desperate need of some good news. Fear had just sent a report back that Africa was looking for missionaries to come minister to the wretched humans. All the wickedness that had been wrought could be for nothing with one evangelistic missionary. Missionaries were beyond annoying.

Deceit called a meeting for the clan of evil. They came in with heads hung low.

"Well, I am ready to hear about the blood bath between Barbara and Susanna." Deceit rubbed his claw like hands together. "Who wants to start?"

Not a peep of sound entered the room.

"May I remind you that Susanna was intending to slay the idol of Barbara's dead son? That couldn't have gone well for her could it?" Deceit hovered over the quivering form of Despair.

Despair became engrossed in biting her nails. "No, sir, it should not have gone well at all."

Deceit had a sinking feeling. He spun around to look at Bitterness. "You had your roots around the heart of Barbara since that nasty little baby died, right?"

Bitterness lumbered forward, his twisted trunk bent in defeat. "Yes, sir. I did. I had her hating God for the death of that child. I turned her into a cold perfectionist."

Rejection slithered to the center of the chamber. "I enticed Barbara to insult Susanna right after Susanna had given her a compliment." Rejection twirled his tail around to scratch his forehead, as if somewhat confused. "Something about her being able to make a coffee cake because it was so simple."

Envy started bouncing up and down. "I lured Barbara into going on and on about her new hire. She said she was thinking about grooming her for management. That should have irritated Susanna because Barbara has never given *her* a word of praise."

"Yes, yes, you are right about that," Deceit said.

Despair skipped to center stage. "I brought to the forefront of Susanna's mind the memory of that horrible beating she suffered as a child."

"Well, then what happened?" Deceit said, pacing with impatience.

"Susanna forgave Barbara." Despair whispered, her greasy head hung in defeat.

"What? Speak up a little louder. I don't think I heard you right." Deceit said perplexed.

"Susanna forgave Barbara for the beating."

"She did what?!" Deceit screamed.

"She forgave her mother for the beating, the coldness, and the perfectionism." Despair screamed in exasperation.

"Why on earth would she forgive that wretched woman?" Deceit said, his voice quivering with rage.

"Because she is beginning to understand her," Despair muttered.

"That is nonsense. Absolute nonsense. We have been present in Barbara's heart since Stevie died and there is no logic or understanding to us," Deceit said. "How can child abuse ever be understood?"

"Couldn't tell you sir, don't understand those humans myself," Despair muttered.

MONEY PROBLEMS

THE DAY WAS A BLUR OF ACTIVITY AND JOY. SUZIE FELT as if a huge burden was lifted off of her shoulders. She was so excited to start the process of understanding and loving a mother who had always been off limits to her.

She tucked the children into bed and then remembered the envelope her mother had given to her from her father. She felt a bit jaded now when thinking about her father. He seemed to have been a bit harsh when her mother was grieving the loss of Stevie. He was still her father though, and she loved him. She didn't want him to become the villain in this story. Sometimes in life everyone is a victim and life itself can be villainous.

She opened the envelope and saw a check for $5,000.00. She was so grateful. That would help her for a few months at least. But what would she do when that ran out? She really needed to find a job. There were so many things she needed to consider. If she worked, who would take care of the children? She knew that Grace and Mr. Mercy would be delighted to babysit but she didn't want to take advantage of them. It was one thing to have children come over every now and then but an entirely different thing for them to be there every day. Plus, they were elderly and although still quite active, they needed to take care of themselves.

It had been a bit of time since she had heard from Joe. She needed to know what the divorce agreement said and then she could decide what kind of job she could do. Calling Joe was not something she wanted to do. Confronting her mother had turned out well but confronting her ex-husband may not have the same outcome. Somehow tearing down an idol of a dead brother seemed like a piece of cake next to confronting a man who had idolized his mistress over two years.

Her mind was a whirl of conflict when the phone rang. She rushed to pick it up, silently praying that this phone call would provide some answers to the nagging questions that cluttered her mind.

"Hello?" Suzie asked, a bit breathless from the effort of rushing.

"Hello, Susanna. This is Joe."

"Yes, I know, Joe. I used to be married to you and, believe it or not, I do recognize your voice," Suzie replied.

"I believe that our lawyers have come to a collective decision about the divorce agreement. I was wondering if your attorney had contacted you?" Joe asked.

"No, he hasn't." Suzie said, momentarily thinking that Mr. Vanderpool had deceived her into thinking he actually gave a flip.

"Well, I think you should call him. If you agree to the terms we could avoid going to court. It would be in your best interest to agree because if we went to court I promise you one thing: You will lose custody of the children."

"Joe, I don't know why you think it is necessary to use threats. I know you don't love me anymore. Your threats don't hurt," Suzie responded. "So would you please stop being a jerk?"

"Just call your attorney so we can get this behind us." Joe said as he slammed down the phone.

Suzie paused and took a deep breath. She wasn't shaking, she didn't feel as if her heart had dropped to the pit of her stomach, she didn't feel anything. She had heard it said that the opposite of love is not hate, it is indifference. Maybe she was at the end of her rope with Joe and the tethers of heartache had been cut.

Nonetheless, this may not be about the loss of her marriage but more importantly the potential loss of custody. She needed to call Mr. Vanderpool and she had better do it first thing in the morning.

The night closed in on the house and the land of dreams gently stole the worry, fear, and trepidation that were closing in on the mind of Suzie.

HELP WANTED

SUZIE WOKE UP THE NEXT MORNING WITH ONE THING on her mind: She needed to talk with Mr. Vanderpool. She rushed Michael and Sarah off to school, then challenged Jonathan to build the tallest building he possibly could with his Legos.

Suzie didn't think the outcome of the divorce was going to be in her favor. She had a gut feeling about it. After the phone call with Joe last night, her priority was to retain custody of the children. She didn't care about the child support. She would figure out a way to pay the bills.

She dialed the number of Mr. Vanderpool. Her fingers were shaking as she punched the numbers.

"Hello? This is the law office of Mr. Vanderpool, Angie speaking." Angie's voice was as smooth as velvet.

"Hello Angie. This is Susanna Whatley. Is Mr. Vanderpool available?" Suzie asked.

"No, he is in court this morning," Angie replied.

"Could you please tell him to call me? My ex-husband, Joe Whatley, has said that if I don't sign the divorce agreement immediately he would pursue custody of my children." Suzie said, with an edge of panic in her voice.

"I told you he is in court this morning and I don't know when he will be finished." Angie's voice had lost the velvet sheen and taken on a nasty tone.

Suzie paused for a moment. She knew that Angie didn't like her because, in her deluded mind, Suzie was a threat for the affection of her boss. There was only one way to handle this woman and that was to play into her delusion.

"Well, I guess I will have to clear my schedule for tomorrow morning and come in to see Mr. Vanderpool to get this straightened out." Suzie's tone became seductive in nature, intending to incite Angie to react.

"He will be in court tomorrow morning, too. This is a big case he is working on and he has given it top priority. I am sure he will get around to your divorce agreement when he has the time." Angie spit the words out with venom.

"I understand," Suzie responded. "I think my dad may have his personal cell phone number. I will just call him and see if he can meet me for coffee, that is… before he goes into court. He said to call him if I ever needed anything." Suzie's tone beckoned for Angie to become jealous.

"Oh, my. I can't believe it. He just walked in the office. Let me see if I can get him on the phone." Angie's voice turned upbeat and pleasant.

"You lying bitch," Suzie muttered.

There was some muted conversation and then Mr. Vanderpool got on the phone.

"Susanna Whatley! How are you dear?" Mr. Vanderpool exclaimed.

"To be honest, I am a bit concerned. Joe called me last night and said that an agreement had been made regarding my divorce. He threatened to go for custody if I didn't sign the papers immediately. I guess I was expecting you to keep me informed." Suzie held her temper in check.

"I received them this morning and just now had a chance to review them. Do you want the good news or the bad news first?"

"Bad news first please," Suzie responded.

"Well, they are using the joint custody clause to petition for a measly amount of child support. They are only willing to pay $600.00 per month for your children, which is a small fraction of their income. They are demanding joint custody also," Mr. Vanderpool stated. "The good news is that they are only wanting the children every weekend."

"Every weekend?" Suzie asked.

"Yes, don't worry. I imagine once the novelty of having children every weekend wears off, that will diminish."

"Okay, I will agree to those terms. I don't want to risk losing custody of my children. Can I come in tomorrow morning and sign the papers?" Suzie asked.

"Yes, you can; and I will represent you in court so that you don't have to make an additional drive."

"Thank you, Mr. Vanderpool."

"You are welcome, dear," Mr. Vanderpool stated.

Suzie started calculating her monthly expenses. She would come up short of funds in a span of four months. She really needed to find a job. She got the newspaper from the front porch. She looked through the "help wanted" ads. She didn't see anything for nursing. She imagined most of the ads were listed on a website. She didn't have a computer. Joe had taken that when he moved out. She couldn't afford to buy a computer without having an income.

Maybe she could stop by a library and use a computer there. If she could leave Jonathan at Grace and Mr. Mercy's house tomorrow morning, she could sign the divorce papers and then locate a library in the same town. She felt better now that she had a plan. She hoped that her need for babysitting was not becoming a burden for her gracious neighbors.

She checked on Jonathan. "Hey there buddy. You are really building a big building aren't you?" Suzie was amazed at the detail that Jonathan had put into his Lego construction.

She looked at the clock and realized that the morning had slipped away. She needed to head out the door to check with Grace and Mr. Mercy to see if they could watch Jonathan tomorrow. "Honey, do you want to put your Legos up now or would you rather show your work to Michael before you put them away?"

"Wait to show Michael." Jonathan said, furrowing his brow with concentration as he put the last Lego into place. "I done now." Jonathan looked up at his mother and reached for his coat, giving the monstrosity of creativity one last critical glance as he walked out the door.

Suzie crossed the country road and pulled into the yard of Grace and Mr. Mercy. The arrangements for Jonathan were made quickly.

Jacob was the only one who would be home but he was happy to look after Jonathan. He even offered to take him first thing in the morning so that Suzie could travel to Mr. Vanderpool's office straight from the school. Suzie breathed a sigh of relief. She could not believe how blessed she was to have such good neighbors. She left to go pick up Michael with a heart full of gratitude.

As soon as Michael walked in the front door, Jonathan showed him his masterpiece. Michael was quite impressed and played with Jonathan for the rest of the afternoon.

Sarah even stopped to admire the handiwork of Jonathan before she went into her bedroom to do her homework.

The evening crawled slowly into nighttime with the usual routine of homework, dinner, baths, and nighttime reading, along with bedtime prayers.

The next morning, Suzie beat the alarm clock in her race to start the day. She paused for a moment to whisper a prayer of praise. It wasn't that her life was so grand. She was still worried about how she was going to pay her bills but she had so much to be thankful for. Her healthy children, her dad's generosity, her precious neighbors, and a mother whom she was eager to begin loving.

When she got up she had a smile on her face. She threw on her bathrobe and peeked in on the children. She was always amused by the tangled web of limbs they wove during the night, and amazed that they could sleep through it.

Sarah had always had a difficult time with sleeping alone. When she was little she would crawl in beside Suzie. Soon she transferred to her brother's bed. Three little ones in a queen size bed could be utter chaos some nights, but Suzie was reluctant to pressure Sarah to sleep in her own room. She knew that Sarah would naturally mature to a point in her life where sleeping with her brothers would be uncomfortable. When that time came, she would move into her bedroom.

Suzie wanted to make a special breakfast for the children today. She hated it when all they had for breakfast was cereal or a granola bar. She had bought a biscuit mix and she had some eggs and bacon. She would make breakfast sandwiches.

She was frying the bacon when she felt two little arms circling her waist. "Smells yummy Mommy." Michael said as he looked up, closing his eyes and puckering his lips for an expected kiss.

"You are such a sweetie." Suzie bent down and planted a kiss on his lips. "If I get the plates out, would you mind setting the table?"

"I'm still sleepy, Mommy. I'm going back to bed." Michael said as he turned around and shuffled back to his bedroom.

Suzie started giggling. "Well, at least he noticed that I was making something yummy and gave me some sugars this morning. Two out of three ain't bad." She opened up the cabinet and set the table while the bacon was sizzling in the frying pan.

The children came stumbling into the kitchen with sleep still clouding their minds. Suzie paused for a moment to put Jonathan in the booster seat and then went back to cooking. It took only a few minutes to finish the sandwiches. She piled them on a plate and set them in the middle of the table. Three hands shot out and eight sandwiches were quickly reduced to five on the serving plate.

As they were eating, Suzie thought it may be wise to apprise Jonathan of her morning plans. "Jonathan, after we are done eating, I will be taking you over to spend some time with Jacob."

Michael stopped in the middle of a bite, put his sandwich down on his plate and squealed. "What?!! How come Jonathan gets to go play ball and I have to go to school?"

"Jonathan is not old enough to go to school, Michael; and I have some errands to run this morning."

Jonathan's eyes lit up as he started shoveling his breakfast sandwich in his mouth.

"That's not fair." Michael got up from the table, strode to the living room and started to kick Jonathan's latest Lego creation into pieces.

Suzie hurried to the living room and pulled Michael away from the destruction. "Honey, you have to realize I am not trying to be mean. I know you like playing ball with Jacob and Mr. Mercy. It is not that I love Jonathan more than you. I have to start looking for a job today, okay?" Suzie picked up Michael and set him in her lap. "I have to go to the library to get on the internet. I don't think I can do that with Jonathan along." Suzie paused for a moment, contemplating how to handle Michael's jealousy. "How about if I buy you a new ball so that you can play ball at our house from now on?"

"Yeah, but I want to pick it out." Michael said, his lower lip jutting out.

"Okay, after I pick you up from school we will swing by Walmart and get you a new ball."

"Alright, Mommy," Michael said.

"Now I want you to go and apologize to Jonathan for destroying some of his work. That wasn't the right way to handle this situation," Suzie said. "And when you come home from shopping with me for a new ball, I want you to help rebuild this with him."

"I will have other things to do, Mommy," Michael countered.

"I think the other things can wait. Now go say you're sorry and get ready for school." Suzie stated with an authoritative tone which defied conflict.

WHERE IS GOD?

AFTER BREAKFAST WAS FINISHED, SUZIE DROVE Jonathan across the country road to stay with Jacob. Suzie wondered if Jacob worked or if he was just going to stay with Grace and Mr. Mercy. He seemed as if he would be good helper but he was young, he needed to have a career. However, if he had a career he wouldn't be able to babysit for her this morning so maybe she should stop judging him.

After Suzie dropped Michael and Sarah off at school, she quickly traversed the country roads until she finally hit the highway. She felt uneasy. She didn't know what Joe and Megan were up to but the threat of a custody battle seemed like a real possibility.

Rain started falling gently on her windshield. Spring was knocking at the door of winter and slowly slipping in with bursts of color. Suzie was glad; she loved spring. The smell of freshly mown grass, the joy of seeds turning into blossoms, and her favorite part of spring-butterflies. The rain started pelting her windshield as if to punish her for being happy.

Suzie heard something strange. It seemed as if something was following her. It sounded like a helicopter but it was close, very close. As cars whizzed past her, a few honked at her. What was wrong? Should she stop? Maybe if she slowed down, the noise would disappear. She pulled off on the shoulder and tried going slower. The sound mimicked her; it slowed down but it didn't disappear. She would have to stop on the shoulder.

The rain was becoming torrential and she had no umbrella in her car. She didn't even know if she had an umbrella at home. She had put extra effort into her makeup and hair this morning because she wanted to make Angie jealous. Now she would look like a drowned rat.

She had to check to see what was wrong with her car, there was no two ways about it. She stopped on the shoulder and the sound disappeared. She would have to get out in this horrible rain and see what was going on. Maybe she had driven over something and it had attached to her car.

She dissolved into tears as the rain continued to bombard her windshield. She transferred every bit of mascara that had been on her lashes to her cheeks. She looked in the rearview mirror and realized that she was a mess. She had nothing in her car to wipe the mascara from her cheeks. Oh well, maybe the rain would be good for something.

She took a deep breath, opened the car door and slithered out into the rain. There was nothing wrong with the driver's side. She edged around the back of the car and looked at the right side of the car. She found the culprit; it was the back right tire. That tire was flat as a pancake and was starting to shred.

She looked back at the highway, making sure there was no oncoming traffic, then scampered back to the driver's seat. She sat in her car, sobbing. She became angry at God. "Where are you God? I am trying so hard to survive and if you are God almighty then why did you allow my tire to become flat? This could have serious consequences. I could lose custody of my children and if I don't get a job; I could lose my house and I could be homeless in six months. All because of a stupid flat tire that you allowed."

Somewhere in the back of her mind a bit of logic started creeping in her thoughts. It wasn't God's fault that her tire was flat and her tirade against God was not fixing it.

She had a flat tire and she thought that Joe had always had a spare in the trunk. What good would that do her? She didn't know the first thing about changing a flat and even if she did know, there was no way she could change it in this rain. If someone was nice enough to stop and offer aid, they wouldn't be able to change it either. The shoulder of the highway she was on dropped off into a deep ravine.

There was no way she could call anyone. She didn't have a cell phone. Joe had said she didn't need one if she stayed at home with the kids.

Her only option was to keep going until she reached the town where Mr. Vanderpool was and see if there was a tire shop there.

She plugged along, trying to remember if she had seen a tire store in that town. The traffic was speeding past her and more than one car honked at her. "Why on earth are they honking at me? Do they honestly think I am unaware of the flat and that I am driving on the shoulder at 20 miles an hour for the heck of it?" Suzie spit the words out with disgust.

She kept crawling along the side of the road, praying that driving on a flat tire was not going to mess up her car. She thought she was about a mile from town, surely driving on a flat tire for that distance should do no harm. She really didn't want to spend what little money she had on a tire. Maybe the tire store could put the spare on her car and they wouldn't have to charge her for a new tire.

She entered the town searching with anxiety for a tire shop. It might serve her well if she asked someone. She pulled into a cozy little restaurant on the corner of a block. The name fit the restaurant: Kozy Korner.

A busty blonde greeted her at the door and asked her how many was in her party.

"Oh, I am not here to eat. I was just wondering if I could use your restroom to freshen up? I was caught out in the rain because I had a flat tire."

"Well, of course you can use our restroom. I am so sorry about the tire. Do you have a spare? My husband could try his hand at changing the tire if you have a spare."

"Oh my goodness, that would be so nice of you. I think I have a spare," Suzie said. "Could you please point me to the restroom?"

"Yes, it is in the back, to the right of the kitchen."

"Thank you so much." Suzie said, scurrying to the back of the café, trying hard not to let anyone see her face.

Suzie scrubbed her face till it was blush red in the bathroom and came out with a smile on her face. "Thank you so much for letting me use your restroom."

"Certainly. My husband is the chef here and he is changing into other clothes to see if he can help you. You're lucky, you arrived at the very time we have a lull in business. In between our breakfast and lunch crowd is the only time we can even sit down. By the way, my name is Dolly." Dolly extended her hand in friendship.

Suzie shook her hand and gave her a warm smile. "My name is Suzie. Thank you so much for helping me out."

"No problem, hon." Dolly turned to look at her husband, a broad shouldered man, who looked like he had eaten plenty of meals which he had also served to others.

"Hello, my name is Jack. Let's see what happened to your tire. Do you have a spare?" Jack said as he held open the restaurant door for Suzie to venture outside into the rain.

"I think I do. I think my ex-husband kept a spare in the trunk but I couldn't say for sure." Suzie shielded her eyes from the rain with her hand. She felt someone tugging on her coat. She turned around and saw Dolly holding out an umbrella for her. "Oh my goodness, how sweet, I didn't think to bring an umbrella along."

"I figured that was the case. We have a few extra in the restaurant. Customers forget them when the sun starts shining. You can keep this if you need it," Dolly said.

"Oh, thank you so much." Suzie gave Dolly a hug and took the umbrella.

"Jack and I just always try to do what we think Jesus would do. Living life through Jesus makes us so happy." Dolly said as she gave Suzie a warm smile.

"I believe in Jesus too. It is so nice to find someone who lives like Jesus would," Suzie said.

"We wouldn't have it any other way," Dolly said.

"I think I am going to need some keys if I am to look in the trunk for a spare." Jack said, winking at Dolly.

"Oh, my, I guess that would help, wouldn't it?" Suzie said, with a giggle, as she handed Jack the keys.

Jack opened the trunk and a frown crossed his kind face. "There is no spare in this trunk, Ma'am."

Suzie's heart sank. She knew when she was married that Joe had always kept a spare in the trunk. Would he be so heartless that he even took that?

"Is there a tire shop in this town?" Suzie asked, on the verge of breaking down into tears again.

"Yes. You go up one block, make a right then go five blocks and make a left. The street is called Murphy Drive." Jack said, glancing with a worried look towards the restaurant. "I would show you but as you can see people are already trickling into the restaurant. If I don't start cooking, there may be a riot." Jack said smiling.

"Oh, no, you have done plenty to help me. Thank you so much." Suzie flashed him a tear worn smile and quickly slid in her driver's seat, putting the umbrella on the seat beside her.

She inched her disabled car along the streets until she got to the tire shop. She stepped out of her car, ducked under the umbrella and walked briskly to the door.

The shop was small with just a few dirty chairs to sit on. There was only one chair left for Suzie. She lumbered across the room and plopped down in the chair, running a hand through her rain-soaked head of hair.

One by one, the chairs became empty and soon Suzie was the only one left in the shop. The guy behind the counter had oil and grease oozing from his pores. He seemed young, maybe in his early 20's. Pleasant looking, even with the smear of oil on his cheeks. "Ma'am would you mind telling me what brought you here today?"

"I have a right rear tire which is flat and I don't have a spare. I guess my ex-husband took that when he moved out."

"If you could give me the keys. I will look at it." He walked around the counter and held out his hand.

Suzie smiled at the young man and gave him the keys.

It was a few minutes before the young man walked back in. Shaking his head, he said. "I am sorry Ma'am that tire is way beyond fixing. I have a new one in back that I can put on. It will cost you around eighty to ninety dollars."

"Okay." Suzie looked beside her. She hadn't brought her purse in the store. It must be in her car. "Hold on a minute. I need to find my purse. Is my car unlocked?"

"Yes, Ma'am but I didn't see no purse in there." The young man said with furrowed brow.

"Surely I didn't leave it at home." Suzie said as she strode toward her car. The feeling of horror and shame settled in the pit of her stomach. Suzie looked through every square inch of her car. Her purse was not in the car.

Suzie trudged through the tire shop and entered the store with her head hanging low. "I don't know what to do." Suzie said as the tears started flowing down her cheeks. "I don't normally leave without my purse. It's just that the last few weeks have been so difficult." She paused to take the Kleenex that the young man handed to her. "My husband left me for another woman. I found out that I had an older brother who died as an infant. I was on my way to sign my divorce papers and my ex said if I didn't sign them right away he would go after custody." She paused to look at her watch. "I am running out of time. I won't make it to the lawyer's office now. I will be lucky if I can make it to pick my son up from kindergarten." She started sobbing uncontrollably, plopping down into a chair by the counter.

The young man came around the counter and laid his hand on Suzie's shoulder. "Listen, I know that times can be hard for a single mother. My mom left my dad when I was six. He had beaten her and he was starting to beat us. She had to work two jobs to make ends meet but she raised five good kids."

"Five?" Suzie looked up at the young man with wide eyes.

"Yes, five."

"Wow, I only have three and I haven't even started working one job much less two. She must have been amazing."

"She was. She has passed on but her legacy lives on through her children." The young man paused for a moment and then a look of peace settled the furrows in his brow. "How about if I put on a new tire for you and you come back and pay for it when you find your purse?"

"You would do that for me?" Suzie asked.

"Yes, I would. By the way, my name is Chris." The young man said as he extended his hand.

Suzie shook his hand. "Thank you, Chris, thank you so much."

The tire was on in minutes. The young man watched as Suzie drove away with a smile and a wave. Then he reached into his back pocket, took out his wallet and extracted eighty-six dollars which he put into the till.

"Here's to you, Mom." He said, looking up to the heavens, as one lone tear slid down his oily cheek.

THE COMPANY PICNIC

SUZIE HAD TO RUSH TO PICK UP MICHAEL FROM school. She was so disappointed in how this morning had turned out. She was terrified that Joe would follow through with a custody battle. She still didn't have a job. Desperation was starting to seep into her thoughts.

It wasn't only desperation though; it was a bit of disappointment that she had not been able to put Angie in her place. She was sure that there was something going on between Angie and Mr. Vanderpool and she was certain that something wasn't good.

Since the day she met Megan, she had a feeling about these kind of things. Her mind skipped back to that horrible day.

Joe had asked her to come to a company picnic. She was excited. It would be fun. The children hadn't yet had a picnic. Although Jonathan was just a baby, Michael and Sarah would enjoy the frivolity of a picnic. Suzie was hoping there would be a playground for them to explore.

The day was perfect. The sun hopscotched in-between clouds. The breeze was like a tender caress which brushed across the skin with cool but not cold air. Flowers were breaking free from the cage of soil to explode into blossoms of color.

Suzie made wonderful chicken salad sandwiches, cut up some watermelon, and added some cupcakes to share with others. Suzie tried hard to present the food in an appealing manner.

The minute they drove into the parking lot, Joe became tense. Suzie couldn't understand it. There was no reason to be tense, this was a day of fun. She ignored his demeanor and the occasional insult.

As soon as they parked, Joe grabbed the children and started off with them. Suzie was shocked. Joe had spent little time with the children lately. He had treated Suzie and his children as if they were an inconvenience. Suzie shook her head. Her husband was becoming an enigma.

She grabbed the picnic basket full of food and lumbered clumsily to the picnic area. She set her mind to laying out her food in the best possible light and noticed that very few people were at the picnic table. She raised her head and gazed over the horizon. There seemed to be a cluster of men close to the woods. They appeared to be talking to someone who was clearly the focus of their attention.

Where was Joe? Furthermore, where were her children? Suzie's heart started racing. She didn't see them anywhere. She quickly left her food and started frantically pacing around the park.

As she became more frantic, she noticed that someone was breaking free of the cluster of men. As she looked closer she saw a woman, who sauntered like a tigress, walking towards her. The woman had a golden tan, emerald green eyes, and coal black hair which fell in perfect waves down her back. She was wearing a low cut, skin tight, turquoise top and a black miniskirt. Her perfectly toned legs were set in black stilettoes that were rimmed with rhinestones.

Suzie looked down at her jeans and gingham top and realized that either she had underdressed or the other lady had clearly overdressed for the occasion. Suzie bit her lip. She felt a sense of doom descending over her. The feeling grew more ominous with each step the woman took.

The space between the woman and Suzie closed in. The other woman reached out her perfectly manicured hand, saying in a sultry voice. "Hello, I am Megan, Joe's boss. You must be his wife. Am I right?"

Suzie shook her hand, smiling broadly. "Yes, I am his wife. So glad to meet you. I hope you liked the fragrance I picked out for your birthday present." She had been very proud of herself for even buying a gift for Megan, much less one which was valuable.

"Hmmm, I am trying to remember which one that was. I got so many presents that day… it was hard to keep them sorted in my mind."

"It was White Diamonds." Suzie said with a twang of envy. Joe had forgotten to buy her a gift on her recent birthday.

"Oh, yes… Now I remember. I told Joe it was my favorite fragrance because it came from him." Megan looked over her shoulder to ensure that no one else was near. "Can I tell you a secret?"

Suzie nodded, captured by the spell of Megan's beauty.

"I never wear American fragrances. I only wear ones from France." Megan whispered as she subtly drew closer to Suzie. "The way they make the perfumes in France is just so delicate. They are meticulous. You can smell the difference. But please don't tell Joe anything about our secret." Megan winked at Suzie.

"You can count on me to keep my mouth shut on that one." Suzie said, wondering why in heaven's name she was being so nice to Megan. Megan had clearly given her an underhanded insult. She looked up and saw Joe walking towards them, with the children following.

"I go to Paris at least once a year to buy clothes, shoes and other items." Megan said flipping her hair over her shoulder and targeting Joe with her gaze. She turned to him. He was walking straight to her, as if they were magnets.

Suzie had had enough by now and she was preparing to spar with Megan. "You go to Paris to buy clothes, shoes and other items?" Suzie asked, as she frantically picked up her pace, trying to slide ahead of Megan in the race to get to Joe.

"Yes, that is the only place I shop."

"You do it only once a year?" Suzie asked, catching up to Megan.

"Well, sometimes twice a year."

"Funny, you have to fly all the way to Paris for the same kind of items I buy at Walmart, except I don't go once a year. I go weekly." Suzie said, flipping her golden hair over her shoulder, trying her best to sway her hips with seduction. She pulled ahead of Megan, interrupting the gaze of lust that was lasciviously dancing between Megan and Joe.

She stayed glued to Joe's side for the rest of the picnic, trying hard to be an obstacle between Joe and Megan. Suzie gained a new understanding that day…

If you want to strut your stuff and act like you are a diva, it is damn hard in tennis shoes.

The bright yellow of a school bus yanked Suzie away from the closet of painful memories. As she looked in the rear-view mirror, the outline of Michael's school was diminishing.

"Oh, shit." She said, whipping her car around on the country road. "First I leave my purse at home and then I shoot past the school as if I didn't have a child to pick up."

That got her started thinking. She had promised Michael he would be able to go shopping for a ball but she didn't have her purse with her so she would have to go home to get that. What would Jacob think if he saw her pulling in to her driveway and then not come over to pick Jonathan up?

She didn't think he would care. He seemed to really like hanging out with her boys and it wouldn't take that long to pop back home, pick up her purse, and then quickly drive to Walmart.

She drove into the horseshoe of the school parking lot. Michael was one of a few students who was nervously waiting to be picked up by parents.

Michael jumped in the car. "Mom, why did you drive past the school?"

"I am sorry Michael. I was distracted. How was your day?"

"Good. Are we going to get a ball today?"

"Yes, we will but I got to drive by home first and pick up my purse. I accidentally left it at home this morning," Suzie said as she turned onto the country road leading back to her home.

"And you wonder why I left my shoes at home." Michael muttered, as he rolled his eyes.

Suzie smiled as she reached over to tousle Michael's hair. "I guess we are just two peas in a pod. Is school going okay for you?"

"Yea, kinda." Michael paused for a moment. "There is just one thing that bothers me."

"What is that?"

"Well, there is this one boy, named Johnny, and he always does just a bit better than me. He always gets better grades than me and he is just a bit faster than me in races. I am really good at most things, but he is better," Michael frowned.

"Do you work hard to try to beat him?" Suzie asked, driving down the country road to her house. "You know if someone is always just a touch ahead of you in most things and you are striving to beat them, something really wonderful happens."

Michael turned to look at his mother with expectation. "Will I finally beat him?"

"I don't know if you will beat him or not but you will try harder than you would have if he wasn't beating you all the time. You don't have a hard time beating anyone else in your class do you?"

"Nah, not really. I usually do really good on my homework and tests. When we run races I am right behind Johnny but no one is even close to me," Michael said. His brows furrowed as he was trying to figure out what was so wonderful about Johnny winning.

"The wonderful thing that is happening to you, Michael, is that you are being challenged. Johnny is actually pushing you to be better than you would be if he wasn't in your class."

"I still don't like him, Mommy. I don't like losing or being second place."

"I know you don't honey; you don't have to like him but you may learn to appreciate him."

"What does that mean?" Michael looked at Suzie.

"It means that you don't view him with anger because you realize that he is actually making you a better person. Do you understand what I am saying?"

"Kind of." Michael said as they were pulling in the driveway. "Hey Mom, since we are already home could I just go over to see Jacob? I really don't want a new ball."

"Well, we can see if Jacob would allow that. He has been watching Jonathan all morning and I don't know if he...." Suzie stopped as Michael jetted out of the parked car and sprinted across the road to the house of Grace and Mercy.

Suzie ran inside her house to freshen up a bit and then went to pick up her boys. Her heart grew warm as she drove into the front yard. The house looked more like home each time she approached it. Someone had painted a lovely trim on the house. If it snowed again, it was beautiful enough that it could be on the front of a Christmas card.

As Suzie approached the porch, she reflected on what a difference these neighbors had made in her life. They had accepted her with no trepidation. When she was around them she felt confident of one thing and that was that God loved her. She thanked God for these neighbors and also for her friends: Hope, Faith and Joy. She was blessed in so many ways.

Suzie felt bad that she had been so angry at God over the flat tire but there was a lot at stake in her life right now. She really needed a job because she was running out of money and the thought that a custody battle could ensue terrified her.

Grace opened the door before Suzie could knock. "Hello dear. How was your morning?"

Suzie paused for a moment and then with a sigh said. "Well, it wasn't what I expected. I got a flat tire on the way to my lawyer's office."

"Oh, no. I am so sorry." Grace said as she looked at Suzie's car with a puzzled look. "Which tire was it?"

"The back right rear." Suzie said as she plopped down on the porch swing. "I am exhausted and I didn't even get anything done."

Grace chuckled, as she peered over the porch railing. "Well, it looks like you got your tire fixed at least."

"Yes, I ran across the sweetest bunch of people ever." Suzie smiled at Grace. "I knew I needed to find a tire shop but I am not familiar with that town, so I stopped in at a restaurant. There was a Christian couple that owned the restaurant and the man told me where the tire shop was." Suzie paused a minute to wipe a stray hair out of her eyes. "It was pouring down rain and his sweet wife gave me an extra umbrella they had."

"That was nice. That was very nice." Grace nodded in agreement, as she sat beside Suzie on the swing.

"When I got to the tire shop, I found out that I had left my purse at home. I had no way of paying the young kid who was running the shop," Suzie paused. "I didn't know what to do."

"Oh my, I left my purse at home just a few days ago, it is such an easy thing to overlook. Especially when you have little ones underfoot." Grace said with an understanding smile.

"I was so upset at that tire shop I actually broke down and cried. The young man at the shop was so nice to me. Apparently, he had been raised by a single mother too and he put a new tire on the car. Then he told me to come back and pay when I found my purse."

"It is so wonderful when people allow the love of God to flow through them," Grace said.

"Yes, it is." Suzie grasped the hand of Grace and gave it a squeeze. "You have been so nice to let Jonathan and Michael come over to play. I really appreciate you."

Grace waved her hands in a dismissive gesture. "We have been delighted to have them. They are so well behaved."

"Well, they are when they are over here at least." Suzie winked at Grace. "Not so much when we cross the road to home. I better go get them. Thank you again for watching them." Suzie gave Grace a hug and gathered her boys to take them across the road to home.

THE PROBLEM WITH ANGIE

AS THE EVENING MATURED, SUZIE'S THOUGHTS became tortured with fear. Would Joe and Megan really fight for custody? If they did, would she have any chance of hanging on to her children? Was her lawyer good enough to fight for her if it came to that? If Joe and Megan took her children, how would she survive? Her mind became a frenzy of scattered and disjointed thoughts.

After the kids were in bed, Suzie went to her bedroom, sat on the bed and dissolved into a mess of tears. After crying for a good ten minutes she wiped her eyes and saw her Bible on her nightstand. Maybe she could open it up and see if God had something to say on this.

Suzie reached for her Bible with trembling fingers. The Bible fell open to Psalms 37. Suzie started reading out loud. "Don't worry about the wicked, or envy those who do wrong. For like grass, they soon fade away. Like spring flowers, they soon wither. Trust in the Lord and do good. Then you will live safely in the land and prosper.

Take delight in the Lord and He will give you your heart's desires. Commit everything you do to the Lord. Trust Him and He will help you. He will make your innocence radiate like the dawn and the justice of your cause will shine like the noonday sun. Be still in the presence of the Lord and wait patiently for Him to act."

Suzie closed the Bible and took a deep breath as she bowed her head in prayer.

"Wow, if my brain was a target you just hit the bull's eye, God. I will admit I am terrified that there will be a trial to determine the custody of my children. Heavenly Father, I know that you gave these children to me. I also believe that they are supposed to be trained in your Word and your ways. I would be so grateful if I could be the one to continue to raise these children. I can't imagine that it would be good for them to be raised by Joe and Megan but I acknowledge that you are God and you know best. I pray that your will be done and I want you to know that I trust you with my children, as well as myself."

Suzie fell asleep immediately. She slept peacefully throughout the night as her mind skipped through the land of dreams.

In the morning, she revisited Psalms 37. She wanted to pick out one verse to write on a card so that she could meditate on it during the day. She picked the third verse: "Trust in the Lord and do good. Then you will live safely in the land and prosper."

So, what could she do that would be good?

She needed to go to Dr. Vanderpool's office to sign the divorce decree. Then she needed to stop by the tire store and pay her bill. Neither of those activities would she categorize as being good. They were more obligations, not exactly doing a good deed.

"God, I am at a loss. I am going to trust you to help me do good." Suzie whispered as she made her way to wake up her children.

The hustle and bustle of the morning routine slyly stole the worry of doing good from Suzie's mind. It wasn't till she got back home and started to prepare for her errands that she became aware of a gentle nudging, urging her to be a blessing to someone else. Suzie knew that she could have dropped Jonathan off again at her neighbor's house. For some reason, on this morning, she felt as if he should be with her.

Maybe she should call Mr Vanderpool's office and apologize for not making it yesterday.

It seemed as if her attitude towards Angie had changed overnight. The change had occurred the minute she had walked onto the porch of Grace and Mr. Mercy's house. She had felt the condemnation slipping away and an eerie sense of sadness replacing it. If Angie was sinning with Mr. Vanderpool, she was to be pitied and prayed for, not hated and condemned.

Suzie dialed her attorney's number.

"Mr. Vanderpool's office. Angie speaking. May I help you?"

"Hello Angie, this is Susanna Whatley. I want to apologize for not making it in yesterday to sign my divorce decree. I had a flat tire. I hope that I can make it in today. Would today be too late?" Suzie said a silent prayer that Joe had not pushed the issue of a custody battle.

"Let me check. Could I put you on a brief hold?" Angie asked.

"Yes, of course." Suzie responded, still praying.

"It looks like the hearing was delayed because Joe could not make it to the courthouse either. He had two flat tires apparently," Angie said.

"Thank God for tire gremlins." Suzie took a deep breath and let it out in a giggle. "So, this morning would be soon enough right?"

"I would suggest you make it no later than this morning. These cases can turn on a dime and become very nasty custody battles. The sooner we get this divorce decree signed, the better off you will be." Angie's tone turned ominous.

"Okay, I will be on my way in a second. Thank you so much Angie."

"Sure thing." Angie responded as she hung up the phone.

Suzie rushed out the door with Jonathan in her arms and her purse on her shoulder. She needed to go to the lawyer's office and then she needed to pay for her tire. A fleeting thought that she should be more focused on doing good, than doing tasks, flew through her mind.

"I don't know what you want me to do that is good, God. It is hard for me to understand how I can do good for anyone else. I am barely hanging on myself but I am going to trust you to show me what good I can do." Suzie muttered the prayer as she was backing out of her driveway.

As Suzie was pulling up to the door of Mr. Vanderpool's office Jonathan started fussing.

"Oh, great. I should have left him at the neighbor's I guess."

By the time she arrived at the office of her attorney, Jonathan was screeching with discontent. The hysterical crying continued until Suzie entered the office. The minute Suzie entered, Angie got up from behind her desk and held her arms open for Jonathan. Jonathan stopped screeching, looked up at his mother and then held his arms out for Angie to grab him.

Suzie was speechless as Jonathan's pouty lips went topsy turvy and ended up in a smile.

Angie looked at Jonathan with adoration and picked up the phone to notify Mr Vanderpool that "Jonathan's Mom" was here to sign the papers.

Suzie couldn't make any sense out of this. Angie had seemed to hate her and Jonathan on the previous visit. What had changed?

Her mind was a whirl of confusion as she walked into the office of Mr. Vanderpool. She had just closed his door when a horrible thought came slashing through her reality.

Joe had threatened a custody battle. She had just been stupid enough to hand Jonathan over to a woman who had previously detested her. What if she had lost custody without knowing it and Jonathan was now being handed over to Joe and Megan? Her heart dropped down to her stomach and a sense of panic stole her breath.

Mr. Vanderpool looked up from the papers he was reading and gave Suzie a heartwarming smile.

"Hello there, Suzie. I guess we are almost done with this, aren't we?"

"I hope so. I am sorry that I could not come yesterday. I hope that Joe didn't use my tardiness as an excuse to file for custody." Suzie said, desperately trying to hold the looming sense of panic in check.

Mr. Vanderpool chuckled. "Must have been a day for flat tires yesterday. We plan on meeting at the courthouse this afternoon to get the divorce finalized." Mr. Vanderpool put a pen in his desk drawer. "Did you bring your son with you today?"

"Yes." Suzie answered thinking it was strange and a bit disturbing that Mr. Vanderpool would be asking about Jonathan.

"How did Angie respond to your son?"

"She seemed to welcome him." Suzie responded, wondering where in God's name, this conversation was going. Was this some sinister plot to take Jonathan from her and give him to Angie?

"Good." Mr. Vanderpool put the papers on his desk in a neat pile beside him. "Angie lost her little boy and husband several years back. A drunk driver killed them. Her husband was taking the little boy on a drive because he was teething and he wouldn't stop crying." Mr. Vanderpool looked out the window as if he were gazing back in time. "It was midnight when they left for their drive. It took one hour and one poor drunken fool for my granddaughters' world to shatter." Mr. Vanderpool returned his gaze to rest on Suzie's face. "Angie is my granddaughter."

"Angie's grief took her to the brink of suicide." Mr. Vanderpool shook his head. "She couldn't forgive herself for asking her husband to take her baby on that drive."

"After the accident, she moved in with her grandmother and I. Her grandmother died a few months after she joined us. She lost almost everyone she loved within the span of a year. I am the only one close to her that is still alive. She has become very protective of me since all of this happened."

"Oh my goodness. I don't blame her. I am so sorry for her loss." Suzie responded, trying to keep her tears in check.

"She hasn't dated anyone since but that doesn't bother me. What disturbs me is that she couldn't bear to be around little children anymore. I know she was cold to your son initially but I talked with her about this and she said she would change."

"I would say by the looks of this morning she has changed. She was very welcoming to Jonathan; and Jonathan responded without any hesitation." Suzie said nodding her head.

"Good... Good," Mr. Vanderpool said. "Angie is not meant to be a receptionist. She used to be a daycare director and the children adored her but after the accident... well, she just couldn't."

"I understand," Suzie said.

"She got fired from her position as director of the daycare. They said she was emotionally unstable." Mr Vanderpool shook his head and slyly wiped a tear from his cheek. "I thought she handled it as well as could be expected. Emotionally unstable... my ass." Mr. Vanderpool said as his wrinkles creviced into lines of grief.

"Anyhow, that is why I am still working." Mr. Vanderpool said, rearranging a pile of papers on his desk. "She needed something to distract her, so I kept my practice open and hired her as a receptionist. I was hoping she would go back to working with children but it has been two years... and until today she couldn't even hold another child," Mr Vanderpool frowned. "To be honest with you, I would like to retire."

"It must be horrible to lose a child and to lose a husband also... I can't imagine. I know my mother had a difficult time dealing with the loss of her son but she still had my dad." Suzie dropped her head to hide a lone tear which was caressing her cheek.

"It was good that you brought Jonathan back today. I know Angie can be very cold at times and to expose your son to that possibility took guts."

Suzie lifted her head. "You know; I don't think I can take credit for that. I believe the credit belongs to God. I asked God this morning to show me where I could do good. I felt a gentle nudge to bring Jonathan with me." Suzie swiped a stray hair from her face and caught the tear in the crossfire. "It is interesting that he wasn't with me yesterday when I had the flat tire. I believe that God is just as concerned about your granddaughter as you are, sir."

"I hope so. When my wife died, Angie was such a comfort. It would be easy for me to allow things to continue as they have been. I know the joy that Angie has when she works with children. When she is ready, I intend to get her started in her own childcare center. I will make sure it is state of the art and the best daycare center in this town." Mr. Vanderpool said with his mouth set in grim determination.

"I am sure you will, sir." Suzie said with a smile.

Mr. Vanderpool shook his head as if to force the memories of grief out of his mind. "Well, if you will sign these papers. I will file them at the courthouse this afternoon." Mr. Vanderpool said as he stood up to hand her the papers and a pen.

Suzie took the pen and signed her name. A million thoughts went through her mind as she was signing.

This is the start of a life I never chose. I will miss Joe so much. I wonder if this marriage to Megan will last? What will the children do without a father in the home? How on earth do so many single mothers survive? I don't know who I am if I am not Joe's wife.

As she handed the papers back to Mr. Vanderpool a voice inside her head spoke. "*I am your Father and your King, your eternal bridegroom is my Son. Do not be dismayed we will never leave you.*" A sense of peace settled into the heart and mind of Suzie as she let this truth sink deep into her soul.

As Suzie walked out of the office into the reception area she was surprised that Jonathan did not come running to her. She looked at Angie and saw him nestled in her arms fast asleep. Angie was looking at him with adoration in her eyes and for just a moment Suzie's heart skipped a beat.

To see another woman love her son gave rise to a conflict of emotions. She was happy that he could elicit love from others but a bit upset that she may have competition for his affection. She would have to deal with this conflict when Megan started assuming her rightful role as his stepmom.

"Thank you so much for watching him, Angie." Suzie said as she circled around the desk and held out her hands to take Jonathan.

"Could I please take him down to your car and put him in the car seat?" Angie asked, her eyes pleading. "He just fell asleep."

"Of course, you can," Suzie said. "Don't you need a coat? It is pretty cold out there."

"No, I don't want to take the chance on waking him up." Angie whispered as she slowly got up from her chair and started walking towards the door.

Suzie looked at Mr. Vanderpool, who was standing in the doorway of his office with a huge grin on his face. Suzie shrugged her shoulders as Mr. Vanderpool threw her a wink. Suzie turned, following Angie out the door.

MERCY TRIUMPHS OVER JUDGEMENT

JONATHAN WAS TUCKED INTO HIS CAR SEAT WITH SUCH compassion that Angie didn't even wake him up. She gave him a kiss on his forehead and then slowly pulled out of the car and turned to look at Suzie.

"Thank you… thank you…" Angie started crying and Suzie quickly embraced her with love and acceptance.

"I know you lost your husband and your son but you didn't lose the love of your heavenly Father. God still loves you," Suzie whispered.

"Oh my God. How did you know I walked away from God?" Angie pulled out of the embrace of Suzie, staring at her with disbelief.

"Because I have been tempted to do the same through my divorce. It is in our darkest hours when we need Him most."

"Yes, but I didn't feel Him then. At first I cried out to God but I felt only emptiness," Angie sobbed. "I miss Him, but I feel like He abandoned me when I needed Him most."

"Sometimes grief can be such a dark valley that it difficult to see any light. God is the creator of light though, and He is the only one who can lead us to truth. He gave you your grandfather to love."

"My grandfather? He doesn't even know God. What would God have to do with him? He doesn't go to church. He doesn't pray or read his Bible. He's lost." Angie said wiping the tears from her face.

"That is exactly why you are living with him. Jesus didn't hang out with church people. He hung out with sinners. He taught in the Synagogues but He didn't even like the Pharisees or Sadducees. He pursued the lost." Suzie took her coat off and wrapped it around Angie, who was shivering.

"Angie, what I saw in that office was a man who has put all of his dreams on hold because he is dreaming for your future. You have a chance to give him a key to eternal life and you are missing the boat. He is concerned about your future in this life but I think you should be more concerned about His future *after* this life."

"You know what? I think you're right. I know without a doubt that my husband and my son are in heaven. I know I will meet them there someday. Although my grandfather is a good man, I know he can't get to heaven without the blood of Jesus covering his sins." Angie paused and took a deep breath. "I may just have a reason to live after all."

"You have more than one reason to live." Suzie pointed to the office of Mr. Vanderpool. "That sweet man has a wonderful future that he is planning for you. I think you two may need to have a heart to heart talk."

"You are an amazing woman of God." Angie said as she hugged Suzie.

"And you, my dear, are a sweet child of God." Suzie said as she returned the embrace and checked her watch. "I am sorry but I must jet off to pick up my other son from school. I will keep you in my prayers."

"Thank you and I will keep you in mine." Angie winked at Suzie and took off the coat to put it around Suzie's shoulders.

Suzie drove off with her heart bursting with joy. "Trust in the Lord and do good. I had no earthly idea that doing good could be so much fun, God."

Now to go to the tire store to pay her overdue bill. Suzie had made her mind up to pay Chris more than what he had quoted. To let her drive off without even paying a cent, was such a sweet act of mercy she wanted to make it worth his while.

She pulled into the lot and grabbed Jonathan. She didn't see Chris behind the counter but a gruff looking older man. There was no one in the shop other than her.

"Sir, I was in this shop the other day and unfortunately I didn't have my purse with me. The young man who put a new tire on my car allowed me to have an IOU. I believe I owe you some money." Suzie said as she retrieved her wallet from her purse.

"Ma'am, I check the balance every day and there is not one day that I have been short." The older man looked at her as if she were missing more than one marble in her brain.

"Sir, I can assure you that I owe Chris some money. I can show you the tire he put on my car. I promised him I would come back and pay him the money for that new tire and that is what I intend to do." Suzie said, with a flicker of anger rising in her breast.

"Ever since I hired that young man things have changed around here." The man shook his head. "I have more business than I have ever had when he is working. You are not the first person that has claimed that they have gotten a new tire for free. Yet, I am never shorted on the balance sheet." The older man wiped his sweaty brow. "When I am working, as you can see, no one comes into my store. They all wait until he is working. He says most of the people that come in are from his church. He keeps inviting me to go." The old man shook his head. "I don't think God would want a sinful man like me to attend church. I have so many skeletons in my closet, I could populate a whole graveyard." A low rumble of a chuckle shook his belly.

"Are you kidding me? You obviously don't know Jesus. A friend of mine just told me a story about two sheep. One was safe in the fold and the other was on a cliff being pelted by hail and wind. Guess which lamb the shepherd went after?"

"Well, Ma'am, I imagine the shepherd went after the one on the cliff."

"That is exactly right. If I know the Lord like I think I know him; I would say that He may have stationed Chris in this tire shop for one reason. That reason was to share His love with you." Suzie swung Jonathan to her other hip and continued. "Now I intend to pay for that tire sir. Could you please tell me how much it would be?"

"Nothing. Not a cent. It is obvious that it has already been paid for."

"Just like all those sins you have committed, sir. All you must do is believe that Jesus died on a cross for your sins. Your penalty has already been paid." Suzie paused to take a breath. "Are you sure I don't owe you anything for the tire?" Suzie asked.

"No, ma'am, I think you may have just convinced me to do what Chris has been telling me to do for… well… ever since I met the young man. If what you say is true, I may be able to spend eternity in heaven. That is much more precious and worthy than the price of a tire." The old man's face broke into a smile. "Furthermore, anytime you need a tire you can come to my shop and it will be on me."

"Wow. Thank you so much. You don't know what that means to me." Suzie said, her eyes moistening with tears of gratitude.

"You helped convince me to accept forgiveness from God and you want to pay me for a tire? Believe me, I am more indebted to you than you are to me." The old man said as he closed his till with a finality which defied argument.

Suzie's heart was about ready to explode into a fountain of joy. She was so excited. She had never helped someone accept Christ. This was a kind of joy she had never experienced. She scurried out the door of the tire shop, put Jonathan in his car seat and then raised her hands and jumping up and down screamed at the top of her lungs. "Yay God!" Suzie didn't care who saw her or what they thought of her. She had no idea that there could be this much fun in doing good.

Suzie was in the car and driving home when a thought occurred to her. *What was the last part of the verse she had meditated on*? She looked down on the passenger seat and saw the verse written on a recipe card. The verse said, "she should live in the land safely and prosper."

She hadn't been worried about anything other than her part, which was doing good. It appeared as if God was fulfilling His end of the bargain. Apparently flat tires would not be an issue for her anymore.

THE THEFT OF JOY

SUZIE WANTED TO SHARE THE EXPERIENCE SHE HAD just had with someone. She thought about calling her mother, Faith, Hope, or Joy. They would have been so good to talk with but she really yearned to talk with Jacob again. For some reason, even the thought of Jacob brought her a sense of peace.

Soon she had picked Michael up and they were all home again. She made the boys a light lunch and started to pick up the house. After lunch, the boys fell asleep on the couch. The educational channel on TV hummed in the background.

Suzie knew she should try to find a job somehow. Without a computer, it was difficult to know what was available much less apply for a job.

Suzie felt an ache for the simplicity of the past. She used to just check the "help wanted" ads in the newspaper, make a few phone calls, and then apply for the job. Computers made life so much more difficult in some ways.

Joe was an expert with computers. She could ask him anything about a computer and he could always provide a suitable answer. Suzie really missed him at times.

She needed to go into town again and stop by the library. Maybe Jonathan could stay at the neighbor's tomorrow and she could start looking for a job. Today though, she was going to make some cookies. As she reached up into the cabinet to grab the flour, her phone started ringing. Suzie quickly snatched the flour and then answered the phone.

"Hello?" Suzie asked.

"Hello, Susanna, this is Joe. My lawyer says that you signed the divorce. In the divorce decree, I get the kids every weekend. I want you to bring them over this weekend. Megan is eager to meet them."

Suzie's heart sank. "Joe, I don't even know where you live. Would it be possible for you to come pick them up? I don't have a job yet and I have to watch my expenses."

"I am giving you child support. Susanna. That child support is meant to be spent on the children. I think that driving them over to my house is not asking too much," Joe said.

"I haven't gotten any child support yet, Joe and the amount that you offered is not enough to allow me any waste. Three hundred dollars every two weeks barely pays for the necessities, Joe. I am sure that you and Megan don't have to worry about sticking to a budget, but that is my reality," Suzie pleaded.

"In the decree, it states that you are to drop them off and pick them up every weekend. I think we should follow the divorce decree. That way there will be no misunderstanding." Joe said, with a calm tone to his voice.

Suzie could have kicked herself for not going through the divorce decree with a fine-toothed comb before signing. “Alright, Joe. Just give me a second to grab a pencil and a piece of paper. I will need you to give me directions.”

“Seriously? You haven’t gotten a cell phone yet? My God, there are apps on a cell phone which can direct you to my home. Suzie, you need to modernize.” Joe said with disgust.

“Joe remember when we were married? I begged you for a cell phone. I asked you to teach me about the computer. You refused to let me have a cell phone because you said I didn’t need it and you were always too busy to teach me how to use a computer.” Suzie hung her head in shame. “I know… I feel as if I am not connecting with the modern age. I will try to do better but it will take me a few weeks to get that sorted out. In the meantime, could you please tell me how to get to your new home? I know the children miss you.” Suzie swallowed the lump that was growing in her throat. .

“Ok, well coming from your place you would turn left out of the driveway….” Joe continued to detail the route to his new home.

When the conversation was finished and Suzie had settled the phone into its cradle, she took a deep breath. Her mind was overrun by emotions; none of which were comforting.

She needed distraction. What was she doing before Joe called? The flour on the counter beckoned her.

Suzie whirled around and swung open the refrigerator. She grabbed two sticks of butter and threw them unwrapped into a mixing bowl. It was one thing to lose a husband to another woman but a far greater insult to have to share children with that same woman.

She searched through her cabinet and grabbed the sugar and brown sugar. After the sugar was measured, she slung it into the bowl. What on earth did Joe see in Megan?

The two eggs were cracked with such force the shells threatened to evaporate. Silicone and collagen were enough to lure a man from a good woman? The mixer began to vibrate as Suzie dissipated the butter into the sugar and eggs.

Suzie washed her hands and grabbed flour, baking soda, and salt; along with the sifter. She didn't know that Joe had wanted a successful career woman. She had always preferred the role of mother as opposed to being a career woman. She had thought Joe had been pleased with her skill as a mother. How absurd her assumptions had become.

She sifted the flour with such vigor that her top and face were covered with the fine silt of it. She could only imagine the mansion that Megan and Joe lived in. The mixer started again, slashing through every part of the dough, as thoughts of envy, bitterness, and despair trampled through the mind of Suzie.

She looked at the oven and realized she had forgotten to preheat it. As she turned the oven to 350 degrees, the evil entities in hell were collecting for yet another meeting.

THE TWISTED PATH OF EVIL

DECEIT WAS THE LAST TO ENTER THE CHAMBER OF Darkness on this occasion. He strode into the chamber with arrogance riding on the shoulders of his black cloak.

"I believe the reason for this meeting was to rejoice in the absolute end of Susanna Whatley. Who has the death certificate?" He pounced upon Despair, who was cowering in the corner.

"I am in her mind, sir. Right as we speak. I am covering her thoughts with my slime."

"Covering her thoughts?!! That means she is still alive! Why on earth have you not succeeded?"

The tree of Bitterness lumbered across the chamber and held Deceit in check. "Why don't you ask for the whole story? We have all tried our best to defeat this woman and she has thwarted our every intention."

Deceit swatted the limb of Bitterness off his chest and stood still for a moment, pondering what his next step should be.

"If you knew the whole story you may be able to plan a more efficient attack next time sir." Condemnation said, readjusting his judicial robe and straightening his collar.

"Hmmm, okay.. then someone had better start quickly." Deceit sat on a large boulder in the chamber.

"She had a meeting to sign her divorce decree and she got a flat tire on the way to the meeting," Despair whined. "She was really busted up about that flat tire. She was worried she would lose custody. She cried buckets of tears. She made such a mess of her makeup she had to go into a restaurant to wash her face."

"Good, good," Deceit interrupted. "So, now that she does not have custody of the children we can start pulling her into severe depression, right?" Deceit straightened out his cloak of evil then proceeded to check his to do list for the rest of the day. "Depression leads her into insanity and insanity into suicide. Simple pimple. Then we go after the children."

"Didn't happen like that, sir. Joe got two flat tires because God was present when a new addition was being added to Megan's house. The carpenters dropped a box of nails right in his driveway." Bitterness shivered as if a cold wind had blown through its limbs. "There was no custody battle."

Deceit started to slump.

"Yes, but she had left her purse at home. She had no way to pay for a new tire. You know how forgetful she is at times," Rejection hissed. "Tires can be very expensive and even more so when you don't have a way to pay for them." Rejection winked at Deceit.

"So, she got thrown into jail for a flat tire?" Deceit started to laugh. "That is a good one. A very good one. Good job fellow comrades.

Now I must fly off to Africa. Fear has just requested my presence there." Deceit started to stride, with exuberance, to the entrance.

Bitterness blocked the exit. "You said you wanted the whole story, didn't you?"

"Yes, I believe that is right but I also said I wanted it quickly. If Susanna is in jail because she didn't pay for a tire, then I can surmise she will not have custody of her children. Boom! Mission accomplished!" Deceit raised his arms in a victory salute.

Bitterness shook with agitation and kicked Rejection against the chamber walls. "She is not in jail. She got the tire for free."

Deceit retracted his victory salute. "What? No one gets a tire for free! People only get songs, books, movies for free. You know, the stuff that takes years of blood, sweat and tears to produce. Tires? Well, they cost some serious money."

"Not in this case, sir. The other side has a warrior working in a tire shop. He has "blessed" more than one person with a free tire. He grew up with a single mother and had mercy on Susanna. She got the tire for free." The limbs of Bitterness were drooping.

Deceit muddled about for a moment. "Susanna doesn't strike me as someone who takes charity. She would feel too guilty about that."

"You are right on that count, sir. She went back to the tire shop, insisting on payment and led the owner of the shop to accept Christ," Condemnation said.

The mention of Christ caused all hell to break loose in the chambers. The walls started crumbling. Despair screamed out with pain as the jagged rocks slashed through her skin. Envy was in complete chaos bouncing against the walls and others in the chamber. Bitterness lost all its bark. Rejection was molting out of season. The judicial robes of Condemnation became a shredded mess. Deceit was shaking with fear.

Upon this chaotic mess, Adultery came striding in. Her beautiful blonde curls, ample cleavage and long legs kicked a pathway for her to take center stage.

"I have no idea what happened here but I have been working on the mind of a doctor to leave his marriage. He just hasn't found the right nurse yet. If you know what I mean." Adultery looked down at the crumpled heap of Deceit with disdain. "I told you before. I got this one wrapped up." She flipped her hair over her shoulder and sashayed out the exit.

THE "OTHER" SIDE

As Suzie was pouring the chocolate chips into the cookie mixture she heard a knock on the back door. Suzie glanced at the door and dismissed the idea that anyone would be coming to visit her on this cold day. She bent over to grab the cookie sheets from the cabinet and another round of knocking sliced through the stillness of her kitchen. The last thing that Suzie wanted was company. She put a round of cookies on a cookie sheet and slid them into the oven. Another knock, this one a bit more persistent. Why couldn't some people just give up?

Suzie wiped her hands on a dish towel and stomped to the back door. She opened it just a crack and peaked out. "Who's there?"

"It's Jacob, ma'am."

Suzie swung the door wide open and threw her arms around Jacob. "My goodness, what are you doing out in the cold?"

"Well, if you want to know the truth, I was waiting for you to open the door. I didn't know if your kids were taking a nap or not, so

I didn't want to chance using the front door." Jacob whispered as he slipped inside the kitchen.

"Thank you. Just earlier I was wishing I could talk with you. Maybe if I close the door to the dining room they won't wake up." Suzie said as she tiptoed to the other end of the kitchen to close the door.

"I have so much to tell you." Suzie pulled a chair out from the kitchen table and motioned to Jacob. "Please sit down. You timed your arrival perfectly to be the royal taster of my cookies." Suzie winked at Jacob. "You sly devil, you."

"Thank God for my hidden powers of ESP. Those cookies are smelling delicious!" Jacob said with a smile, as he slid into the chair by the table. "So, what has happened and why are you all white like a ghost?"

Suzie stopped for a moment, looked down at her flour tinted shirt and realized that a layer of flour dust had transformed her into a ghost. "Oh blazes. I didn't mean for that to happen. I don't want to go wash it off because then I may wake up the boys. Do you mind?"

"No, not at all," Jacob said. "You look kind of cute as a ghost."

Suzie was surprised that Jacob said anything about her looks. He had never mentioned anything about her looks before.

"Thanks…I think. Remember a couple of days ago, when I got a flat tire?" Suzie asked as she took some cookies out of the oven, placing them on a cooling rack right under Jacob's nose.

Jacob nodded. "Yes, Grace had mentioned that to me."

"I was so irritated because I needed to get my divorce decree signed. I also had to go to the library to use their computer system, Joe took ours when he left. So, I was really put out over the flat tire."

Suzie grabbed a spatula and loosened the cookies, placing them on a plate.

"Well, because of that flat tire I was able to meet a very wonderful Christian couple at a restaurant who gave me directions to a tire shop in the town. When I got to the tire shop I got my tire changed. Then I realized I didn't have my purse to pay the young man who was running the shop. You know what he did?"

Jacob was entranced. "No, Grace didn't tell me what he did. Do you mind if I have a cookie?"

"Of course I don't mind if you have a cookie." Suzie replied, pushing the plate of cookies closer to Jacob. "That man at that tire shop *gave* me a free tire." Suzie took her apron to wipe the flour dust off her face. "Can you believe that?"

"Mmmm, No, ma'am. By the way these cookies are delicious." Jacob said as he licked his lips. "May I have another?"

"Here." Suzie pushed the plate of cookies toward Jacob. "Have as many as you want. I have plenty for my family. But that isn't all... there is much more to this story than just a free tire. Would you like some milk with those cookies?"

"Yes, I would love some milk," Jacob said. "These may even rank as being a slight bit better than Grace's cookies."

"Well, don't tell Grace that but you may want to mention that to Michael. He thought Grace's cookies beat mine when he first met Grace." Suzie poured a glass of milk for Jacob. "The best part of the story is what happened to Angie. Angie was my lawyer's receptionist. On the day that I had the flat tire I was going to try and make her angry because I had assumed that she was having an affair with my lawyer. They just seemed too close, you know? After what happened to my marriage I thought I had a right to interfere if someone else's marriage was about to implode. I was all pumped up with self-righteous indignation." Suzie stuck her nose up in the air in a haughty gesture. "I felt it was my Christian duty."

Jacob took a drink of milk. "I can understand your motivation for that Suzie. A lot of people react that way when they have been hurt by sin."

"Yes, well when I went to pick up Jonathan from Grace and Mercy all of that judgement and condemnation fell off me. I couldn't get it back either. It was just gone, like it had never even entered my mind. Then that evening I read Psalms 37 and I picked out a verse to memorize which said, 'Trust in the Lord and do good.'"

Suzie started putting more cookie dough on a cookie sheet. "How was I supposed to trust God? I had missed an appointment with my lawyer. I could be losing custody of my children. How come God always asks us to trust him when we are in a storm? Not only that but on top of trusting Him, I was to do good! Well, I didn't know what kind of good I could do. Just the day before I had wanted to strangle Angie with condemnation and now I felt sorry for her in some strange way." Suzie bent down to put the cookies in the oven, setting the timer for six minutes. "I had to schedule another appointment with my lawyer and I had a problem. I didn't know what to do with Jonathan."

Suzie sat down at the table and grabbed a cookie. "You were so nice to have babysat Jonathan the first day when I had the flat tire but I didn't want to ask you two days in a row."

"We wouldn't have minded one bit. Our house comes alive when your boys come over," Jacob responded.

"Thank you for that but I must admit something. I felt a nudging from the Holy Spirit to take Jonathan along. Well, when I got to the office of my attorney Angie took Jonathan and they bonded like glue. I couldn't believe it! When Angie saw Jonathan the first time, I could have sworn that she didn't like him or me one bit." Suzie took a bite of her cookie. "Well, when I started talking to Mr. Vanderpool, he gave me the scoop on Angie. She isn't his *lover*, she is his *granddaughter.* She lost both her husband and baby boy to a drunk driver. That is why she dismissed Jonathan to begin with. He must have reminded her of her son who died."

"That is tragic." Jacob said, fully captured by Suzie's story. "What happened next?"

"I signed my divorce papers and while I was in his office Mr. Vanderpool told me that he had wanted to set Angie up in her own child care center. You see after her husband and baby died, she got fired from the daycare center she had directed. He really wants to retire but can't until Angie rediscovers her passion for children." Suzie took another bite of a cookie. "You should have seen Jonathan when he was in Angie's arms. He melted like butter and fell asleep. I was just a teensy bit jealous of her magic with him." The timer went off. Suzie got up from the table and switched the cookie sheet from the bottom oven rack to the top. "I had no idea that she was a Christian. She told me she had fallen away from the Lord after the accident. Who could blame her? Then she said her grandfather didn't know the Lord."

Suzie set the timer for another six minutes. "Jacob to be honest with you, I would have reckoned that the grandfather was a Christian and that Angie was lost." Suzie shook her head. "Boy, was my radar wrong on that assumption. I encouraged Angie to share her faith with her grandfather. It is never too late to show someone the light of God's love through faith in Jesus Christ, right?"

"You got that right." Jacob said as he grabbed another cookie. "Did you ever pay for your tire?"

"No, I didn't. That was the craziest thing. I drove to the tire shop and the young man wasn't there. The owner of the tire shop was there. He refused to let me pay. He said he had not been shorted any money. He implied that Chris, the man who had given me the tire, must have paid for it out of his personal funds. Jacob, I talked to the owner about Jesus too. I think he may have accepted Christ because of Chris's influence and my witness." Suzie was smiling so much her cheeks hurt. "Jacob, I had never felt the amount of joy I felt walking out of that tire shop. To know that in some small way I may have increased the kingdom of God and someone new is destined for an eternity in heaven… well, it was just about to bust me wide open." Suzie started giggling. "All I had to do was trust in the Lord and do good and God took it from there."

Jacob was grinning from ear to ear. "Back when I was in seminary, you would have been a legend. We learned all kinds of formulas for preaching and evangelizing to bring other people to a belief in Christ. You did it, with no effort, by standing on the Word of God and going forth with confidence. You did more than good though." Jacob took a drink of milk.

"In James 2:13 the Word of God says, 'For judgment is without mercy to one who has shown no mercy. Mercy triumphs over judgment.' You approached Angie with grace and mercy, sensing that she needed compassion, not judgment. It was that spirit which opened the door for God to walk back into her life."

Suzie murmured, "'Mercy Triumphs over judgement.'"

"You know, I just remembered what I said to the man at the tire shop. He said that God wouldn't want him because he had too many skeletons in his closet. I told him that story that you told me about the sheep, inferring that he was the sheep out on the cliff. Somehow not judging him and instead having compassion on him may have crushed his resolve not to accept God's love. Mercy does indeed triumph over judgement."

Suzie's face transformed from one of joy to conflict. "You know when all of this happened I was so happy. Then I got a call from Joe, my ex-husband, and my joy disappeared."

"The devil has great timing, doesn't he? Every time we have a parade of praise for God there is someone waiting in the wings to rain on our parade." Jacob wiped his milk moustache off with a napkin. "Why does he still bother you? Do you still love him?"

"That is a good question." Suzie replied, her brows furrowed in introspection. "I don't think I love him anymore. I mean, I miss him because he was my husband but I don't love him like I used to." Suzie got up from the table and started wiping the counters with a dish rag. "The call today was about him having the kids." Suzie paused to brush a stray hair out of her eyes. "Jacob, I don't even know this woman he left me for. I met her once at a company picnic. She was a striking beauty but she had different values than I have. She said she went to Paris to buy all of her clothes." Suzie threw the dishrag in the sink. "I mean, who does that? That is crazy extravagant and to be honest, I am green with envy. I would love to go overseas; to Italy,

Paris, London…anywhere. Instead I am stuck with three kids, hardly any money, no job, and a house which always seems cluttered." Suzie said as she put the last of the cookie dough on the cookie sheet.

"Joe seems to have hit the lottery and I am sinking into a mire of poverty. I don't mean to complain but I wonder if there is any reward for doing good? There sure seems to be a tremendous pay out for a man who has left his family for another woman."

Jacob was speechless for a moment. "You are blatantly honest, Suzie. That is so refreshing. Many times, in Christian circles people hide behind the mask of positive thinking. I think that God wants us to have hope but he desires honesty first and foremost. If you read the Psalms you will know that David told it like it was and God called him a man after His own heart." Jacob pushed the plate of cookies aside and reached into his coat pocket for a Bible.

"I know I am skating on thin ice when I show you this verse because right now you want to see a materialistic reward. That is very understandable but can I show you the window that God may be looking through?" Jacob asked as he motioned for Suzie to sit down next to him.

Suzie nodded as she sat next to Jacob. "Yes, I guess that would be okay."

Jacob opened the Bible to 1 Peter and pointed out in the first chapter the verses of 6-7. "So be truly glad, there is wonderful joy ahead, even though you have to endure many trials for a little while. (7) These trials will show that your faith is genuine. It is being tested as fire tests and purifies gold-though your faith is far more precious than pure gold."

"Can I be honest with you Jacob?" Suzie said, her eyes filling with tears.

"Of course," Jacob said.

"I am still jealous of Megan. She got my husband, she gets to go to Paris and now she gets to play mommy to my three precious children without having one second of labor pain. It stinks." Suzie said as tears streamed down her cheeks.

Jacob reached across the table and held the hand of Suzie. With tenderness in his voice he spoke. "You don't know how long this marriage will last. Marriage that is sprouted from sin often grows the weed of divorce. Every bit of clothing that she wears will eventually wear out. Faith is eternal." Jacob gently wiped the tears from Suzie's face with a napkin and lifted her chin so he could look in her eyes. "You have three children. God only had one Son. Your children are going to be parented by someone else every weekend. I know that is difficult because you are one terrific mother. God gave up His Son to a family on earth for an entire lifetime, which is more than a weekend. Your children are going to their father's house and I believe that he still loves them am I right?"

"Yes, he loves them and they love him. I don't have a problem with them seeing Joe; it's just Megan." Suzie blew her nose in a napkin.

"God sent His one and only Son to earth to be crucified so that we would have no separation from Him. Do you honestly think that your children going to the house of Joe and Megan is going to faze God?"

"No. I guess I have to have faith in Him that He will watch over them." Suzie was silent for a moment. "Jacob, can I ask you a question?"

"Yes of course."

"I have had a very painful past. One in which I didn't understand my mother's love. Then I fell in love with my husband, only to have him leave me after giving birth to three of his children. I have been through many trials as it says in this passage. Yet, I know now, more than at any time in my life, that God is real. He is watching over me and that He cares for me. Does this mean that my faith is genuine?"

"I can't answer that, Suzie. God is the only one who can testify as to how great your faith is." Jacob paused for a moment, resting his head in his hand, as if in deep thought. "Wait a minute. God is bringing to my mind another verse. "Likewise, every good tree bears good fruit." You just encouraged two people in their Christian walk. Your faith may be so genuine that it is already bearing good fruit. That is exceptional. Just exceptional."

Suzie's face blossomed into a grin. "Better than shopping in Paris I would say. I am sowing seeds which are growing fruit which will expand the kingdom of God. I'd say that was far, far, better than shopping in Paris!"

THE HOUSE OF ENVY

JACOB SLIPPED OUT OF THE HOUSE WHILE THE BOYS were still sleeping. He had some errands to run. Suzie always felt at peace after she had talked to Jacob.

The boys were thrilled to wake up to chocolate chip cookies. Suzie knew she needed to let them know that they would be seeing their dad tonight. She thought it may be good to wait for Sarah to come home.

As soon as Sarah walked in the door, Suzie offered her some cookies and milk and asked the boys to come into the kitchen.

"I have something to tell you. I think you will be excited."

Michael looked at her with skepticism. "It isn't Christmas yet, Mommy. Can I go back to play in the bedroom?"

"No, you can't. I wanted to tell you that you will be going to your dad's new house this weekend."

Sarah stopped in mid-bite. "Really?"

"Yes, really."

"Do we need to pack clothes?"

Suzie stopped for a moment to consider the question. "I think that might be a good idea. At least, at first, you could take an overnight bag with a couple sets of clothes. I didn't think to ask your dad if he had bought any clothes for you. You may want to take some toiletries."

"What is that?" Michael asked.

"Stuff like shampoo, lotion, toothbrushes and toothpaste. The things you would need if you went on a trip." Suzie replied as she wiped cookie crumbs off the table.

Jonathan's eyes filled with tears. "We not staying long aw we?"

"No, darling. Just a couple of days. That's all."

"Yippee! I get to see my daddy!" Michael jumped up and down with joy.

Suzie bit her lip. She was not going to burst into tears. To be overjoyed at the prospect of sharing the children was not an option either. She was going to have to park her emotions in neutral. Maybe helping the children pack their bags for the weekend would be a good distraction.

Wait a minute. She had never bought suitcases for the children. They had never gone on a trip. Joe had not been interested in traveling, other than going on his many hunting trips. She wouldn't have time to go to the store and buy any. She didn't even have any overnight bags. Maybe she had some grocery sacks that she could use. She rummaged through her kitchen closet and found some paper grocery sacks.

Sarah looked at the sack with sheer disdain. "I thought you said we should take an overnight bag. I wouldn't consider a paper bag an overnight bag."

Suzie was mortified. "I know honey. I know. I am sorry I didn't think about this before this afternoon. To be honest with you, I don't have the time or the money to go get some suitcases. Once I get a job, then maybe we can go shopping and get you a cute bag. Okay?"

"Don't worry. I am sure that Daddy can take us shopping. He always made sure we were well taken care of when he lived here." Sarah said with a sneer.

"Wow. I don't remember that he ever cooked a meal. He never washed your clothes or checked your homework. He didn't take you to one single doctor's appointment but I guess that doesn't count as taking care of you, does it?" Suzie retorted.

Sarah rolled her eyes. "Mom, you need to get a job."

"I know that honey. I will try to work on that while you are at your dad's house."

"You better do that, Mommy. One of my friends got taken away from her mother because she couldn't find a job. She has to stay with a foster family now." Sarah turned away from Suzie and started fiddling with her hair. "She misses her mommy so much and hates her foster family."

Sarah whipped around and looked at Suzie with tears glistening in her eyes. "I already lost my daddy. I don't know what I would do if I didn't have you, Mommy." Sarah wrapped her arms around Suzie and nestled her silky hair into Suzie's waist. Her shoulders were quivering as silent tears streamed down her young face.

"Oh, honey. I hope and pray that doesn't happen to us. I love you so much." Suzie was coming to the stark realization that Sarah's harsh exterior was an ineffective mask for a scared little girl. She bent down to look in Sarah's eyes and held her face in her hands. "I know that there have been a lot of changes lately in your life but I will always be your mother. Nothing will ever change that, or the fact that I love you." Suzie gave Sarah a kiss and a hug.

Suzie glanced at her watch. She needed to move things along to get the children to their Dad's house in a timely fashion. "Do you think you could rummage through your closet and pick out what you would like to wear at your daddy's house?" Suzie asked.

"I guess I could do that," Sarah said. "Can I pack the boys' bags, too?"

Suzie sighed with relief. "Oh, sweetie, I would appreciate that. I'm a bit frazzled today. If you pack the clothes, I can round up some toiletries. Thanks so much for your help, honey," Suzie said.

"Sure thing, Mom." Sarah got busy packing the grocery bags, while Suzie made a sweep through the bathroom for toiletries.

Suzie looked at the clock and realized it was time to load the kids in the car. She had to put on a good front even though her heart was torn.

"Alright boys, get your coats on and let's get ready to go see your dad's new home." Suzie said as she dumped her toiletry stash into a plastic sack.

Suzie peeked in the living room. Michael had his coat on and was about ready to pop at the seams with anticipation. Jonathan looked a bit more pensive.

Suzie racked her brain for a way to reassure Jonathan. He loved cookies. Maybe if she packed some cookies for the ride he would feel comforted. Suzie scurried to the kitchen, grabbed some cookies and then poured some milk into some sippy cups.

"Ok, let's get into the car." Suzie said as she shooed the children out the front door. She settled Jonathan into the car seat and gave him a bag of cookies with a cup of milk. Then handed the same treats to the other children.

A fleeting thought that she may be spoiling their appetite knocked on the window of her thoughts. She pushed it aside. She didn't really care. The important thing was that Jonathan would have a pleasant experience associated with leaving her and going to his dad's house. She didn't want this to be traumatic for him.

It was only a forty-five-minute drive, but when she pulled up to Joe's house she felt as if she had entered another world. A world of perfection. The house was probably four to five times as big as hers. The trees were evergreen and the lighting on the house was exquisite. There was not a smudge of dirt on the windows nor even a stray leaf on the driveway. The turrets on the house transformed the elegant abode into a make-believe castle.

"No need to go to Disneyland for vacation when you live at a castle daily," Suzie muttered.

Sarah let a long whistle escape her lips. Michael was mesmerized. Jonathan was still engrossed in eating his cookie and drinking his milk. Suzie kind of wished that she was staying there for the weekend also. Joe's new house was at the high end of magnificent.

As the children tumbled out of the car, Suzie became aware of an unsettling feeling. One of envy. How on earth did someone who left his family deserve this kind of favor from God? She handed the grocery sacks to her children and walked them to the front door of the castle.

She rang the elegant doorbell, praying that Megan wouldn't answer the door.

Joe opened the door wide. The children were ecstatic to see him. There was plenty of kisses and hugs to go around for everyone but Suzie. She felt as if she was a fish out of water, struggling to catch her breath.

She looked down at the grocery bags which had been discarded on the front porch. "I don't know if you or Megan had time to go shopping for the children; so I had them pack some items for the weekend."

Joe looked at the grocery bags and a look of amusement crossed his face. "Really, Suzie? Megan bought them a selection of clothes last summer when she was in Paris." In a split second, Joe's face transformed from one of amusement to one of horror. He quickly closed the door behind him as he stepped out onto the porch. "Please don't let Megan see those grocery bags. You are an embarrassment, Suzie. We have so much better than that." With that Joe spun a 180, walked through his front door and slammed it soundly in the face of Suzie.

Suzie tried scooping up the grocery bags but her arms were so burdened with grief that they could not hold on to the flimsy bags. She was tempted to leave them on the front porch but that might embarrass the children and incite Joe's anger. She didn't want to do anything which may reflect badly on the children. She had to pull herself together, take one step at a time, while juggling the different bags, until she got to the car.

She trudged to the car, head down, shoulders slumped. She barely had enough energy to open the car door. She gently put the grocery bags beside her and slowly turned the ignition. The car crawled out of the perfectly manicured front lawn and into the dark of night.

If crying was an Olympic event, Suzie would have won a gold medal as she drove home from Joe's house. She felt drenched with depression and despair but it was more than that. She was angry. In fact, she could feel a seething anger at God boiling inside her chest.

If God was so good, then why did wickedness get rewarded? If he was a just and righteous God, then where in heaven's name was justice for her? She stewed in bitterness and anger until a bit of honesty started knocking on the door of her thoughts.

It wasn't God's fault that she hadn't been a superstar in her career. It was hers. She was the one who had walked away from her career. The moment she thought her children needed her more than her boss did, she had given her resignation. Now she was left with a run-down house and car in the country, no job, bills to pay, and three children to provide for.

She thought that God would have punished Joe for leaving his family. Instead, He had showered Joe with a fabulous house, a stunning wife, and probably more money than he had ever seen in his life.

The thoughts of Envy tormented Suzie into the wee hours of the morning. Then a still small voice said, "You need to stop looking at what they have and start looking at what I have done for you."

Envy was shattered in that moment and understanding started to seep into the consciousness of Suzie. As she drifted off to sleep Suzie knew the first item on her list tomorrow was to make a phone call. She needed to talk with Hope.

THE IDOL OF MATERIALISM

THE RING OF THE PHONE SHATTERED THE STILLNESS of morning. Suzie rolled over and stumbled out of bed. She rushed to the kitchen and caught the phone on the last ring.

"Hello?" She said, as she lumbered back to her bed.

"Hello, sweet child of God." The soothing voice of Hope crooned.

"Wow, I don't know how you do it but you are always right on time when I need you." Suzie said, as she pondered the choice between staying in bed, or getting up and making some coffee. "I had another meltdown last night."

"What happened?" Hope said with empathy.

"Dropped the kids off at Joe's house. Well, it wasn't really his *house.* More like a castle, not a house." Suzie said as she yawned and crawled back into her bed.

"Hmmm, how did you feel when you saw where he lived?"

"I felt worthless, Hope. I felt as if my life was a waste of time." Suzie said with blatant honesty.

"Do you consider your children worthless?" Hope asked.

"NO, of course not!" Suzie said with indignation.

"You have invested the last few years into the wellbeing of your children," Hope said.

"Yes, but I wasn't rewarded with a castle… as it seems Joe was," Suzie frowned.

"Yes, that is a mighty fine reward. I have to admit that." Hope paused for a moment. "Can your children talk?" Hope asked.

"Yes, they can talk Hope. You know that," Suzie answered.

"Can they see?" Hope asked.

"Yes." Suzie rolled her eyes.

"Can they hear?" Hope asked. "And do they have hands and feet?"

Suzie was getting perturbed. "Yes, Hope, but what does that have to do with Joe living in a castle?"

"Do you have your Bible handy?" Hope asked.

Suzie glanced at her nightstand and grabbed her Bible. "Yes." Suzie said with obvious irritation in her voice.

"Turn to Psalms 115:4-8 and read it to me." Hope said with excitement quickening her speech.

Suzie flipped through the pages of her Bible, with an anger that was about to erupt.

She spoke the word of God with a staccato crispness. "Their idols are merely things of silver and gold, shaped by human hands. (5) They have mouths but cannot speak, and eyes but cannot see. (6) They have ears but cannot hear, and noses but cannot smell. (7) They have hands but cannot feel, and feet but cannot walk, and throats but cannot make a sound. (8) And those who make idols are just like them, as are all who trust in them."

"How would you characterize the items in this passage which so entice worship from humans?" Hope asked.

"They are things which don't have a heart and they don't have any life," Suzie replied.

"Do you realize that when God looks upon you he sees a beautiful princess who lives in a castle of love?" Hope paused a moment for emphasis. "Suzie, you have such a vibrant love that you have opened the door to healing for your mother. You have comforted a young woman who lost everything that was dear to her. You have sealed the deal on eternity for a man who merely owned a tire shop. Do you have any idea how much your love has breathed life into those around you?"

Suzie stared at the Bible, holding it in her hands as if it was gold. "Well, I never thought of it that way, Hope."

"Have your children gone hungry, been too cold or too warm, or gone without clothes even one day in their life?" Hope pressed on.

"No," Suzie answered.

"Have they suffered any horrendous disease?" Hope asked.

Suzie paused for a moment. "No, not anything other than a common cold."

"You look out the window of envy at Joe and Megan, thinking that their cold house will bring them happiness. If you keep looking out that window you will fail to see the magnificence of your own home. Their house is full of death, Suzie. Yours is full of life."

"Hope, you didn't see it. It had turrets like a castle. It was beyond gorgeous," Suzie whined.

"Do you have any idea how much time and money it takes to tend to a house of that magnificence?"

"No, but I bet that Megan is a perfectionist and she probably doesn't have a problem with keeping things clean like I do," Suzie replied. "Either that or she has a host of maids and landscapers that do the work for her."

"That is neither here, nor there, Suzie. The Lord has put boundaries around you so that you will trust in Him and not some stupid mansion. Your house is adequate and it shelters you and your children. It is not lavish but is what a house should be, it is a home full of love and laughter."

"Well, I do love my children and we do have a sense of joy and laughter. What if my children don't see that though? What if they are mesmerized by the grandeur of their father's home?" Beck asked with a worried tone of voice.

"Children are smarter than you think. They know where love resides. It does not reside in gold or silver, nor in homes which resemble castles." Hope said with force. "There is a simplicity to poverty which fosters a deeper realization of what things are precious in life. There is a song that we used to sing when I invited you to Daily Vacation Bible School. Let me see if I can remember it."

Hope started singing the verses of an old Shaker hymn:

"'Tis the gift to be simple, 'tis the gift to be free
'Tis the gift to come down where we ought to be,
And when we find ourselves in the place just right,
'Twill be in the valley of love and delight.
When true simplicity is gained,

To bow and to bend we shan't be ashamed,
To turn, turn will be our delight,
Till by turning, turning we come 'round right."

Suzie giggled and then joined in to sing the song with Hope. "I remember that song, Hope. That was one of my favorites. It had such rhythm that I wanted to dance when I sang it."

"Do you understand that wealth can be a cage for people? Material possessions and the success needed to obtain them can steal precious time," Hope said.

"I understand that Hope but I still don't understand why it seems that Joe is getting rewarded for sin. It just doesn't seem fair," Suzie responded.

"Everyone has a choice to make in this life, Suzie. You can choose to go after worldly things or you can choose God. In 1 John 2:15 the Bible says, "Do not love the world or the things in the world. If anyone loves the world, the love of the Father is not in him."

"It's just that Joe's new house was so beautiful." Suzie said, with a touch of wistfulness.

"Worldly beauty is deceitful. It gives the appearance of contentment but hides stress and worry beyond the castle walls." Hope paused as if collecting her thoughts. "You are at a crossroads Suzie. I know you are looking for a job. I know that you are intelligent enough that you could go far in your career if you put that as a priority. You also have three children which are in their formative years. They need your love and your guidance to accept God's love. You can choose money or God but it is rare that you can have both."

"Are you implying that I should give up my job search? The last thing I want to do is to be on welfare. I *detest* people who live off the government." Suzie spit the words out with indignation.

"No, in the Bible it says you should not eat if you do not work. Commit your ways unto the Lord and He shall make your pathways straight." Hope stopped talking for a moment to take a drink of water. "Suzie, you have so much to be thankful for. You have a roof over your head, clothes enough to wear and food to eat. What you don't have is a lot of things to distract you from your two most important priorities which is to love God and nurture your children. You are surrounded by the Spirit of God. Grace and Mr. Mercy, Faith, Joy and even me, Hope, are continually near you. If you start running after materialism you may forfeit that which has nurtured you. Do you really want a castle now?"

Suzie glanced around her room and realized it was quite pretty. She reflected on the comfort that she felt when she crossed the road to the house of Grace and Mercy. She knew she would feel lost without Hope, Faith, and even Joy. Her mind skipped down the path of memories to visit her talk with Angie and the tire shop owner. She had so much fun drawing them closer to God.

"No, Hope, I don't want a castle. I want God more than anything. I realize that although Joe has been rewarded with material possessions, I am the one who has really gained victory because I have become closer to God," Suzie said.

Hope breathed a deep sigh of relief, knowing how close she came to losing Suzie to the lure of the world. "That is a wise choice, sweet child of God. A very wise choice. May I offer a suggestion?"

"Yes, of course you can, Hope."

"Every time you are tempted to disregard the house which you live in as being unworthy, turn that around into an offering of praise to God that you have a house. That will cause the slime of Envy to slip off your mind."

"I can do that, Hope." Suzie said with assurance.

"There is one more thing that may help you become less envious," Hope mused.

"What is that?" Suzie said as her eyes scanned her bedroom taking in all the items which she intended to give thanks for.

"When you pray, ask God to bless Joe and Megan." Hope said, knowing she had just dropped a bomb into the arena of envy.

"WHAT?!! ARE YOU CRAZY?!! They don't need any more blessings. I am the one who needs to be blessed. My God, Hope, you should have seen that house." Suzie was fuming.

"You see things through the eyes of a human, Suzie. I see things as God sees them. Your home *is* the *castle* because it is filled with unconditional love and acceptance of God." Hope paused to say a silent prayer that Suzie would be given understanding. "The home of Joe and Megan is just a house filled with the death of materialism and rejection. The walls of their 'castle' will not last for eternity but the love that you have received from God is eternal. This love breathes life and joy into you and into everyone surrounding you."

Suzie broke down into tears. "I am trying, Hope. I am really trying to view life through the lens of God but I will be honest, it is the most difficult path I have ever walked. I have gone through so much these past few months. Some days I feel like giving up." Suzie paused for a moment to reflect on the past few months. "But each day I feel just a bit stronger and more loved by God. The joy I felt when I was witnessing to Angie and the tire shop owner was the closest thing to heaven I have ever felt."

"Remember the dream that you had about heaven?" Hope asked.

"Yes, I do. That was such a surreal moment. I hope I never forget that the way to heaven is through Jesus." Suzie stated.

"Remember when Faith told you that you had a harvest to gather and that was what the women in the field symbolized?" Hope asked.

"Yes, I do remember that." Suzie said, wondering what Hope was getting at.

"You have already started to harvest souls for the kingdom of God." Hope stated. "You are fulfilling your destiny."

The tears started streaming down the cheeks of Suzie. "I get it Hope. It doesn't really matter what kind of home I live in, does it?"

"You are right, sweet child of God. It matters nothing what house you live in. What matters most is that you gather the harvest that God has set before you. His desire is for you to expand His kingdom and to grow His family."

"Thy kingdom come, they will be done, on earth, as it is in heaven." Suzie spoke softly, recalling the words of the Lord's prayer. "Wow, I really don't get much joy out of things anyway do I? Nothing like what I felt when I went to the tire shop."

"You have the Spirit of God surrounding you, Suzie, and the joy of the Lord is your strength," Hope said.

"I agree with that Hope. I really do. Thank you so much for listening to me whine about that stupid castle that Joe and Megan live in. I would absolutely hate having to clean or maintain a house that size," Suzie said.

Hope giggled. "I am aware of that my sweet. So, what do you have planned for today?"

"I am going to find a job. I don't want to use up all of the money my dad gave me and I certainly do not want to be a welfare mom." Suzie paused for a moment to reflect on the conversation with Hope. "I appreciate your counsel, Hope. I think I will try to look for a job where I can just work the weekends. That way I can be home to nurture my children during the week."

"That sounds like a very wise choice. I better go, my children are waking up," Hope said.

"Wow, I didn't realize what a strange feeling silence is. My house seems bizzare without the children being here. I miss them," Suzie said.

"They will be home soon. Use your time wisely. If you get a job on the weekends you will be very busy," Hope said.

"Busy and exhausted. I better get going. Time is slipping away," Suzie said.

"Yes, I know. I love you, sweet child of God," Hope said.

"I love you too, Hope," Suzie said.

ONE LAST TRY

DECEIT WAS IN A STATE OF BLISS. HE HAD JUST COME back from Africa. There was so much violence and bloodshed in that country. He felt as if he had been feasting on a buffet of evil.There was still a nagging discontent in the recesses of his thoughts though. He had not ensured the death of Susanna Whatley. The sooner this happened, the greater his access was to those children.

He was on his last nerve with this lady. She had continually turned to God every time he had rendered an attack on her. She was now looking to the Bible for her guidance, when he had made it so very easy for her to jump into the abyss of envy and despair. What on earth was wrong with her?

Adultery said she had a plan. It had better be a good one.

He needed to call the forces together for one last try to put an end to the life of Susanna Whatley. He dreaded those meetings. To corral the focus of his underlings was his greatest challenge. Well, maybe the second greatest challenge. That poverty stricken, unemployed, destitute single mother, Susanna Whatley, trumped everything in the challenge department.

He clanged the bell to call the meeting.

Envy was the first to arrive. The green glob of vomit bounced into the room as if it had won a battle. Soon the snake of Rejection slighted in, followed by Insecurity and Doubt. The peacock of Arrogance strutted in with feathers spread wide. Bitterness lumbered in with a bit of new growth on its branches. Condemnation strode in with his cloak of Guilt freshly laundered. Despair skipped in, tripped over Rejection and landed face first in the vomit of Envy.

Deceit was about ready to call the meeting to order when he noticed the most important entity had not yet arrived. Adultery was nowhere to be found.

Deceit became enraged and started clanging the bell louder and louder. Despair covered her ears with her spindly fingers and began screaming out in pain. "Stop! Stop! That hurts my ears!"

Soon Adultery sauntered in, sashaying her broad hips as if they were a seesaw.

"This meeting is called to order for the purpose of securing the death certificate for Susanna Whatley." Deceit stated as he glared at Adultery with disgust.

Envy began bouncing erratically. "I got inside her mind! Yes I did. She was covered in my vomit!"

The lips of Deceit started to curl upwards. "Finally some success in this battle. Tell me how you succeeded."

"Well, you know how Susanna does not have a good home. I mean despicable would be an accurate term for the shack she lives in. She does the best that she can but Joe never gave her any money for their home. He was too busy hiding money to finance his coupling with Megan." Envy said with glee."So Joe made Susanna bring the children to his new home. He detests her so much that he has allowed Arrogance to enter his heart," Envy said.

"Hold on a minute there, dear. I have been in Joe's heart for quite awhile. In fact, since the first time he caught sight of our star pupil, Megan." The Peacock fanned his feathers in indignation.

"Well, I didn't mean that you hadn't been present all of the time but you were just more apparent when Joe insisted that Susanna see his new home." Envy said, as her glob of vomit started to quiver.

"That is NOT what you said!" Arrogance started striding to Envy as if to start a fight.

"STOP! Blazes, do you really think any of this matters?" Deceit said. "I asked Envy how she had succeeded in entering Susanna's mind. I did NOT ask how long you had residence in the mind of Joe." Deceit stepped in to avert the potential conflict. "Now do go on, Envy."

"Thank you." Envy glared at Arrogance. "Well, Megan and Joe worked like slaves to make everything appear as if it was perfect. The lighting on their home was exquisite. The lawn was perfectly manicured. The windows were sparkling clean. They attended to each and every detail I placed in their mind. All for the purpose of convincing Susanna that they were so, so much better than her." Envy took a pause to collect her thoughts.

"Susanna drove up as the sunset was exploding across the sky. Joe designed this house to appear as if it was a castle. In reality, he had only gone on one hunting trip. All of the other "hunting trips" had been meetings with architects, construction crews and interior decorators. He was constructing his second home while still married to his first wife." Deceit chimed in."Wasn't that brilliant?"

Adultery held up her hand to stop Deceit. "You mean when he told Susanna he was going hunting that was a lie?"

"A pure and blantant lie." Deceit announced with pride.

"Wow, I need to write that down." Adultery pulled a pen and notepad out of her cleavage and began taking notes. "Sometimes humans can be so wicked."

Insecurity slipped into the middle of the chamber with Doubt as her sidekick. "Joe was so insecure in himself that he doubted his ability to keep Megan interested."

"So he figured if they both worked on their new home together and he put up some of the money for the 'castle,' Megan wouldn't leave him," Doubt said. "She has a habit of that, you know, leaving men that is."

Deceit stomped his foot. "Can we focus on Susanna? Joe is *clearly* not our adversary; Susanna is."

Envy resumed her tale. "Her heart sunk when she saw the grandeur that Joe and Megan were living in. Despair and I were so close together in her heart that we literally could have grasped hands."

Despair started twirling around the room crooning. "Susanna thought she was a princess as a little girl. When she grew up she realized that she never was, nor ever will be a princess because someone stole her prince." At which point she dissolved into heinous laughter.

"So… she is sitting there in her car, gazing at the grandeur before her and I placed the thought. 'Wow, Joe does everything that is wrong and he gets a castle. I am trying my hardest to do everything right and what do I get? A delapidated shack out in the country. I wonder why God would be so unfair?'" Envy quivered with excitement.

"Brilliant, brilliant!" Deceit said. "So did she drive away with Rejection, Despair, Bitterness, Doubt and Insecurity riding shot gun in her heart?"

"She sure did." Envy was trying to slide past Bitterness so she could leave before the bomb of Hope dropped.

"Great. So I imagine she went home feeling worthless and drown herself in tears. Then she sat down at the kitchen table, wrote a suicide note and took her life, right?" Deceit was so happy he was jumping up and down. "So where is her death certificate?" He continued to jump up and down looking this way and that.

The judge of Condemnation strode to the center of the chamber, kicking the vomit of Envy savagely against a wall. "There is no death certificate. Susanna did her usual insane escape. She went to sleep. The very next morning Hope called her."

"WHAT??!!!" Deceit screamed.

"Yes, Hope told her that she was already fulfilling her destiny. Apparently God has a harvest of souls for her to collect and she is already bearing fruit." The cloak of guilt covering Condemnation became worthless shreds with the mention of God.

"Would you please calm down?" Adultery said, flipping her blonde hair over her shoulder with an air of conficence. "I told you, I got this covered."

She paused for a moment to look around the chamber as if she was searching for something. "Is there a stool or something I could sit on? Because you are seriously wearing me out with all of your worrying about this stupid single mother." Adultery fanned herself and sat down on a stool provided by Doubt and Insecurity.

"Alright, this is the plan. That stupid wench has been going to the Bible for each and every little thing that has gone wrong. She has clearly learned to protect her mind with the helmet of salvation if she thinks that asking God to bless her ex-husband is the right thing to do. I mean he has a castle, a Barbie doll wife, and a hell of a bank account, and she thinks he needs blessing? Seriously, that is just creepy." Adultery shivered with disgust.

"How is she doing with Faith?" Adultery asked Doubt.

"I can't seem to get a grasp on her mind. Faith is very present. Faith is almost like a shield for her body. I just can't keep hold." Doubt muttered, his brow tangled in frustration.

"If I am correct, I believe she has rendered you quite incapable also?" Adultery glared at the form of Deceit. "Winning is so easy for you in most cases but this single mother has been one of your most difficult fights. Am I right?"

"Yes, you are right." Deceit hung his head.

"The reason why we can not penetrate this woman's spirit is because she has been gaining the armor of God. There is only one item that she is missing. This is the breastplate of righteousness. If we lure her into sin she is vulnerable to attack." Adultery stated with decisiveness. "Sexual sin is the most alluring sin for humans to succumb to."

"Here is my plan: First of all, Susanna has not been told how beautiful she is for quite some time. She has been so busy with her children that she has taken no time for herself. She has a limited amount of money saved up and no job." Adultery readjusted her gown. "Arrogance has been released to capture the thoughts of a doctor who works in a nursing home. This same nursing home has just fired their weekend supervisor, leaving open a position which would be perfect for Susanna. All I have to do is lead her to apply for this position, have her catch the eye of the doctor, and soon Susanna Whatley will be a page in our history books as a battle won."

"Well, we can't really win her. I mean the other side already has claim on her eternal life because she believes in…." Despair started to tremble, remembering the chaos that the mention of Jesus could bring. "You know… you know… that guy who thought He was God."

"Yes, yes, we have clearly lost *her*, but if she dies she will not be able to bring in the harvest of souls; nor will she be able to influence her children. Sounds like a win-win to me." Condemnation said, straightening out his cloak of judgement.

"Clearly you are right on that, but I don't know that she could fall for someone this fast after losing Joe." Doubt's eyebrows furrowed in frustration.

"Believe me, once I enter her mind and give her the delusions of how fabulous it would be to be married to a doctor, the door to Adultery will be wide open," Arrogance screeched.

Deceit was visibly pleased with this meeting and plan. He hadn't even had to put much effort into this meeting. Yet, he couldn't be complacent. They still had not signed the death certificate for Susanna Whatley. He had a feeling it would be coming soon.

"Alright, go forth and create havoc, heartache, and wickedness; and do so with great haste in response to Susanna Whatley."

JOB HUNTING

SUZIE LOOKED AT HERSELF IN THE MIRROR WHEN SHE stepped out of the shower. She looked so different than she had eight years ago. Her abdominal muscles had softened. There was a peppering of cellulites on her legs and the wrinkles around her eyes and mouth had propagated.

She was just going to the library today, but she wanted to look a bit better than normal. She washed her face with some facial cleanser and searched through her medicine cabinet until she found some old moisturizer. She massaged the cream into the crevices of her face, vowing to take better care of herself.

After she went to the library she may stop by a storefront and try to buy a cellular phone. It seemed as if everyone had one these days and she thought it would be good to have one for safety. She still had enough money to survive for a few months. If she got a phone she could use the navigational system to get to work.

She felt so helpless in the current world of computers. She had been stupid enough to assume that Joe would always be there to help her figure out the intracacies of IT. What a fool she had been to become so dependent on him.

It seemed as if Joe had given her a ticket for a magic carpet ride to enter domestic bliss. She had been flying high until Megan pulled the carpet out from under her. Now she felt as if she was floundering in midair trying to find her footing again. Maybe if she had a job she would feel more grounded, Suzie thought as she walked past her Bible.

"Wait a minute." She said as she did a double take and picked up the Bible. "I am sorry God, for even thinking that a job should be my foundation for life. Your word and your love are what I stand on. Please give me a verse which I can reflect on today and guide me as I seek to do your will."

As the Bible fell open to Matthew six, Suzie's eyes became focused on verse 33."But seek first the Kingdom of God and His righteousness and all of these things shall be added unto you."

"Dear Lord, let me please make you my first priority today. Then I ask that you help me find a job." Suzie jotted down the verse on a index card and then grabbed her purse and her resume'.

When she got into her car she placed the index card on the console, so that she could view it when she was at a stop light.

She realized as she was driving out of her yard that the car was silent without the children. She really missed them, but as Hope said it was only two days and she intended to make the weekend a productive one.

As she stopped at the rural intersection she noticed that Mr. Mercy was sitting in his old jalopy pickup at the corner. She wondered if he needed help. He flashed her a winning smile and waved her on her way. As she turned the corner she saw him speeding home.

"Poor guy, he is probably thrilled that I am leaving for the day. He may actually be able to get something done at his house for a change, without me and the boys constantly interrupting him."

As she entered the town she passed by Dolly's restaurant. She intended to buy some cookies or a pie for Grace and Mr Mercy on the way home. That way she could say "hello" to Dolly and bless her neighbors all in one fell swoop.

She would have liked to stop in and say "hello" to her new friends at the tire shop also but that would have to be done on a different day. The morning was slipping away and she felt pressed to get to the library.

As she entered the library she received no warm welcome from the lone librarian. Suzie felt out of her element and would need some help to navigate through the foreign land of computers.

"Hello. I hate to bother you but I need help navigating through the computer system in order to find a job. I need to find a job in nursing. Could you possibly help me?" Suzie asked in the kindest tone she could muster.

"Listen, lady. We close in twenty minutes. It would take me at least thirty minutes to teach you how to do it. Like I said, we close in twenty minutes." The librarian said without looking up from her phone.

A fire started raging inside of Suzie as she looked at the name tag of the librarian. "Listen, Katie, I drove quite a long ways to get here.

I do not have a computer at home. Even if I did have a computer, I wouldn't know how to use it." Still no reaction from the librarian. "Now, if I am not mistaken I believe you are employed by the city which means that some of my tax dollars help pay your salary. So could you please interrupt your fascination with your phone and do your job?"

Katie looked up from her phone with contempt at the forefront of her glare but Suzie sensed a sadness lingering in the background.

The librarian disengaged from her chair as if her buttocks was glued to the seat. Her thick thighs rubbed together like sandpaper as she lumbered slowly to the back of the library.

Once she sat down in front of the computer, her fingers started flying across the keys as if they were lightening.

Suzie stood beside her, mesmerized by the speed and competency of her skill.

"Which site do you want to use? Careerbuilder, Monster, or Indeed?"

"Umm, Careerbuilder sounds like a good choice. I don't know what that Monster site is but I am a nurse. I didn't know why they would have a site to take care of monsters. Are there really jobs for that?" Suzie asked.

Katie's fingers stopped in mid air. She turned and looked at Suzie as if she had just flew in from Mars. "You're serious right? You don't know about Monsterjobs.com?"

Suzie felt a blush color her cheeks. "No, I guess I am kind of in the dark regarding that. My husband left me and took my computer. He was in IT, so he was always on it anyhow. I have been so busy raising our children I hardly have time to watch TV." Suzie stopped to brush a stray hair out of her eyes. “When I watch TV it is with the kids. So it is usually Barney or some other kind of kids’ show. I guess I am not as in touch with current affairs as I should be.”

Katie looked at Suzie and merely shook her head. “I think I found a job for you. I could only find one in nursing but it is on the weekends. I doubt you want to work every weekend.” The librarian reached for the power switch to turn off the computer.

“Wait a minute!” Suzie shouted. “A weekend position is exactly what I want. Please write down the information for me so that I can contact them on Monday.”

The librarian quickly jotted down the information, turned the computer off and got up so quick that Suzie thought she had just morphed into a superhero.

“So if you got kids, where are they at today?” The libarian said as she turned to walk towards the front door.

“They are at their dad’s house.” Suzie said as she gathered her items and made sure she didn’t leave anything behind.

“Wow. Their dad wants to see them?”

“Yes, he is demanding them every weekend.” Suzie said as she tucked her new job lead into her wallet. “I guess his new girlfriend hasn’t had the opportunity to have children yet.”

“They’re lucky. I never saw my dad. My mother had to work so much I rarely got to see her either.” Katie hung her head as if weighted down by sad memories.

“Wow. That would be tough. I am so sorry. I wasn’t that thrilled about them seeing him every weekend. It’s not him that I am worried about. It is just that I don’t know much about his new girlfriend. It’s kind of hard having someone be in charge of your kids when you haven't even done a background check on them," Suzie said.

"I could see that that would be a little unsettling but he is their dad. I am sure he loves them enough to watch out for them if he wants them every weekend." The librarian said as she looked down at her cell phone with worry etched in her facial lines.

"What is on your phone? You look worried when you look at it." Suzie said with compassion.

"Aww, my dog is sick. He is really the only thing I love. My mother passed away last year. We were just starting to get close, then she got cancer. She bought me a dog to help comfort me, for when she passed on." The librarian went behind the counter to get her car keys. "I got a camera hooked up in my apartment and I am streaming a live video of my dog. I don't know why I am doing this. I can't afford to take him to a vet. It kills me that he is hurting." The librarian wiped a tear from her cheek.

"Can I see him?" Suzie asked.

"Yeah," Katie handed Suzie the phone.

The dog was squirming as if in pain. "How much would a vet visit cost?"

"Close to $100. I just don't have that kind of money."

"I don't either on a normal basis. I brought some money along because I wanted to buy a cell phone. I feel as if God wants me to give you the 100$ bill. That way you can take care of your dog." Suzie said as she took a hundred dollar bill out of her wallet and gave it to Katie.

Katie started crying. "No one has ever showed that they cared about me. If my dog had died, I was going to take my own life. And I was so rude to you. I am sorry."

Suzie reached out her arms to embrace her former foe. "Now, now don't beat yourself up. I probably would have acted the same way if I had your situation. You had a tough childhood and didn't get much love but you don't know what God has in store for you. You have to hold on during the tough times ok?"

The librarian nodded her head and snuggled into the embrace of Suzie. "You believe in God?"

"Yes… yes I do." Suzie replied, searching in her purse for a Kleenex.

"My mother always talked about God but I wondered how she could believe that God was good when her life totally sucked."

"Her life didn't totally suck," Suzie replied.

"Yeah, it did. My dad left as soon as he saw that I was a girl. He had wanted a boy. I was sick a lot when I was a little girl and she had to work so much just to pay the medical bills."

"A lot of people have to work more than one job. Her life didn't suck."

"My mother looked like a beauty queen when she was young but when she got cancer she shriveled down to nothing. I tried as hard as I could to be there for her. She died when she was forty years old. She always said that God had her life in His hands." Katie shook her head. "It would really suck to die that young."

Suzie tenderly lifted the head of her new friend and looked her square in the eye. "The life of your mother did not suck. If she believed in God she is now enjoying time with her heavenly Father. She had the joy of having you as her daughter. She had God and she had you. That is so much more than most people could ever hope to have." Suzie handed out a tissue for the libarian to wipe her face. "Why don't you try connecting with that God she believed in?"

"I doubt that He would want anything to do with me. I'm kind of a bully if you hadn't noticed." Katie shrugged off the suggestion. "My mother was a saint. There is no way God could accept me."

"See that is just it, Katie. Being accepted by God has nothing to do with how good you are. It has everything to do with the sacrifice of Jesus. If you believe that Jesus died on a cross for your sins and you ask Him into your heart, then you are accepted by God. We could never do enough good to equal God, that is why He sacrificed Jesus for our sins. Would you like to ask Jesus into your heart right now?" Suzie was silently pleading with God for an open door to this girl's heart.

"Do I have to be nice immediately? Cause I have been a bully for most of my life."

Suzie giggled. "You can be a bully as long as you like but I think when Jesus takes over, you may want cut down on the bullying."

"You know, I think I want to do this. Do I have to kneel on the ground?"

"No, but it might be kosher to bow our heads." Suzie said as she caught hold of Katie's hands. "Now repeat after me."

"Ok." Katie said, giving a slight squeeze of affirmation to Suzie's hands.

"Heavenly Father, I come before you asking you to forgive my sins. I believe that Jesus was your Son. I believe that He died on the cross for my sins. I pray that the Holy Spirit would enter my heart and begin the process of cleansing me from all unrighteousness. In Jesus name, Amen."

Katie repeated the words. By the end of the confession, tears were flowing freely down her cheeks. "I have always felt so worthless. Now I have God's Spirit dwelling within me." Katie wiped the tears off of her cheeks. "I actually feel lighter, as if a burden was taken off of my shoulders."

"Sin can be an awful burden to bear." Suzie said as she reached out to give Katie a hug. "The most wonderful aspect of accepting Christ is learning to give and receive love from God. When my husband left, I thought my world would end but God has surrounded me with His love. I actually feel more fulfilled with God's love than I felt when I was happily married."

Katie smiled. "I am looking forward to the journey." She looked down at her phone and exclaimed. "Oh my goodness, my dog just got up and he is eating his food."

"You're kidding, right?" Suzie reached for the phone. "Goodness me, he looks perfectly fine."

"I guess I don't need your money anymore." Katie said as she handed the money back to Suzie.

"Wait a minute, I was urged by the Holy Spirit to give you that money. It seems as if He has healed your dog so that you can spend that money on something else you may need," Suzie paused. "Do you have a Bible?"

"No, I don't," Katie said. "My mother gave me hers." Katie hung her head. "I couldn't bear to go through the boxes she left me when she died."

"I think that you should use that money for a new Bible." Suzie said as she opened her car door and took out the recipe card.

"I try to claim a Bible verse each day. This is the one I claimed for today: 'Seek ye first the Kingdom of God and all of these things shall be added unto you.' I wrote my phone number on the back," Suzie said. "I would love to be your friend but more than that I want you to become God's daughter."

"I would like to be both," Katie said. "I don't have very many friends."

"Don't worry. I don't have that many either." Suzie said with a shrug of her shoulders. "Please keep in touch."

"I will," Katie said.

ALL THESE THINGS

As Suzie was driving home from town she thanked God for her new friend, Katie. She was hoping she would hear from her.

She had a new cell phone sitting in the seat beside her along with some cookies for her neighbors. She found it interesting that the young man who had helped her with her cell phone had insisted that she download the app to record conversations. In addition to this, he had put a GPS system on her phone.

She was so glad she had given the cash she had to Katie. The phone was much more expensive than she had thought, so she had put it on a credit card.

She was using the GPS to drive home this time. As she drove out of town she passed a plant nursery. She loved gardening but didn't have the time, nor the money, to engage in such frivolity. A bit of landscaping could do her house good…wish she had the money for that.

As she got closer to home she became anxious. How would it feel to be in the house without the children? Just the thought of them brought tears to her eyes.

She had done well to distract her thinking so far, but she knew that the minute she walked into her house, their absence would come crushing down on her.

As she was driving, she noticed a beautiful little house on the side of the road. It was similar to hers in the frame and the style but the landscaping made it look so much better than her house. As she drove she realized that she had overshot her home. Her thinking became clouded by depression as she realized how deathly silent the car was without the children.

She was approaching the adorable house again. She stopped to study it. Maybe she could replicate the landscaping at her dismal location.

She glanced to the right and noticed a house that looked much like Grace and Mercy's home. By God, there was Jacob and Mr. Mercy standing on the porch waving at her.

Her head whipped to the left in disbelief. What had happened to her home? Someone had painted the trim and put in a couple of flower beds, some trees peppered her lawn and a new railing was on her front porch.

It was an amazing change from what she had left in the morning. Who had done this?

She parked in her driveway and got out to gaze at the wonder in front of her. She could not believe her eyes. The house had never looked so good.

The house was painted with creamy white, a rich emerald green hugging the trim. In her front flower beds were an array of tulips and hyacinths. The luxurious scent of the hyacinths, wafting in on the fresh spring breeze, began caressing her cheeks, as she took it all in. Soon tears were flowing down her cheeks.

A gentle deep voice shattered her moment of awe. "I'm sorry. We thought you might like a redo. We should have asked." Jacob shrugged his shoulders and his head sunk to his chest. "It's just that we care for you so much. This was the only blessing we could think of to do for you."

"Are you kidding me?" Suzie asked. "I was crying because I was happy."

A look of confusion crossed Jacob's face. "You're happy then?"

"I am overjoyed. The house has never looked so good. The flowers and trees are amazing. I love every square inch of what you did. How can I ever repay you?"

"Ahh, you don't have to repay us. My brothers came to help out. We had so much fun we thought this kind of thing should be outlawed." Jacob lifted his head to catch the gaze of Suzie. "I could use a hug though."

Suzie threw her arms around Jacob, hugging him with all of her strength. "Thank you so much! No one has ever done something like this for me. It means so much." Suzie gave one last squeeze to Jacob. "I know it is not much but I bought some cookies for you at Dolly's restaurant. Would you like to come in and have a few?"

"I can never turn down a cookie. Do you need help bringing them inside?" Jacob asked.

Suzie paused for a moment to look at Jacob and a twinkle appeared in her eye. "I think I can handle a dozen cookies after all you did… but nice try on sneaking a bite before we got to my front door." Suzie flashed Jacob a wide tooth grin coupled with a wink.

"Awww shucks. You know me too well," Jacob laughed.

Suzie sprinted up the stairs of her new front porch. She was just about to grab the door handle, when she felt Jacob's hand firmly catch hers.

"Careful, dear lady, the paint may still be wet."

Suzie caught her breath, her heart was racing. What was happening?

Jacob opened the door with one hand as he guided Suzie into her home with the other. He kept his hand on her back as they walked through the living room, the dining room, and then the kitchen.

By the time she got to the kitchen Suzie's hands were shaking. No man had ever had this effect on her. She put the cookies on the table and motioned for Jacob to sit down.

"Here have a cookie." She opened the bag of cookies, still trying to categorize the reaction she had to Jacob. "Do you want some milk?"

"If you have some I would be eternally grateful."

Suzie opened the fridge door and stuck as much of her head into it as possible, gulping the cold air, in a vain attempt to freeze the warming of her heart towards Jacob.

As she was pouring the milk into a glass she studied Jacob's gaze. His gaze was one of pure devotion to Suzie. She had never seen a man look at a woman the way Jacob looked at her. Then in a second it changed and a troubled expression clouded his gaze.

"Ok, what is going on?" Suzie asked.

Jacob looked at Suzie with a desperate longing in his eyes. "I just got word that my application to become a missionary to Africa has been accepted."

"Wow." Suzie felt her heart sink to the floor. "I… I had no idea…"

"I didn't want to say anything about it at first because it was a long shot that I would be accepted." Jacob looked down at his hands. "I have wanted to be a missionary to Africa all of my life," Jacob paused. "Well… no… that is a lie." Jacob looked at Suzie with sincerity. "The minute I met you… that changed. From the first time we met all I wanted to do was spend more time with you." Jacob ran his hands through his dark brown wavy hair in frustration. "You're all I can think about."

"Wow. I don't know what to say. I guess I just assumed you would always be across the road from me." Suzie felt her knees go out and quickly sat down. "I realized this afternoon that I am attracted to you but I have never wanted to go to Africa. Can you say 'No?'"

Jacob got up from the table and started to pace. "Yes, I probably could turn it down. I just don't know if I could live with myself if I did that. I think that being a true Christian sometimes involves sacrifice. I look at the example of Jesus and I see sacrifice. Pure and simple; from the moment of his birth, to his death on a cross, he was a living sacrifice."

Suzie looked down at her hands. "I guess it was stupid of me to think…I should have asked you what your plans were. I was always talking about myself wasn't I?" Suzie looked at Jacob with remorse.

"Ahh, Suzie, don't beat yourself up. I didn't know. I mean I had submitted my application a year ago. I thought they had lost my records or something. At the beginning, I thought it was a test from

God and then I met you." Jacob sat back at the table with his head cradled in his hands. "When I met you I considered withdrawing the application. I thought maybe I could start a church." Jacob raised his head to catch Suzie's gaze. "That way I could be with you, if you wanted that. I had mentioned this to my brothers and they were ready to build a church in the backyard of Grace and Mercy's place." Jacob heaved a big sigh and dropped his gaze. "Then the letter came. They had been working this whole year to get the approval for me to go to the Congo. It wasn't easy. They had to jump through hoops to get the approval."

Jacob paused to take a breath, a look of anguish on his face. "What are you thinking?"

Suzie stared at Jacob. "I am in shock, to be honest with you, Jacob. This is just a lot for me to absorb. It is amazing how one minute I am on top of the world and the next, I am sinking to a new low. I don't know what I am going to do without you."

Suzie looked down at the floor. "I am flooded with emotions right now and none of them are good. I am scared I may say something which could hurt you. Would you mind if I had some time to pray about this and maybe we could talk again tomorrow?"

"I'm sorry, Suzie. I had no intention of hurting you when I first met you. I thought of you as… kind of like a little sister to me. Then my feelings started changing. I tried hard not to feel anything other than a friendship but you are such an amazing woman..."

"Thank you, Jacob. I really need some time alone. I need to sort through all of the chaotic thoughts which are flooding my mind right now. Could you possibly bring the rest of these cookies to Grace and

Mr. Mercy? I will come over when I have sorted things out." Suzie swallowed hard, willing an avalanche of tears to stay put.

"Sure, I'll see you tomorrow, hopefully." Jacob said as he grabbed the cookies. Jacob walked to the back door and closed it gently as he stepped onto the back porch.

CALLING UPON FAITH

As Jacob closed the back door Suzie crumbled into a mess of tears.

"Why would you give me a man who is so wonderful, only to take him away? Haven't I gone through enough to deserve something good for a change?" Suzie screamed out to God in indignation. "Why would you do this? Why?"

After a bout of crying, Suzie attempted to pull herself together. She knew that wallowing in selfpity would not be a productive way to spend her weekend. She started cleaning her house with anger dusting the furniture, indignation vacuuming the floors, and fury cleaning the bathroom and kitchen.

She had just sat down for a rest when the phone rang. Her hands were shaking with exhaustion as she picked up the phone.

"Hello, sweet child of God. How is your first weekend without your children going?" Faith asked.

"Well Faith, it has been a whirlwind and I am not sure what to make of it." Suzie paused and took a deep breath.

"This morning I went to the library and found a lead on a job."

"That is wonderful! What kind of job is it?" Faith asked.

"It is a weekend position at a nursing home. It was just what I was hoping for."

"Terrific. What else happened today?"

"I led the librarian to Christ." Suzie said, as if it was no big deal.

"You did what?" Faith asked.

"I led the librarian to Christ. She was really a pill to deal with at the start but her dog was really sick and she just lost her Mom to cancer. Her mother had always talked with her about God but she had never accepted Christ. At least, not until she met me." Suzie smiled as she recollected the precious memory. "I don't know what it is about leading people to Christ but I sure do get happy when I do that."

"That is because you are fulfilling the calling that God has placed on your heart," Faith said.

"When I was driving home, I passed by a plant nursery. I wanted to stop by and purchase some plants for my house. My house has looked drab for quite some time. I wonder if that is coveting?"

Faith interrupted. "I wouldn't consider that coveting. I would characterize that as a desire to enhance your property with God's natural beauty."

"Yeah, well, then I happened upon a house which looked very similar to mine and I *was* coveting. It had the same shape as my house but a new paint job and the yard was amazing. The yard was a cascade of vibrant colors; purple, red and pink with accents of dark green. I *really* wanted that house. Then I looked around a bit and I realized that house *was* mine." Suzie giggled with joy.

"You're kidding, right? Was it like a mirage or something?" Faith asked.

"No, it was real. Jacob, my neighbor, and his brothers came and did a complete redo in one day. His mother and father, Grace and Mr. Mercy were foster parents. He must have over 100 brothers. I can't believe what a difference it made. I am so thankful."

"I imagine you are. Is that all that happened today? I detected a bit of sadness in your voice when you first answered. Did they pick the wrong colors?" Faith asked.

"No, everything they picked was perfect. I couldn't have asked for anything more. Jacob came over right away to make sure I was happy and I was…until… he told me he was leaving for Africa." Suzie started tearing up.

"Why Africa?" Faith asked.

"He has been called to the mission field." Suzie said, with tears rolling down her cheeks. "Faith, I always thought of him as a friend. I never considered that he might be anything other than that, but today my heart raced when he was near. Today of all days. The day I find out he is leaving is the day I discover I have fallen in love with him. Why would God do this to me?"

"Love is a choice and you have chosen well. Jacob sounds like a man after God's heart. Yet God loves those dear people in Africa just as much as He loves you." Faith paused for a moment. "There is a reason why God has put a calling on Jacob's life for Africa. He desires those who are lost to be found. He is yearning for the lost souls in Africa to return to His fold. Some of His children are being slaughtered and tortured for their belief and love for His Son. Others are being molested and abused by the government officials who are coming in under the disguise of 'peace making.'" Faith took a deep breath. "There is great hardship and suffering in Africa. God hears their prayers. He gave His Son to die on the cross for them and that is a sacrifice which is based on pure love."

"Faith, I feel horrible. Am I being selfish to want Jacob to stay here?" Suzie asked, the tears running in torrents.

"Darling, you are not selfish. You are in love. It is natural for you to yearn to be with someone you love. I believe if you asked Jacob, he would admit he has been in love with you from the moment he laid eyes on you." Faith responded with no condemnation in her voice.

"How am I to survive without him, Faith?" Suzie sobbed. "I have never felt the feelings I have when I am with him."

"What was the verse you chose for today?" Faith asked with gentleness in her tone.

"Seek ye first the kingdom of God and His righteousness, and all of these things shall be added unto you," Suzie responded.

"You seek God first and His righteousness. Then you have faith that all of these things will be added unto you. You have already started to fulfill your destiny, Suzie."

"What do you mean? I don't understand. I want my destiny to be with Jacob." Suzie stated, with a pout.

"Remember the dream you had when you asked for a glimpse of heaven?" Faith asked.

"Yes, I will never forget that," Suzie said.

"You were in a field full of women. You are to bring in a harvest of lost souls yourself. You have already opened the door for Katie to enter into heaven. You have many more doors to open."

"Am I supposed to go to Africa?" Suzie asked, clearly searching for a way to be near Jacob.

"Was Katie in Africa?"

"No, she was in a nearby town." Suzie said, her sail of hope deflating.

"You will know the answer when you seek God with all of your heart," Faith replied.

"How do I do that?" Suzie asked. "It is not like God is showing up for breakfast every morning."

"You immerse yourself in His word and you pray until you get peace."

"But what about Jacob? How do I respond to him?"

"You let him go, Suzie. He is devoted to fulling the call of God upon his life in Africa."

"Why can't his calling be in America?" Suzie pleaded.

"You are being tested, Suzie. In Jeremiah 29:11-12 God says, "I know the plans I have for you, plans to prosper you and not to harm you. Plans to give you a hope and a future. Then you will call upon me and pray to me and I will listen to you." Faith said with confidence.

"You need to have faith that God will protect Jacob as he is working in Africa. God needs you to pray for him daily to provide the strength for what he is supposed to do in the mission field. He has allowed the feelings of love to grow in your heart so that your prayers will be passionate and continuous. God needs you in America to pray and support Jacob while he is on the mission field in Africa."

"I understand, Faith. It is just that I am feeling like God is not even considering my needs at all. I lost my husband to another woman and he gets to live in a castle. Then I fall in love with a wonderful man of God and he moves to Africa. Where do I fit in? Where do my needs get met?" Suzie whined.

"Suzie, you are looking at all of the things you have lost. The one thing you have not lost is God's love. Did you ever tell Jacob that your favorite color was purple?"

"No," Suzie replied wondering where this was leading.

"Did you even mention to Jacob that you thought your house could use a new coat of paint?"

"No, I didn't. I knew I couldn't afford it so I didn't even talk about it."

"The Holy Spirit was the one who led Jacob and his brothers to do all of the work on your house and your garden. Were you pleased when you saw your house?"

"I would say ecstatic would be the proper term to describe my reaction."

"God is just as ecstatic about the changes He has seen in you. You have taken the shattered vase of a broken marriage and allowed the light of God's love to shine through your life. You have opened the door to two rooms in God's mansion in heaven. The man at the tire shop and one young woman are now a part of God's family due to your testimony."

"I guess I really have a knack for opening doors in heaven don't I?" Suzie asked with a grin spreading across her face.

"That is why God heard your prayers of righteous indignation when you saw the house that Joe lived in. He put the thought in

Jacob's mind to make your house as beautiful as it could possibly be," Faith replied.

"Well, He certainly did a good job on that front."

"As you seek His kingdom and His righteousness. He will continue to provide for your needs," Faith said.

"I have a decision to make. Either I am on God's team, fighting to increase His kingdom on earth; or I am on Suzie's team, with no eternal goals in mind," Suzie said.

"That is an interesting way to put it but, yes, I think you are at a crossroads in your life. God will still love you no matter which way you go. The question is… how much do you love God?"

"I think I need to get some sleep. It has been an exhausting day. Good, but exhausting. I don't want to make a such an important decision when my mind is clouded with fatigue." Suzie said as a yawn forced her mouth wide open.

"That is a wise decision to make. I will be praying for you Suzie. Good night, sweet child of God."

"Good night, Faith. I love you."

THE LAST BATTLEFRONT

AS NIGHT CLOSED IN, THE ENTITY OF DECEIT HAD only one goal on his mind. The decimation of Susanna Whatley.

Deceit was in a stir. Susanna had thwarted every attack. In the midst of this war she had began to shield herself with the armor of God.

The fact that she delighted in bringing the good news to those who were lost went against every fiber in the realm of evil. To bring the light of truth into darkness made an absolute mess of everything.

Susanna had more than one annoying trait. Not only did she enjoy leading others into salvation through Jesus Christ, she also hungered for the Word of God. Blasted woman, she was even starting to claim a verse daily. What an absolute horror!

She was getting very close to thirsting for righteousness. For a single mother to desire righteousness, instead of fornication and lewd behavior was just so unlike humans.

Susanna had failed to measure up to the expectations of society. She had not applied for welfare, she had not succumbed to the lust of men, she hadn't even abused her snotty-nosed brats. She was becoming worthless to the purpose of evil. Why was she still living?

A nagging thought kept knocking at the door of Deceit. Suzie had been isolated. She hadn't been exposed to the world. Staying at home with her brats left little opportunity for lust to seep into the crevices of her heart. The more she chose God, the harder it was for Deceit to lure her into sin. If he could displace the breastplate of righteousness, he would have access to her heart.

Suppose, just suppose, he could break her heart through fornication. Then he would be able to peel off the other pieces of armor which so shielded her from the attacks of evil.

He needed help. He rang the bell, calling the forces of evil in for yet another meeting.

Soon they were all gathered in the Chamber of Evil.

"I am distraught, dismayed, utterly embarrassed by the lack of progress we have made in securing the demise of Susanna Whatley." Deceit said, as he strolled throughout the chamber, glaring at each entity of evil.

"Adultery, I believe the last time we met you said you had something planned. Could you fill me in?" Deceit asked.

"Well, I have been quite busy with the politicians in Washington D. C. and then those lewd men in Hollywood…" Adultery paused to flip her long blond curly hair over her shoulder. "I mean those are the power brokers in the world, right? Why are you so obsessed with one single mother who lives in a shack out in the country?"

"It may be because she has a calling on her life. You imbecile! She has already secured the entry into heaven for one old man who ran a tire shop. Who knows what else she has done while you were gallavanting among the 'power brokers.'"

Envy quickly checked her records. "Master, according to the latest tally, Susanna Whatley has three souls credited to her for entry into heaven. The tire shop man, her lawyer, and now a librarian." Envy's eyes opened in horror. "The librarian was on the brink of suicide when Susanna presented Christ to her and she accepted."

"The power brokers are NOT in Washington DC or in Hollywood. You idiot! *They* are already on our side. You need to focus on Susanna Whatley."

Adultery held her hands up to ward off the anger of Deceit. "Calm down, calm down." Adultery sat down on a stool, taking center stage.

"I was in the library when the librarian was choosing where Susanna should work. I only allowed one option. The option includes a nursing home with a doctor whose heart is full of arrogance and contempt for his wife. He is a pro at playing the victim and luring young nurses into his bed. If they don't succumb to his advances, he fires them and destroys their career. If they do sleep with him, then the breastplate of righteousness is ripped from their chest and we have access to their heart. You know what I do with hearts, don't you? I break them into a million little pieces." Adultery let out a shrill and haunting laugh.

"In addition to this set up, an unusual event has occurred." Adultery started swaying through the chamber, sashaying her hips as if she was on a run way. "Susanna has fallen in love. Her heart has been captured by a godly man by the name of Jacob."

Deceit exploded in rage and grabbed Adultery, throwing her against the chamber wall. "Are you mocking me, you bitch? There is no evil in a Godly man."

Adultery kept her cool. "How right you are and Jacob is as good as a man gets. He is so good, in fact, that he is going to Africa to be a missionary. He tells Susanna this on the same day that she realizes she has fallen in love with him. First, she loses her husband to another woman. Then she loses the love of her life to God. When the doctor strolls in the door of her life, she will be famished for love. Any kind of love, even if it is covered in sin."

Deceit fell back and took a deep breath. "This might work. This just might work. I want all forces to be involved. I am not leaving this up to you, Adultery. Rejection, I want you to slither into the mind of Susanna, making her feel as if God has abandoned her by sending Jacob to Africa."

Rejection rattled his tale. "I have already entered her thoughts, my master."

Deceit continued on. "Arrogance, I want you to set foot in the doctor's heart so that he places his sexual lust far above any rational thought process."

The peacock feathers of Arrogance fanned out in full display. "Consider it done, sir."

"Doubt, I want you to chip away at the shield of Faith which Susanna has placed in front of her heart. She needs to doubt that God loves her," Deceit stated.

"I will try, but do you know that the Holy Spirit led Jacob and his brothers to do a complete updo on her house and yard? So now, like every time she walks outside or sees her house, she is reminded that God loves her. Kind of hard to chip away at that, sir," Doubt said.

"I don't know why Jacob couldn't be like the majority of Christians. You know, most of them do a good job of ignoring the needs of single mothers. They are first in line to judge them." Doubt swayed back and forth.

"That is due to my baby, Self-righteousness. Together we can stop so many good intentions. Unfortunately, Jacob does not leave an open door for us. He is filled with humility." Arrogance shook his feathers. "What an absolute waste humility is."

Deceit felt his grasp loosening on the group. He started to panic. He needed to redirect and make it quick. "Insecurity, I want you to infuse the thoughts of Susanna with your presence. She lost one husband, now she loses another man. Who will ever love her? Have her keep questioning herself. Point out the cellulite and the wrinkles she has gained. She doesn't have a job. Her house is still a mess. You know, on and on."

Insecurity lifted her wilted head. "Gotcha."

Deceit walked over to Envy. "Envy, oh, Envy, where do you belong in this twisted tale of demise?" Deceit pondered for a moment while Envy quivered with anticipation.

"When Susanna meets this wayward doctor, emphasize all of the lovely things that go along with being a doctor's wife. The prestige, the money, the vacations. Living above the standard of living, instead of below it."

Deceit twirled around in a circle as if to make a point. "Make sure you do not allow reality to filter in. You know, the countless hours of being on call that most doctors do. Nor do I want the reality that he is married to permeate her conscious mind. She is to be filled with envy for the 'lucky' wife of this doctor."

Envy jiggled with excitement for her new venture.

Deceit then stopped in front of Betrayal. "The moment Susanna becomes engaged in sex with this doctor I want you to start ripping her heart to shreds. You will cause the doctor to discard her like used trash once he has had sex with her."

"Condemnation will convict her of her sin." Deceit looked around. "The thought that she was abandoned by not only two men, but now three, will cause her to plunge the dagger of self hate into her heart. The death certificate is a short jaunt from self hate. Just a short jaunt."

Condemnation stepped out from the shadows. "I don't mean to be in opposition to this magnificent plan but I do think there may be one aspect we have not considered."

"What, what, do you mean? What supposed aspect has been overlooked?" Deciet said with agitation.

"It appears to me that Suzie loves God more than she loves any man."

Deceit swirled in anger, it was as if his cloak was fuming. "GET OUT! GET OUT! BRING ME THE DEATH CERTIFICATE OF SUSANNA WHATLEY!" He thundered in a blind rage.

THE SACRIFICE

JACOB AWOKE EARLY THAT SUNDAY MORNING. HE made coffee and sauntered out to the front porch. Sitting on the porch swing, he inhaled the aroma of coffee, contemplating his future.

His heart was yearning to sprint down the path to Suzie's house. His body swayed back and forth on the swing, as his heart see sawed between faith and doubt.

Soon the kind and gentle face of Mr. Mercy appeared, as the front door began to open. "Mind if I join you?"

Jacob looked up from his coffee. "I would welcome the company." Jacob said, as he slid over for Mr. Mercy to sit down.

"I have sensed a change coming over you," Mr. Mercy said.

Jacob looked into the distance. "Yes, change is a good word to describe all that I have gone through since I moved back home."

"You want to tell me what you are thinking?" Mr. Mercy asked.

"I think I have been given a choice. A choice to fulfill my calling or to follow the path of love."

"It is interesting that you would consider it a choice. That word indicates that you would have to choose one over the other. What about trying to interweave the paths?" Mr. Mercy suggested.

"You mean ask Suzie to come to Africa with me? I don't know what it will be like. What if it is dangerous? She has three wonderful children. What is she to do with them?" Jacob got up from the porch swing and walked to the railing of the front porch. "Their natural father wants to see them every weekend. I can't uproot them and force them to go to Africa. Nor can I ask Suzie to leave them here. Suzie would never leave her children to go to another country." Jacob turned around and sat on the porch railing. "I would never ask her to do that."

"So you think that a person must be present to experience love?" Mr. Mercy asked.

Jacob looked at Mr. Mercy as if he had lost his mind. "Of course. I mean isn't that how you nurture a relationship? By spending time with one another?"

Mr. Mercy nodded his head in agreement. "Yes, that is necessary for most humans. Yet, God chose to only become man for thirty-three years. Jesus is the greatest gift of love this world has ever seen and he is not present on earth at this moment in time. It is His Spirit, the Holy Spirit, which tends to His sheep and nurtures those who have professed their love for Him."

"So you are saying that Suzie and I can love each other even when I am not across the road from her?" Jacob shook his head.

"Yes, I am saying just that. Jacob, you have no idea what kind of darkness you will encounter in Africa. Suzie is a warrior in the spiritual realm. She has been buffeted by the devil with one attack after another and with each attack she has sought God's word and come out stronger." Mr. Mercy got up from the swing and stood in front of Jacob. "There are few women who hold the Lord's hand as they walk each step. Suzie clings to God as if He is her only Hope."

"I know, I know. That is what I find so irresistible about her. She lights up when she talks about God. Do you know that within the short time I have known her, she has already led people to Christ?" Jacob said with a look of pride. "Can you imagine what God could do through her in Africa?"

"Yes, yes, I know. She has been assigned a great harvest of lost souls to gather for God." Mr. Mercy covered Jacob's hands with his own and looked into his eyes with understanding. "But, Jacob, Suzie is to remain here."

"Why? Why?" Jacob melted into the embrace of his Father, Mr. Mercy, as his shoulders shook with sobs. "I am going to miss her and her children so much."

"They will miss you also. Suzie has come into awareness of what she feels for you. It is important that you keep your relationship pure and free from sexual sin," Mr. Mercy said. "If you open the door to lust, Satan can wreak havoc in both of your hearts during this time of separation."

"So how do I love her if I can't hold her? How do I provide for her needs if I am not near her? How do I nurture the children if I can not even play catch with them?" Jacob asked, with a pleading heart.

"You trust God that He will show her love. You have Faith that He will provide for her needs and you intercede in prayer that the children will remain blessed in your absence," Mr. Mercy said.

"How can God, who is invisible, love her better than I?" Jacob asked.

"God had only one Son. He sacrificed His only Son to be tortured and to die on a cross for Suzie's sins and you doubt His love?"

Jacob pulled away from Mr. Mercy and wiped the tears from his eyes. "No, I don't doubt God's love. I believe at this moment in my life I must decide whom I love." Jacob took a deep breath and began pacing. "Either my whole life as a Christian is a charade or it is a decision which infuses my love for God into every thought and action. I definitely love Suzie and if God loved her enough to send Jesus to die on the cross for her sins so that He can spend eternity with her, then I am sure He is capable of protecting her."

"She will continue to be a light of Hope for you, Jacob. Where there is the darkness of sin, it is important to have someone who can shed light." Mr. Mercy said, with a gentle smile.

"I don't know how I am going to let go of her." Jacob said, with tears streaming down his face.

"You don't need to let go of her, Jacob. You just need to hand her and her children over to God every day," Mr Mercy said.

Jacob got up in anger. "What if she finds someone else while I am in Africa?."

"If she finds someone else you will need to pray that that person is God's will for her life," Mr. Mercy replied.

"And what if he was abusive?" Jacob's eyes were afire with indignation.

"That is never God's will. Suzie is smarter than that," Mr. Mercy stated.

"Why is this happening to me? Suzie is the only woman I have ever fallen in love with. Now when I find love, I am forced to walk away… to fulfill God's plan for my life?"

"You keep saying you are leaving Suzie. Jacob, your love will never leave Suzie. Just like God's love will never leave you." Mr. Mercy folded his hands as if praying. "You are separated by land and sea but your hearts will choose where your affection lies." Mr. Mercy paused for a moment. "If you survive this time apart you will love deeply, like God loves."

"What do you mean by that?" Jacob asked.

"God loves people so much that he gives them free will to walk away from Him. He loves entirely without manipulation or control. He sacrificed His only Son to allow access to His heart and His love and yet millions of people can and do walk away."

"What if she falls in love with a good man while I am away?" Jacob asked, his face tortured with emotion.

"I am hoping she falls in love with a very good man while you are away." Mr. Mercy said, his eyes ablaze with truth.

Jacob turned to Mr. Mercy with a look of shock on his face. "You don't think I am good enough for her do you?"

"It is not what I think that matters. I am hoping she falls in love with the best man possible. Her eternal husband, Jesus Christ," Mr. Mercy stated.

Jacob was speechless for a moment. "You know what? I hope the same thing."

GOD'S PROVISION

As Suzie sipped her first cup of coffee she looked out her kitchen window. Her eyes feasted on her transformed yard. It was stunning. She wanted to giggle with joy every time she looked outside.

Yet, today was not about the aesthetic quality of her yard and house. It was about her heart and soul. Would she choose to trust God or would she become bitter and resentful over the recent events in her life?

It was hard to question God when the Holy Spirit had been so gracious to her recently.

When Suzie reflected on the changes that had happened since Joe left, she felt a sense of peace. She knew that divorce was not what God would want but she had never felt as close to God as she did now.

There was still an inkling of doubt residing in her heart and mind. Would God really take care of her if Jacob was in Africa?

"Seek ye first the Kingdom of God and His righteousness, and all these things shall be added unto you."

Suzie bowed her head to pray. "God, I know you created the world. I understand that you helped Jacob and his brothers transform my house. For some reason I am still doubtful that you can provide for my children and me. Could you please indulge me and give me one more sign that you will provide?"

Suzie's prayer was interrupted by the phone ringing. "Hello?"

"Hello, Suzie? This is your mother, Barbara."

Suzie's first reaction was to cringe. She discarded that response and answered with a cheerful greeting. "Hello, Mom. I am so sorry I haven't called you. I have been thinking about you every day. How are you doing?"

Barbara gave a sigh. "I am sorting through the baggage of my life, thanks to you."

Suzie paused for a moment, not sure how to react. "Is that a good thing?"

"Ummm, yes, I would say it is a very good thing. It is brutal, but after seeing you and talking with you, I became aware of how bitter I had become," Barbara said.

"Wow, that is a big thing, Mom. So how are you sorting through your baggage?" Suzie asked.

Barabara laughed, "Very slowly. I am going through my entire life and trying to examine every piece of baggage looking for any good remnants. In the Bible it says that *all* things work together for good." Barbara paused for a moment, which hung in the air as if it were a century. "I missed my mother so terribly when she died. Yet, I think of all of the qualities I gained by the responsibility I was given. I was the oldest child in a motherless home. I don't think I would have fulfilled my dream of owning a boutique without that happening."

"That is a good point. What other pieces of baggage have you examined?" Suzie asked.

"I have unpacked and repacked the death of Stevie a million times throughout my life. The only way I can explain it, is that God needed him in heaven and he needed you on earth. When I realized that, something broke loose in me. I had been holding on to him. I have to release him into God's hands. God is more than capable of loving him." Barbara said with resolution.

"That is a big step for you, Mom," Suzie said.

"Yes, it is. It was amazing to me that when I finally released Stevie to God, I felt more love for you. If you are willing, I would like spend a day or two every month with you and my grandchildren." Barbara said with trepidation. "Would that be okay?"

"It wouldn't be okay, Mother. It would be wonderful! I would love to have you come over. You are welcome any time you can fit it in to your busy boutique schedule." Suzie said with a grin.

Barbara breathed a sigh of relief. "There is one more thing I would like to ask."

"Go ahead," Suzie said.

"Would it be okay if I brought some clothes from my boutique that the kids could sort through? They could have whatever they want, I have some really cute clothes for kids," Barbara said.

"Oh, Mom. I would love that. They could really use some new clothes. Thank you so much for offering that." Suzie said with love. "What time would it suit for you to come over?"

"What would be the best time for you?" Barbara asked.

Suzie contemplated for a moment and then replied. "Would tomorrow be okay? I need to go and apply for a job. Would you mind watching Jonathan while I do that?"

"I wouldn't mind at all. What time would you like for me to arrive?"

"Hmmm, how about 9 o' clock in the morning? I get home from dropping the kids off at school around 8:30," Suzie replied.

"That sounds perfect. Do you want me to bring coffee cake again?" Barbara asked.

"Mom, you are bringing clothes over for the kids. Don't you think that is enough?"

"Well, it is such an easy coffee cake. It would be no big deal," Barbara replied.

"Are you sure?" Suzie asked.

"Yes, it takes like two minutes to put it together and a half an hour to bake it. It doesn't take a rocket scientist," Barbara said.

"Alright, I need to be honest with you about something. I am going to be selfish. I want to keep the left overs again if that is okay with you."

Barbara busted out laughing. "Of course you can keep the left overs. I am so glad you enjoyed it."

"'Enjoy it' would be an understatement. I am excited that you are coming over. I am beginning to love you, Mom." Suzie said with sincerity.

"Oh, that is so good to hear, Suzie. I have always loved you. I was scared of it though. Fearful that my love would cause you to die."

"We will work through that fear, Mom. You need to trust God that he will protect me and the children. You can't live life to the fullest if you leave the door open to fear." Suzie said with confidence.

"I am beginning to realize that. Well, I will see you tomorrow morning then, dear."

"Great! See you tomorrow. Oh, and Mom… my house looks different on the outside so just look for my car in the front yard. You might not recognize the house." Suzie said in closing.

"I don't care what your house looks like. I just want to see you and the children," Barbara said.

"That is good to hear. See you tomorrow then," Suzie said.

"Tomorrow it will be. Goodbye, Suzie, I love you." Barbara said, a tear of gratitude trickling down her cheek.

"Goodbye, Mom, I love you too," Suzie said.

As Suzie hung up the phone she realized that God had answered her prayer. Her kids were getting some new clothes and she also was getting a babysitter for free. This was all to be done through a mother whom she had not loved for most of her life.

There was no doubt that He could take care of her and her children and the doubt that her mother could heal was becoming less and less a concern.

BREAKING THE NEWS

SUZIE SKIPPED DOWN HER NEW FRONT PORCH WITH an assurance that had settled in her heart. She knew that if God needed Jacob in Africa then that was where she wanted him to be. She needed to talk with him.

As she approached Jacob's front door, she thanked God for the wonderful time she had spent with him. What a comfort he had been after Joe left. Not only to her but her children.

Suzie stopped in her tracks.

The children… what would the boys think? Jacob had become such a good friend to them. He was almost like a second father to them.

They would be heartbroken.

Tears started trickling down her cheeks.

She had to get a grip before ringing the doorbell. Jacob could NOT see her cry. She was supposed to be excited about his calling to Africa. Maybe she should come over another time. As she turned to walk away, the front door swung open and in a minute she had melted into the arms of Jacob.

"I thought I had my emotions under control. I don't mean to be crying." Suzie said in between sobs. "I hadn't even thought about the boys. They adore you." Suzie said, looking at Jacob. "What are they going to do without you?"

"I know. I know," Jacob said, pulling Suzie back into his arms. "I have been praying about them. Suzie, you have to know that no matter where I am, I will always love you and your children. You mean the world to me. I love your children as if they were mine." Jacob stroked Suzie's long silky hair with tenderness. "I don't know why this is happening but I know my God. I know He has promised that all things work together for good to those who love Him and to those who are called according to His purpose. I know my purpose right now is to serve in Africa."

"I know. I understand. It is just with Joe leaving, I assumed that you were a gift from God to replace him. My bad. I guess my life is not meant to be a Hallmark movie."

"I wouldn't say that. When I see you, I see a miracle," Jacob said.

"A miracle?" Suzie asked. "How could I be a miracle?"

"You have taken a memory from childhood which could be the seed for bitterness and unforgiveness and transformed it into a path of healing for your mother. *That* is a miracle," Jacob stated.

Suzie looked at Jacob for a moment, letting his words sink in. "I guess I did choose that path didn't I? By the way, my mother is coming tomorrow to babysit Jonathan while I apply for a job. She's bringing some new clothes for my children. Can you believe that?" Suzie stopped to wipe the tears from her face. "The craziest thing is that I am so excited about seeing her. I used to dread even getting a call from her. I think God is changing the heart of my mother." Suzie blew her nose into a hanky which Jacob provided.

"I think God may be changing your heart too." Jacob said, with a wink.

Suzie looked at Jacob and smiled. "You know, I think you may be right about that. Now why don't you tell me about Africa?"

Jacob's face broke out in a grin. "On one condition: you come inside and have lunch with me. Grace was fixing a delicious meal when I walked out on the front porch."

"Well you don't have to twist my arm to agree to that plan." Suzie said with gusto.

The afternoon sun melted into a sunset and Suzie was shocked that the time had passed so quickly. She needed to pick up the children. She was glad she had spent the afternoon with Jacob though. She had gained an appreciation for the African people after talking with Jacob at length about his calling. She was sad that he was leaving but she couldn't deny his passion for doing God's will.

As she walked across the road to her home she began dreading the rest of the day. Seeing Joe would have been hard in any circumstance but seeing him reside in such splendor grated on her nerves.

She needed to claim a verse for this journey. She rushed inside and opened her Bible to Ephesians 2. Her gaze settled on verse 10. "For we are God's masterpiece. He has created us anew in Christ Jesus, so we can do the good things He planned for us to do long ago."

The last thing that Suzie wanted to do at this point was something which was good. She wanted vengeance and justice for all that she had been through. Yet she prayed that she would surrender her will to God.

She drove up to the "castle" admiring the beauty of the sunset reflecting on the pond in the front yard. Suzie prayed that admiration was not envy. She did appreciate the beauty before her but after talking with Hope she realized the work this would entail. She didn't have the energy or the focus for this kind of mansion. It was certainly beautiful though. She would be lying if she didn't admit that.

She drove in the circular drive and walked up the stairs. She rang the doorbell and waited a bit. Then she knocked on the door. She rang the doorbell again and the door opened with a flourish of anger.

"Have you ever heard of common courtesy?" Megan asked with a scowl. "Your children are changing into the clothes you sent them in. Could you please be patient?"

Suzie's mouth hung open, no words came out and the door was slammed in her face. She felt about an inch tall. How on earth Megan did it, she couldn't determine, but she had made her feel worthless.

Soon Joe opened the door. The kids were clustered around him, giving him hugs and kisses. They begged him to walk them to the car.

Suzie stood aside in shock. He leaves the family for another woman. He gets a mansion and now, somehow, the children, whom he has ignored for the past few years, are smitten with absolute adoration for him.

She trudged behind Joe, who had two new arms called Michael and Jonathan and a third leg, by the name of Sarah.

Joe helped nestle the children in the car and gave kisses to each young face. He turned to walk back into his "castle" when Suzie grabbed him by the arm.

"Joe, please tell me. Why did you leave?"

Joe's eyes flitted from the mansion back to Suzie's car. "Suzie, when I married you I thought we wanted the same things. Once you had children, you changed. You weren't the wife I wanted anymore."

"You wanted this?" Suzie pointed to the "castle."

"Yes, Suzie. I wanted something better than what you were willing to settle for. Megan has fulfilled every desire I have. I am at peace and content."

Suzie's heart sank. "Joe, if this is what makes you happy, you are right. I don't want this. I want so much more. I want my life to be full of love instead of materialistic items. I want my goals to be eternal not temporal." Suzie got in the car and gunned the motor. As she sped off she saw Joe shaking his head as he turned, walking back to his "castle."

The children settled into bed with little to no fuss. Suzie picked up the house a bit before she went to bed.

She meditated on Ephesians 2:10 before going to bed. As she meditated on the verse she realized that Joe's new mansion was intended to become a distraction for her. She needed to focus on becoming a masterpiece created anew in Christ Jesus. The reason why she was to become a masterpiece was so that she could do good things. What a unique and unusual goal that was.

As her mind drifted off to sleep she asked for God to help her become the masterpiece which He wanted her to be. She had wasted too many years trying to be something less than a masterpiece and working to impress a man who would never know that reality.

GOD'S MASTERPIECE

SUZIE WOKE UP BEFORE THE ALARM COULD JOLT HER out of bed. She said her morning prayers then started brewing the coffee.

So many thoughts were racing through her mind. How was she going to tell her children about Jacob leaving for Africa? Would Jonathan and her mother get along while she was applying for a job? What if she didn't get a job? How was she going to pay her bills if she didn't get a job?

She heard the pitter patter of tiny feet traipsing down the hall.

"Mommy, Daddy lives in a castle!" Michael said with pride.

"I noticed that honey. So how was your weekend in the castle?" Suzie asked, biting her lip.

"Ohhhh… it was interesting. Saturday morning we went out for breakfast. Megan doesn't like cooking because it gets her kitchen dirty." Michael paused to brush a stray crumb off the kitchen table. "I had a humongous waffle. They said the waffle was from a country but I can't remember the name of the country." Michael paused to recollect.

"Could it be a Belgium waffle?" Suzie asked.

"Yes! It was a Belgium waffle. It was really good. Then we went to McDonald's to play and we played in the jungle gym. After we played for awhile we had lunch. Then we went to a movie and on Sunday we did a repeat." Michael said with a smile.

"Did you have any time in the castle?" Suzie asked.

"Well, we slept there but Megan said that was *her* castle and she didn't want it getting dirty. Daddy said your house was a mess and he didn't want his new house looking like yours." Michael said, clearly trying to keep his composure.

Suzie felt her innards starting to boil. "I must admit that my house is not a castle but my house is your home and you don't have to be perfect to be in my house."

"Megan screamed at Daddy a lot when we were there. We felt bad for him." Michael said, wringing his hands.

Suzie felt a bit of satisfaction when she heard that but she could tell that the weekend had been unsettling for Michael. She said a silent prayer to God asking Him how to handle this in a Christian manner.

"Megan has probably never had small children in her home. It may take a bit of time for her to get used to having you around. Why don't you try to be as clean as you possibly can and she might relax over time."

"I don't know Mom, she was pretty tense. She kept saying if we were good she would fly us to Disneyland next Christmas. Jonathan kept spilling his drink." Michael paused to run his fingers through his hair. "I don't think we are going to get to go."

Jonathan came toddling into the kitchen. He looked distraught. Suzie scooped him up in her arms and held him close.

"I got someone special coming to see you today." Suzie said, looking at Jonathan.

"Jacob? Is Jacob coming?" Jonathan's eyes lit up with anticipation.

"No, it's someone you haven't seen in a long time," Suzie said.

Jonathan crinkled his nose and forehead in concentration. "I don't know. I little, I not see that many people yet."

"Yes, I know, but your grandmother wants to see you today." Suzie said with a smile.

A look of absolute horror crossed Jonathan's face. "NO! Gwamma clean! Megan clean! I not clean! I spill things. I make messes." Jonathan let out a heartwrenching sob.

If Megan had been in the room, Suzie would have murdered her. She was surprised by the blatant rage she felt. To steal her husband was one thing but to demean and degrade her children for being children was beyond evil.

The demonic force of perfection was still knocking on her door. How could she prevent it from hurting Jonathan?

Her gaze fell on the verse that she had written down recently. "For we are God's masterpiece, created anew in Christ Jesus, so we can do the good things that He has planned for us long ago."

"Jonathan, I am sorry that Megan gave you a hard time for spilling things. She hasn't had children in her house so it may take her some time to get used to you. I want you to know that you are not a mess. You are a little boy and little boys get dirty and they sometimes spill things. You know what? God doesn't think you are a mess." Suzie said lifting Jonathan's head to make eye contact.

Jonathan wiped the tears from his eyes. "He doesn't?"

"No, he doesn't." Suzie grabbed her Bible from the kitchen counter. She flipped through the Bible and found Ephesians. "He says right here that you are a masterpiece. It also says that He is making you more and more like His son, Jesus every day. Do you know why he is doing this?"

Jonathan was spellbound. "No, why?"

"So that you could do good things that He planned for you to do long ago."

"Waz a mastapiece?" Jonathan asked.

"Well, a masterpiece in this instance is whatever God created you to be. He created you to do good things. We need to start praying that you become the masterpiece that God wants you to be," Suzie said.

"Okay, I not a mess, I am a mastapiece." Jonathan said, as he slipped off of Suzie's lap.

Sarah sauntered into the kitchen as Jonathan was slipping out. She had a beautiful box in her hands. She sat down at the table, opened up the box and started putting eye shadow on her eyelids.

Suzie looked at her with a frown creasing her brows. "What are you doing, Sarah?"

"After the boys went to bed Saturday night, Megan and I had some girl time." Sarah said with a smile. "She taught me how to use makeup. She doesn't want me growing up to be a plain Jane like you, Mom."

Suzie opened her mouth to speak and closed it. Opened it again to say something and closed it again. Finally she found the words that seemed right for the occasion. "Sarah, you are only seven years old. How many girls in your grade wear makeup?"

"Brittany wears makeup and she showed her belly button the other day." Sarah said with an air of indignation. "The boys are crazy about her."

"Sarah, I would prefer you not wear makeup until you get older. You are such a pretty girl and makeup disguises your beauty. God made you beautiful, why would you want to cover that up with makeup?" Suzie asked.

Sarah rolled her eyes. "Mommy, there are girls who follow the rules, girls who break the rules, and girls that write their own rules. Brittany writes her own rules. She is a trendsetter."

"So I guess you want to be a follower. Is that right? Because I thought you were someone who didn't follow. I always considered you more of a leader. I was sharing with Jonathan a verse in the Bible. In this verse it says that you are a masterpiece. If you believe in Jesus, you are becoming more like Him every day. Do you know why God is doing this?"

Sarah had a petulant pout smeared across her beautiful face. "No, why would I want to be like Jesus? He was crucified. I don't see what this has to do with wearing makeup."

"It has everything in the world to do with wearing makeup at seven years old. God created you to be a beautiful young girl and you need to appreciate your natural beauty." Suzie paused for a moment. "If you are changing how you look for boys, then you are changing who you are for something other than God. God, who created you, thinks you are a masterpiece."

Sarah's crumpled into tears and threw back her chair from the kitchen table. She stomped to her room, in a fury of indignation, slamming the door in the face of Suzie.

Suzie's first impulse was to barge through the closed door and scream at Sarah. She stopped for a moment to consider what Jesus would do in this circumstance. How could she preach Jesus to her children if she didn't first show them the nature of Jesus herself?

Suzie knocked gently on the door. "Sarah, could I please come in?"

No answer. Suzie knocked again. "Sarah, please let me in. I love you. I would like to talk with you."

Through sobs, Sarah muttered. "You can come in."

Sarah was in a fetal position. Tears streaming down her face. The mascara had long since left her lashes and the blue eyeshadow was beginning its descent into the abyss of nothingness.

"Listen honey. I'm concerned about how you view yourself. To be constantly comparing yourself to Brittany is not healthy for you. When your daddy left I realized how much I had tried to become something I wasn't to keep him here. I tried so hard to have a perfect house. I tried to remain slender." Suzie said stroking Sarah's hair. "I stopped going to church. I stopped reading the Bible. I hardly prayed at all. I turned my back on God. I had become an empty and shallow person because I was trying to fight what God had created me to be. I don't want you to change who you are for anyone other than God." Suzie stopped and took a deep breath. "Listen, I think it was really wonderful that Megan gave you that makeup. I wouldn't mind you using it when you get older but I think seven years old is just too young to wear makeup."

"Mommy, I look drab. I haven't got any new clothes. If you take me shopping I will put the makeup in my closet until you say I can use it." Sarah said with a determined look.

"Well, I can't afford to buy you new clothes right now but I have a surprise for you that is much better than a shopping trip."

"A surprise? Please tell me what it is." Sarah said, a smile creeping insidiously across her lips.

"Well, your Grandma is coming over today and she asked if she could bring some clothes over for you and the boys to try on. You know her boutique is quite fancy and she wanted to help us out," Suzie said.

"Really? Megan said she bought her clothes in Paris." The smile slowly faded from the face of Sarah.

"Yes, I know. Unfortunately, I can't afford a trip to Paris right now. Would you mind looking at the clothes that my mom brings over?"

"No, I wouldn't mind… I guess." Sarah paused, a frown still planted on her face. "Why are you calling her 'Mom?' I thought we were supposed to call her Barbara." Sarah said, her brows furrowed in confusion.

"God has done a lot of healing between my mother and I," Suzie said. "When God heals a relationship it is important to call that person the name that they prefer."

"I'm glad you made up with your mother," Sarah said. "All of my friends love their grandmas and call them 'Gammy,' 'Gamma,' and 'Grandmother.' It was kind of weird for me to say that mine was called 'Barbara.'"

"I am sorry about that, darling. Now please get ready for school. I intend to go job hunting today." Suzie said with a wink.

"Okay, Mom. You know I think you are right about Brittany. I really don't want to be like her, no matter how crazy the boys are about her." Sarah said, flipping her beautiful long hair over her shoulder.

Suzie chuckled. "That's my girl. We were made for better than impressing boys or men. We are a masterpiece, recreated in the likeness of Jesus, to do good things which God planned for us to do long ago."

A MASTERPIECE

SUZIE HAD TO RUSH TO GET THE KIDS TO SCHOOL ON time. It was amazing how many emotional bombs could have imploded inside her heart and mind if she hadn't had the Word of God protecting her.

Megan seemed to have a flare for criticism and verbal abuse. Suzie said a prayer of thanks to God that that demonic influence had not crept into her soul. She felt a bit of sympathy for Joe but soon got over that. He chose his bed, now he had to lie in it.

As Suzie opened her front door she said a prayer of gratitude. Suzie was so thankful that Jacob had shown her what a true man of God was. She dreaded the day he would leave for Africa but knew that if God wanted him there than that was to be her desire also.

The doorbell jolted her from her thoughts. She was shocked that the morning had flown by so quickly. She rushed to the door and opened it to her beautiful mother standing on the porch with a glistening caramel coffee cake.

Suzie gave her a warm smile. "My goodness, Mom. This coffee cake looks even more scrumptious than the last one you brought over."

Barbara returned the smile. "I hope you don't mind, I copied the recipe for you. Is that being too presumptious?"

Suzie gave a playful scowl. "No, ma'am, I think that is just being thoughtful. Thanks, Mom." She said as she enveloped her mother in a tender hug. As she held her close she whispered in Barbara's ear, "I need to share something with you before I get going. It is about Jonathan. Do you mind going to my bedroom?"

Barbara looked at Suzie with concern and walked very quietly to the bedroom.

"Hey Jonathan, Grandma is here. I need to show her something in my bedroom before she gets to play with you. Would you mind watching the dragons fly for just a bit?" Suzie asked.

Jonathan looked at his mother as if she had lost her mind. "No, Mommy. I don't mind at all." He jumped down from the chair, sprinted to the living room, had the TV on, and picked a spot on the couch in less than five seconds. "Take yo time, Mommy. I will be ok." He said as he stood on the couch and gave his mother a wink.

Suzie busted out in giggles as she made her way to the bedroom. Those flying dragons could be monsters one day and a godsend the next.

She made her way to the bedroom and opened the door to see her mother sitting on her unmade bed. "I don't know how to say this but to just be truthful. Jonathan had a difficult weekend at Joe and Megan's house. Apparently he spilled some milk and Megan hit the roof. She said he was a dirty boy and was always creating messes. The last time we were at your house the children were a bit traumatized by your obsession with cleanliness. As you can see, we don't live in a sterile environment. I want Jonathan's memories of you to be filled with laughter and love, not criticism. Could you please be on board with creating good memories?"

Barbara's face fell. "Was that why you refused to come back over?"

Suzie nodded.

Tears started rolling down the face of Barbara. "I am so sorry, hon. Come here, let me give you a hug. That old witch has been crucified with Jesus. I have asked God to clean out the clutter of rejection I felt from my father, the rejection I felt from the church, and to create in me a clean heart open to love others. I am so sorry for all of the hurt and criticism I have seeded into your life and the life of your children. I intend to change with the help of God."

Suzie embraced her mother. "You are forgiven." Suzie paused for a moment and then said. "I have something I want to share with you." Suzie turned from her mother and walked with haste to the kitchen picking up her index card with Ephesians 2:10 on it.

She walked back into her bedroom with a sword, the Word of God. "The devil is on the attack against my children and he knows he has lost his grip on you. He is using Megan and Joe now. This is a verse which God brought to my attention before I even knew what Megan had said."

Suzie handed the index card to her mother with joy. To be able to share her connection to God with her mother in this way was such a wonderful change. Suzie had not been allowed to talk about God when she had lived with Barbara.

Barbara took a moment to read the card. "That is how I felt about Stevie. He was such a beautiful masterpiece." Tears glistened in her eyes. "I was so blinded by my own grief I didn't see the masterpiece that God was creating in you. So, you want me to treat Jonathan as if he is a masterpiece of God?"

"Yes, Mom. If you don't mind. In that verse it indicates that we are to do this with the goal of doing good things for others. It is not to inflate our pride but to have enough self-confidence that we can do good, as God works to recreate us to be more Christlike." Suzie said with conviction.

"I have never heard of a better parenting technique than what you just proposed. I am totally on board with this and I will enjoy using this technique. You know what? You are a really good mother. I know I said your children were undisciplined but I was wrong to say that," Barbara said. "I am so sorry."

"Mom, you don't have to keep apologizing. I forgive you. Don't look back at how you used to be, look forward to how God can work in your life. In the Bible when Lot left Sodom and Gomorrha, God told him not to look back. Once we repent of our sin it is important that we don't allow the devil to keep condemning us for it. We must move on into the fullness of grace, accepting the forgiveness that Jesus gave us through his sacrificial death." Suzie gazed into the eyes of her mother with pure love.

"I have learned so much from you about God. You have a way of using God's word that is just… remarkable. Have you ever thought about ministering to other women? You would be so good at that." Barbara said as she and Suzie walked out of the bedroom.

"I know that is God's intention for my life. I received that wisdom from a dream but right now, I need to nurture my children. In God's timing I will fulfill His will in my life. I believe He wants me to develop a ministry for women but my first priority is the children He has blessed me with." Suzie said with a smile.

"Like I said, you are a very good mother. I would expect you to put your children first." Barbara said as she began to cut the coffee cake for consumption.

"Thank you, Mom. That means so much to me." Suzie turned her face to the living room. "Jonathan would you like some coffee cake?"

Jonathan bolted from the living room couch to the kitchen as if he hadn't eaten for a month.

The look in Barbara's eyes was one of true devotion when she looked at Jonathan. "Sweetheart, would you like some milk to go with that coffee cake?"

"No, Megan says I spill milk. I can only have wata."

Barbara's eyes turned to a slit of anger. "That bitch." She muttered under her breath. "Can I pour you just a little bit of milk? That way if you spill it, it is only a tiny mess. Tiny messes are easy to clean up."

Jonathan looked at Suzie who nodded her approval. "Ok, just a little though." Jonathan said with a smile.

Suzie looked at her mother with amazement. She would get up and down to pour Jonathan his milk, pouring only a smidgeon at a time.

Suzie needed to set the record straight on milk though. "Jonathan, you can drink milk at our house any time you want. I don't care if you spill it. We don't live in a castle, so we don't have to be worried about spilled milk okay? But I really love the way you handled this, Mom." Suzie said as she gave her mother a kiss on the cheek. "You are amazing." She whispered in the ear of her mother.

"Now I got to get ready for the day. Mom, could you please pray that I get the job that God wants me to have? I really would like a job on the weekends. Joe wants the children every weekend. If he takes them on the weekend and I take them during the week we wouldn't have to worry about the expense of daycare."

Barbara sighed. "Every weekend. Really?"

"Yes, that is how he got by with paying such a small amount of child support. Our great politicians at work again, trying to make it as hard as they can for single mothers."

"How much child support did you get?" Barabara asked.

Suzie looked at Jonathan and then looked at her mother and mouthed the words. "Not now."

Barbara nodded her head in understanding. "Well, I know that God will provide for you and the children. Jonathan what do you want to play today?"

Jonathan's face lit up. "I want to play with Legos. I love building things."

"That sounds like a wonderful plan for the day. Why don't you go get them?" Barbara said as she began to clean up the breakfast dishes. As she put the milk in the fridge, she noticed the bare shelves. After playing with Legos she was going to go grocery shopping with Jonathan.

"By the way, Suzie, I love the redo on the house. It is adorable! How were you able to afford that?" Barbara didn't mean to judge but she thought that food in the fridge may be more important than painting a house and planting trees and flowers.

Suzie came out of her bedroom with her wet hair draped in a towel turban. "You wouldn't believe this, Mom. I have a neighbor across the road who has become very dear to me. He and his brothers did this while I was running errands one day. I didn't even recognize the house. Drove right past it to begin with." Suzie busted out in giggles.

Barbara started laughing. "You know, I almost did the same thing. If I hadn't seen your car in the front yard I would have sped right past."

"God has been so good to me. He has protected me in so many ways since Joe left." Suzie looked up towards the heavens.

"I am only beginning to realize just how great our heavenly Father is, Suzie. I feel as if I am being reborn as I let go of the bitterness and unforgiving cage I lived in for so long."

"We are to be a masterpiece, recreated in the likeness of Jesus, for the purpose of doing good." Suzie said, with joy. "We are not to be enslaved in sin."

"Amen to that, sister." Barbara said, as she wiped the last crumb off the kitchen table.

THE JOB INTERVIEW

"DO I LOOK ALRIGHT, MOM?" SUZIE SAID AS SHE CAME out of her bedroom, wearing a casual pant suit.

"Well, let me see," Barbara walked into the hallway and twirled Suzie around. "You look wonderful. When did you start pulling your hair back into a bun?"

"As soon as it got long enough. I don't like hair getting into my cooking and if it is in a bun I don't intimidate other nurses. They seem to freak out when they see my long hair," Suzie replied.

"They're just jealous."

"Maybe, but I really need this job so I am not taking any chances." Suzie said, as she collected her resume' and purse from the formal dining table. "If I don't get home by 11:30 a.m. would you mind picking Michael up from school? I will call on the way to tell them that you may pick him up. Jonathan, you be good for Grandma, okay?"

Jonathan did not divert his gaze from the Legos. "Okay, Mommy."

Suzie put the address for the nursing home into her GPS and about jumped out of her skin when it started telling her how to get there.

She was heading out onto the country road when she realized she hadn't told her mother where Michael was going to school. She quickly dialed her home phone.

"Hello?" Barbara answered the phone with a cheerful tone.

"Hi, Mom. Hey, I am sorry but I didn't think to tell you how to get to Michael's school."

Suzie said, fumbling with her phone.

"That is okay. When you were married I got all of that information from Joe in case there were any emergencies. I have kept it in my wallet for safe keeping," Barbara said.

"Why didn't you ask me?" Suzie asked, feeling more than a little hurt.

"I never knew how to communicate with you, Suzie. Every time I tried to talk with you, I would criticize you. Then you would fight back and I would end up getting hurt. It seemed like a vicious circle. I do care about my grandchildren but I knew you didn't want me around them. The only reason why I asked Joe for the address of Michael and Sarah's school was in the case of emergencies." Barbara said, a tear trickling down her cheek.

"Mom, I'm sorry that I made you feel that way and thank you for caring enough about my children to ask for that information," Suzie said with compassion.

"You mean you're not mad at me for talking to Joe and not you?" Barbara asked wiping the tears from her cheek.

"How could I be mad at you? You were just trying to make sure my children were safe in an emergency. I think that is sweet."

Barbara gave a sigh of relief. "Oh, thank God. I thought I had messed up again by talking to Joe even when you were married. I don't talk to him anymore. I haven't talked with him since he told me Megan was a superstar in her career field."

"That's okay Mom. I know you miss him. I just think it would be easier for him and Megan to form a good relationship if you didn't call him. Apparently, the grass on the other side of the fence is not as green as Joe thought it would be. He made his bed though and now he has to lie in it. Please don't call him again." Suzie said, praying that her mom would understand and not be offended.

"Oh, don't worry. I have no intention of doing that," Barbara said. "Now go get that job."

"Yes, ma'am!" Suzie said with a cheerful giggle.

Suzie drove down the country roads till she arrived at the town where the nursing home was located. She put a fresh coat of lipstick on her lips and checked to make sure no stray hairs were escaping her bun. She grabbed her resume' and purse, then walked into the nursing home with an air of confidence.

She walked up to the front desk and could see that the nurse was playing a game on her phone. "Excuse me. I am looking for a job. I found an ad for a weekend supervisory position. Do you know if that is still available?"

"Couldn't tell you." The nurse said, not looking up from her phone.

"Well, if you couldn't tell me, perhaps you could direct me to who could." Suzie said using her most polite voice.

"The Director of Nurses office is down the hall. The closed door on your right."

The nurse looked up from her phone and sized up Suzie. "Good thing you are slender, cause that heifer is so big she can barely get through the door."

"Thank you so much," Suzie said. She turned to walk down the hallway and almost ran smack dab into a tall man with a white lab coat on. "Excuse me."

"NO, exccuuussee me. Wow! Where did you come from?" The man asked, clearly undressing her with his gaze.

"I am here to apply for the weekend supervisor position." Suzie said, as she felt the warmth of a blush covering her cheeks.

"Delores is our Director of Nurses. She is down the hall on the right." He said as he pointed down the hall. "I'll put in a good word for you, okay?"

Suzie didn't know how to interpret this man. "Thanks, I appreciate that. Considering we have never met before I don't know how you could do that but I appreciate the sentiment."

"Oh, believe me, we have met. Weren't you the latest playboy centerfold? Cause if you weren't, you sure as hell should have been." The doctor whispered in her ear.

Suzie was shocked. She felt as if she had been assaulted.

Maybe if she introduced herself the doctor would start treating her like a human instead of a sex object. "Hello, my name is Suzie Whatley."

The doctor looked like he had been slapped. His inappropriate word choice hadn't fazed this young beauty. "And my name is Dr. Statler. I am the medical director of this fine facility."

"*Fine facility?*" Suzie thought. "*It smells like a sewer.*"

"Well, I best be getting on to see Delores. I have a son to pick up from kindergarten. Nice to meet you, Dr. Statler." Suzie said, hoping the mention of a son would keep Dr. Statler's libido in check.

Dr. Statler looked at his watch. "I do hope you have time to stop by my office before you leave. I would like to inform you of the requirements for the job."

Suzie glanced at her watch. "I am sorry, sir, but I will do good to have time for an interview with Delores. I doubt I will have any time to spare. Maybe another day?"

Dr. Statler looked crushed. "Yes, another day would be fine."

Suzie felt like vomiting. Jacob and Dr. Statler were so different. When Suzie spent time with Jacob she felt encouraged, uplifted and respected. Within the few moments she had spent getting to know Dr. Statler she felt filthy and unworthy of respect. She had never been so turned off by a man.

She knocked on Delores' door. The nurse at the front was correct. Delores and her excess adipose tissue filled all the air spaces behind the desk, with little room to spare. She looked as if she had just woken up from a nap.

"Hello, my name is Susanna Whatley. I saw you had an ad for a weekend supervisor. I wanted to give you my résumé, and if possible discuss the position with you. Do you have time?" Suzie asked.

Delores flipped her long black wavy hair over her shoulder and gave a sigh of disgust. "I was beginning to audit the charts." She held her hand out. "Let me take a look at your résumé."

Suzie handed Delores her résumé, biting her lip and praying fervently.

"So, you haven't worked in two years?" Delores asked.

"No, ma'am, um... When my last baby was born, my husband and I decided I could stay home." Suzie said, wringing her hands.

"So what happened? Did the baby die? Did you get bored? Why would you take two years off to stay at home and then want to jump right in as a weekend supervisor?" Delores asked.

"My husband left me for another woman. I was not awarded much child support, so it is a necessity that I work," Suzie said.

"Men are all bastards. My husband left me after thirty-five years for a stripper. He was a deacon in the church. Still is, in fact, the church asked me to resign as head of the children's department, so that his new wife wouldn't feel uncomfortable." Delores said with a scowl.

"My goodness, that doesn't sound right," Suzie said.

"I don't usually air my dirty laundry out when I interview someone. I am sorry. Today was our wedding anniversary and it would have been our 40th." Delores brushed a stray hair out of her eyes. "Now back to your résumé. You don't have a lot of experience and with this lapse of unemployment for the past two years I am reluctant to consider you." Delores said with a look of concern.

At this point her phone rang. "Hello?" Delores began tapping her pen on her desk. "Yes, this is Delores. Yes, she is sitting right in front of me." Delores winked at Suzie. "I can see that is one way to look at it. Yes, I agree. I will do as you say, sir."

Delores hung up the phone. "It appears our medical director, Dr. Statler, has taken a fancy to you and he demanded that I hire you. He said if there was any problem with you he would assume full responsibility."

Suzie grew tense. She didn't want to be under Dr. Statler's authority but there were no other options and she needed to work. "Thank you, ma'am. Is there any paperwork I need to fill out?"

"Yes, there is. You need to fill out a formal application and we also need to drug test you." Delores opened up her bottom desk drawer and took out a urine specimen container and a small plastic bag. "Urinate in this cup, put it in this bag, and then bring it back to me. I will get it sent off before I leave for the day. When can you start work?"

"I could start next weekend. Is there someone who could train me?" Suzie asked.

Delores sighed with exasperation. "I could come in for a little on Saturday. I am so tired of working seven days a week though. The other nurses can help you also."

"If I am supposed to be the supervisor wouldn't it be best for me to learn from you, instead of other nurses?" Suzie asked.

"Yes, I guess so." Delores sighed again with exhaustion. "I will try to help you out as much as I can."

"Thank you and I look forward to working with you and for you." Suzie said as she reached for the urine specimen container and bag.

"Some things never change." Suzie muttered under her breath as she walked down the hallway.

A lack of training was characteristic for the nursing home industry. She had hoped that she would receive proper training since she had not worked for a few years. She knew the patients were old. That didn't mean they were not worthy of the most excellent care she could give. That goal would require a sufficient amount of training.

Suzie obtained the urine specimen and brought it to Delores in the bag. “What are the hours for the weekend shift?”

Delores looked up from a chart. “You will be working two 16 hour shifts. You will start on Saturday morning at six a.m, and finish at ten p.m. that evening. Then on Sunday it will be the same.”

“Wow! That will be a challenge,” Suzie exclaimed.

“Tell me about it. I have been working seven days a week for three months now. I really need you to catch on quick so that I can get some rest,” Delores said.

“I will try my best.” Suzie said with a reassuring smile. Suzie rushed down the hall and nearly sprinted to her car. She didn’t want to run into Dr. Statler again.

THE NEW "GAMMA"

SUZIE THANKED GOD ON THE WAY HOME FOR THE healing which had transpired between her and her mother. She used to dread visits or calls from her. Now she looked forward to them.

Until this morning she didn't realize that her mother had ever been scared of her. Barbara had actually seemed to be afraid of Suzie's response to the call Barbara had made to Joe.

As Suzie walked in the front door of her house. She saw her mother whispering to Jonathan. Jonathan had a look of exuberance. He seemed just about ready to burst with joy.

Barbara looked at Jonathan with such admiration, it almost brought tears to the eyes of Suzie. "Jonathan made a very big decision today. He decided he wanted to be a masterpiece. So we discussed what things we could do that would be good. Part of being recreated through Jesus Christ is doing good." Barbara said, standing by Jonathan. "Jonathan, do you want to show your mom the first good thing you decided to do today?"

Jonathan nodded his head emphatically and then pulled down his sweatpants. The Pull-Ups were gone and some very nice underwear was covering his private parts. "I'm a big boy now!" He exclaimed, putting his hands up in a victory salute.

Suzie was taken aback for a moment when he had pulled his pants down. Once she understood the reason for this unusual action she flew across the room, scooped Jonathan up and twirled him around the living room in joy. "I am so proud of you, Jonathan." She said giggling with joy.

Suzie mouthed to Barbara, "How did you do this?"

Barbara pointed to Jonathan, "It was all Jonathan. He decided he wanted to do good things today and chose that as his first good thing."

Suzie placed Jonathan on the ground and hugged her mother. "Thank you so much for embracing the Word of God in my home."

Jonathan pulled his sweatpants back up, standing tall and proud, he said. "I think God been planning fo me to do this fo a long time."

"Knowing God like I do, I think you may just be right on that count. You are just one step closer to becoming a masterpiece now." Suzie winked at Jonathan.

"Mom, would you like to ride along with Jonathan and me? We need to go pick up Michael from school." Suzie said, glancing at her watch.

"I would love to do that," Barbara replied.

"Great, I need to talk with you about something." Suzie said quietly.

When Barbara looked at Suzie there was a flicker of fear that clouded her gaze. Yet, she followed Suzie out to the car with confidence in her step.

Suzie backed the car out of the driveway and by the time she had turned on the country road, Jonathan was fast asleep.

"I want to thank you for baby sitting Jonathan this morning, Mom. The fact that he gave up his reliance on Pull-Ups is amazing. I tried several months ago to get him to go to the toilet but he was dead set against it. Then the divorce happened and it slid to the bottom of my priority list," Suzie said.

"I don't think I can take any credit for that, Suzie. It was all Jonathan and God. I did bring along some underwear with flying dragons on it, though. He seemed super excited about that." Barabara said with a slight bit of confusion.

Suzie started laughing. "God *must* have been involved then because there is no way you could have known that that is his favorite television program."

"You're kidding, right?" Barbara guffawed.

"No, God's truth, he loves that program." Suzie flashed her mom a warm smile. "I wanted to talk with you about something." Suzie paused to collect her thoughts. "I know we have processed life differently. I think you used the boutique as an escape from your grief. I think my devotion to be a stay-at-home mother was, in some way, a rebound reaction to your success in the business world."

"Now, because of the divorce, I am being forced out of my comfort zone. I am scared about reentering the field of nursing. I got the job today but I think I got it because the medical director took a fancy to me. He said some very inappropriate things to me and he had just met me."

Barbara sighed in disgust. "Men can be so vile at times."

Suzie shook her head. "The other thing which concerns me is that the director of nurses did not commit to actually training me. Mom, being a nurse in a nursing home doesn't require a PHD but I do need to be trained."

"Wow, seems like you jumped right into the lake of fire with this job, right?" Barbara asked.

"Yes, and in addition to that, I have to work two sixteen hour shifts back-to-back with little time to sleep in between. I am sorry, I know I should be thankful for this job. They are really taking a chance on me." Suzie said with fear furrowing her brow.

Barbara took a deep breath. "You may want to consider the value of what you have done over the past few years. Raising three children with a man who is distracted by a mistress is no easy feat. You continued to love your children, providing a safe and healthy environment for them, when you were getting no support from anyone. That takes an enormous amount of strength and character."

Suzie looked at Barbara with astonishment. "I always thought you didn't realize how hard it was to be a stay-at-home mom."

"It is a job which takes the patience of Job, the wisdom of Solomon, and the compassion of Mother Mary. It is a very difficult job. I sensed that Joe was being lured away from you in my talks with him. That is why I encouraged you to go back to work. I didn't want you to suffer," Barbara said.

"Wow, I thought you wanted me to be a career woman so that I could emulate your success," Suzie said.

"To be honest with you, I would give up the boutique in a second if I could have the love that your children have for you. They simply adore you." Barbara said, with longing in her eyes."If I could replay my life, I would have done things so differently."

"Mom, you can't keep looking back. Regret is a very cruel master. We must look forward to how God is healing our relationship. I survived your mothering. We don't know how much of my mothering techniques are based on my reaction to how I was raised. That may be why I am all about my children and not a bit about the cleanliness of my house. As long as Martha Stewart doesn't come to visit, we are all good." Suzie started laughing.

"You know that is one thing that has always bothered me. The respect I got when I was owner of a boutique was so much more than the respect I got from other women when I was a stay-at-home mother. I almost had to apologize for staying home to take care of you when you were a baby," Barbara said.

"Yes, I know, I don't get the whole feminist movement. It seems as if their main objective is to make us more like men. Yet, God made us unique in our femininity and the role of motherhood is so special. I wish they would focus on the respect that mothers deserve, whether they work or stay at home. It is such a wonderful role to play." Suzie said as she reached across the seat to take hold of her mother's hand.

"I have got a sneaky suspicion that being a mother isn't half as much fun as being a grandmother." Barbara said as she squeezed Suzie's hand with a warmth that Suzie had never known her mother was capable of.

Suzie picked up Michael from school and when Sarah got home, Barbara produced a fashion show with the children as models.

Sarah was absolutely smitten with the clothes that Barbara had brought over.

Michael was a bit more reserved. He considered which clothes would be appropriate for school and which would be more suitable for his weekends at the "castle."

Jonathan was dismayed. "I neva gonna be able to drink milk in this. It too pwetty."

Suzie and Barbara exchanged a look of indignation for the wounds which Megan had inflicted on Jonathan. "Honey, the best thing about these clothes is that they can be washed. It doesn't matter if you spill milk on them."

Jonathan looked down at his cute outfit and then diverted his gaze to Suzie. "These clothes special. I want to save them. Is that okay?"

"Sure. That's just fine. You can tell me when you would like to use them. I think it would be nice if you would wear some of the clothes to your dad's home though. I think he would be very pleased to see you dressed in such high fashion." Suzie said, winking at Barbara.

After the fashion show was done, Barbara helped Suzie hang up all of the new clothes.

"What did you plan on having for dinner?" Barbara asked.

"Shoot. I didn't even think of that. I should have went grocery shopping when I was applying for a job." Suzie said with dismay. "I am sorry, Mom. I don't have any good food in the fridge. I would love for you to stay for dinner after all that you have done. All I have is peanut butter and jelly sandwiches."

Barbara smiled slyly. "Well, I saw more than that when I looked in your fridge. Why don't you go look."

Suzie started to argue but decided she would succumb to her mother's wishes. When Suzie looked in her fridge she saw it brimming over with healthy food. "Mom, did you do this?"

Barbara nodded with a smile. "I couldn't have left knowing you had little to no food in the fridge."

"Thank you!" Suzie said as she gave her mother a bear hug. "I can't tell you what your visit today has meant to me."

"I can't tell you what your forgiveness has meant to me, dear," Barbara said.

"I give God all of the credit for that, Mom. Without the guidance of the Holy Spirit I may have held a grudge. I would have missed out on so much if I would have chosen bitterness over forgiveness," Suzie said, kissing Barbara on the cheek. "Would you like to help me make dinner?"

"I would love that." Barbara said as she began pulling things out of the fridge.

Mother and daughter made chicken lasagna, tossed salad, and French bread for dinner that night.

Before Barbara left she received loads of kisses and hugs from her grandchildren and daughter. As she drove away, she left with thankfulness in her heart for all that God had done, through a daughter who was clearly more His to claim than hers.

JACOB'S CALLING

SUZIE HAD JUST FINISHED CLEANING UP BREAKFAST. Michael and Sarah were already at school when she heard a knock on the back door.

Suzie rushed to open the door. "Jacob! Come in." Suzie said with arms outstretched for a hug.

Jacob walked into the hug and returned the embrace. "I thought it may be easier for me to tell Jonathan first and then break the news to Michael later."

"You mean about Africa?" Suzie asked.

Jacob nodded. "I was thinking of presenting it to them as an adventure. You know little boys are always up for an adventure."

Suzie looked into Jacob's eyes and saw pure torture in his gaze. "Oh, Jacob. We are going to miss you." She pulled him into an embrace once more.

"And I you." Jacob said as he gently slipped out of her embrace. His gaze went to the kitchen door, where Jonathan was standing with a look of astonishment.

"Jacob!" Jonathan exclaimed, his hands going up, as if a reflex, reaching for Jacob.

"Hey there, little buddy." Jacob strode, in long strides, across the kitchen and swooped Jonathan up into his arms.

"I missed you." Jonathan said as he leaned out of the embrace to plant a kiss on Jacob's lips.

Jacob began laughing. "I bet you didn't miss me as much as I missed you. What have you been doing?"

Jonathan wiggled out of the embrace. "I became a big boy. Come look!" Jonathan tugged on Jacob's hand to lead him to his bedroom. He pulled out the bottom drawer of his chest and displayed a drawer full of underwear. "I not need those anymo.'" Jonathan said, as he motioned to a sack of pullups in the corner with a dismissive gesture. "Gwamma got me some new big boy pants!" He said, as he proudly waved a pair of flying dinosaur underpants through the air.

"That's awesome!" Jacob said as he applauded.

"I becoming a masta'piece fo' God. This is my fewst good thing but I gonna do lots of good things." Jonathan said with pride.

Jacob looked at Suzie standing in the doorway of the bedroom. His gaze begged for understanding.

"We had quite the Monday, yesterday." Suzie flashed Jacob a reassuring smile. "God had placed on my heart a verse in Ephesians. This verse says that we are a masterpiece, recreated in the likeness of Christ. The reason for this is so that we can do good things which God planned for us to do long ago."

"My good thing was to be a big boy," Johathan exclaimed.

"Wow! I have never even noticed that verse. That really has impact." Jacob said as he grabbed Jonathan's hand and led him out of the bedroom.

Jonathan sat down at the kitchen table and motioned for Jacob to sit down next to him. "I need to tell you something."

Jacob smiled and said. "Go ahead and tell me."

"I think you gonna be my daddy Numba 2." Jonathan said, with a grin as bright as the sun.

Jacob's face fell. He threw a pained glance to Suzie. "Jonathan, come sit in my lap."

Jonathan got off his chair and crawled into the embrace of Jacob. "I know you love my momma. I saw you hugging. I know you love me. You gonna be daddy numba 2."

Jacob looked out the kitchen window at the house of Grace and Mercy and collected his thoughts. "Jonathan, you are a smart boy and you are right. I love your momma. I also love you. But you know how you had to become a big boy to become a masterpiece?" Jacob lowered his gaze to meet the eyes of Jonathan.

Jonathan nodded.

"Well, God wants me to move to Africa in order to do good there. That is how I am to become a big boy."

"You alweady a big boy Jacob. You don't need to go to Afwica to do good. You do good fo my Momma." Jonathan said, shaking his head with disbelief.

Jacob looked at Suzie, silently beckoning her to help him.

Suzie sat down at the kitchen table and grasped Jonathan's tiny hand. "Jonathan, before Jacob met you and I, he had promised God that he would be a missionary to Africa. There are little children in Africa who don't even know about Jesus. They don't know God loves them. Jacob felt as if God wanted him to go to Africa so that those children and others in Africa could accept Jesus. That way they could be masterpieces, too."

Jonathan paused for a moment. "Can I go too? I could teach the little boys how to become big boys." His face lit up in expectation.

"No, Jonathan, Africa is a country which is far away from where we live. They live very differently there. They don't have television and some of them don't even have houses. Plus, you can't go that far from your daddy. Your daddy wants to see you every weekend," Suzie said.

Jonathan started breaking down into tears. "Being a mastapiece isn't easy."

Jacob embraced Jonathan with tenderness, tears streaming down his own face. "It can sometimes be the most difficult path in life. If we are truly being recreated through Christ we must be willing to sacrifice. Christ laid down his life so that we could one day be with God in heaven."

"How long you gonna stay? One week?" Jonathan asked grasping Jacob's face in his hands.

"No, buddy, it will be a lot longer than that. Before I met your mom I would have stayed my whole life. Now I am asking for specific goals and timelines to accomplish those goals from the missionary agency. I have asked for leave of my commitment once those goals are accomplished." Jacob stated, looking at Suzie, who had dissolved into a puddle of tears.

Suzie's head shot up. "Really? You asked them for that?"

"Yes, I told them about you and what a wonderful woman of God you are. I told them that I loved you and yet I loved God more. I was willing to fulfill my calling but I also intend to marry you one day, Suzie." Jacob said with decisiveness.

"Wow! How did they respond to that?" Suzie asked.

"We had a long discussion about the mission field. I proposed to them that they may get more volunteers to go into the mission field if they had shorter time frames. Say a one year, two year, five year and ten year mission commitments. They may also find financial support to be more forthcoming if the time allottments were shorter." As Jacob spoke, the tears were replaced by a confident demeanor.

"You know, that really makes a lot of sense," Suzie said.

"One of the frustrations I consistently hear from my friends who are in the mission field, is that they are thrown into another country and culture with no direction or firm goals. In addition to this, many of them face a language barrier. I shared this with them and asked for a translator and specific goals with time frames," Jacob said.

"Were they open to your suggestions?" Suzie asked.

"They were so grateful for me speaking my mind. I did it with gentleness and compassion. Asking, more than telling. They were grateful for my input. They said that once I had accomplished my goals that they wanted to meet with me in person."

"Sounds like they were impressed with you," Suzie said.

Jacob reached out to hold Suzie's hand. "I don't know that I could have been as assertive in that conversation if I hadn't met you. I have seen such strength in you, Suzie, your dependence upon God's Word has given you such confidence."

"I don't think it is right for me to take credit for that, Jacob. I was a shattered vase at first. God was the one who chose to use my brokenness for healing. I give Him all of the credit." Suzie said, with her gaze looking up to the heavens.

Jacob's gaze returned to Jonathan. "Do you know what I need for you to do for me?"

Jonathan looked at Jacob with tears in his eyes, as he nodded and said, "Keep loving you even if you go to Afwica?"

"Well, I hope you do that but I also need you to pray for me okay? So when you go to bed, you can talk to God about me and ask Him to keep me safe."

"I alweady do that," Jonathan said, as he snuggled into the arms of Jacob, wiped the tears from his eyes and fell asleep.

"Would you mind watching him while I go and pick up Michael from school?" Suzie whispered.

"Not a bit." Jacob said, as he slowly got up from the kitchen chair and settled into the comfort of the living room sectional.

"Thank you." Suzie mouthed to Jacob as she scurried out the front door to pick up Michael.

Michael jumped into Suzie's car with excitement. "I beat him! I finally beat him! Just by a little but I leaned forward in the race and I beat Johnny. I did better than him on the math quiz too. I got a 100 on my math test. He got a 98. I had such a good day, Mom. I love trying my best." Michael's face was ablaze with joy. "You know, I think what you said about him being a challenge for me makes sense.

If Johnny wasn't in my class, I wouldn't work as hard. I am trying to become friends with him."

Suzie reached across the seat to squeeze Michael's hand. "I am so glad you are seeing it that way. Competition has the potential to draw the best out of you." A tear trickled down Suzie's cheek. Suzie quickly wiped it away, as if to chide it for coming out of the cage of her tear duct.

"What's wrong, Mom?" Michael asked. Michael was so observant of every nuance in life. One tear could not escape his attention.

"Jacob's moving to Africa to become a missionary, honey." Suzie said as she forced a fake smile to lessen the impact.

"He is moving to Africa?" Michael asked. "That is amazing! Africa has so many animals which are fantastic. Elephants, tigers, lions, cheetahs.... When can we go visit him?"

Suzie wiped the tear from her face. "Well, dear. He hasn't left yet. I am sure it costs quite a bit to go there. It is also dangerous because there is a lot of fighting in Africa."

"Yes, but to go to Africa is an amazing opportunity, Mom. How many Americans get that chance?" Michael asked.

"One more than I would like..." Suzie muttered under her breath.

"So when is he leaving and how long is he staying?" Michael asked. "This is fantastic! What an adventure! Hey, I am supposed to pick a foreign country and give a presentation on it at school. My teacher is really pushing this. She is from a foreign country. I think India is where she is from. She says that Americans should be concerned about what is happening in the world." Michael paused for a moment. "She is nice about it though. She never says anything bad about America, just that we should be interested in other nations. Do you think Jacob would want to help me?"

Suzie looked at Michael with admiration. "I think you should ask him."

Michael bounded up the stairs of their front porch, went flying through the door and stopped dead in his tracks. Jonathan and Jacob were cuddled together on the couch, snoozing like a couple of contented cats. Michael shot a questioning look at Suzie.

"Why don't you go in the kitchen and do your homework? I will bake some cookies. I bet the smell of fresh baked cookies will wake them up." Suzie whispered in his ear.

Michael gave a thumbs up signal and tiptoed to the kitchen.

Suzie tenderly removed the cookie sheets and mixing bowls from her cupboards. She put the butter, sugar, and eggs in the bowl and took it to her bathroom to mix with her hand mixer. She then added the flour, baking soda, and salt; stirring it well before she put some crushed corn flakes and chocolate chips into the dough. Soon her kitchen smelled like delicious chocoloate chip cookies. The scent wafted through the kitchen, skipped merrily through the formal dining room and then gently tickled the nose of Jonathan.

The scent of cookies started luring Jonathan to wrestle away from the clutches of sleep. He fought it for a moment because he wanted to linger in the arms of Jacob but the cookies soon won the wrestling match.

Jonathan pulled himself up to a sitting position, then leaned over to whisper in Jacob's ear. "Momma baked us some cookies."

Jacob woke up. Before he could sit up, a plate of warm, freshly baked cookies appeared on the coffee table before him. "Wow! What a way to wake up."

Michael sprinted to the living room and jumped on the couch right beside Jacob as soon as he heard him say, 'Wow!'" Michael grabbed a cookie, then yelled. "Hey, Mom, could we have some milk with these cookies?"

"Sweetheart, I think you may have forgot your manners. "Please may we have some milk with our cookies?" would be the correct way to ask." Suzie said, as she held two glasses of milk in limbo.

Michael said, with a slight blush. "I'm sorry, Mom. Please may we have some milk with our cookies?"

Suzie winked at Michael. "Yes, of course you can."

Michael took a look at the cookie in his hand and the milk on the table and ignored both. He instead turned his entire focus to Jacob. "So, Mom says you are moving to Africa. That is going to be an adventure. I am so excited for you. Most Americans don't have a chance to go to another country, much less one as amazing as Africa."

Jacob looked at Suzie with astonishment. "You know that is exactly how I felt before I met your mom. It is nice to be reminded of how I felt at first."

"My kindergarten teacher is from India. She tells us stories about India all of the time. It is so interesting to hear how she grew up. She wants us to each pick a country and kind of adopt that country as our own. We will give a report on our country sometime during the year. She always says that America is the greatest though. She loves living in America. I was wondering if you could help me on preparing that project? It would be so much fun to do with you." Michael said as he bit into his cookie and then took a gulp of milk.

"I would love to do that. I think I have a month to prepare before I go to Africa. I should have plenty of time to help you out with that." Jacob said, winking at Suzie.

"Great!" Michael said.

Soon the excitement that Michael brought to the table regarding Jacob's trip to Africa became infectious. The whole family got involved in studying Africa. Sarah was mesmerized by the beautiful fabrics that African women wore. Michael was obsessed with the amazing wildlife that roamed the safari. Jonathan prayed every night for the children in Africa, hoping that they would know the love of Jesus. Suzie began studying the political climate and began praying for peace. With each passing day, the passion for Africa grew in Jacob's heart, as he prepared to leave the family he had grown to love.

WORKING ON THE WEEKEND

THE WEEK WAS A BLUR OF ACTIVITY. THE CHILDREN came home from school and after doing homework, they quickly jetted out the door to the home of Grace and Mercy.

Suzie was so relieved at the excitement that her children felt for Jacob. To go to Africa seemed to be the highest form of adventure. She had little time to reflect upon how much she would miss Jacob. They were all so caught up in learning about this wonderful continent that there left little room for Despair to slip in.

Soon the weekend approached and it was time to drive the children to the 'castle' once again. This time they proudly wore the clothes which Barbara had so graciously given them. Suzie didn't want them thinking that they were better than others, but she also did not want them to feel inferior to Megan's ideals.

She had a talk with Jonathan on Friday morning, explaining to him that children were not bad if they spilled milk or got dirty. Then she dressed him up in the cutest little outfit she could find. He held his head high with confidence as he crossed the threshold to his daddy's new castle that evening.

Suzie did not feel ashamed of her house in comparison to Joe's castle. She was thankful for what she had. The work that Jacob did on the house gave it such a warm and appealing appearance. It was truly an adorable cottage in the country now. So different than how Joe had left it.

Suzie was excited to go back to work. Yet, she was also scared. A mistake in the medical field could cause serious harm to a patient. She prayed that Delores would be there to train her.

Suzie went to bed on Friday night with thankfulness in her heart. She awoke at 4:30 a.m.and arrived at the nursing home fifteen minutes before her shift started.

She walked in with a sense of foreboding. The nurse at the front desk looked exhausted.

"Hello," Suzie said. "I am the new weekend nurse. Could you possibly tell me where I can clock in and where I could put my lunch?"

The nurse rubbed the sleep out of her eyes. "Hello, my name is Amy. The break room is right over there." She said as she pointed to her right and across the hall. "Your time card should be in the rack. You can put your lunch in the fridge. Good thing you brought your lunch. The food they serve here is not worth eating."

Suzie smiled. "Thanks for the warning, Amy. My name is Suzie. I'll go clock in and put my food away." Suzie walked to the break room, searched for her time card and didn't find it. She put her food in the fridge and went back to Amy. "I'm sorry I didn't find my time card."

Amy rolled her eyes. "Oh, no, not again. They did the same thing to a CNA last week and then said she didn't report for work. That poor girl worked all weekend, like a dog, and they refused to pay her."

"You're kidding. That is illegal." Suzie said, getting angry.

"Yeah, I know, but what is she going to do about it? The sad thing about it is that she was the best CNA I have seen. They lost a good worker," Amy said. "She will be snatched up quickly by someone who values her. This company… they don't value any of the workers."

Suzie felt her stomach go into knots. "Well, they had better not try that with me. I have a good lawyer that is a friend of mine and they would regret it."

Amy looked unimpressed. "So, I think Delores said you were going to work the back hall. The night nurse on that hall left early. I have had to take care of the whole facility for the past hour."

"Wow! That is quite a responsibility," Suzie said. "I will need someone to show me the ropes. Is Delores coming in?"

"Nancy should be coming in soon. She is the nurse who takes care of the front hall. She is really nice. She can show you," Amy said. "So glad you showed up early. I got to run. Nancy usually drags in around 6:30 or 6:45 a.m. I can't leave the facility with no nursing staff but Dr. Statler said if just one nurse was here I could leave early." Amy said as she slipped on her coat.

Suzie was horrified and speechless for a moment. Then she began to think clearly. "If I don't have a time card and they cannot verify my presence, then there is no record of another nurse being here when you leave." Suzie said, with anger in her gaze. "Furthermore, I don't know if I have stated my case clear enough for you to understand. I have not worked as a nurse for several years. This is my first shift at this facility. I am now not asking nicely for some training but I am *demanding* it. If you leave before Nancy arrives, I will walk out right on your heels. Nobody will know I even arrived because I have not been able to clock in. Though I believe that you can be charged with abandoning your patients."

"There is no need for you to be a bitch about this." Amy said as she took off her coat and sat back down.

"I didn't mean to be a bitch, Amy. But these old folks deserve good quality care and without proper training I can't ensure that." Suzie said, as she tried to calm herself down. "I will go to the back hall and try to get orientated. When Nancy comes in, can you tell her I would like to speak with her?"

"Yes, I will, but you need to realize the goal of this nursing facility is to make money. The management doesn't really care about how well these patients are taken care of," Amy said.

"That's a shame, Amy. An absolute shame." Suzie said as she made her way to the back hall.

Nancy soon arrived and after greeting Amy, she introduced herself to Suzie. "Amy says that you haven't had recent nursing experience."

Suzie nodded. "Yes, I took several years off of my career to have children. Then my husband left me for someone else and I find that a career is now a necessity and not an option."

Nancy smiled with warmth. "I am sorry that happened to you but I am so thankful to have you here as a weekend nurse. We really needed the help. We have been using temp nurses since our last nurse quit. Never know what kind of crazy you get when you hire a temp. There were some good ones but they were few and far between. It will be nice to have some stability on the back hall."

"I hope I can provide stability and good nursing care," Suzie said.

"Let me show you the medicine cart and get you orientated to this hall. All of the patients should have ID bands on their left wrist. I want you to check the ID band before giving anyone medication." Nancy motioned Suzie to enter into the med room. "The insulin is in the fridge. There are five patients on this back hall which get a standard dose of insulin. Delores says we don't have to check their blood sugars because the insulin is not given on a sliding scale. I usually check their fasting blood sugar just to make sure they don't become hypoglycemic. It is your choice. Do what time allows you to do."

"Thank you. I was wondering where or how I could get a time card? I have heard that if I don't have a time card they will not pay me but I didn't find one in the break room," Suzie said.

"That is the director of nurses' responsibility. She said she would be stopping by this afternoon." Nancy said as she glanced at her watch. "You better get started on that insulin administration. Remember to check the ID bands, especially with insulin."

"I will, but I warn you if I do not get a time card this afternoon, I will not be coming back tomorrow." Suzie said with an unusual firmness to her voice.

Nancy face turned from compassionate to stern. "Like I said, that is not my job."

Suzie lumbered through the morning administering medications to the thirty patients on the back hall. As soon as she was done with the morning round, the noon meds were to be given. She noticed that some of the patients had wound care orders on the medication sheet. She would have to ask Delores about that if she ever showed up.

She finally got done with the noon meds at 2:30 p.m. She asked Nancy if it would be okay to take a break.

Nancy replied in the affirmative but told her that it had better be a quick one. The evening medication pass was supposed to start at 3 p.m.

Suzie had no idea how tired she was until she sat down in the break room. She quickly ate her food and then got back to passing out the evening medications.

Delores walked in at 4 p.m. Suzie could hear Nancy and Delores whispering in the hallway. She only heard snippets but "lawyer and time card" were repeated frequently.

Delores approached the nursing station. "So word has it that you expect to be paid. Is that right?" She said with a smile.

Suzie smiled back. "Yes, ma'am. If I wanted to volunteer I would have opted for less hours and a shorter distance from my home. I need to develop an income stream in order to pay my bills."

"I can understand that. I have put a time card in the break room. Just write in when you arrived and I will initial it when I come in on Monday." Delores said as she started back down the hallway.

"Why don't I do that right now?" Suzie asked, scurrying out from the nurses station and into the breakroom. She found her time card hidden behind Amy's. She got it out and wrote in her time of arrival. She handed it to Delores as she was leaving the facility and got the necessary verification of initials.

Suzie was dismayed that Delores hadn't come to check on her work. She was a bit uneasy in this new atmosphere. She still had those wound care orders to address.After she was done with the evening medication pass she enquired about the wound care orders.

"Nancy, I have seen some wound care orders on the medication administration sheets. It appears as if they are to be done daily. Where are the supplies?"

Nancy looked up from charting at Suzie with a perturbed frown on her face. "Darling, how long have you been out of nursing school?"

"I graduated eight years ago." Suzie said, wondering what this piece of information had to do with the price of beans in China.

"In nursing college, they teach you to be perfect, as if the real world was a bubble of idealism." Nancy wiped sweat off of her brow. "This is reality. During the week, the nurses have eight hour shifts. They have more support staff and administration available to troubleshoot. We have to work two sixteen hour shifts back-to-back with no support staff other than a couple of certified nurse assistants. It is important to prioritize the tasks and if you have time to do them all; then please do. If you don't get the wound care done, don't worry about it. They can do it during the week."

Suzie paused for a moment to regain her calm demeanor, let out a big sigh and said. "I appreciate your perspective but you didn't answer my question. Where are the supplies for the wound care?"

Nancy rolled her eyes and got up from her chair. "Follow me."

Suzie hadn't noticed the tiny hall closet where all of the wound care supplies were kept. It was in a bit of an upheavel. With a bit of digging, Suzie soon found the supplies which were called for. She hurried to do the wound care after the patients were bathed and before they were put into bed.

Carol, a CNA, noticed the tenderness with which Suzie performed the wound care.

"You are so gentle with them. The last weekend nurse we had here was from Nigeria. She ripped the old dressings off and made the patients scream with pain. One of the patients finally called her daughter and complained about that nurse. She was fired soon after. She was so mean."

Suzie paused and looked up at Carol, seeing such compassion in her eyes. "I am sorry that happened. The elderly deserve the best in life and seldom get it." Suzie brushed some hair out of her eyes. "Would you mind holding up this patient's leg so that I can look on the back side to see how bad the wound is?"

"No, not at all." Carol said as she picked up the stiff leg.

"I have friend who is going to the Congo as a missionary. I am studying the politics of that continent. There is so much violence..." Suzie said as she cleaned the wound with wound cleanser. "She may have become desensitized to pain. We can never tell what people in other countries have to do just to survive. We are so blessed to live in America."

"You know, I never thought about it that way. I don't think anyone ever bothered to ask about her life in Nigeria. I bet she felt isolated and like an outsider," Carol said.

"She may have. She may have responded differently if someone had showed her kindness." Suzie said as she applied wound care to the wound.

"You know, I have never considered myself to be prejudiced. I wonder if I was quick to judge her because she was black?" Carol asked.

"I doubt it, you seem so sweet. I am sure you were just worried about the pain that the patients were experiencing. Yet, you know the famous quote, "hurt people hurt others." If somone had shown this Nigerian nurse that they cared about her, then showed her the proper technique of soaking a bandage before removing it, you may have killed two birds with one stone." Suzie stated as she began wrapping the leg with a gauze bandage.

"What do you mean?" Carol asked.

"If Delores had taken the time to train this nurse adequately and she had been shown compassion by other workers. She may have become a nicer person and done the wound care in a manner which did not cause pain." Suzie taped the gauze in place.

"You know, I never thought about it that way. Are you a Christian?" Carol answered.

"Yes, I am," Suzie said.

"Which church do you go to?" Carol asked.

"None, right now. It's not that I don't want to go. When I was married, my husband had no interest. Now that he has left me, I would like to go to church but as you can see I am working on the weekends," Suzie said. "Do you need help transferring this patient into bed?"

"Yes, that would be great. I didn't mean to pry about the church thing. It's just that you are a lot nicer than the people I go to church with." Carol said as she lifted the patient out of the wheelchair and transferred her into bed.

"Thanks. I think people find God in different ways. I am blessed to be so close to Him without attending church. I would really love to find a church though." Suzie said as she pulled the covers up over the patient.

The first sixteen hour day flew by. Suzie got five hours of sleep and then started on her second long day.

She hadn't even thought about Dr. Statler until she heard Carol giggling inside a patient's room. Dr. Statler soon came out of that room. He looked like he had been caught with his hand in the cookie jar.

"Well, if it isn't our new nurse. How are you doing Mrs. Whatley?" Dr. Statler said with a smug grin on his face.

"Fine, thank you." Suzie replied, wondering what on earth Carol had been giggling about.

"Carol had been telling me that you actually did the wound care. That is pretty impressive. However, the supplies you used are quite expensive. You may want to cut back on that next weekend. No need to drive this company in the red just to take care of skin which no one even sees," Dr. Statler said.

"Sir, if you feel that way then I suggest you change the doctor's orders. It is my responsibility as a nurse to follow the doctor's orders," Suzie said.

"Nancy mentioned to me that you were acting like you were just out of nursing college. What a shame you have not had more experience."

"Dr. Statler, I graduated from nursing college several years ago but I believe that these patients deserve quality care. If that means we operate at a loss, then so be it." Suzie turned on her heel and walked back to the nursing station.

Dr. Statler mosied around the building until the end of Suzie's shift. When he saw a patient's family he was all smiles and congeniality, appearing as if he really cared for their family members. The minute the family members walked out the door, the patients were cast aside.

Suzie had finished all of her medication rounds, documented on all of the charts, and was about ready to fetch her coat and walk out of the facility when Dr. Statler appeared at her nursing station.

"Are you all done for the day?" He asked.

"Yes, I believe so." Suzie said, feeling her stomach cramp with disgust.

"How did you like working here?" Dr. Statler asked.

"It was a challenge but I have always liked a challenge." Suzie said, choosing her words wisely.

"I'll walk you out to your car. This neighborhood is crime-ridden and I don't want my new nurse being attacked," Dr. Statler said.

Suzie felt uneasy about this, but allowed Dr. Statler to walk her to her car. She tried hard to wipe the inappropriate comments he had greeted her with from her mind.

"You seem to have done a good job this weekend." Dr. Statler said as he helped her on with her coat.

"Thank you. I have ruffled a few feathers, I think," Suzie replied.

"It takes a while to fit in." Dr. Statler said as he removed her time card and punched her out. "Where is your car?"

"I hope you don't mind. I parked in front," Suzie said.

"That is okay on the first weekend. From now on, I would prefer you parked in back of the facility. The family members like parking in front." Dr. Statler said as he opened the front door of the facility to let Suzie outside.

"It's dark back there isn't it? Why would you have the employees park in the dark when this is a crime-ridden area? Don't the family members come during the day when it is light outside?" Suzie asked.

Dr. Statler grabbed Suzie by the arm. "Are you always this difficult?"

"I don't mean to be. Yet I think that the safety of your employees should be something to consider. Maybe you could have them move their cars from the back parking lot to the front once the sun is starting to set. That way you could accommodate both concerns."

Dr. Statler loosened his grip and laughed. "It seems as if you are a pro at killing two birds with one stone, as Carol put it."

Suzie didn't know if she should take that as a compliment or an insult. "Yes, I guess so."

They were approaching her car and Suzie was eager to get away from Dr. Statler.

"Did you get to know Carol well?" Dr. Statler asked.

"Fairly well, we shared some," Suzie replied.

"Did you exchange phone numbers?" Dr. Statler asked.

"No, I didn't even think about that." Suzie asked, searching her purse for her keys.

"Good. I don't really approve of my employees getting together outside of work." Dr. Statler turned to walk away, then did a 180. "Oh, by the way, there is something I forgot to mention. We have a mandatory staff meeting this Friday evening. It is being held at Angelo's Italian Restaurant." Dr. Statler opened the car door for Suzie the minute she unlocked it. "It is a chance for me to apprise everyone of the financial goals the corporation has set for our facility. The meeting will start at six p.m. There is a motel close by if you drink too much wine. It's not far from the nursing home. I would suggest bringing a change of clothes and staying the night."

"I am sorry, Dr. Statler. I must drop my children off at their dad's house. I don't think I could arrive by six. I could probably get there by seven. Would that be okay?" Suzie asked.

"Oh, I didn't know you were divorced. Yes, seven will be fine. See you then." Dr. Statler said as he closed her car door and returned to the nursing home.

SEEKING WISDOM

SUZIE REFLECTED ON THE WEEKEND AFTER SHE HAD tucked the children back into bed. She was so thankful to God for the guidance she felt from Him.

Nevertheless, she still couldn't shake that sense of foreboding. It seemed as if the nursing home had not been managed well. She really didn't know whom to blame for that. It seemed as if no one was supposed to care about the patients. Profit was the main priority.

She didn't know what to make of Dr. Statler. He had not said one inappropriate comment to her all weekend. After the way he had greeted her, she expected much worse.

She felt uneasy about Carol, hidden away in a room with him, giggling like a school girl. She needed to be careful how much she shared about herself.

As she searched the Bible for guidance she kept coming to Mattew 7:6 "Do not give what is holy to the dogs; nor cast your pearls before swine, lest they trample them under their feet, and turn and tear you into pieces."

She needed to talk with someone about this. She didn't want to alarm Jacob with her fears regarding Dr. Statler. Jacob would be upset over the way Dr. Statler had greeted her. Besides, Jacob was going to Africa soon. She needed to learn how to handle things by herself.

She thought about sharing it with her mother but she didn't want to worry her.

She would call Faith in the morning. Faith always seemed to know just what to say.

Soon the shrill sound of the alarm was slicing through Suzie's slumber. Waking the children up in the morning was a bit difficult. They had fallen asleep at Joe's house, then woke up, put in the car, fallen asleep in the car, then had to get up, walk to the house, put their jammies on, get back into bed and fall asleep all over again.

Suzie wished that Joe would help out with the transport of the children but he was being stubborn and selfish. After speaking with Katie at the library she assumed she should be thankful that her children had a father who wanted to see them. Wishing for Joe to think of someone other than himself may be pushing her luck.

With a bit of prodding, Suzie finally detached her children from their bedsheets. They immediately got into a fight. Suzie had to separate them and put them all in a time-out. Her house wasn't large but the walls were thick enough to stop flying fists.

They appeared to have settled down after the time-out.

"If you can eat breakfast without fighting you can come out of your time-out," Suzie said.

"Mom, Sarah sleeps in her own room at Daddy's house. Can't she do that here?" Michael asked.

"Did you have a problem with Sarah sleeping with you before you went to your daddy's house?"

"No, but it's getting a bit crowded." Michael said, as he sat down at the table to eat cereal.

"Sarah, how do you feel about the idea of sleeping by yourself?" Suzie asked Sarah, whose eyes were red from crying.

"I don't like sleeping by myself. I could hardly get to sleep at Daddy's house. His house is so big, it is terrifying," Sarah exclaimed.

"Well, if you don't want to sleep by yourself and the boys don't want you sleeping with them, I can think of only one other option." Suzie said, setting out two more bowls for cereal. "How about you sleep with me?"

Sarah's face lit up. "Really, Mommy?"

"Yes, I don't see why that would be a problem at all."

"Moomm…that is not fair." Michael screeched as if he were a wounded fox in a trap.

"Michael, you get to sleep with Jonathan. Sarah will get to sleep with me because you are crowded with her in your bed." Suzie said as she poured milk into the bowls of cereal.

"I DON'T WANT TO SLEEP WITH JONATHAN!" Michael screamed.

"You don't wanna sleep with me?" Jonathan dissolved into hysterical sobs.

"It is clear to me that this may be something we can discuss at a later time. We have all day to solve this apparent dilemma but only ten minutes to get ready for school. So I propose we shelve the sleeping arrangements until you get home from school. Is that agreed?" Suzie said praying for peace.

"Fine by me." Sarah said, flipping her hair over her shoulder while exiting the kitchen and throwing her mother a wink in the process.

Suzie couldn't help but laugh. "Okay boys, now hurry up and get ready for school. I bet Jacob will want to see you this afternoon."

"Yeah, I was telling Dad about Jacob. He asked if he was black," Michael said.

Suzie rolled her eyes. "Really? Just because someone loves Africa and the people of Africa doesn't mean they are black. A lot of white people love black people just as much as they love other whites."

"Yeah, I know. He asked me how much time we spent with Jacob. I told him we went over there almost every day. I told him Jacob was helping me put together a project on Africa. He asked me what you were doing when we were over there. I told him you always went with us unless you had errands to run."

"Wow looks like you went through quite the questioning. Did you go to McDonald's again?"

"No, we stayed at the house this weekend. Megan left to go to Mexico with some of her friends. We had to be very careful but we stayed home. To be honest, it was kind of boring. We couldn't do much, for fear of breaking something." Michael said with a frown furrowing his brows.

"Awww, I am sorry dear. Now please get your coat and backpack. We will be leaving soon." Suzie said, wondering if the charm of being a stepmother had already worn thin for Megan.

As soon as the children were at school and Jonathan was settled into watching those blasted flying dragons, Suzie slipped to the bedroom with her new cell phone.

Faith answered on the first ring.

"Hello?" Faith answered the phone with her calm and soothing voice.

Suzie took a deep breath. "Hello, Faith. I need your advice."

"Hello, Suzie. I am so glad you called. What can I do to help you?"

"You know I got that job I wanted at the nursing home. But I feel unsettled there." Suzie said, smoothing out a wrinkle on her bedspread.

"I thought that was the job you wanted," Faith replied.

"Yes, I thought so too. It was a weekend position and although I work thirty two hours in two days, I still thought it would work out fine. I really want to be home with the children during the week." Suzie said, wondering if she had any right to be concerned.

"Then what is the problem?" Faith asked.

"To start off, the day I applied for the job, the physician was there. He was very inappropriate with some of the comments he made. He said I looked like I should be a playboy centerfold."

Faith gasped. "That is horrible. Did you report it?"

"No, to be honest. I was in shock. I didn't know how to respond. I was praying that he wouldn't come in during my weekend shift." Suzie paused to take a breath. "He didn't come in until last night. It was like he was a different person last night. Totally professional. Although he was in a patient's room with a CNA and she was giggling like a school girl."

"Why was she giggling?" Faith asked.

"I don't know. The door was closed," Suzie replied. "He insisted on walking me out to my car because he said the neighborhood was crime-ridden. Then he asked me to park in back of the building next weekend. He said the front was for family members. I said it wasn't safe for his employees to park in back."

"That sounds like a reasonable concern," Faith said.

"He said I was being difficult," Suzie said. "I don't feel that I was being difficult, Faith. I suggested to him that the employees on the weekends park their cars in the back during the day and once the sun started to set they could move them to the front for their safety."

"That sounds like a perfect solution." Faith said, with a bit of pride for her friend.

"Yes, that's what I thought. But there is more. When I was getting in the car he said there was a mandatory staff meeting next Friday. It's at an Italian restaurant," Suzie said.

"That sounds nice," Faith said.

"Yes, it should be. I can't remember the last time I had a meal at a restaurant. He said if I drank too much I could stay at a motel nearby and that I should bring a change of clothes."

"That is not nice, that is dangerous. Why on earth would drinking be allowed at a mandatory staff meeting?" Faith asked.

"That's what I was thinking," Suzie replied. "Should I go?"

"If it is mandatory I don't know that you have a choice. I would suggest only drinking water and keeping an eye on your glass at all times. Too bad you don't have a way to record this supposed meeting, in case the jerk gets vulgar again," Faith said.

"No kidding," Suzie said. "Hey, wait a minute. The guy who sold me this phone told me I could do that with my phone."

"I suggest you get very comfortable with that feature. Do you have a camera on it also?" Faith asked.

"Yes, I do," Suzie replied.

"Then take a picture of everything you do next weekend. Sign and date all of your wound care dressings. Then take a picture of the dressing. Try to do this without being observed. Also try and document the medications you pass with a picture." Faith said with a firm edge to her voice.

"I don't know if I will have time to do that but I will try," Suzie said.

"There is more to this than what it appears to be, Suzie." Faith said in a grave tone.

"What do you mean?" Suzie asked.

"You have encountered one trial after another recently. With each trial you have responded by drawing close to God and seeking wisdom from His spirit. You have even used the Word of God as a weapon against the attack of the devil. There is only one area where you have not been tested." Faith said with sincerity.

Suzie was floored. She truly thought she had gone through enough testing. "Which area is that?"

"It is the area of your heart," Faith said.

"My heart was broken when Joe left. How can you say my heart has not been tested?" Suzie asked.

"You have not been lured into sexual immorality. Jacob is a godly man. He would never consider that an option for showing you his love." Faith spoke with assurance.

"I am still confused," Suzie said.

"So far you have been righteous in the area of sexual immorality. The breastplate of righteousness is covering your heart. The devil is trying to steal that from you, so that evil can enter your heart and wage havoc in your life." Faith spoke with wisdom.

"But as a Christian isn't my righteousness from Christ?" Suzie asked.

"Yes, it is, but when you knowingly sin, you disrespect His sacrifice. The easiest way to explain this is to go back to the Bible. In I Corinthians 6:19-20 the Word of the Lord says, 'Do you not know that your body is a temple of the Holy Spirit, who is in you, whom you have received from God? You are not your own;(20) You were bought at a price. Therefore honor God with your body.'"

"Wow! So sexual purity is kind of important, isn't it?" Suzie asked.

"Yes, very important. Especially in relation to you, Suzie. God has chosen you for a special purpose. Because you will be teaching others, it is important that you are protected by the Armor of God."

"I don't understand, Faith," Suzie said.

"Read Ephesians 6:14-18 when you have time this week. I have to go, but I need you to read that passage." Faith said, trying to draw the conversation to a close.

"Okay, I will, Faith. Thanks for the advice," Suzie said.

"Of course, sweet child of God." Faith said, as she hung up.

PREVENTION OF A HEART "ATTACK"

As soon as Suzie hung up the house phone with Faith, she bustled to the kitchen and grabbed her cell phone. She said a prayer of thanks for the employee who had showed her how to download the app for recording conversations. As she was walking back to her bedroom, she made a detour through the living room to check on Jonathan. He was fast asleep.

She experimented with the phone; checking to see how loud she needed to speak, whether the phone could be left in her purse and at what distance the phone needed to be, in order to record speech.

Then she started learning how to take pictures. She was fascinated with this device and a bit angry that Joe had always assumed that she was too "stupid" to have a cell phone.

She checked the clock before picking up her Bible. She had fifteen minutes before she needed to start the process of picking Michael up. She needed to allow more time than normal since she would have to wake Jonathan up from a nap.

She settled down on her bed and opened the Bible to Ephesians 6:14-18.

"Stand therefore, having girded your waist with truth, having put on the breastplate of righteousness, and having shod your feet with the preparation of the gospel of peace; above all, taking the shield of faith with you which will be able to quench all of the fiery darts of the wicked one. And take the helmet of salvation, and the sword of the Spirit, which is the word of God; praying always with all prayer and supplication in the Spirit, being watchful to this end with all perserverance and supplication for all the saints."

"That is quite a lot to digest," Suzie thought. "The benefit to using symbolism is that so many different interpretations can be drawn from it. Paul was quite the literary genius."

As Suzie closed the Bible and laid it on her bedstand, she still couldn't understand why it was so important for her to read this passage. The breastplate of righteousness applied to her present circumstance but the rest of it seemed a bit much.

That was the wonder of Faith. One day she could be as clear as the sun and the next as mysterious as a shooting star. Yet Suzie didn't know what she would have done without her.

The week skipped by as if it was on a race to the weekend. Suzie and the children were invited to Grace and Mr. Mercy's house for an African dinner on Wednesday evening.

As Suzie looked across the table at Jacob, she realized how much he had meant to her over the past few months. Without him and the presence of Grace and Mr. Mercy in her life she may have chosen a different path. He always led her to a deeper understanding of life.

She was going to miss him but she had Hope, Faith, Joy, Grace and Mr. Mercy to run to when he left.

The children were excited to eat the Congolese chicken stew. Suzie couldn't believe it. They had never in their life liked stew. When Grace started ladling the stew into their bowls they devoured it.

"Grace, I don't know what you put in this stew but my children are loving it. You will have to give me the recipe." Suzie said, as she took her first bite. "Hmmm, this is really good."

"You know I have been studying the diet of the Congo and they eat much differently than we do. I must admit, I think it is a healthier diet. They eat a lot of vegetables, small amounts of meat and I couldn't find any recipes for sweets." Grace said as she put some more stew in the bowl of Mr. Mercy.

"Mom, if you made vegetables taste this good. I don't think I would have a problem eating them," Sarah said.

Suzie smiled at Sarah. "If Grace would be willing, maybe she could teach both of us how to cook this stew. I think sometimes it is not only what you eat but how you package it that makes the difference."

Grace lit up with joy. "I couldn't have said that better myself. I used to make carrot bread using pineapples and carrots just to get Jacob to eat some vegetables."

Jacob laughed. "I remember that, Mom. That was so delicious. You didn't let up on those vegetables though. I used to hate broccoli but you kept making it. When you started serving it with cheese sauce I couldn't resist."

Mr. Mercy busted out laughing. "I think we have a picture of you eating that. I am not sure how much cheese sauce got in your tummy because there was a lot on your cheeks."

"Sounds like our meal with Hope doesn't it, Mom? We had a contest to see who could eat spaghetti without getting the sauce everywhere." Michael said, motioning to Grace for some more stew.

Sarah sat up straight in her chair with pride. "I won that contest. I gave my prize, which was a cookie, to Hope."

Suzie started giggling. "Yes, you did honey and that was so sweet. That dear cookie got passed from one to another at the table with a blessing added on. Finally it ended up back with Sarah."

"That sounds like a wonderful way to share a meal," Jacob said.

"Everything with Hope is wonderful," Suzie said. "In fact, having Hope over is almost as lovely as being over here."

"Wherever God's Spirit is, there is love." Grace said with an enchanting smile. "I hope you don't mind, I couldn't find any African recipes for dessert. So, I made an Oreo cake to top off our African meal."

Jonathan piped up the minute he heard Oreo and said, "I don't mind."

"No complaints here." Michael said, as he got up from his chair and helped clean the plates off.

"I have never heard of an Oreo cake but it is a delicious idea." Sarah said, as she politely patted crumbs off of her mouth with her napkin.

Grace brought the cake to the table as Mr. Mercy went to get the ice cream. Silence soon engulfed the dining room as each person was engaged in polishing off their cake and ice cream.

"Grace, could you please teach my mother and I how to cook like you do?" Sarah pleaded.

"Goodness, I don't think I cook that well but it would be a privilege to share what I do know," Grace replied.

"Yippee!" Sarah said, as she sprung up from her chair and began helping Michael clean the rest of the plates off the dining table.

Jonathan quickly slid off of his booster chair, toddled into the kitchen and asked Grace what he could do to help.

Jacob motioned for Suzie to step outside on the front porch.

"I want to thank you for allowing your children to come over here so much." Jacob said as he patted the porch swing and motioned for Suzie to sit down beside him.

"It was their choice. They are really excited about your mission in Africa. I thought they would be sad but they have embraced the sense of adventure. I am so proud of you, Jacob, for caring enough about the people in Africa that you are willing to minister to them." Suzie said as she nestled in beside him on the porch swing.

"I was a lot more excited about it before I met you. I have thought a lot about how I should process my feelings for you, Suzie. I considered proposing to you." Jacob wrung his hands in frustration. "I think that would be selfish. You have just gone through a divorce and you may want to date other men while I am gone," Jacob said.

"To be honest, Jacob. I don't know how I will feel once you leave. I haven't even thought about dating. I guess I have been focusing on my kids, my mom, and my job," Suzie stated.

"I forgot to ask you. How did your job go this weekend?" Jacob asked.

"It was good. That place is a mess. They care more about profit than their patients. I have a mandatory staff meeting to go to this

Friday. I was thinking that I could give some suggestions if I was asked." Suzie said, looking towards the yard.

"You seemed to tense up when you talked about your job. Is something wrong? Is there something you would like me to pray about?" Jacob asked.

Suzie took a deep breath. "Jacob, I feel uneasy about working there. The medical director said some inappropriate things to me on the day I applied." Suzie looked down at her lap. "I don't know. Maybe he was just joking. 'Cause when I was working he was Mr. Professional."

"Inappropriate in what way?" Jacob said, getting angry.

"Sexually inappropriate," Suzie said. "I am so used to the way you treat me, Jacob. When a man says things which are disrespectful to me, it really offends me."

"It should offend you. Not only because of being around me but because you should be treated as if you are a princess. You are the daughter of the most high King," Jacob paused. "Do you want me to address this man and put him in his place?"

"No, I don't think I need that. My friend, Faith, gave me some verses. I am meditating on them. There is one which says that our bodies are holy and a temple of God." Suzie grabbed Jacob's hand. "He just doesn't understand, Jacob. He is blind to the truth of Christ. He wouldn't know how to treat a woman in the right way."

Jacob tighted his grip in Suzie's hand. "I hate that I am leaving, when you have to deal with a jerk like that."

"That's okay, Jacob." Suzie said as she patted his hand. "The Holy Spirit will guide me. I think I need to rely on God first before I start relying on another man."

"I am so glad you said that, Suzie." Jacob said as he reached in the pocket of his coat. "I wanted to get you a ring but I felt led to get you this instead." Jacob pulled out a jewelry box and gave it to Suzie.

"Jacob, you didn't need to get me anything," Suzie exclaimed as she opened the box. "Jacob, this is beautiful! It is so stunning." Suzie said as she held a beautiful cross filled with sparkling jewels.

"So you like it?" Jacob asked.

"Like it? I love it!' Suzie said as she put on the necklace.

"When I am in Africa I need to trust God to take care of you. I will pray every day that the Holy Spirit will protect and guide you." Jacob said, as he lifted Suzie's hands to his mouth and kissed her hand.

"And I will do the same for you, my sweet man of God." Suzie said as she kissed the top of Jacob's hand.

THE "MANDATORY" STAFF MEETING

SUZIE WORE HER CROSS NECKLACE THROUGHOUT THE day Thursday. She kept looking at her reflection in the mirror and admiring the beauty of the jewelry.

The day was skipping along like a daydream until the phone rang in the middle of the afternoon. Sarah had just gotten home from school and Suzie was checking her test scores.

"Hello?"

"Hello, Mrs. Whatley, this is Dr.Statler. I just wanted to confirm that you would be at the staff meeting tomorrow night at 7 p.m. Will you be able to make it?"

"I was planning on it, Dr. Statler. You said it was mandatory, right?" Suzie asked wondering why he was calling to check up on her.

"Yes, yes, of course it is mandatory." Dr. Statler paused, as if distracted by something. "Oh, by the way, the dress is casual. No need to get all gussied up."

"Okay, thank you for the reminder, I will see you then." Suzie said, anxious to get off of the phone.

"Yes, you could come early if you want to," Dr. Statler said.

"I think seven is good. Remember, I have to drop my children off at their dad's house," Suzie said, rolling her eyes.

"Okay then. Seven it will be." Dr. Statler said as he hung up.

Suzie could have sworn she heard Carol giggling in the background as Dr. Statler was hanging up.

Suzie turned her attention to Sarah's school work. "Sarah, you are doing very good in all of your classes. I am so proud of you," Suzie said.

"Thanks, Mom. Brittany didn't do that well at all." Sarah said as she sat down beside Suzie.

Suzie took a deep breath. "Sweetheart, I want to talk with you about something. In Ephesians 2:10 God says we are a masterpiece. He is trying to recreate you in the image of His Son. I think you may have an unhealthy fascination with Brittany."

"Mommmm, she is popular and she is so pretty. She wears the cutest outfits and she has that smoky eye look because her mother lets her wear eye makeup." Sarah said with exasperation.

"I understand that it is nice to be popular but as a Christian it shouldn't matter what clothes we wear or what makeup we use. What matters is our likeness to Christ. We are supposed to be like Christ so that we can do good things for others." Suzie continued as she tenderly grasped Sarah's hand in hers.

"Brittany doesn't do anything good. In fact, she made fun of a girl in my class who has Down's Syndrome. She made her cry. She told her to go to the back of the line because she was an idiot and she didn't deserve to stand by her," Sarah said.

"Do you think that is how Jesus would have treated that girl?" Suzie asked.

Sarah shook her head. "No, I think he would have asked that girl to stand in line beside Him."

"Sarah, each of us have a choice to make in life. We must choose who we want to be like. We must also choose who we worship. If we are blessed, we will choose someone who is good." Suzie patted Sarah's hand. "It is your choice, Sarah, and I will love you no matter who you choose."

Sarah paused for a moment. "I choose Jesus. I know he came down to earth to die on a cross for my sins. I think He was a good person while he was here. So I need to start doing good things don't I?"

Suzie nodded her head. "I think that would make God and Jesus very happy."

Sarah's face lit up with excitement. "I know what I am going to do. Valentine's Day is next week. Brittany said she expected everyone to give her 'their best Valentine card ever.' I'm going to give my best one to the girl who has Down's Syndrome." Sarah paused to catch her breath. "In fact, I am going to tell as many people as I can to give a card to the girl who has Down's Syndrome and forget Brittany." She sprung up from her chair with renewed energy.

Suzie caught her before she left the room. "I think giving the girl with Down's Syndrome a Valentine's card is a wonderful idea. But I don't think you should tell people not to give a card to Brittany. God wouldn't want Brittany to have her feelings hurt. You never know what she is going through at her home. To be sexualized at such a young age reveals that there is brokenness in her family. Be gentle with her. God isn't finished with her yet."

Sarah had a flicker of indecision which crossed her brow then said. "Okay, Mom. You know what? It is kind of fun trying to become a masterpiece for God isn't it?"

"It definitely beats working for the devil," Suzie said.

Soon Friday had slipped through the cracks of the week and Suzie was driving the children to Joe's house.

The castle had lost its luster in the eyes of the children. They missed their daddy but hadn't figured out how to love Megan as a stepmother. Suzie was as supportive as possible of their relationship with Megan but she was not going to stand by and let Megan demean them without a fight.

The children were met at the door by a perfectly tanned and stunningly beautiful stepmother. Suzie had to keep reminding herself of her conversation with Sarah. Megan was not her role model, Jesus was. Megan seemed happy to see the children and dismissed Suzie as if she were an irritating insect.

Suzie was so thankful for the presence of God in her life. A year ago if Megan had treated her in that manner, Suzie may have decked her.

Suzie drove to the restaurant that Dr. Statler had specified. She said a prayer in the car pleading with God to keep her from temptation.

She was there early, so she went to the bathroom to freshen up. She made sure her blouse was buttoned enough to conceal her cleavage. Her pants were loose enough that they didn't reveal what beautiful legs she had. Her makeup was light and barely noticeable. She put a light pink lipstick on to keep her lips moist. Then she turned on her phone for audio recording and placed it in an outside pocket of her purse.

She walked back to the lobby of the restaurant. "I believe there is a staff meeting under the name of Dr. Statler. Has anyone arrived yet?"

The hostess looked at Suzie as if she had lost her mind. "That meeting was at five. Dr. Statler may be in the back. He is a good friend of Angelo, the owner of the restaurant." The hostess looked at her list of waiting guests. "I will check after I get these other people seated."

Suzie's heart dropped to her stomach. She was sure they had agreed upon seven as the time of the meeting. If Dr. Statler changed it, why didn't he let her know?

Soon the hostess was done seating everyone waiting in the lobby. "I will see if he is with Angelo." She walked to the back of the restaurant. In a few minutes the hostess returned to the lobby. "He will be here in a few minutes. Angelo and Dr. Statler go way back. They had a lot of catching up to do. He told me to go ahead and seat you."

"I should probably just go home. I was under the impression that we had a mandatory staff meeting at seven. I guess it was at five." Suzie said, gathering her purse and turning to walk out the door.

"Oh, no you don't. If Dr. Statler was nice enough to reserve a table for you, then you are going to stay here and eat a meal. He doesn't do that for all of his employees." The hostess said as she grabbed the elbow of Suzie and steered her to the back of the restaurant. "Only the pretty ones." She said as she pulled out the chair for Suzie and handed her a menu.

Soon Dr. Statler sat down next to Suzie. "I am sorry that we could not accommodate your schedule tonight. But I am so glad you came. I would like to get to know you better. So you said you had children to drop off at their dad's house? How many children?"

"I have three children, Dr. Statler. One daughter and two sons," Suzie said.

"Are they young? My wife and I have one child. He is disabled." Dr. Statler said, as he poured himself a glass of wine.

"Yes, they are young. My daughter is seven years old, one of my sons is five, and the other is two. I am sorry that your son is disabled." Suzie said, her heart melting just a smidgeon.

"Yes, he had complications at birth. I was on a trip for a medical convention. The poor fella can't walk. My wife has to feed him and take care of him twenty four hours a day. Of course, I have to put in a lot of hours to pay for all of the medical expenses." Dr. Statler said as he took a garlic knot out of the basket.

"I am so sorry," Suzie said. "That must be a real burden for your wife and you to handle."

"Yes, you know when friends of mine like Angelo talk about their sons… healthy sons… well, it just kind of cuts through my heart." Dr. Statler said, as he teared up. "So you have two healthy sons right?"

"Yes, and a wonderful daughter too." Suzie said as she helped herself to the garlic knots.

"I just can't see leaving a woman who has three children who are healthy. What was your husband thinking?" Dr. Statler said, looking into Suzie's eyes with compassion.

"I don't know what he was thinking." Suzie paused, as if this was the first time she had tried to figure out why Joe left. "His new wife is very beautiful. She has a lovely home which looks like a castle. Apparently he values that more than he valued me or our family as a unit." Suzie said as she took a drink of water. "He insists on seeing the children every weekend though. So it's not like he left them. He just left me." Suzie said as she fumbled with the napkin.

"I bet it is hard for you to get a date," Dr. Statler said.

Suzie's head shot up in indignation. "Why would you say that?"

"Well, not because you are ugly," Dr. Statler said. "You are definitely attractive but most men aren't like me. They don't want the responsibility of raising someone else's children."

"Actually I don't have any problem getting dates. My children are a delight to be around and any man who doesn't think so, needn't waste my time." Suzie said as she picked up the menu. "Are you ready to order? Because I have to get home soon to get some sleep before I go into work."

"I'm sorry if I offended you. I guess being a step-parent to three healthy children is much easier than taking care of one which is disabled." Dr. Statler said as he took another drink of wine.

"You didn't offend me. I imagine having a disabled child presents many challenges but I am sure that you and your wife handle it just fine." Suzie said as she beckoned a waitress to their table. "I would like the lasagna please."

"I will take the chicken Alfredo," Dr. Statler said. "You see, ever since that child was born it is like a wall was erected between my wife and I." Dr. Statler folded his hands in front of him and feigned a mournful look. "It's like once our son was born I ceased to exist."

Dr. Statler conveniently left out the reason why there was a wall. He had not been at a medical convention but with a stripper on the night of his son's birth. His wife had almost died in childbirth. When he did finally arrive back home he had some unsavory companions, Gonorrhea and Syphilis.

"Have you tried family counseling?" Suzie asked with concern.

"I have begged her to go to counseling with me. She refuses. All she is after is my money. She said if I divorce her she will clean me out financially," Dr. Statler said. "Every time I see someone with normal, healthy children I just want to jump in as dad. She doesn't let me do anything with my son. She says he is fragile."

Once again, Dr. Statler left out pertinent information. Like the time he slapped his son so hard that a red hand imprint was on his cheek two hours later. He had traumatized his son, even when he was just a baby. As a toddler, his son would start shaking the minute he heard his father walk in the front door. His wife finally put a lock on her son's door and refused to give Dr. Statler the key.

Suzie began to smell a rat. "That is tragic. I am so sorry that you have gone through all of that. I hope you don't consider me rude but one of the reasons why I accepted this invitation was to speak with you about the facility. Do you mind if we focus on professional topics now?"

"Yes, I am sorry. Sometimes my personal life just gets the better of me. Let me tell you the mission statement of the facility. We are basically a holding place for the elderly. Kind of a transition platform for them. They transition from being a productive member of society to one that is worthless. Most of the families couldn't give a shit about the people we take care of." Dr. Statler said as he took a gulp of wine. "We are a warehouse for people who haven't had the guts to give up and die."

Suzie was shocked. She stopped chewing her lasagna because she thought she may vomit. "That explains some of the difficulty I was facing this weekend. It seemed as if the nursing staff didn't care about the patients. They weren't doing the dressing changes on the wounds. When I took the dressings off I could see that they had not been changed on a frequent basis."

Dr. Statler grabbed Suzie's hands. "Dear, you musn't delude yourself. The medical industry is NOT about taking care of people. It is about taking advantage of people and making a shitload of money in the process. Wound care is expensive and I must watch the amount of money we spend on the patients. If we spend all of our money on wound care I can not pay the salaries of my employees. Comprehende? That means you, my dear lady, would not be able to feed your children." He kissed Suzie's hands.

Suzie slipped out of his grip. "It seems as if good budgeting could accommodate both objectives, sir."

"Yes, but sometimes I need to get away. Last time I went on a trip, I took the weekend supervisor to Belize. There was a medical convention there. Of course we attended some of the seminars but we spent a good deal of time frolicking on the beach." Dr. Statler smiled as if he were in a dream. "Such fun we had. I think there may be another convention in Mexico coming up this summer. I was thinking you could come with me."

"I can't afford that," Suzie said.

"Well, it would be on the company's bill. See if you start fudging more on the wound care, there may be a trip to Mexico in the cards for you." Dr. Statler winked at Suzie.

"Sir, I think I will pass. I would prefer that my patients had quality care. Mexico can wait until I can pay for it out of my own pocket." Suzie folded her napkin up and laid it on the table. "Now as I was saying, I have to get some sleep. I want to thank you for the excellent meal. Tell your friend, Angelo, he has an award winning lasagna."

Suzie started to get up from the table and was grabbed by Dr. Statler. "I don't want you to go yet. I am so lonely in my marriage. Could you spend one night with me?" Dr. Statler said as some drunken slobber slid down his chin.

"Are you propositioning me?" Suzie asked.

"No, if you just held me. My wife is so cold." Dr. Statler looked as if he was on the verge of tears.

"I am sorry about that, but I am more than just a single mother. I am more than a nurse. My body is the holy temple of God. My body was bought at the cost of another person's life and that person was Jesus Christ. Because of this, I must honor Him with my body. To allow myself to be placed in a compromising situation with a man who is married, would not reflect honor upon Jesus." Suzie said as she broke free of Dr. Statler.

"You self-righteous bitch. I will have you fired," Dr. Statler snarled.

Suzie leaned down and looked into Dr. Statler's eyes. "There is one more verse from the Bible which I would like you to be mindful of. That is the verse where it cautions me to not throw what is holy before dogs, nor cast my pearls before swine."

Dr. Statler's face turned beet red. "Are you calling me a dog?"

"No, I didn't say that but it's fascinating that you would come to that conclusion," Suzie said. Then she turned on her heels and strutted out of the restaurant.

THE FULL ARMOR OF GOD

SUZIE WAS UNAWARE OF THE POWER THAT SHE NOW could lay claim to. She had passed the last test. As she was walking out of the restaurant, the Breastplate of Righteousness clicked into place.

Grace, Mercy, Faith, Hope and Joy were rejoicing in the heavenly realms.

"She has done it," Hope exclaimed.

"Yes, she has." Grace said with a smile.

Mr. Mercy held Grace's hand tightly. "There were times I was a bit concerned. Yet every time I nudged Jacob to comfort her, he said just the right thing. I am glad the armor is in place before he goes to Africa."

Faith sighed. "Me too. Being a single mother is no piece of cake. She needed to go through all of these trials to get stronger for when he leaves. She has earned my shield. The Shield of Faith."

"As it says in 1 Peter 1:6-9 'So be truly glad. There is wonderful joy ahead, even though you have to endure many trials for a little while. (7) These trials will show that your faith is genuine. It is being tested as fire tests and purifies gold-though your faith is far more precious than mere gold. So when your faith remains strong through many trials, it will bring you much praise and glory and honor on the day when Jesus Christ is revealed to the whole world.'"

Faith paused for a moment, then continued. "(8) Suzie will love Him, even though she has never seen Him. Though she does not see him now, she trusts Him; and she will rejoice with a glorious, inexpressible joy. (9) The reward for trusting Him will be the salvation of her soul."

"She has proven to be worthy of the Shoes of Peace. She has drawn several people into a saving knowledge of Christ through her compassionate nature," Mr. Mercy said. "We have two old men and a young lady who have been added in the Book of Life due to the testimony of Suzie."

Joy was excuberant. "This is just the start of her harvest. Suzie will harvest many more lost souls. She has learned the value of truth. She has not fallen for the deception of materialism, nor sexual immorality. She is wearing the Belt of Truth."

"Although she struggled with envy and unforgiveness she did not allow the evil of those entities to enslave her. She has chosen to forgive Joe and Megan for the pain which their sin has caused her. The Helmet of Salvation is now protecting her every thought." Grace stated with conviction.

Hope spoke with authority. "She is covered from head to toe with the armor of God but she is not only a defensive player she is savvy in offense, too. Did you see how she put Dr. Statler in his place using the Word of God?" Hope busted out giggling. "I personally think he is a dog and a pig."

Faith smiled at Hope. "Now, now dear. He is lost and blind. Which means he has a target on his back as far as Suzie is concerned."

Soon everyone in the heavenly realm was laughing.

However, laughing was the last thing that Deceit had on his mind…

It had been a few days since a meeting had occurred regarding that worthless woman, Susanna Whatley.

Deceit was confident that Adultery would have ripped the breastplate of righteousness from this woman's heart.

He began fantasizing. If he had access to her heart, his poison could invade her mind and her body. It wouldn't be long before he had the death certificate in his hands. He needed to call another meeting.

The entities of evil filed in one after another. Rejection, Envy, Doubt, Insecurity, Condemnation, Bitterness and Despair were all present. Deceit scanned the room. Adultery and Betrayal were nowhere to be found.

Deceit cleared his throat. "Does anyone know where Betrayal and Adultery are?"

Silence.

Deceit stated in a louder tone. "Where are Betrayal and Adultery?

Not a peep.

Deceit screeched at the top of his voice. “BETRAYAL AND ADULTERY WHERE ARE YOU?!!!!

“Shut the hell up,” Adultery said as she sauntered into the cavern with a torn gown exposing a gash in her leg. “You seriously need to rip those damn fangs out of the mouth of Betrayal. He has marred my gorgeous leg.”

Deceit glared at Adultery in annoyance. “Excuse me, this is not about you. I am at the end of my rope. Did you get into her heart? Did she commit adultery?” Deceit asked, licking his lips.

Adultery sauntered across the cavern. “Not exactly.” Adultery readjusted her gown to try and distract Deceit with her ample cleavage.

“NOT EXACTLY? What does that mean?” Deceit was seething with fury.

Despair pranced to the middle of the cavern. “I did what I could boss. I had Dr. Statler tell his side of the story regarding his miserable existence with a disabled child. He admitted that his wife had put up a wall in their relationship. I didn’t mention that she prayed for his salvation every day. Nope, I didn’t mention that at all. I painted her as a cold-hearted witch.”

Deceit brushed Despair aside. “Well done. You have worked very hard on this case. I think you deserve a vacation.”

Despair lit up like a firecracker. “Oh that should be fun!”

Deceit cornered Adultery. “I thought you had this one in the bag. If you had cracked the breastplate of righteousness we would have a chance.”

“Does she have everything else?” Adultery asked, looking at her nails.

“Yes.” Deceit stated with a scowl.

Adultery hemmed and hawed for a moment. "Well, I think maybe we should work on someone else for a change. Megan is starting to get bored with Joe. She ran across a handsome millionaire in Mexico. Just saying…"

Betrayal was fuming with rage. "Suzie has submitted to God. She has resisted us on every count! I feel like running away from her. She is like some kind of nasty disease."

Deceit shuffled to the center of the Cavern of Evil. "The attack on Susanna Whatley has ended. The last piece of Armor has been fastened over her heart. She is now off limits. There is not one millimeter of opening for us to slip into her heart or mind. She and God have won this battle." Defeat crumpled to the floor in defeat.

A GIFT OF LOVE

SUZIE'S WEEKEND WENT WELL AT THE NURSING HOME. Dr. Statler did not come in during the weekend.

Suzie was so happy to be back home on Sunday night with the children nestled back in her nest. She knew that Jacob would be leaving for the Congo on Thursday. Thursday was also Valentine's Day.

She invited Grace, Mr. Mercy, and Jacob over for dinner on Wednesday night. She wanted to make sure that Jacob had some American food in his stomach while he was on his flight to Africa.

The lasagna she made turned out fabulous and the children helped set the table.

Michael insisted on sitting right by Jacob in the formal dining foom. "My teacher said that Jacob was a courageous man. She said she didn't know anyone who had gone to Africa, much less go as a missionary. She gave me an A+ on my report." Michael said, gleaming with pride.

"Well, you did a very good job on the report, Michael. All I did was tell you a few things. Then we found some pictures. You put it all together, though." Jacob said, smiling at Michael.

Sarah piped up as she put some lasagna on her plate. "If there is any way you could send me some of that African fabric, Jacob, I would love to make a scarf for my new friend, Cassidy."

"Who's Cassidy?" Michael asked.

"She's this girl in my class who has Down's Syndrome. Everyone always made fun of her but Mom said I should be her friend. She is sweet and fun. I really enjoy her." Sarah said with a smile.

Grace looked at Sarah with love. "Sarah, I am so happy you are being a friend to Cassidy. Mr. Mercy and I once had a daughter named Charity. She had Down's Syndrome too."

"Really?" Michael asked.

Mr. Mercy nodded, with a faint hint of sadness at the mention of Charity.

"That is so cool. What happened to her?" Michael asked.

"She went to heaven." Grace said, a smile of serenity caressing her face.

Sarah's face fell. "I am so sorry."

"Thank you for that sentiment, Sarah." Mr. Mercy said, his eyes glistening. "Without Charity we would have never adopted Jacob. She was the special child who opened our hearts and home for foster children."

"I wish I had known her," Jacob said. "I am so grateful to her for what she meant to both of you."

"She would have loved you," Grace said. "Suzie, this lasagna is delicious. How did you know that this is Jacob's favorite dish?"

“The same way he knew my favorite color was purple. Through prayer.” Suzie winked at Grace.

The dinner lingered on into the early evening hours. As the small home filled with love and laughter, Suzie’s eyes moistend at the prospect of Jacob’s future.

Jacob motioned Suzie aside. “Would it be okay with you if I spoke a blessing over your children before I left?”

Suzie’s face lit up with joy. “Jacob, that would be wonderful. What a sweet way to say good bye.”

Jacob gathered the children into the living room. “I want to thank you for allowing me to come over and spend time with you. Being able to play ball with you guys has reminded me of how much I enjoy children.” Jacob said as he looked at Michael and Jonathan.

“You three children are all a masterpiece in the making.” Jacob turned his gaze to Sarah. “Sarah, you have such a natural beauty and sweetness that you are going to melt hearts wherever you go. You are the spitting image of your beautiful mother and if you turn out half as wondeful as her, you are better than most women.” Sarah was beaming, as she looked at Suzie and gave her a wink.

“Michael, you embraced the calling of God on my life with such a sense of adventure, that I am more excited about going to Africa than I have ever been. With your energy and intelligence you will do great and mighty acts for the Lord.” Jacob said as he gave a high five to Michael.

“Jonathan, I need you to pray for me. I think God has something wonderful planned for your life. I hope I can one day be a part of that. Even at your young age I see the masterpiece of Christ being recreated in you." Jonathan was bravely wiping tears from his cheeks, trying desperately to maintain his composure.

Jacob looked at Suzie. "Would it be okay if I prayed with everyone before I left?"

"Of course, it would be okay." Suzie said, slyly wiping a stray tear from her cheek.

Grace and Mr. Mercy came into the living room and hands were held as Jacob started his prayer. "Dear God I thank you for your majesty and your power. I pray that you would watch over Suzie and her children while I am in Africa. I pray your hedge of protection, your financial blessing, and your wisdom to keep this family in your will. I ask that you give Suzie the strength and endurance as a single mother to put you first in her life. I ask that you would give her wisdom for discipline, abundance for love, and patience if the children are disobedient. I ask that you provide enough income to keep a roof over her head, clothes on their backs, and healthy food in their stomachs. I pray that you would protect the children from evil and lead them not into temptation. May your Holy Spirit be ever present in each of their lives. You are the only God who is worthy of worship and we bow before you in humility, with gratefulness that you consider our petition of prayer. Amen."

Suzie squeezed the hand of Jacob. "Heavenly Father, I thank you for the blessing of Jacob. I thank you for his Christ-like counsel and demeanor. He has meant so much to us and we are going to miss him. I pray that you would make his paths straight in Africa. Keep him safe from violence. Provide healthy food which he can eat and a safe place to stay. I pray most of all that your Holy Spirit will guide and direct him as he ministers to the African people. I pray that their hearts are ready to receive Jesus as their Savior, and that Jacob will accomplish the goals which you have set before him. We commit his life to your calling as we commit our hearts to you. We love you, heavenly Father and are eternally grateful for the sacrifice of your son. Amen." Suzie stated as she squeezed Sarah's hand.

"Dear God. I thank you for Jacob. When Daddy left, I had a hole in my heart. Jacob kind of filled that hole. Now that he is leaving, I expect that Jesus is gonna have to start filling that hole. I am thankful for Jacob and also Jesus. Keep Jacob safe in Africa." Sarah said, squeezing Michael's hand.

"God, I need to confess something. I am kind of jealous that Jacob gets to go to Africa. I haven't been anywhere exciting yet. I pray that Jacob will have the time of his life in Africa. I pray that he will be safe but not bored. I hope he likes those African children as much as he likes me. Amen." Michael said looking at Jonathan and giving him a nod.

"I hope Jacob gets done in Afwica quick, cuz I want him to be my daddy numba two." Jonathan said as he broke rank with the hand holding, ran to Jacob and hugged his leg with tears exploding down his cheeks.

Mr. Mercy came over to Jacob. "Son? Would you mind kneeling down in the middle of the room so that we can all lay hands on you?"

Jacob knelt down and the children laid their hands on his back. Suzie knelt down in front of him and placed her hand on his heart and Grace and Mr. Mercy placed their hands on his head. The children were nestled around him like baby birds in a nest.

"Heavenly Father. We come before you with hearts full of gratitude for our son, Jacob. What a privilege it has been to raise this child of God with your Word lighting the path. Now, it is as if we are giving him back to you God and that is not easy to do." Mr. Mercy paused to wipe the tears from his face. "I pray that you put your hedge of protection around him. Keep his heart from evil. Please keep every thought captive to Christ. Give him energy and passion to serve those who are lost. Give him the ability to lure those lost sheep of yours back into your fold. May his harvest be great and may your name be praised through his Christian service."

Grace took in a deep breath. "God, from the time Jacob was just a young boy I could see he was favored in your eyes. I pray that your favor will continue with him as he leaves for Africa. I pray you will guide and direct him and keep him safe. I pray that his harvest of souls for your kingdom will be abundant. I ask that you be with him as he is adjusting to a new language, country, and culture. Give him wisdom in every difficult trial. In Jesus' name, Amen."

Jacob looked at Mr. Mercy and Mr. Mercy nodded. The children said their farewells to Jacob. Grace and Mr. Mercy kept them entertained while Jacob lured Suzie out in the backyard.

The moon was full, the stars were bright and Suzie's tears were shining like diamonds in the night.

Jacob took Suzie's hands in his, as he pulled her close. "I have no right to ask you to be mine. If you find someone who makes you happy and you want to marry them, you have my blessing. I will pray for you and the children every day. I hope I can come back and marry you but there is a lot of violence in the Congo. I do not know if I will survive. So go as God leads you."

"Jacob, I will pray for you every day. I will continue to seek God and His guidance and I hope He brings you back home to me. I don't know what path is before me. I don't feel the need to replace you with anyone else. You have comforted my heart with God's love when it was shattered. You have led me not only to love you but to love God more. I will try my hardest to keep my mind and my heart focused on God." Suzie said, as her hands went to the cross necklace that was laying against her chest.

Jacob bent down to kiss Suzie, as his arms wrapped around her in a tender embrace.

The kiss was long enough to assure true love. Love which could cross oceans and continents.

As Jacob pulled away from Suzie, he gently wiped the tears from her face, then grabbed her hand and led her up the back stairs of her home.

In the darkness of night, Jacob left for Africa.

Suzie had a restless night and at daybreak was awakend by thunder and pelting rain. She got up and noticed that the cross necklace was still wrapped around her neck.

She wanted to find a special place to put this necklace. She knew exactly where it should go. She pulled out the drawer where the picture of Stevie had been kept.

"All of my life I have been searching for my prince. First I thought it was Stevie, then Joe. When Jacob came I was sure it was him but Jesus… I think what I really wanted…. is for you to be my Prince. Because you are the only One who has truly captured my heart." Suzie said as she kissed the cross necklace and tucked it away in the drawer.

A flash of lightening blazed through the dusky sky. The clouds parted and a brilliant rainbow embraced the sunrise.

Suzie inhaled deeply and suddenly became aware that there was a delightful scent surrounding her.

It was the fragrance of roses.

The End